MacGREGOR'S GATHERING

This was the time when the famous Rob Roy MacGregor and his swaggering nephew Gregor led the landless clan of the MacGregors. Their very name was proscribed and outlawed, but they still clung to Glengyle, one small remaining corner of their ancient territories, and held fast in their loyalty to the King over the water.

Both Rob Roy and his nephew opposed the plan to unite the English and the Scottish Parliaments, a scheme that would send any self-respecting MacGregor reaching for his dirk. But in the midst of the political struggle young Gregor still managed to find time to pay court to Mary Hamilton, a lovely girl from the Lowlands who at first rejected his rough Highland ways . . .

MacGregor's Gathering

Nigel Tranter

CORONET BOOKS
Hodder and Stoughton

Printed and bound in Great Britain for Hodder and Stoughton Paperbacks, a division of Hodder and Stoughton Ltd., Mill Road, Dunton Green, Sevenoaks, Kent TN13 2YA (Editorial Office: 47 Bedford Square, London WC1B 3DP) by Clays Ltd., St Ives plc.

ISBN 0-340-34914-X

MACGREGOR'S GATHERING

The moon's on the lake, and the mist's on the brae,
And the clan has a name that is nameless by day.
    Then gather, gather, gather, Gregalach!
    Gather, gather, gather.

Our signal for fight, which from monarchs we drew,
Must be heard but by night in our vengeful halloo,
    Then halloo, halloo, halloo, Gregalach!
    Halloo, halloo, halloo.

Glen Orchy's proud mountains, Kilchurn and her towers,
Glen Strae and Glen Lyon no longer are ours.
    We're landless, landless, landless, Gregalach!
    Landless, landless, landless.

But doomed and deserted by vassal and lord,
MacGregor has still both his heart and his sword.
    Then courage, courage, courage, Gregalach!
    Courage, courage, courage.

If they rob us of name and pursue us with beagles,
Give their roofs to the flames and their flesh to the eagles.
    Then vengeance, vengeance, vengeance, Gregalach!
    Vengeance, vengeance, vengeance.

While there's leaves in the forest and foam on the river,
MacGregor despite them shall flourish for ever.
    Come then, Gregalach! Come then, Gregalach!
    Come then, come then, come then.

Through the depths of Loch Katrine the steed shall career'
O'er the peak of Ben Lomond the galley shall steer,
And the rocks of Craigroyston like icicles melt,
Ere our wrongs be forgot or our vengeance unfelt.
    Then halloo, halloo, halloo, Gregalach!
    Halloo, halloo, halloo.

WALTER SCOTT.

AUTHOR'S FOREWORD

THIS is fiction – though the background and most of the characters are factual. The legends adhering to Rob Roy MacGregor's name are legion, some of them fairly well authenticated, others less so. Vastly less has been written about his nephew, Gregor Ghlun Dubh (Black Knee) Mac-Gregor of Glengyle. The character of Rob Roy was obviously a highly complex one, that of his nephew considerably less so. I have sought to cull, from the mass of lore and legend and history, such incidents as seem to me to present a recognisable and fairly consistent picture of these two men, set against the stormy background of Scotland in the first decade of the eighteenth century, not hesitating to invent wholly imaginary incidents and individuals where such seem necessary for my story and for the fuller delineation of the characters that I conceive these two to have borne.

Much herein, therefore, is no more than a product of my fancy – but I have sought to keep the background of the times as accurate as I know how, and not to traduce any historical character unduly. John Campbell, first Earl of Breadalbane, is the villain of the piece, and while this tale may do his memory less than justice in some respects, in others it holds a more charitable silence. All authorities seem to be unanimous that he was a man whom no one in Scotland trusted and everyone feared, and his dexterity at changing sides was unrivalled in an age when such gymnastics were commonplace. He had his reward.

Rob Roy led his clan again in the next Jacobite rising of 1715 – and suffered some diminution of esteem in the process. Gregor, his fame unsullied, fought both in that affair and in the later attempt of the Forty-five.

The politics of the day ought not to be wholly without their lesson for us today. Politics, indeed, seem to change but little with the centuries.

NIGEL TRANTER.

ABERLADY, 1956.

CHAPTER ONE

YOUNG Gregor Ghlun Dubh MacGregor of Glengyle uplifted his golden head and hearty voice and shouted great
laughter to an understanding heaven – the pure unsullied
and spontaneous laughter of a happy soul. Not the laughter
inspired by amusement or humour or mockery or still less
worthy emotions, but the joyous variety born of sheer goodwill towards all, and a lively appreciation of the excellence of
life. Gregor Ghlun Dubh was a great appreciator of life, and
consequently a notably happy young man.

And certainly the scene was an inspiring one. Indeed, seldom could the little market-place of Drymen have seen anything more lively and altogether heartening. Cattle milled
everywhere in glorious and loud-voiced confusion – not only
the small black kyloes of the glens but the more substantial
products of fat Lowland pastures – steers, bullocks, milch-
cows and calves, in an endless variety of size, colour, shape
and temperament. There were hundreds of beasts there, un-
countable – though undoubtedly Gregor's puissant uncle
would be having a count kept somewhere – and their
bellowing protest ascended up as a hymn of praise to a
benign Providence, and the steaming throat-catching scent
of them was as incense in a MacGregor's nostrils. Laugh?
The tall young man in his best tartans slapped his bare knee
– the same that bore the hairy black birth-mark, so strange
on a young blond giant, that gave him his by-name of Ghlun
Dubh, or Black Knee – slapped and out-bellowed the
cattle.

It was Lammas quarter-day, the year of Our Lord seventeen hundred and six, and the Captain of the Highland
Watch was at the receipt of his dues and customs – the Mac-

Gregors' Watch, Rob Roy's Watch – Gregor of Glengyle assisting for the first time since coming of age.

A less vigorous and lusty young man than Glengyle might have been weary of it all by this time – for this business had been going on all day, and now the August sun was beginning to sink behind Duncryne and all the serried blue hills beyond Loch Lomond. These cattle had come from far and near, in droves great and small – for Rob Roy MacGregor cut a wide swathe. From the Graham lands of Aberfoyle and Killearn to the Buchanan territories of Touch and Kippen, from the uplands of Fintry and Kilsyth to the green plains of Stirling and Airth, from Menteith to Callander and Allan Water to the Vale of Leven, the droves great and small had come to this convenient tryst of Drymen – convenient for the MacGregors, that is – representing the tribute of some seven hundred and fifty square miles of fair Scotland to Robert MacGregor Campbell, alias Robert Ruadh MacGregor of Inversnaid, alias Rob Roy, Captain of the Glengyle Highland Watch, or, as his own Clan Alpine put it, Himself. Proud earls had contributed – even a marquis, said to be in line for a dukedom – lairds of large acres and small, fine Lowland gentlemen and canny Highland drovers, the Church and the State, all were represented there. Which was as it should be. Rob Roy was worth paying tribute to – and he made a point of leaving none in doubt of it.

It was the Church speaking now, just at the young man's back, in the sober, indeed somewhat lugubrious person of the Reverend Ludovic Erskine, Minister of Drymen. 'Man, Glengyle – that's a terrible lot of beasts,' he said, without proper enthusiasm – undoubtedly because there was a cow of his own included somewhere in the total. 'I canna think what your uncle can be needing with them all.' He shook a grizzled foreboding head. 'There is danger in it, mind. The grievous danger of greed, of the worship of Mammon, Glengyle.'

Gregor Ghlun Dubh, like his uncle, was a great respecter of the Church, as of all worthy and proper things. Also he was newly enough of age to appreciate that introductory 'Man, Glengyle' of the minister's. Therefore he did not turn and rend the maker of such infamous suggestions as undoubtedly he deserved. Moreover, the man had recently lost his wife, and Gregor was of a soft heart.

'There are many MacGregor mouths to feed,' he mentioned, still smiling. 'You would not be having them starve in the midst of plenty?'

'Starve, is it!' Mr Erskine cried, his harsh voice vibrant with power and emotion. It had to be to counter the bawling of the beasts. 'The starving will be nearer home, I doubt! And there will be no plenty in Drymen after this day.'

Gregor knew what was coming, of course. The minister was not the first to seek to approach Rob Roy through his nephew, as the less alarming individual. All men knew of Rob's affection for his dead brother's son, the young chieftain of Glengyle, whom he had cherished and brought up from the age of ten. Tutor of Glengyle had been one of his uncle's proud titles, only recently relinquished – and, if the truth was known, sometimes relinquished only in name at that.

'I am thinking the good folk of Drymen will not be letting their shepherd starve,' he observed.

'Little you ken them, Glengyle – backsliders, reprobates, withholders of God's portion! And now my cow is riven from me – my best cow, the only brute-beast that is worth its keep, indeed! It is hard, hard. If you would but speak a word into your uncle's lug, Glengyle. He is namely as a man respectful to the Kirk, kindly towards the poor and the widow. Och, and the widower is the worse off, indeed . . .'

Young Gregor groaned in spirit. That the creature should spoil this bonny day and its good work with such shameful whining! He shook his yellow head impatiently. 'Himself is throng with business, *Mhinistear*. Later, may be . . .'

Glengyle paused, grateful for a diversion. A new drove was coming at the trot up the little hill from the south-west into Drymen's slantwise market-place, mixed beasts as Rob liked them, stirks, cows and followers, but all prime conditioned stock. He pointed.

'Oho – see you!' he cried. 'My Lord of Aberuchill is late. But better late than sorry, as they say!'

'Aberuchill . . . ?' the minister echoed. 'Man – does the Lord Justice-Clerk of Scotland himself pay your Hielant blackmail?'

'Blackmail, sirrah!' Gregor's voice rose menacingly, all laughter gone. 'As Royal's my Race – I'd have you remember to whom you speak, *Mhinistear*!' His uncle could hardly have improved on that himself. 'Choose you your words to a Highland gentleman, see you, with more care . . . !'

As well for the Reverend Erskine and any hopes in the matter of his cow, perhaps, that just then a sudden high-pitched squealing overbore even the speaker's vehemence. At the trotting heels of the new herd a six-month calf was outdoing all rivals in ear-piercing protest, as a burly drover twisted its tail savagely as a means of propulsion. The press of beasts in the market-place was already so great that the newcomers were holding back, and the fellow was using this method to urge them on past the narrows of the street which sundry MacGregor gillies were endeavouring to keep open for incoming traffic from the east.

Gregor wasted neither breath, time nor opportunity. Leaving the minister without a word, he strode down through the little crowd of gaping townsfolk and round the near edge of the milling throng, thrusting aside men and cattle with equal disregard. This was more in his line. That calf could be injured by such treatment, for tails could break – and a broken tail took the value off a beast. Moreover, its bawling was an offence to the ear, and unsuitable. Again, the offending drover was obviously nothing but a Lowlander. And, as has been seen, Glengyle was of a notably soft heart.

The last few yards to Lord Aberuchill's drover were covered at a pace which allowed little opportunity for Gregor's rawhide brogans to touch the cobbles. One of the hulking fellow's two colleagues cried a warning. But it was too late. Before the man could turn, Gregor's arm reached out and did the turning for him, swinging him round with such force as almost to overbalance him. As he staggered, still clutching the calf's tail, Glengyle's other hand grabbed the substantial stick that the other held, and wrenched it from his grasp.

'Fool! Knave! Scum!' he cried indignantly. 'Would you damage MacGregor's cattle? Hands off, lout!' And without allowing even a moment for the transgressor to question the authority of that, he swung the heavy stick and brought it down with a resounding thwack upon the creature's forearm.

The drover yelled, in tune with the calf, and both arm and tail dropped limply. A spluttered volley of oaths, incomplete and incoherent but nevertheless hoarsely heartfelt, followed on.

But the Lord Justice-Clerk's drover did more than swear. He lashed out with a great ham-like left fist for Gregor's head – which branded him for a rash and impetuous fellow indeed. Perhaps he was so much of a Lowlander that he did not recognise the significance of two eagle's feathers in a Highland bonnet. Though probably his folly was the result of mere spontaneous reaction.

It was as well, undoubtedly, for all concerned, that the blow did not strike home – for the consequences would scarcely have borne consideration. As it was, Gregor avoided it with a full inch to spare – despite the shock that such a thing could be possible. And quicker than thought, of course, he drove home the much-needed lesson.

Coming up from his hasty sideways duck, he clutched the other's shoulder to slew him round into a more convenient position, and drove down the staff in his other hand with all his force on the man's bullet head. The stick broke, too.

The drover grunted, swayed drunkenly, tottered on his toes, and then slumped full length on the dung-spattered cobbles, mouth open and eyes shut.

Gregor Ghlun Dubh tossed the two sections of the stick on to the body of the unconscious miscreant, wiping fastidious hands thereafter on the seat of his philamore or great kilt, as though to avoid contamination.

'Remove it,' he jerked, in the Gaelic, to the nearest of the gillies. And to the two remaining gaping drovers, in English, 'Begone'. And without further ado he stalked off to return to the minister.

Not unnaturally he felt considerably better. He was prepared even to be patient with the Church-Supplicant. But as he approached his former stance before the ale-house door, a third man came hurrying from the other direction, another gillie, naked save for short kilt and brogans. They met in front of Mr Erskine.

'Himself would be having a word with you, Glengyle,' the newcomer said, panting a little. 'Down in the church.'

'Yes. I will come,' Gregor assured, and almost started off there and then. But he recollected. Those days were past and done with. He was Glengyle now, chieftain of his house. 'Tell Himself that I will be there very shortly, MacAlastair,' he amended graciously. And repeated the message in English for the benefit of the minister, without the 'very'. 'Off with you.'

The dark-avised and sombre-browed messenger gave him a meaning look. He was Rob Roy's own foot-gillie, and something of a privileged character. He nodded, unspeaking, and padded away silently whence he had come.

'About this cow of yours, *Mhinistear*,' Gregor mentioned handsomely. 'What colour did you say it was ? Is it a kyloe ?'

The other eyed him a little askance. 'That man . . . ?' he began, and swallowed. 'Is he . . . ? Was it needful to be so . . . so hasty, Glengyle ?'

'Hasty . . . ?' The younger man wrinkled his brow. 'Myself hasty – to MacAlastair ?'

'Not him. The other man. Down there. The herd . . . '

'I do not follow you, sir.' That was said with deliberation and a remarkable clarity of diction.

'Oh. I . . . ah . . . ummm.' The minister glanced sidelong at the young chieftain's elevated profile – and decided to revert to the subject of cattle. 'My cow, yes. Och, she is just

14

an ordinary sort of a dun-coloured creature. But a grand milker, man – a grand milker.'

'Indeed. I am going to speak a word with, er, Inversnaid. I think it best that you accompany me, sir,' Gregor said, somewhat stiffly formal.

'Me . . . ? Och – no, no. Not at all. No need, Glengyle. Yourself will do fine. Just a word in his lug, like I said. . . .'

'Come,' the other commanded, and turning on his heel, strode off.

Reluctantly, with no urgency upon him, Mr Erskine followed on, the space between them growing at every step. They made quite a notable contrast, the tall, gallant and swaggering young Highlander, in his vivid red-and-green tartans, stepping Drymen's cobbles as though very much upon his native heath, and the lanky stooping divine, clad in patched and sober grey, shuffling doubtfully after, out of the market-place and down the curving brae towards his own parish kirk.

*   *   *

The Kirk of Drymen could hardly have been more conveniently placed. It sat squarely above the climbing narrow road which led into the little town from the west, and nothing could pass its door unseen. Moreover, directly across the trough that the road had worn for itself was another ale-house, Drymen being namely for its numerous places of refreshment. Again, around the back, a lane encircled the town, by the water-meadows, linking up with the road that came in from the east and all the wide lands of Forth. So all that was necessary was to have a couple of stout fellows stationed at the east end of the town, directing the flow of traffic from that side down the lane to where it must join the west-coming droves, and all had thus to come surging up the hill below the kirk door, where it could be scrutinised, counted and received in business-like fashion.

Rob Roy MacGregor sat decently in the church doorway behind a table, quills, ink and paper before him – for he was almost as good a hand with pen as with claymore and dirk.

These latter, of course, also lay upon the table. He was something of a stickler for the niceties of procedure. Mac-Alastair stood at his back, another man sat counting silver at the board, and three or four plaided gentlemen of the name lounged around. As Gregor came up the steps from the roadway, his uncle was in process of interviewing a stout red-faced little Lowland laird in cocked hat and good broadcloth, who appeared to be essaying the difficult task of keeping civil, paying over hard cash, and suggesting a rebate, all at the same time. Some clients of the Watch elected to pay their dues in silver.

'Er . . . just that, Buchlyvie,' Rob said pleasantly. 'My nephew, Glengyle. Mr Graham of Buchlyvie, Greg.' And he got to his feet as he spoke.

Rob Roy seated and standing gave two very different impressions. Seated, he looked a huge man, for he had enormous breadth of shoulder, a barrel-like chest, and arms so long that he could tie the garters of his tartan hose without stooping. Standing, he proved to be less tall than might have been anticipated – though nowise small – with stocky and just slightly bowed legs that gave an extraordinary impression of strength. That impression of strength, indeed, was the most notable quality about the man – and it was not confined to his peculiar physique. A man in his late thirties, he radiated personal power and a latent energy. His fiery red hair, fierce down-curving moustaches, and the rufus fur that clothed wrists and knees as thickly as on one of his own Highland stirks, did not lessen the effect. He was not a good-looking man, as his nephew Gregor Ghlun Dubh was good-looking, but no one who glanced once at Rob Roy MacGregor failed to look again. The brilliance of his pale blue eyes saw to that, if nothing else did. He was clad now, like Glengyle, in the full panoply of Highland dress, great kilt and plaid, tartan doublet, otter-skin sporran, silver buttons, jewelled brooches, buckles and sword-belt. Only, his bonnet, which lay on the table, flaunted but the one eagle's feather to Gregor's two.

'Nephew,' he said now, quizzically, in the English,

'Buchlyvie here poses us a nice problem. He contends that since there has been no villainous thievery of his cattle, nor raids on his district, this past year, we ought to be reducing his rate of payment. From five percentum of rateable value, he suggests, to four. How think you?' He sounded genuinely interested in the proposal.

'*Dia* – I think Mr Graham is ungrateful!' Gregor declared strongly, as required. 'Because our Watch is successful, and preserves him in peace and plenty, he would deny us our poor sustenance. I cannot congratulate him on his reasoning!'

'And there you have it, Buchlyvie!' his uncle laughed genially. 'My nephew has the clearer brain to us oldsters. *Maxima debetur puero reverentia.*' Rob was a great one for Latin tags – for education and all its benefits indeed, and so had brought up young Gregor. 'I cannot think that there is any more to discuss, eh? Unless indeed you would have us withdraw the Watch from you altogether?' He was glancing down at the end of the table where one of his henchmen had the silver coins all neatly counted and stacked, and who nodded his head briefly that the tally was correct. 'Now is the time, whatever, if you would wish it, Mr Graham?'

'No, no! Mercy on us – never think it, Rob . . . Inversnaid!' the laird assured hurriedly. 'The thought never crossed my mind.'

'That is well. We are of one mind, then?' The MacGregor signed the handsome receipt under his hand, with a flourish, and passed it over – a document worthy of Edinburgh's Parliament House. 'Eh, hey – it is good to deal with reasonable men. I bid you a very good e'en, Buchlyvie.'

'I do also,' Glengyle agreed.

All the MacGregor gentlemen did likewise, as the little man bumbled out. Politeness was a great matter with Rob, and none laughed out loud.

'Well now, Greg,' his uncle said, in their own tongue, resuming his seat. 'It was not to listen to such as Buchlyvie that I brought you here. Would you be after liking a small bit of a task, and this something of a special occasion for yourself?' Taking his nephew's acceptance for granted, the Captain of the Watch went on. 'It has been a good day, and all has gone well. The tally has been kept, and only three droves have not come in. Ballikinrain, Kerse and Gallangad. But Ballikinrain and Kerse are on the way. They have been spied from up the tower, there. There is nothing from the direction of Gallangad.'

'Ah!'

'And only last quarter-day, see you, Graham of Gallangad was after grumbling about his payments – just the way Buchlyvie was at just now. I am thinking that it is maybe a little small lesson that he needs.'

'That could be,' the younger man acceded gravely. 'And you would have me teach him it?'

'The notion occurred to me that you might welcome the exercise, Greg. It serves no good purpose when cocklairdies grow too cocky, whatever. The disease could be catching! You know the place?'

'Surely. No great distance off. Behind Duncryne, yonder. Five miles, or six?'

'Eight, make it, and the ford to cross. It will be sundown within the hour. If his beasts were to be here in time, they should have been in sight ere this. Man, Gregor – go you and fetch them in for me. All of them, you will understand? All. It will keep you from wearying.'

'Yes, then. They are as good as here, just.'

'No – not here, lad. Bring them to Inversnaid – to Glen Arklet. We shall be gone long before you win them back here. But . . . see you, Gregor – is that the minister that is dodging and skulking down the steps there, like a rock-rabbit?'

'Och, yes – I had forgotten him. The man is desolate because of his bit cow that has been taken. Bewailing like all the daughters of Babylon!' Gregor glanced sidelong to see how the other MacGregors had taken this erudite allusion. 'God's shadow – it is a great plague for one small cow!'

'Ministers' cows always low the loudest,' Rob Roy observed. 'But you are speaking for him, Greg?'

'Och, well . . . '

'Call him up, then.'

The Reverend Erskine came up to his own kirk with little of the Church-Militant about him. 'Mr MacGregor,' he began, with an incipient bow, 'you'll forgie me, I hope? I winna waste your time forbye ae meenit.' Perturbation, it is to be presumed, was driving him into his broadest Fife doric. 'I was just speiring at Glengyle here . . . '

'See you, *Mhinistear*,' Rob Roy interrupted, but easily. 'Let us be discussing your matter, be it what it may, on a right footing, whatever. Myself, you may name me a number of things – but not Mister! Inversnaid would be proper, or Captain maybe. But Rob I will answer to – or even Mac-Gregor. But, as Royal's my Race – no man shall Mister me within my hearing or the reach of my arm, *Mister* Erskine!' It was mildly said, but there was a certain sibilance of enunciation, which had a notable effect.

The growl of approval that arose came from all in hearing save Mr Erskine.

That unhappy man all but choked. 'I . . . I . . . och, nae offence, Inversnaid! Nae offence meant, I assure you. A slip o' the tongue, nae mair. Just oor Scots usage. . . . '

'Are you for informing me, sir, what is Scots usage?'

'Na, na – guidsakes! You'll have to forgie me, Captain. I'm a right donnert man become since my wife died on me. And noo the coo . . . '

Somewhat donnert he certainly sounded. Gregor, beside him, perceived that the lean veined hand actually trembled as it gestured feebly – the same hand that undoubtedly would beat the Good Book in thunderous authority in the pulpit back there of a Sabbath. And soft-hearted as ever, he intervened.

'It is but a little small matter, Uncle, to be wasting our time over. One small bit of a cow! Think you we could spare . . . ?'

'The cow is nothing, Nephew – but the principle is everything, whatever,' Rob Roy declared, sternly now. 'Mr Erskine, like others, has had my protection, and gained

19

thereby. He cries penury now – but so does every subscriber, from my Lord Marquis downwards. Restore him his cow, see you, and I should have a tail of others demanding the like. The thing is not to be considered. But . . . ' He paused, toying with his silver-mounted dirk, his glance switching between the faces of his nephew and the alarmed presbyter. ' . . . my respect for God's Kirk and religion is known. Mac-Alastair – take you Mr Erskine and let him be choosing any two beasts from the *spreagh* that he will. *Two* – you hear me ? As free gift and thank offering, from Robert MacGregor of Inversnaid.'

Into the divine's subsequent incoherent babble of gratitude and blessing, and Gregor's great laughter, Rob Roy held up his hand. 'Wheesht you, *Mhinistear* !' he commanded. 'What is that outcry ? A truce to your belling, Greg – what is the to-do upbye ?'

They all listened. Sure enough there came down to them a considerable din other than the day's norm of bovine protest. There was much shouting, the clatter of shod hooves and the unmistakable cracking of a whip.

'See you to it,' Rob directed, with a brief jerk of his red head in the direction of one of his lounging gentry.

'I will go,' young Glengyle announced, born an optimist, and turned him about.

*　　　*　　　*

It was a large travelling-coach that was the cause of the pother – a heavy, brightly painted affair drawn by four matching greys and equipped with whip-cracking jehu and shouting postillions. It was jammed in the throat of the market-place where the road from the east came in, along with perhaps fifty miscellaneous cattle-beasts, and making nothing of the business. Sundry gillies were hallooing round about, and cocked hats were poking through the coach windows. An interesting situation.

Gregor strode thitherwards laughing, pushing his way amongst the beasts. The coach doors were emblazoned with a florid coat-of-arms, ermine cinquefoils on a red field. How the equipage had got even thus far was a mystery. Determined folk, evidently.

A heavy-featured handsome man, handsomely clad and bewigged, beckoned imperiously to Gregor from one of the windows as he approached. 'Is this a fair, or what ? A tryst ?' he called out. 'Young man – these damned animals are not yours, by chance ?'

'They are not mine, no. But a tryst it is, after a manner of speaking.'

'Thank the Lord that you speak the Queen's English, at any rate!' the gentleman exclaimed. 'Will you kindly request these jabbering heathen to clear me a passage. 'Fore God, it should be obvious enough even to such as these! I believe that they are wilfully misunderstanding me!'

'What was it that you were after calling them, sir ?' Gregor Ghlun Dubh enquired interestedly.

'I said jabbering . . . ' The other's masterful voice tailed away as his arm was grasped from behind and another and older man's face appeared near his own, to mutter in his ear. Gregor heard only the words ' . . . MacGregor tartan . . . ' of whatever was said. But the effect of the whispering was on the whole beneficial. 'Well, dammit . . . we can't have this! Shrive me, it's a scandal, just the same. This is Drymen, is it not ? In the same Sheriffdom of Stirling as is Bardowie! Not some Hieland clachan! Blocking the Queen's highway . . . !'

'To which Queen do you refer, sir ?' Gregor asked then, more interestedly than ever. To counter the press of bullocks around him, he was now holding on to the handle of the coach door.

There was a musical tinkle of laughter from within. '*Touché*, John!' a woman's voice said, as with enjoyment.

The heavy gentleman swallowed, all but gobbled, and drew back from the window a little, turning his head. Gregor took the opportunity to jump up on the step and peer within.

He found the coach to contain two women as well as the two men, both young and both merry-eyed. But the younger, and the larger-eyed if anything, was sitting at this side of the vehicle, only a yard from Gregor's face. And he recognised her there and then, with a decision and certainty that his uncle must have commended, as quite the most lovely and desirable creature upon which his chiefly grey eyes had yet fallen. In token whereof, despite the difficulty and the balancing feat involved, he swept off his feathered bonnet in an impressive sweep – a thing that could have been done for no man save only the unfortunate Archibald MacGregor of Kilmanan, High Chief of Clan Alpine.

'Your servant, ladies!' he announced happily. And though he included them both, courteously, he rather concentrated upon her who was nearest. The Gregorach had always been notably impressionable as regards the sex – as centuries of blood and tears bore witness.

'Enchanted, sir,' one of the ladies said – the other one. 'You are an improvement, I swear, on the other faces that have been examining us! Is he not, Mary?' She was a plumpish comely creature, patched and prinked and powerfully well dressed for travelling – save over a bulging bosom.

Despite the bosom, Gregor's eyes still were magnetised by the other female attraction whom she called Mary, a less voluble young woman, and much less fussily dressed, but still more spectacular in her own way. Tall and slender, though dark-eyed and dark-haired and of a sculptured and arch-browed patrician loveliness, there was nothing of the chill and aloofness that frequently complements such beauty. Indeed, conversely, she had a lively warm eagerness of expression, a gaiety of spirit, that was as notable as her good looks. From her comparatively plain attire, and the fashion in which the curling masses of her seemingly unruly hair were ineffectually enclosed in a mere kerchief, instead of the elaborate headgear of the other woman, she might have been a superior servant, or perhaps a paid gentlewoman-companion – only, no one with half an eye could have taken that one for any sort of servant; certainly not Gregor Ghlun Dubh MacGregor of Glengyle.

'But still more dangerous, I would say!' this other

charmer declared – without by any means cringing back in her corner.

'Oh, most assuredly. The others, after all, were only bullocks!' The rounded lady veiled her eyes momentarily, and with effect. 'And a Jacobite into the bargain, if I mistake not. A *professing* Jacobite . . . unlike some!'

Both the men opposite cleared their throats. 'That's enough, Meg,' the younger heavily handsome man jerked. To Gregor he said: 'I'll wager the ladies will esteem your service the higher, sir, when you set about removing them from the God-offending stink of these cattle!' And he treated himself to a couple of liberal pinches of snuff, as deodorant.

Gregor managed to withdraw his gaze from the young woman – but sufficient of the effect remained to markedly tone down the automatic resentment aroused in any Mac-Gregor by a derogatory remark anent their staple and stock-in-trade. 'The Mother of God took no offence at the smell of cattle – in Bethlehem!' he mentioned levelly. And silenced all in that coach very thoroughly.

Which was the state in which Rob Roy found them. His great shoulders suddenly filled the other window, and he gazed in, from amongst the cattle, frowning just a little. Then his glance lightened.

'Arnprior!' he cried. 'Well, well – here is an unexpected pleasure. And Miss Meg, it will be? Beautiful as was her mother, too!' Rob's eyes did not miss the other young woman either, on their way round to the fourth traveller. 'A coachload of worth and beauty, whatever!' And he smiled that guileless smile of his that so little matched his reputation.

'Rob! Yourself, is it!' That was the older man speaking, and he thrust his hand out of the open window to shake the red-furred fist of the MacGregor. 'Well met, indeed. Man – you're looking fine and prosperous. Better than the last time we forgathered, eh! You mind, in that damnable business in Edinburgh – when they pulled Atholl down with the forgeries, and near got some others

23

o' us, forbye! Three years past, it would be . . . ?'

'Three years, yes. Seventeen and three. Three bad years for the Cause, too. But . . . ' The Highlander shrugged those shoulders. 'Och, for myself, I have managed, man – I've managed! And you, Arnprior – you've been furth the country, they tell me?'

'Aye, aye, Rob – I thought it wise-like, after you-know-what. France, where I saw you-know-who. Then to the Americas – to try to save something from the Darien business, see you. Then London itself – the lions' den. But och, the lions are purring now, with plenty to digest in their bellies, and auld Scotland dead just, dead – save maybe for yourself, Rob. . . . '

'Sleeping,' the other amended mildly.

'Well . . . maybe. But here's no place to discuss politics. Man, I saw the MacGregor tartans, and wondered what was all the stour. And this young man . . . '

'This young man, Arnprior, is my nephew Glengyle.' That was significantly said.

'Ha – the Colonel's grandson!' Rob Roy and Robert Buchanan of Arnprior had served as comrades-in-arms under the former's father, Lieutenant-Colonel Donald MacGregor of Glengyle, in the bad stirring days after Killiecrankie. 'I am proud to shake your hand, Glengyle.'

'Buchanan of Arnprior, Greg. And Mistress Meg Buchanan. . . . '

'Alas, no,' the plump young lady declared, pulling a face. 'No longer, I'm afraid!'

'Och, mercy on us, and my manners all gone gyte!' Arnprior cried. 'Here is my son-in-law, John Hamilton of Bardowie. And Miss Mary Hamilton, his sister. Rob Roy MacGregor.'

The impact of this introduction on the Hamiltons was noteworthy. John Hamilton half rose from his seat, recovered himself, made as if to thrust out his hand, thought better of it, and bowed his full-bottomed wig instead – a

24

strangely uncertain performance for such a substantial citizen. His sister was more forthright.

'Rob Roy MacGregor – the noted . . . er . . . !' Her forthrightness faltered there, and she bit a red lip lest any more should emerge.

'Exactly, Miss!' Rob laughed, and slapped the side of the coach so that the entire affair shook alarmingly. 'None other.' He turned to her brother. 'Bardowie is a known name to all men,' he said civilly. 'Myself, I thought that I recognised the red and white of the Hamilton scutcheon. Arnprior travels in better company than sometimes he has done, sir!'

'In more cautious company, anyhow,' Mrs Hamilton amended, smiling. 'You will have poor John quite dumbfounert with all your seditious talk! Though not Mary, I think . . . !'

Her father changed the subject. 'But what do you here, Rob – in Drymen? And whose are all these cattle? Is it some new fair, established since I've been gone?'

'The beasts are mine – or, say, the Gregorach's. Though, if you are after looking closer, friend, you'll maybe can make out your own mark on two-three of them, whatever! Your factor at Arnprior, I thank God, has an excellent memory!'

'Save us all – you mean . . . ? Don't say . . . ? Not all these, man . . . ?'

'Business is expanding, yes.' Rob shrugged. 'A man must keep pace with the times, as they say. It is Lammas quarterday, see you, and the dues fall to be collected. And youknow-who gets his share, too.'

'Eh . . . ? Ah! Ummm.'

'Also, your Arnprior herds, sir, have not lost a beast in these three years,' Gregor mentioned, coming back into the conversation after a feast of pulchritude. 'Ask you your factor when you get there.'

'Aye. I see. Just so.' The laird did not sound just entirely converted even so, perhaps.

'Come – we will have to be getting you out of this,' Rob Roy declared, in suitably businesslike tone. 'A plague on't Greg – we'll need more gillies. Where's MacAlastair . . . ?',

*   *   *

That coach was extricated from the bottleneck of Drymen only by means of a major operation wherein cattle were coaxed, cajoled, whacked and manhandled by a vociferous host of wiry and half-naked Gregorach – and during which stirring proceedings the young chieftain of Glengyle contrived, amidst much buffeting, to remain at the desired window of the coach, and from there to point out much that was amusing and edifying. And that some part of his audience at least was fully appreciative of his show and his showmanship seemed to be established by the consistency of the laughter, melodious but little constrained, that rose to join his own throughout.

It was with a distinct sense of disappointment and anti-climax, indeed, that Gregor at last saw the way clear for the coach to take its onwards road eastwards round the lower rim of the great Flanders Moss, to Kippen and Arnprior. He did suggest to his uncle thereafter, as a matter of some urgency, that a mounted escort to conduct the equipage for the remaining dozen miles or so might be a wise precaution – but the older man did not seem just wholly convinced of its necessity. If his nephew insisted, needless to say, they could always send along one of the MacGregor gentlemen . . . ? But meanwhile wasn't it time and more that Gregor went off about the serious business of Gallangad? Unless, of course, Glengyle preferred squiring Lowland females around the country to the man's work of teaching Gallangad his lesson?

After that, naturally, there was no more that could be said with dignity. Gregor bade an abruptly stiff and formal farewell to the travellers, and curtly ordered MacAlastair to find him half a dozen sturdy gillies – insisting with a stern loftiness that when he said half a dozen he meant only half a dozen; wasn't he only going to doff the bonnet of a mere bonnet-laird for him? Thereafter he stalked off to collect his garron.

His uncle smiled after him, stroking his small red beard.

CHAPTER TWO

GREGOR got over his disappointment with commendable speed, of course, for as has been stressed he was of a cheerful disposition and no repiner. Also, it falls to be admitted, he was on a ploy that any young MacGregor, any Highlandman almost, would relish. Moreover, the sunset into which he rode was particularly fine – and, as has been made equally clear, he was a young man with an eye for beauty.

He rode south-westwards through the August evening, then, on his sturdy short-legged Highland garron, his own long shanks trailing in the already turning bracken. Six deep-breathing but tireless gillies ran at his heels. They would do the eight miles in well under the hour, thus – for this was a tame country of gentle green slopes and whinny knowes, of patches of tilth and winding purling burns, and these men would run forty steep mountain miles in a day – and then ten more after supper; also they had been townbound all that day, and now rejoiced in the fine freedom of flexing muscles. And at *their* heels loped two lean and shaggy deerhounds, trained to cattle working. So ran the Gregorach.

Gregor maintained the bold steep sugarloaf of Duncryne on his right front, where it thrust like a jagged black fang out of the green braes, dividing the level rays of the dying sun, keeping between its base and the shallow valley of the Catter Water. They rode through a blaze of gold and crimson, with inky shadow brimming from every hollow and dip, and magnifying every least projection. Away in front, across the loch, the massive hunched shoulders of the Mac-farlane hills above Glen Fruin were etched jetty black against the glare. To the right, their own Ben Lomond and all its stalwart satellites thrust noble brows into the burning heaven to win crowns of glory. And to the left, southwards, the gentler rolling Lowland hills of Kilpatrick lifted round bare breasts out of long purple-brown shelving moors. It was a fair scene – and the fairer for the good work that was toward.

Gallangad sat amongst the green skirts of those long brown moors, across the Catter Water, an open breezy place amidst wide cattle-dotted pastures, visible for miles off. No sort of cover did its approaches boast, save for a few crooked wind-tortured trees – not that Gregor, of course, contemplated for a moment approaching the place under any other cover than his own chiefly bonnet. The house itself, set amongst the huddle of its farmery, was a modest two-storeyed crow-step gabled place grown out of a squat square tower, whitewashed but solid and without pretensions.

The MacGregors forded the Catter at a point actually slightly west of their objective, for Gregor desired to assure himself that they could get cattle across the stream here, on the best line for his eventual formidable droving back to Inversnaid so many rough miles to the north-west. Then up over all the green braes to the house they went, their leader whistling blithely as he rode.

There were cattle scattered about those braes, however, and it seemed a pity to be passing them by. So Glengyle gave the word, and the gillies and dogs spread out, working together in a nice harmony – the consequence being that young Gregor approached Gallangad House with a tail of a round dozen fine heifers. Nobody was going to accuse him of being underhand or ungentlemanly about the business.

Graham of Gallangad thus had fair notification of what was to do, and the size of his problem. He was out in front of his steading as Gregor rode up, a big raw-boned glowering man, clad in hodden-grey homespuns and blue bonnet, a stout blackthorn cudgel in his hand. At his back was only an old cattleman – yet there had been two others only a minute or so before, Gregor had noted. From the windows of the house female faces peered anxiously.

'Hech, sirs – what's the meaning o' this, ava?' Graham grated – though he must have had a fairly shrewd idea. 'I'll thank ye, whaesiver ye are, to leave my beasts alane, b'Goad!'

Gregor tut-tutted, mainly to himself, at the harsh coarse Lowland manner and voice, so unlike his own soft and sibilant Highland tongue. But he greeted the man civilly nevertheless. 'A good e'en to you, Gallangad,' he said. 'Dry it is, and the brackens going back early.' The fellow, however rude and uncouth, was laird of his own heired thousand acres, and the rights of property and line fell to be respected. 'I am Glengyle.'

'I care'na whae ye are, Hielantman – but thae queys are mine, and I'll hae ye return them whaur ye got them!'

Gregor was interested. This was not the reaction that might have been expected. After all, the fellow knew that he had flouted Rob Roy and the Highland Watch. He would hardly have expected his defection to be overlooked. And yet he was apparently prepared to be defiant. Which could only mean, surely, that he believed himself to be able to defend himself and his cattle? With what? He had sent two men away, presumably to bring up support. But from where? Gallangad himself would not have more than four or five cattlemen and herds on his thousand or so acres of rough grazing. Had he then been brash enough to raise some sort of a confederacy against the Gregorach? The thing was next to unthinkable – but what else would serve? His neighbours, small farmers, cottagers, the miller at Mavie, merest peasants all, would scarce dare lift their hands against Rob Roy – however little they had to lose. Who else could Gallangad have got, then? Not any minions of the law or the government, certainly, when even the Lord Justice-Clerk himself had to pay for protection. They were much too near to the Highland Line for Edinburgh's writ to run.

Intrigued, Gregor considered the man in relation to all this. A modicum of circumspection might be indicated. Though naturally the fellow must be taught how to speak to such as himself. 'I think you forget, sir,' he observed, pleasantly enough. 'Perhaps your memory is failing on you – a thing that could be happening to any man? But these beasts – and of course two-three others forbye – now belong to Robert Ruadh MacGregor of Inversnaid . . . and to my-self. As witness our bond and agreement. The agreement said, moreover, that you should deliver eight prime beasts to Drymen at Lammas-day – that is today – before sundown.' Noting the other's swift glance to the left and behind him, Gregor bethought him to gesture to his own henchmen, in-dicating further cattle which grazed on the slopes above the house. Four gillies and the dogs slipped off unobtrusively forthwith, leaving two with the heifers they already had. 'Alas that your memory has played you false, Gallangad – and caused the Watch no little inconvenience, whatever. But, as between gentlemen, matters may always be settled decently, and we shall say no more about it . . . save to recoup our extra trouble with a poor extra beast or two.'

'Y'will, will ye – dirty Hielant stots!' the other cried. 'I'll see you damned first! You with your saft mincing words and your gentrice – ye're nae mair'n a wheen red-leggit robbers and thieving sorners! I've paid enough o' your mail, and mair.'

Sitting his pony, Gregor sighed – for he greatly disliked unseemly bickering. 'Not quite enough, Gallangad – not quite. A year of Rob Roy's peace you have had – and that's a thing better men than you esteem worth paying for.' He could not help noting that the man was for ever glancing over to his left, westwards. There was a dip over there, some three hundred yards off, tree-filled – a dene of some sort. 'And I must urge you, sir, to mend your manners – or I shall be forced to have my gillies teach you better with, say, your blackthorn there!'

Gallangad took a wary pace or two backwards, so that he might slip into the narrows of the steading if necessary. 'It'll need mair'n you and your like, my fine fellow!' he said. 'I've gien you the last beast you'll hae frae Gallangad.'

'You prefer that I select them myself . . . ?'

There was an interruption to drown Gregor's soft Highland voice. Up beyond there, where the deerhounds were circling to bring in a mixed scattering of milch-cows and followers to the gillies, a grey-and-white half-collie had appeared out of nowhere and launched itself, barking and snarling, on one of the busy hounds. As dog-fights went it was a brief and inglorious affair, a short sharp tussle wherein the lean and long-legged deerhound seemed to coil itself round the shorter body of its attacker, silently, almost as a snake might, fangs flashing. The other dog's snarling ceased abruptly in a strangled yelp, and then there was no sound from the heaving rolling squirming pair for a few seconds. Then, seemingly leisurely, the deerhound appeared to disentangle and shake itself, before leaping in great springing bounds on its interrupted task with the cattle, leaving an only faintly twitching ragged bundle on the grass.

'Aye,' Gregor sighed. 'Sorry about that I am, man – for I am fond of dogs. I am hoping that you will have no more of them loose, to be getting hurt, at all? There could be a lesson in it, too, for a wise man. How think you . . . ?'

But Gallangad's attention was on him no more, nor even on his unfortunate dog. He was looking away to his left again, and this time with no furtive squinting. The speaker followed his glance. A group of men, indeed a company of men, had emerged from the tree-lined dene and were advancing towards them with an easy resolution – as well they might, for there must have been between two dozen and thirty of them. Moreover, they were tartan-clad men, ragged, dirty, unkempt, but indubitably tartan-clad – a red-blue sett, as far as the grime let it be seen, as distinct from the MacGregor's red-and-green. They seemed to be very liberally armed, too, with staves and billhooks and sickles and knives. Two Lowland cattlemen escorted them from well to the rear.

'Well, now,' Gregor Ghlun Dubh said to himself softly,

in his own tongue. 'The unwashed Sons of Parlan the Wild!' And he laughed – not his usual hearty bellowing, but a soundless brief chuckling. And he loosened his claymore in the silver-mounted sheath that hung from his gleaming shoulder-belt – quite unnecessarily. MacGregor swords seldom needed loosening.

*　　*　　*

Gregor knew who they must be, of course, the only people they *could* be, there and then – Macfarlanes from across the loch, of the broken clan of Glen Fruin, dispossessed these many years by the Colquhouns, landless and little better than tinklers. The Gregorach knew what it was to be land-less – not his own sept of Glengyle, of course, God be praised – even nameless, and they were theoretically out-lawed with a price on every MacGregor head even now; but they had never degenerated to ditch-dodging bog-wallopers who would sell their swords for Lowland silver against their own kind.

Swords was wrong, Gregor amended. There did not seem to be a single sword or claymore amongst the advancing throng – only dirks; as was only suitable, of course, for none could possibly be gentlemen.

Gallangad must have dug deeper into his pouch than any eight stirks to buy this crew.

Gregor spoke to Graham, quite gently. 'I think it would have been less costly to keep faith with MacGregor, Sassun-ach,' he said.

He did more than that, of course. He raised his voice, and cried powerfully, 'Ardchoille! Ardchoille!' the dreaded rallying cry of his clan – partly to bring back to his side the four gillies with the hounds, and partly to help strike caution into the minds of the oncoming Macfarlanes.

Up on the braes behind the house his henchmen, already on the return with another dozen cows and calves, res-ponded by yelping high yittering versions of the same slogan, and came racing downhill, driving the affrighted cattle in a lumbering gallop before them.

The Macfarlanes came on steadily, secure in their numbers, a little dark lively monkey of a man seemingly their leader.

Gregor sat his garron motionless, even if his eyes were busy. He noted swiftly, automatically, such features of the layout of the buildings and the lie of the land as might be useful if this foolish affair came to blows. Seven to thirty, such considerations might have their value.

Gallangad was biding his time, just waiting and glowering, like one of his own bullocks. As the Macfarlanes came up in a solid phalanx, silent but menacing, however ragged, he turned towards them heavily.

But Gregor forestalled him, speaking easily in the Gaelic. 'You are on the wrong side of the loch, are you not, Sons of Parlan?' he wondered. 'What do you amongst the Sassunach?'

'We eat,' the small dark fellow answered him swiftly, briefly.

The MacGregor nodded. 'All must do that,' he agreed. 'But dog does not eat dog – much less eagle eat eagle! I hope that you feed well on Gallangad's beef?'

The other looked just a little uncertain at this line of talk. He glanced along at some of his fellows, and then over at Graham. That individual raised a hand to jab at Gregor.

'Yon's your man!' he cried hoarsely. 'Dirty thieving MacGregor scum! Gie him his paiks, lads – and teach him to come lifting honest men's gear. . . . '

Gregor ignored the creature, addressing himself, in the older tongue, still to the little Macfarlane. 'I am Glengyle,' he mentioned. 'It may be that you have come to help us lift our dues from this close-fisted borach? In which case, my thanks . . . and there are beasts enough for us all!'

'You are generous, Glengyle – with other men's goods,' the dark man said, in his quick squeaky voice. 'But we mind of other times when the Gregorach were less generous. In our own glens!' There was a rumbled growl behind and around him, and an incipient but distinct edging forward.

The Macfarlanes and the MacGregors had ever been un-friends – and Highland memories are long.

'Hae at them, damn their red hides!' Gallangad roared. 'I didna pey ye tae blether, ye gangerels. . . . '

There was a commotion behind Gregor, as the cows from upbye came plunging down to join the heifers, and, more quietly, the four gillies at their heels slipped into their places at their chieftain's flanks, bare chests heaving with their running, but hands on their dirks. The deerhounds loped round and round the augmented herd, red tongues hanging, with the strange effortless tittuping motion of their kind.

The young man on the pony emitted a sigh of relief – though not visibly, of course. His talking had gained what had been required – time to gather his little force tightly about him. Now, he need be less painfully diplomatic.

'Are you with MacGregor, or against MacGregor, Sons of Parlan ?' he shouted, then, and whipped out his claymore with a thin high-pitched skreak of steel. 'Choose you!'

He did not give them long for the choosing, either – not so had the renowned Tutor of Glengyle brought him up. While still the Macfarlanes shuffled and muttered, he dug bare knees into his garron's broad sides, and the beast plunged forward. Close and tight as an arrowhead, at his flanks and rear his six gillies moved with him, herding-staves in one hand, dirks in the other. 'Ardcho-o-o-oile!' they yelled in unison, a fine heartening shout.

That first notable charge was as great a success as was usual – and the Gregorach were namely for their first charges, which in fact not infrequently won the day for them; not with the odds at thirty to seven, of course. But their tight arrowhead formation would bore through any throng not unreasonably deep, and when the point of it was mounted and the opposition was not, and moreover was the only man with a sword in his hand, the thing was child's play. Gregor plunged straight at the little dark fellow, flash-ing his great blade in a beautiful and symmetrical down-bent figure-of-eight pattern – left and right, left and right, the back stroke just clearing his nearest gillies' noses by inches, the forward reaching well out and round in an arc wide enough to ensure that no man could use anything shorter than a billhook against them, with effect. And billhooks are unhandy things to wield in a crowd. Only once did the claymore falter in its sweet rhythm, and that was when, passing Gallangad himself, Gregor turned it sideways-on to give the laird a good whacking buffet with the flat of it, and send him spinning to the ground satisfactorily. It would have been more satisfactory still, of course, to have given him the edge of it, but Glengyle realised well enough that running through even a low-country cock-laird such as this, in the way of business, might arouse all sorts of troublesome repercussions and enquiries, whereas nobody in all the land was going to worry about a few bare-shanked chiefless Macfarlanes more or less.

They drove through the tinkler rabble then, like a knife through cheese, men going down like ninepins on either side, falling back against their fellows, getting in each other's way, billhooks being sheared off by that terrible slicing blade, their butt-ends even doing their own damage in the rear. The gillies actually had little to do, save in the way of dotting an i or crossing a t, only the two rearmost managing to really redden their dirks. They were through the mass in almost less time than it takes to tell, with no more hurt than a long scratch on Gregor's bare thigh caused by a splintering billhook shaft, and a glancing wound on one gillie's cheek made by a thrown sickle, bloody but insignificant.

This sort of manoeuvre was simple, satisfactory, and could be repeated till either the enemy was largely dispersed and scattered or till the chargers became exhausted. But it had one weakness, and that was when each rush was immediately through, and when the arrowhead bared its more or less unprotected rear – that, and the subsequent period of reforming when the components thereof turned around and steadied, regaining their wind. Gregor knew of these possibilities, needless to say, and had chosen to drive through towards a certain alleyway in the line of the steading, a narrow dung-strewn gap between a byre and a stable. Herein they could turn and pause and pant a little, their flanks and rear protected by the walling.

Gregor was laughing again, though a shade gustily with the vigour of his swording. 'How . . . choose you . . . now . . . Parlanach ?' he called out.

No one actually answered his enquiry this time, either. The Macfarlanes were too busy picking themselves up, sorting themselves out, examining their hurts, tripping over their fallen, and generally cursing. Their evident confusion indicated that they were not used to fighting in a body; broken men seldom were, of course. Moreover, Gregor had made certain in the first rush that their monkey-like leader would do no more leading. Also indicated, at least to his uncle's nephew, was the precept that in war confusion in the enemy was a thing to be encouraged. Therefore he jerked a brief word forthwith to his faithful tail, and once more the Ardchoille slogan rang out as the arrowhead bored forward again.

This time they were not quite so successful – not through any failure or lack of vigour on the part of the Gregorach but solely because the Macfarlanes were still involuntarily scattered and uncertain, and therefore less conveniently compacted. As a result, the charge swept through them almost without opposition, and only those unfortunate enough to actually get in the way tended to fall – a disappointing business. Perceiving that most of the throng had drawn away over to the left of them, Gregor gestured and pulled his little cohort round in that direction, in as tight a circling movement as they could make it, causing considerably more of the admirable dispersal and confusion. They returned to their gap beside the byre breathless but intact.

They waited a little longer, now, for the recovery of wind. But the Macfarlanes were undoubtedly rallying, to some extent getting over their first bedevilment. Somebody seemed to be taking the lead. The last memory of the sun had gone, and though the August night was not dark, individuals were becoming difficult to identify at any distance. Gregor gave them a minute or so to decide whether or no they had had enough.

It quickly became clear that that stage had not yet been reached. Despite all the spectacular tumbling and chaos, they had suffered very few real casualties and still outnumbered the invaders by more than three to one. Further lessons were going to be necessary.

Gregor was about to give the order for still another sweep, when a sound behind them drew their glances. A man was darting about at the other end of this alley in which they were wedged. It was deep in shadow there, but by his jerky stiff motions it seemed to be the old cattleman who had stood at Gallangad's side when first they arrived. It was unlikely that such could be of any danger to them, however, and when the character promptly disappeared into one of the sheds, Gregor forthwith dismissed him from his mind. There were more potent folk to deal with.

Strangely enough, he was wrong there, as it happened. Just as Gregor filled his lungs to bellow their slogan once more, a different and still more deep-throated bellow sounded at their backs, jerking all heads round. A great white shape had emerged from a doorway at the head of the alley, and had turned down its narrow length, prodded on apparently at the back by the old man with a pitchfork. It was a bull, most obviously, a massive white and dauntingly horned bull – even allowing for the magnifying effect of the twilight, quite the most bulky and brawny specimen of its kind that even these experts in cattle had ever set eyes upon. And it had its great head hanging low, swaying from side to side, while it scrape-scraped at the ground with an angry forefoot.

Even as they stared, the brute's bellowing rose a degree or two, in tone as in volume, so that it became more like a savage trumpeting. It seemed to try to lash out to the rear at its tormentor there, but could not turn in the confined space of the alley. So, instead, it started off down the passageway at a lumbering gallop, roaring its fury, while the ground and the buildings shook to its challenge.

Gregor Ghlun Dubh delayed no longer. Swallowing whatever it was that had risen into his throat, he gestured forward with his blade – and at that barely beat his gillies to it. The Ardchoille that rose from those lips as they plunged out into the open once more was a poor and wavering effort that Rob Roy would never have recognised. Like the charge that accompanied it. Even a MacGregor charge is seldom up to standard when the chargers' glances are apt to be as much rearwards as front.

CHAPTER THREE

GALLANGAD's white bull changed the whole aspect of that battlefield, changed it radically and entirely and in a ridiculously short space of time. It was a great evil-tempered brainless brute undoubtedly, and what was more, did not know one clan from another. Perhaps the fact that both tartans had a deal of red about them confused even as it enraged the creature, dusk or not, for it hated and attacked them all with equal blind ferocity. From the moment that it came charging out of that alleyway at the heels of the somewhat malformed arrowhead, the interest and enthusiasm went out of the entire battle, as such. It was every man for himself.

At first, the animal merely thundered in the wake of the MacGregors – and the Macfarlanes, with a spontaneous appreciation of the situation, drew aside respectfully to give the whole procession space and passage. The thing thus might have remained attached to the charging Gregorach as a sort of rearguard had it not developed such an unsuit-

38

able turn of speed for so clumsy a brute. As it was, with the spray and draught of its puffing snorts beginning to reach the backs of their bare legs, the running gillies became increasingly preoccupied with other issues than keeping due tight formation and uniform pace. In fact, Gregor began to find them actually passing him on his horse – which was no way to conduct a charge, at all. It was not as if he was going slowly himself – for good garrons were valuable beasts, and not to be lightly hazarded. Gradually, then – at least, in so far as anything so headlong and breakneck could be termed gradual – the MacGregors fanned out, and since those on the flanks quickly perceived that the bull seemed to be considering the pony and its rider as its ultimate objective, they kept on fanning. Soon Glengyle discovered himself, his mount and the bull to be assuming the roles of major actors while everybody else looked on enthralled. Presumably the creature had an objection to horseflesh, or else the extra quantity of red tartan represented by his philamore and plaid acted as magnet.

Needless to say, Gregor found all this both unseemly and quite unfair. He was not quite sure, in a race, whether his short-legged stocky garron would have the heels of the short-legged stocky bull, or vice versa. Certainly the latter seemed to be uncommonly nimble for its weight. Or again, whether he might not be better on his own feet, he who was neither stocky nor short-shanked ? But dignity and prestige entered into that, of course. He was Glengyle, after all, and could not be seen actually running away from anything under heaven. Moreover, he was in process of teaching Gallangad and this Macfarlane riff-raff a lesson, and was not to be distracted. Therefore, he ascertained where the somewhat farflung enemy was thickest, and thitherwards slewed his pony at maximum speed. He managed a rudimentary Ardchoille too, claymore waving.

It was to be hoped that once amongst the Macfarlanes the annoying animal behind would become suitably involved.

Gregor was not disappointed in this, at least. The Macfarlanes on this occasion saw no reason to impede the Mac-

Gregor's progress, and gave way on either side with an alacrity worthy of better men. Two of them, indeed, in a haste unbecoming in Highlanders, collided with such force as to lose their balances and fall. The more agile was up and off again before you could say Loch Sloy. But the other was less effective at getting to his feet in time. Over this miserable specimen Gregor lifted his garron in a jump, disdaining even to poke him with his sword in the by-going. The bull, however, allowed itself to be distracted by the squirming and convulsing red apparition in its path. Which was no less than the foolish fellow deserved, probably.

Gregor knew almost a momentary pique at the lack of attention that his single-minded charge seemed to be receiving from the Parlanach. They all appeared to be much more interested in how their grounded fellow dealt with a rapidly developing situation. And to give the creature his due, he rather redeemed himself, managing now to leap to his feet as though spring-loaded, and so effectively to take to his heels that only the ragged folds of his stained kilt caught on one of the hurtling bull's thrusting horns – where it remained. Fortunately or otherwise, the wretch was not too firmly attached to this his only garment, and leapt off, naked but vociferous. The bull, disappointed and temporarily blinded by this tattered tartan draped over its face, slewed round and charged hither and yonder in short rushes, tossing its head, stamping its feet, and bellowing. Gregor was able to pull up, a short distance off, evidently forgotten for the moment by all and sundry.

There could be no point in seeking to chronicle any coherent and consecutive account of what happened thereafter. A state of general, stirring but quite chaotic activity ensued. The bull quickly got rid of most of its kilt – though it retained one fragment which fluttered like captured colours from its horn – and thereupon hurled itself at anyone and everyone that came within its range of vision. And it had a wide-ranging if choleric eye. Entirely catholic and quite unpredictable, it flung itself around, attacking Macfarlanes, MacGregors and its own Lowland keepers with a fine impartiality and with an unflagging vigour that indicated a virility patently quite unsatisfied by the demands of Gallangad's paltry herd.

Occasionally, of course, some brave fellow would take a whack at the brute, as it were in passing, with billhook or cudgel. But such were few and far between – and apt to be unplanned. It was extraordinary how swiftly everybody lost their identity too – the deepening dusk assisting, of course. Gregor alone, because he was mounted, remained kenspeckle. For the rest, it was quite impossible to establish who was which, all being merely identical and individual targets for an angry quadruped.

Very soon it was apparent to Gregor that there was no hope of restoring the field to anything like order, or even of resuming the battle. Everybody had lost interest. Already there seemed to be markedly fewer folk about – which, since there was no routh of bodies lying about the scene either, must mean that the combatants were just quietly betaking themselves off as occasion offered. A reasonable and sensible attitude, he decided, for the Macfarlanes. But for the Gregorach, of course, it was different. They had their errand to fulfil, and the cattle to consider. . . .

He considered these, then, scattered around eastwards, but none far away, ghostly shapes in the gloom, apparently watching the entire affray with interest. It occurred to him that if he could just get this lot rounded up and on their way, leaving the remaining Macfarlanes to the bull, it would probably be the best outcome of the situation. The trouble was – where were those miserable gillies of his?

Raising his voice, Gregor emitted a sort of modified Ardchoille – nothing that would sound too like a challenge to either bull or Macfarlanes, not so much a warrior's rallying-cry indeed as the call of say a hen eagle for her errant chicks.

There was no audible response. But presently he found a couple of somewhat hang-dog-seeming individuals at his side. He gestured imperiously in the direction of the cattle, and, uttering brief high yelps for the hounds, the pair darted thankfully off. Other shamefaced miscreants appeared, one by one, out of the mirk and confusion, and were sent about the same business. The only thing – Gregor was not quite certain that the odd Macfarlane might not have got included amongst them.

In a gratifyingly short space of time the unified herd of some two dozen beasts was on the move – not directly towards Gregor admittedly, with beyond him the bull's circus, but aslant and northwards – which after all was the way in which they had to go eventually. Which was all right. But one of the young heifers, white also and by her behaviour almost certainly a daughter of the wretched bull itself, chose to be awkward. Breaking away from the others, she came lolloping across, as though to join her sire, mooing warm invitation.

Gregor managed to nip that in the bud, turning the creature back a little. But unfortunately the damage had been done. Perhaps the bull had been getting tired, not physically most assuredly, but of chasing shadows; perhaps it was pining for its own kind; perhaps it just recognised that flutelike lowing, and deep responded to not-so-deep? At any rate the big brute abruptly gave up the harrying of elusive Macfarlanes, produced a really major but quite touching bellow, very different from all its angry trumpetings hitherto, and came pounding over to join the gentle heifer. And therefore, unhappily, the heifer's herders.

Gregor Ghlun Dubh found himself faced with a nice problem. That bull was not to be shooed away – but unfortunately neither was the heifer. She was cavorting joyfully to his right, ululating urgent goodwill. Gregor's abuse and gesticulations and sword-slapping were of less than no effect. The foolish animal would not go away, but only bawled the louder. And the bull, bearing down on his other side at full ground-shaking speed, made answer.

Gregor came to a decision at commendable speed, too. What was one heifer, more or less? Gallangad could be left with one beast to him – or, rather, two. The rest of the herd was streaming away downhill northwards at a fine pace, gillies well up – disappearing into the gloom, in fact. Without further debate, the chieftain dug his knees into his garron and set off in pursuit.

And with a high-pitched silvery belling of sheer *joie de vivre* the heifer followed on, kicking up her heels.

Farther back the deep roar of infatuated maturity intimated that the bull had duly noted the change of course and was now heading northwards also.

Grègor cursed vehemently and comprehensively. He cantered after the herd, and the white heifer cantered after him, and the bull cantered after the heifer. In such fashion the Gregorach retired from Gallangad.

*　　*　　*

The long half-mile down to the Catter Water was covered in what must have been record time, with the rear gaining noticeably on the van. What would happen at the riverside was a matter for real speculation.

Gregor had joined up with the gillies ere that. No hearty greetings were exchanged. There was a definite tendency for the drovers to spread out, left and right, leaving ample space for the white heifer to rejoin her sisters. Glengyle did nothing to discourage this. Unfortunately, the frolicsome creature seemed to have taken a fancy, like the bull before her, either to the young chieftain or to his horse, and now insisted on clinging to his heels with annoying fidelity. The bull, ignoring the rest of the herd, lumbered in her wake.

By the time that Gregor and his immediate tail reached the waterside, the remainder of the cavalcade, now unaccountably slackening speed, had dropped fully a hundred yards behind. The young man rather blessed that dark and chuckling water. He put the pony straight at it, and splashed across its thirty feet or so in fine style – making as much pother as possible, in fact. Now they would see. . . .

But when he got to the far bank and looked back, the heifer was already half-way across, and loving it, even kicking up her hindquarters skittishly as the water splashed her underparts. Her faithful sire plunged in after her, unhesitant.

Gregor groaned.

Up the rather steeper gorse-grown slopes beyond he urged his garron, hoping somewhat desperately that the climb would deter and weary either progeny or progenitor. It did nothing of the sort, only too clearly. The heifer was apparently in the same elevated state in which young females of other sorts, for instance, frail and delicate as they may seem, can dance away the entire night and appear with the dawn fresh and lively as kittens beside their tottering and haggard-eyed escorts. And the bull most obviously was nothing less than a manufactory of energy and vigour, the devil damn it! It was the rider, and possibly to some extent the mount, that began to weary. And there were still fully twenty-five rough and difficult miles to Inversnaid.

It was not until he and his personal procession was high on its long hummocky ascent to the base of Duncryne, round the east side of which lay their route – and the stodgy and uninspired remainder of his retinue had long been lost to sight and sound, far below – that it began to dawn on Gregor MacGregor that this might not all be quite so humiliating and unsuitable as it seemed. Suppose, instead of seeking to shake off this vast and terrible bull, he considered delivering it intact at Inversnaid, as a personal and monumental booty, an epic of single-handed valour and devotion? Might not that be something truly heroic, so much more worthy of his stature and name than merely to bring home the few cows and stirks that his uncle had ordered – or rather, requested? Indeed, might it not be just the sort of thing that the sennachies and song-makers in time to come would sing about and hand down to on-coming generations – how Gregor Ghlun Dubh brought the Great White Bull of Gallangad to Glengyle? That would sound very fine, magnificent.

The notion did not require any period of gestation and growth in Gregor's mind – it flowered forthwith and im-mediately, fully grown, and was as promptly accepted, MacGregor like. And, of course, thereupon the whole situa-tion was changed, transformed. The bull became at once a

44

subject for coaxing and managing, not for terror, a source of possible triumph instead of a menace. From being afraid that the brute might overtake or outrun his garron, the man incontinently began to fear that it would soon grow tired, lose interest, give up the chase. The heifer, from being an infuriating little nuisance, was translated at once into a major blessing, the essential bait for the trap, to be cajoled and cherished instead of shooed away. The human mind is a truly exceptional mechanism.

As they climbed, Gregor was now looking back over his shoulder even more frequently and anxiously than heretofore – in case the creatures behind him should be slackening pace and falling off. But the heifer did not fail him, right up to the low ridge between Duncryne Hill and the lonely place of Cambusmoon – and though the bull's heavy puffings were now more indicative of laboured breathing than majestic wrath, its interests still seemed to be wholly engaged.

It was downhill thereafter, happily, all the way to the Endrick's levels around the tail of the loch. Keeping the few lights of the village of Gartocharn well to his left, Gregor plunged on north-eastwards, having to even restrain his garron a little – it apparently not yet having discovered that they were now leading and not running away. But at least the beast was notably sure-footed, like all its kind, so that its rider needed only to give it the general direction and leave it to pick its own route over the shadowy broken shelving ground – which was a great convenience for a man whose head was turned rearwards for most of the time. It would be a tragic thing, he now was perceiving, if the bull was to fall and break a leg in any of the numerous holes, burns and steps with which this benighted territory was littered. Or the heifer either, of course. . . .

Once across the Dumbarton turnpike, new problems arose to worry the leader of the little procession – literally arose, and went lumbering off affrighted into the night. Cattle. These broad lush flats and water-meadows flanking the mouth of the Endrick were dotted with sleeping beasts,

My Lord Marquis of Montrose's beasts – and who could tell whether one of these might not at any moment take the bull's fancy, in place of the heifer, and divert it off into the gloom?

But that bull was of a worthily tenacious mind, undoubtedly, and not to be turned aside from whatever it was doing. And for the time being it was following and pining after its own little white heifer. Other bovine charmers might plunge off with inviting woofs, or low siren songs from all around, but her sire, that most adequate animal, that was even now butting and bull-heading its way into legend, folklore, even into history itself, just kept boring on, head down, breathing gustily, short thick stamping legs shaking the soft ground.

And that was Gregor Ghlun Dubh's next worry. The nearer that they came to the sluggish mouth of the coiling Endrick Water, the marshier became the terrain. Would his bull perhaps sink into the mire, get bogged, and have to be abandoned like a stranded leviathan from the loch? Fortunately the season had been a dry one, and the place was not nearly so wet as he had known it; he had been perfectly content to lead a herd of ordinary beasts across these flats and over a ford he knew of. But this bull must weigh three times as much as any normal beast. . . .

In the event, however, it was the heifer that got into trouble, not her sire. At the very edge of the river, as Gregor did some quick prospecting for the ford, she came up, still skittish and fancy-dancing, and seeking to cut off a corner that the garron's turning up the river's bank had made, plunged straight into a quaking pot of black mire covered by a skin of moss, and sank almost to her belly. Promptly a piteous heart-rending plaint rang out, markedly different from her previous utterance, to which the faithful bull made loud and confident answer. But the big brute had more sense than to lumber in beside her, just the same, and came to a halt a few yards off, testing the ground with tramping forefeet, great head stretched forward towards the other, snuffling and bellowing by turns.

This was where Gregor of Glengyle's calibre rather fell to be tested. It was one thing to lead the way, keeping a discreet distance between himself and his self-attached tail, and altogether another to turn back and actually approach that bull. He did not do so off-hand or without consideration, either. But he did it. Let that stand. What was more, he went on his own two feet – since the garron would on no account co-operate. Dismounting, and without exactly striding, he moved back to the heifer.

Actually, the bull paid him not the slightest heed. The brute's entire attention was concentrated on the bleating animal in the pot of the bog. After a few wary moments, so was Gregor's. Man and bull stood on opposite sides of the little quagmire, considering the situation.

The heifer was not struggling nor floundering about, just standing still and wailing her dismay. Gregor scratched his head. Just what to do was less than crystal-clear. He could not reach out sufficiently far to touch the creature without falling into the hole himself – not that touching would have been a lot of use anyway. He had no rope with him, to loop round her and seek to tug her out. He tried speaking coaxingly to her, urging her to make the effort to get out herself. But that produced only enhanced complaints – each answered by a sort of groaning blast from the sympathetic bull, the draught of which reached across to the man distinctly.

Then he had an idea. Unlooping his sheathed claymore, which hung on its silver-mounted shoulder-belt, he held the weapon out by its tip, and after the third throw managed to toss the loop of the belt over the heifer's head. Twisting the thing, and moving a little to the side so that it did not slip off, he tugged. It was not the sort of thing that he would have liked anyone to have seen him doing with MacGregor of Glengyle's broadsword.

He tugged to no purpose for a few moments – and it was galling to consider the power and vigour represented by the great brainless brute standing there at the other side of the hole, useless, and that yet could have hauled this cry-baby

47

out in two shakes could it only have been harnessed. Then suddenly his efforts had effect. The pressure on the heifer's neck evidently decided her to do something for herself, for after a series of convulsions she got first one foreleg out on to firm ground, and then the other, and finally, with a great slaister and splattering of mud – much of it over Glengyle's finery – she heaved herself right out, to stand, bemused, bemired and trembling, on the brink. And silent for the moment.

The bull moved round the hole, now, with a sort of sober circumspection noteworthy in so rampant a brute – and Gregor, detaching his sword, moved back to his garron with similar circumspection. But there, looking round, he discovered that the heifer had not moved at all, but was standing still, apparently all the wanton whimsey-whamsey drained out of her into the bog. The bull was nuzzling her rear tentatively.

Gregor compressed his lips, sighed and shrugged in one, and taking the reluctant garron by its shaggy forelock, led it back to the cattle. He had to tug hard here, too. He elected to come up on the other side of the heifer from her sire, the which was making a deep rumbling noise in its throat, that sounded daunting in the extreme but was probably a species of purring; and went only close enough to reach out his sword and its belt once more, loop it over the heifer's head, and vault on to the pony's back. That wise animal was nothing loth to continue its northward journey promptly; the heifer came along meekly, deflatedly, at the pressure; and, chin resting contentedly on her rump, great puffs from its nostrils blowing along her back, the bull came too, waddling grotesquely.

Thus, in sober file, they walked down and into the Endrick Water, and across, with no more fuss than might the Senators of the College of Justice proceed to a hanging, and up on to the firmer ground at the far side. And thus they continued across the darkling flats, to the drove road beyond that led to Balmaha. And every now and again the bull sighed mightily, the heifer coiled a long tongue round the chased sheath of the noble brand that led her, and the garron blew doubtfully through flaring nostrils.

Presently Gregor began to sing, gently to himself, to them all. He made up the words and the tune as he went along, since there was nobody in all the night to hear him – save a bull, a heifer and a pony. And it had the makings of a good, a noble song in it, too.

*　　*　　*

There is no need to tell of the long long walk that they all had thereafter – for that was in fact all it was. Crossing the Endrick had amounted to crossing the Highland Line, and the drove road that they followed took them northwards between towering dark mountains on their right hand and the great isle-strewn expanse of Loch Lomond on their left. Once through the narrow Pass of Balmaha the un-relenting rampart of the hills drew even closer, until it was pressing them for much of the time almost on to the loch shore itself. But despite the constriction of their going, the climbing and the plunging and the twisting of the track, the innumerable streams draining the land mass that they had to cross, and the endless wooded bays and headlands that fell to be circumnavigated, the heifer and the bull followed steadily on behind the pacing garron, the one with a mild acceptance, the other with a growing but determined stolidity. And at the one side the tiny wavelets whispered and sighed, and at the other the muted singing of a hundred burns accompanied them, to fill in the periods when Gregor's nocturne died on him. Otherwise, only the occasional lost cry of some bird of the night interrupted the even clop and scuffle of hooves.

They did not make any great speed now, of course; pro-bably if they averaged two twisting coiling miles in an hour they were doing as much as could be expected. Gregor cal-culated that they had all of eighteen difficult miles to cover after reaching the drove road – which was of course no road at all, but only a rough track for most of the way and sometimes not even that – a long walk for a stiff-legged heavy-built bull indeed.

Before long, the rest of the herd had caught up with them – or almost. When the gillies perceived the white shapes in the gloom in front, they slackened pace judiciously behind, so that a suitable interval should be preserved between the chiefly and the merely subordinate sections of the expedition. And that they maintained throughout, whatsoever the difficulties.

It was at least a couple of hours past midnight before they reached the clachan of Rowardennan, half-road to Inversnaid, and a MacGregor outpost. Gregor would much have liked to knock up the ale-house, whatever the hour, for well-deserved refreshment, but regretfully decided against it; who knew, if once the rhythm of this tranquil progress was disturbed, when and how the bull could be got to resume it? His people behind him, under no such pressure, were some time in reaching their due station in the rear thereafter.

Beyond Rowardennan the mountains pressed still closer and the track deteriorated accordingly, so that now they were merely clinging to a steep hillside grown with oak and birch and hazel, now high above the wan glimmering floor of the loch, now down at its dark wrack-littered beach. They were, in fact, here circling the massive base of soaring Ben Lomond itself. It was hereabouts that the white bull began at last to show signs of weariness, to stumble on its knee occasionally, and to grumble abysmally in its throat. But it kept doggedly on after the tireless heifer, nevertheless.

The pale dawn found them at the lonely place of Cailness, crouching under the great sleeping hills, the house of a sort of cousin of Glengyle's own. And here the bull decided that it had really had enough for one night. But with Inversnaid a mere three miles farther, Gregor was determined to complete his epic. The wills of tired bull and tired man clashed – and the man's won. MacGregor of Cailness was roused out of his bed, a rope and a pitchfork required of him, and the hounds and gillies whistled up. The bull and the heifer were tied loosely together, and another rope looped round the former's horns. Gregor redonned his sword and belt, and took the end of the rope, while dogs and gillies whooped and yelped discreetly in the rear. Only a couple of prods with the pitchfork were required. The party resumed its weary progress up the side of surely the longest loch in all Scotland, the bull led on like a lamb. Cailness, in parting, mentioned that he had never seen such a gentle animal.

Strangely enough, Gregor found himself to be somewhat nettled by this remark. The unsuitability of it remained with him for all the rest of the way over the rock-strewn wooded mountainside that the track was now slowly but surely climbing. His sleep-starved mind was perhaps less nimble than heretofore, but by the time that they had at last turned away from the loch altogether, and were making a laboured slantwise ascent of the precipitous pass of the Arklet Burn, he recognised what he must do to put the matter right. Admittedly, the just-awakened folk that peered at them from the doorways of the grouped croft houses of Clashbuie, first of the Inversnaid townships, gaped in awe at their white monster – but that was not enough. He and his men were now dragging and even pushing the drooping wayworn brute up that gruelling climb, hoisting it almost by main force, a labour of Hercules indeed. So, at the crest, with the level new-risen sun pouring golden light in their faces down the high east-lying trough of Glen Arklet, Gregor, panting, ordered thistles and whins to be collected from the hillside around. A bundle of these was then tied under the tail of the gasping heaving colossus, Glengyle remounting his garron the while. At first the creature merely stood, head sunk, exhausted. But when the gillies, bold now, slapped and poked it with their sticks, it rumbled, swung its head – and swished its tail. The startling hurt widened its dulled eyes. It emitted a cracked bellow. It took a pace or two forward, swished its tail again, and roared its pain and ire. Like milk on the boil, its fury rose within it and poured over. Lashing its spike-loaded tail now, and shaking all the enclosing hillsides with its trumpeted indignation, quite outsoaring and drowning the widespread lowing of beasts that came out of the valley ahead of them, it tore the turf with its forefeet, ripped it with its horns, and then lurched forward at the only live objects visible in front – Gregor and his garron. Neither required the gillies' shouted warning. They proceeded.

And so they tore out through the scattered birches, over the rushy levels where the Arklet and the Snaid Burns met, and round into the lovely green glen of Inversnaid itself, the bull temporarily recovered its strength in its choler, Gregor keeping ahead of it with a nice judgment, the heifer dragged along willy-nilly sprawling and stumbling, and the rest of the herd streaming behind amidst yelling men and baying hounds.

It was a notable entry, worthy of any chieftain of all the long line of Glengyle, or Clan Alpine itself. From all the profusion of the hump-backed cot-houses of the glen floor the folk emerged, to point and shout and laugh and cheer. 'Ardchoille!' Gregor ululated, above the din, and again 'Ardchoille!' and all the watchers in that valley took it up, the men chanting, the women skirling, the children screaming. Straight for the grassy terrace formed above a wide bend in the burn, where Rob Roy's two-storeyed house stood, Gregor rode, and the bull charged. Rob, stripped to the waist, in short kilt, scratching his red-furred chest, was outside his door, head back, laughing his strange silent laughter. At his side a man stood, open-mouthed, clad in once elegant breeches and once white frilled shirt. And from behind their legs children peeked.

Across the shallows the peculiar cavalcade swept, almost to the watchers' feet. There Gregor leapt lightly from his horse, casting away the rope that linked him to bull and heifer at the same time. For a grievous moment he knew doubt, the spectators knew doubt, possibly even the bull knew doubt, as to which it would follow – the careering pony, or the red-tartaned man? But the moment passed, and so did the bull – on at the affrighted garron's heels, pounding the earth and driving itself into further paroxysms of fury by the lashing and liberal self-application of whin-prickles to its tenderest parts, the heifer dragged alongside.

Gregor let them go without so much as a backward glance. No harm in the brute giving the glen a taste of its calibre, he decided – no harm at all. Travel-stained, mud-spattered, heavy-eyed, but chin even a degree higher than his wont perhaps, he swung his plaid back over his shoulder, and strode up to his uncle, hand on the guard of his claymore.

'I have fetched you a few beasts from Gallangad,' he mentioned. 'Just like you said, whatever.'

'As Royal's my Race – you have so, Greg!' Rob Roy cried. 'Yon bull, now – did you fetch it, or did it fetch you, I'm wondering?'

'Sir!' Young Glengyle frowned. 'I'd have you to know . . .' Then he stopped, eyed his uncle from under one raised eyebrow, and then opened his mouth and laughed loud and long, Gregor Ghlun Dubh's own laughter. 'Shadow of God – I couldn't be telling you that my own self!' he declared. 'And that's a fact.'

Uncle smote nephew on the back, then, and despite the younger man's notable size he all but went sprawling. 'Bless you, boy,' he chuckled. 'You're a MacGregor, whatever!' And then, sobering quickly, he turned to the other man in the Lowland garb, a gentleman, and mystified obviously. 'But we are not all MacGregors. Colonel – my nephew, Glengyle, Chieftain of our branch of Clan Alpine. Greg – Colonel Hooke . . . from St Germains!'

'Oh! Ah!' said Gregor, and swallowed his laughter. 'Your servant, sir.'

Perhaps that swallowing of his laughter was symbolic, there and then. For the man before him sought to bring not laughter to the glens but blood and tears.

It might be said indeed that, between them, the White Bull of Gallangad and Colonel Hooke closed the door on

Gregor's carefree youth. The bull galloped away with that chapter, and the Colonel pointed through into the next. Man's estate opened before Glengyle. There are more ways of coming of age than one.

CHAPTER FOUR

GREGOR MACGREGOR had earned his sleep out, surely – but he was denied it nevertheless. Rob Roy would drive men hard, on occasion – though seldom as hard as he would drive himself – and when events were astir, he had scant patience with slumber. By noon he had his nephew shaken out of the log-like sleep into which he had sunk immediately after the merest gesture at breakfasting, and hailed owlishly down to the groaning littered board set outside the front door of Inversnaid House, whereat Rob and his guest were just finishing their dining. He was not much of a man for being indoors, either, when he could be out. Gregor's Aunt Helen-Mary, a quiet but striking-featured woman with a very direct eye – indeed, it was said, the only living eye which could quell that of her husband – gathered the amplitude of broken meats, cold salmon, venison, oatcakes and curds laced with whisky, round her nephew's place, patted his shoulder, and withdrew indoors with her seven-year-old son Coll. Which meant men's talk.

'See you, Greg,' Rob Roy said, feeding his deerhounds scraps from the table now that his wife was safely out of the way. 'Colonel Hooke here has work for us to do. The word has been long of coming, but now it is here at last, God be praised. He was here awaiting me last night, when I was after reaching home from Drymen. He has come from Fife, and requires of us swift action, in the name of the King.'

'Fife . . . ? King . . . ?' Gregor mumbled, blinking the sleep out of his eyes. The noonday sun set up a great dazzle from the plashing Snaid Burn below their terrace. 'You mean the Chevalier . . . ?'

'Tut, lad – wake you! The King – our only king, Jamie Stewart the Eighth, by the grace of God. The Colonel has come from his Court of St Germains, in France, with the word that we have been awaiting. . . . '

'From Fife, did you not say. . . . ?'

'Och, from Fife, yes,' Rob explained patiently. 'He was after sailing from France to Anster, in Fife. He has been talking to the lairds in the Kingdom and in Angus, and now comes to raise the clans, Greg. The King will make a bid for his own, at last.'

'We are rising, then – now?' Gregor's voice rose a little, as his mind rose to shake itself free of the cobwebs of slumber.

'Not quite, young man – not yet.' That was Colonel Nathaniel Hooke speaking, a lean, sober, unsmiling man of middle years, liker the Kirk in looks than the battlefield, yet an old soldier of Dundee's and an Irishman into the bargain. 'Pray it will come to that. But as yet it is plans and promises that we are drawing, not swords.'

'But you said swift action, Uncle, did you not . . . ?'

'To be sure – but there is other action, whatever, than just drawing swords, *a dhuine*,' Rob said. 'We are to be getting the chiefs assembled to a great meeting, a gathering, so that the clans may be raised. Myself, I am to go round them, it seems . . . '

'You are the best man for the task, MacGregor,' Hooke assured. 'No man can cover the ground as you can – especially these wild mountains. You will do in a week what would take me a month and more.' That was no more than the truth, at any rate. 'Moreover, your name and your fame are known to all. You will be able to act as ambassador, my deputy, not merely my messenger. I have His Majesty's commission for you in my bag. And again, you are Breadalbane's kinsman, which, since he is to be host to the gathering, is of advantage. For, h'mm, not all men unfortunately love my Lord Breadalbane!'

Rob frowned. His mother, the Lady Glengyle, had indeed been Margaret Campbell of Glenlyon, first cousin to John Campbell, first Earl of Breadalbane – but it was not every day and in all company that Rob liked to be reminded of the fact. The connection could be useful at times, of course – indeed, had he not had to take the name of Campbell in lieu of his own, in 1693, when the Clan Gregor was outlawed and proscribed again so that no man might legally bear the name of MacGregor? In the eyes of the law – but only the law, to be sure – he was still Robert Campbell. But the Campbell connection had its disadvantages, as Rob was the first to admit – and Breadalbane was kittle-cattle even for a Campbell. Had he not been the main instigator of the MacDonalds' massacre at Glen Coe, of ill memory? Powerful as he might be, no man was less trusted in all Scotland.

'I mislike this forgathering with Breadalbane,' Rob declared gravely. 'Myself, I misdoubt his attachment to the King's cause. It is something sudden, is it not? He stood neutral in 'Ninety, and came out for Dutch William after Cromdale fight. Kinsman or no, I'd liefer see the gathering held some other where, Colonel.'

'You must allow His Majesty's advisers to be the best judges of that, MacGregor,' Hooke asserted, a little stiffly. 'And you will recollect that whatever Dutch William's attitude may have been, Anne's present Government has not looked over-kindly on Breadalbane. In politics, men in high places must sometimes be, h'mm, allowed to change their minds!' He sipped at his horn beaker of whisky fastidiously. 'Moreover, if Clan Campbell can be persuaded to declare for King James, then Scotland at least is as good as won.'

'Man – you are right there, whatever!' Rob Roy cried, but jeeringly. 'Breadalbane may do what he will, but Argyll himself will never declare himself till Scotland *has* been won! As my Race is Royal – that is the way it will be! Man, I know the Campbells, see you – I know them fine.'

It was his guest's turn to frown. 'Maybe you do, Mac-Gregor – but I think perhaps that you do not fully realise the present state of Scotland, which will force the Campbells' hands for them, force Argyll's as it has already forced Breadalbane's. This Act of Union that they are forcing on the Scots Parliament, this surrender of Scotland's independence – it will be signed before the year is out, and the whole country will rise in revolt. . . . '

'It will *not* be signed, in God's name! Scotland will never sign her own death warrant, whatever!' That was Gregor Ghlun Dubh, awake at last.

His uncle eyed him thoughtfully.

Hooke's long upper lip seemed to grow the longer. 'There speaks innocence! Scotland's death warrant will be signed, never doubt it, Glengyle. Enough pens have been bought to ensure it! Already the golden guineas are flowing north. A flood, it is. The Scots Parliament will meet for the last time in October . . . '

'The dastards! The traitors!' the young man cried. 'There are not crawling renegades enough, even in Edinburgh, to carry the day.'

'Think you so?' The other actually smiled, if thinly. 'Many bearing the noblest names in Scotland have already come out for the Union. All thirty-two Scots Commissioners have already agreed it, in London . . . at a price! But *we* need not distress ourselves, my young friend. Leal men should rather rejoice, and grasp the opportunity with both hands – while these others are grasping the English gold! Scotland will be aflame with resentment by the spring. And then King James will come – and when he lands, the entire country will flock to him. It is all, h'mm, most opportune.' That, from Nathaniel Hooke, might be esteemed as enthusiasm. 'Argyll, like Breadalbane, is no fool, whatever else he may be. He is one of the leaders of the Union party, yes – and who knows what his share of the guineas may be – but he knows the temper of the people very well, and what will happen if King James were to land at the right moment. It would not be beyond him to keep his gold, and yet to be ready to join the winning side in time to undo the deed that the gold had wrought!'

'God's death – do men sink so low?' Gregor gasped.

Rob Roy cleared his throat strongly. 'That may or may not be so, Colonel. Time will tell. I agree with you that if the Union is signed there will be trouble from one end of Scotland to the other. Even the Lowlanders may find themselves a modicum of spirit! And that will be the time for Jamie Stewart to land, indeed. But still I mislike this gathering to Breadalbane. I fear the other clans will mislike it also. . . . '

'Tush, man – you misjudge not only your kinsman but the situation,' the Jacobite emissary declared, almost impatiently. 'Do you not see – it is a sign of success? That the tide is with us. Breadalbane will not adhere to a losing cause. All will see that, and take heart. Indeed, the Earl has been most helpful. I had much converse with him at Blair-in-Atholl. This hunting match at Kinloch Rannoch is his own suggestion. All may attend it as his guests, without fear of suspicion.'

'Aye,' Rob said heavily. 'Aye. I'ph'mm. Maybe. And what says Atholl?'

'Atholl is, er, somewhat indisposed. A sick man. But he is with us in spirit. . . . '

'Aye,' the MacGregor said again, significantly. 'That is Atholl. Och, well – *non omnia possumus omnes*, eh? We all have our limitations, whatever. I will do what I can to bring the chiefs in to your hunting match, Colonel. But it will take time – for I will have half the Highlands to be covering.'

'I will come with you,' Glengyle declared, then.

'No, Greg – I think not,' his uncle said. 'There is other work for you. The King's army will be needing gold as well as men – and it will not get its gold out of the heather. Save for my cattle, that is – much of our fine haul here can be turned into good Scots pounds at the Crieff and Falkirk Trysts. The Colonel will go talking with the lairds in Gowrie and Strathearn and the Carse of Stirling. But the real money in this land is otherwhere – what is left of it after the Darien business! It lies with the merchants in Glasgow. Their poor shilpit souls are with their ledgers, whatever – but not all of them will look kindly on this Union. To tap them, we need the help of such as Buchanan of Arnprior and Hamilton of Bardowie, men with their fingers in the pie of the Indies trade. Ha – I see your eye light up, boy! I wonder why? You took a fancy to Arnprior, or maybe his goodson Bardowie, yesternight, did you? Aye, so.'

His nephew examined the stripped haunch of roebuck that he held in his hand, before passing it on to the hounds. 'I preferred his ladies,' he said, judiciously frank. 'They seemed . . . more fervent for the cause.'

'Is that so? Oh, aye. Anyway, I jaloused that you might not be averse to taking a message to Arnprior? And maybe to Stirling of Garden too, who has his links with Glasgow. And to two-three others that I can think on. Fine, then. And again, see you, something more. The Colonel thinks – and I am agreeing with him – that the chiefs and captains of clans that I will be after assembling at this Kinloch Rannoch ploy might be heartened and stablished and in some degree convinced if, as well as seeing Colonel Hooke and each other there, they were to see a sizeable body of armed and determined men!' Rob smiled gently. 'Gillies for the hunting match, of course – entirely necessary, whatever! Now, it so happens that in the deplorable and downholden state of our Highlands today there is only our own Gregorach that could be making such a muster at short notice, belike! A coincidence. It is against the law, of course – but, *dia*, are we not outlawed and proscribed anyhow! So gather you, Greg . . . ' His uncle recollected, and stroked his beard. 'So if Glengyle will be so kindly as to gather his sept, and such other of the Gregorach as he can raise betwixt here and Balquhidder, to the number of, say, three hundred, and bring them to Kinloch Rannoch three weeks from now – och, that will be fine, just fine, see you.'

'And His Majesty will be duly grateful, Glengyle,' Nathaniel Hooke added gravely.

Gregor was on his feet, eyes shining. '*Dia* – I shall be leading the first men under arms for the King in all Scotland, then?' he cried.

'You could put it that way,' Hooke agreed.

'*Ro mhath* – I will do it! Do it all. This will be better than droving cattle, whatever. I will go now. At once. . . . '

'Wait you. Wait for the message, at least!' Rob Roy laughed. 'And think you it would not be kindly to go say farewell to the Lady Christian your mother, over at Glengyle?'

'M'mmmm.'

'And the bull? You will wish to take your bull to Glengyle?'

'I . . . ah . . . I will go see my mother,' Gregor said handsomely. 'Give me your message, and let me be gone. And, Uncle . . . you may keep the bull!'

*　　*　　*

The green valley of Inversnaid, fair and grassy and spreading open to the south and the sun, was in fact little more than a high sheltered corrie and no real glen at all, some two miles in length before it tailed off into the lofty crags and rocky buttresses of Maol an Fhithich, the Bluff of the Ravens. A thousand-foot ridge separated it on the west from long Loch Lomond, and to the east a higher barrier of three tall hills divided it first from Corryarklet and then from Glen Gyle. To reach his home from Inversnaid, then, Gregor Ghlun Dubh could either go the long way round the hill masses, by Loch Arklet and Loch Katrine, or over them by a high bealach between Stob an Fainne, the Peak of the Ring, and Beinn a Choin, the Mountain of Weeping. Needless to say, as a matter of principle he chose the latter. Seldom indeed were conditions such as to force the former upon him, practically two thousand feet high though the saddle lay.

It was not all a matter of youthful masculine esteem, or a point of honour. Aesthetics entered into it too, for assuredly the vista from the lofty pass was something to move even

the dullest perception. And Gregor's was not that —
especially when, as now, a fierce pride in it all possessed
him, and an aching, yearning yet eternally unsatisfied sense
of identity with all that prospect. On every hand the
mountains stretched away into purple infinity — save to the
south, which was blocked out anyway by the majestic bulk
of Ben Lomond. No fewer than eight lochs lay below him,
in blue tranquillity, sparkling in the sun, or glooming deep
in shade. Far down the stretching arm of salt Loch Long
the Firth of Clyde reached out to the western sea, past all
the peaks of Arran. Through the great gap of Glen Falloch
and Strath Fillan to the north, the vast Moor of Rannoch
sprawled, the playground of the . winds, flanked by the
serried mountains of Black Mount and Glen Coe and
Mamore, with, far beyond, the shadowy giants of the
remote north-west, pale and austere and streaked even now
with the white of eternal snows. In every other direction the
jagged succession of countless summits and spurs and
ranges, green with deer-hair, purple with heather, brown
with peat and raw earth, and black-and-white with naked
quartz-shot rock, shouldered and jostled and enclosed this
verdant sanctuary of Clan Gregor, and, over all, the cloud
shadows sailed and flitted. It was a panorama that could
speak with many voices to the beholder. To Gregor that
day it represented Scotland, the ideal, the lovely and forlorn, the betrayed but inviolate Alba, mother and mistress
both, the land to draw sword for, if necessary, to die for.

Thus uplifted, he slanted down into his own Glen Gyle.
Here was a very different valley from that of Inversnaid, a
true glen, deep and narrow, between soaring rugged peaks,
through which raced a sizeable river in rushes and falls and
linked gleaming pools. It was a place of scattered open
birch-woods and hazel-fringed water-meadows, of great
outcropping rocks as big as houses, and long sweeping
grassy aprons scored by burnlets innumerable. Five miles
it stretched, all seen clearly from up here, from the head of
fair Loch Katrine at its foot, to where the thrusting shoulder
of a mountain divided it neatly into two upper corries that

rose fully five hundred feet above its floor, where the twin headwaters were born. And the whole was dotted with croft-houses with their patches of tilth and their peat-stacks, and cattle grazed high on all the hills. Down near the loch shore Gregor's own House of Glengyle stood amidst its sheltering trees, surrounded by its orchard, its herb garden, its steading and offices, its smiddy and its tannery and its duck-pond, like a hen amongst her brood. Heritage enough for any man – and an excellent place for coming back to.

Gregor had soft-heartedly walked his garron up to the bealach, for it could have been tired from its night's cantrips, but he rode it down all the long sweeping slopes to his home in the glen, letting it pick its own way, what time he sent cattle plunging left and right with his cheerful shouting, called and waved to such of his people as were to be seen about their crofts, and fetched his hounds racing up to meet him from the House by his long ululant halloos that the hillsides tossed to and fro in blithesome echo.

Glengyle House was a much superior place to Rob Roy's fairly recently built establishment at Inversnaid, three storeys high, narrow, whitewashed, with a steep crow-step gabled roof, stone-slated not reed-thatched, however much moss-grown. Moreover, it had a stair-tower attached, wherein was the handsome moulded doorway surmounted by a weather-worn heraldic stone panel showing, even though dimly, the crossed tree and sword of his race – bearing suitably the crown on the top of the sword – and the motto S'RIOGHAL MO DHREAM, My Race is Royal. Slapping his mount away to find its own place, Gregor strode in under this ancient stone, all his leaping barking hounds around him, to shout for his mother and acquaint her of the good tidings.

The Lady Christian was a gentle soul who had tackled the business of being wife and mother to MacGregors rather more acceptingly than had, say, Rob Roy's Helen-Mary – who of course was of the Gregorach herself. Six years a widow, she was still under forty, with no grey in the golden hair that was one of the few non-Gregorach characteristics which she had managed to transmit to her elder son. She listened now to his excited and joyous tale, did not seek to chasten his enthusiasm, swallowed her own mother's fears, and sighed a small sigh. For herself, King Jamie could have bided very happily in France.

There was much to tell, much to envisage, many instructions to give, not a few immediate demands to make. Christian MacGregor received all with the quiet compliance that was expected of her. Indeed, her son would have been quite put out had she done otherwise. Nevertheless, even as he made it all known to her, Gregor was looking at his mother as he had never quite looked at her before – as an individual rather than as a sort of comfortable institution to be taken for granted, as a woman indeed – and as at least temporary mistress of his domain of Glengyle. For the first time some detached portion of his mind was contemplating it as a possibility that one day she might be displaced in that mistress-ship. It was a strange and exciting conception – if mildly perturbing too.

As it happened, in all the flood of his talk, the enchanting Mary Hamilton of Bardowie quite escaped mention. There were so many other issues to be dealt with, of course. . . .

To the Lady Christian's highly mother-like if tentative suggestion that King James's cause might not suffer irretrievably if her son did not rush off on it that very afternoon, but spent one night in his own bed, Gregor of course gave short shrift. When Scotland's future was at stake, it behoved men to be up and doing. He was, after all, Gregor Black Knee of Glengyle, and no slug-abed. Had not his Uncle Rob demanded – or at least urged – prompt action? Well, then. With a fresh garron he could cover the twenty-five miles to Arnprior, by the Pass of Aberfoyle and across the Moss, in four hours. He could be there well before dark. A whole day saved. . . .

Christian MacGregor understood, of course.

CHAPTER FIVE

GREGOR GHLUN DUBH rode at a steady mile-eating trot, up hill and down, by track and no track, by lochside and bog, by birken brae and bracken dene, by ford and narrow pass, till at the Clachan of Aberfoyle they won out of the mountains and into the green and spreading plain of the great Carse of Stirling. At his pony's heels loped two running gillies, their bare chests heaving rhythmically, like well-regulated bellows. They ran thus from preference, for they could have ridden ponies also had they wished – indeed, the elder, Ian Beg, who had been foster-brother and body servant to Gregor's young lamented father Ian More of Glengyle, and now liked on occasion to serve his son in the same capacity, actually possessed a couple of garrons of his own. These clansmen were no bidden slaves, but name-proud cousins of their chieftain – however far removed – who served of choice and esteemed it honour.

This matter of the size of his tail had been Gregor's major problem before coming away. Going through and into populous country as he was, it behoved Glengyle to sustain his dignity and status with a suitably large following of armed supporters – especially when, at least theoretically, he was the representative of an outlawed and proscribed clan entering settled country, whose members were forbidden by law to carry anything more lethal than a broken-pointed eating-knife, or to assemble in numbers exceeding four. On the other hand, this business that he was engaged upon was in the first instance highly secret, confidential and not to be shouted about. The time for shouting would undoubtedly come later. That did not mean, of course, that MacGregor of Glengyle was going to skulk about like any tinkler or Colquhoun or something of that sort. He had decided that just a pair of gillies probably would be best –

distinguishing him as a Highland gentleman deserving of due respect without actually drawing unnecessary attention to himself. So that quality should compensate for quantity, he had them armed suitably, with claymores, large and small dirks, and metal-studded leather targes. Here was no cattle droving.

A pair of Gregor's own deerhounds completed the little procession.

With the hills behind them, they took to the lonely empty wilderness of Flanders Moss, that vast waterlogged plain of sedge and reeds, of willow and alder and general quaking bog, that practically filled all the western half of the wide carse, and through which the River Forth linked and coiled and doubled fantastically, an uncertain and daunting quagmire of some fifty square miles, wherein whole armies might enter and never reappear – the Gregorach's first line of defence, indeed. The routes across its mighty and treacherous expanse – for routes there were – remained jealously guarded secrets, some of them known only to a select few, all of them, with the fords of Forth which complemented them, known only to one man – Rob Roy himself. There were islands of firm ground in that huge morass where whole herds of cattle could be hidden and maintained; lochans without number whose waters could be loosed and decanted to flood great new areas; causeways of stone set unseen a foot deep under peat-stained water, the pattern of which was the key to territories as large as a lairdship.

Across this trembling haunted place, where the reeds nodded and whispered and sighed endlessly, where the roe-deer slipped away silently like russet shadows into deeper shade, and the wildfowl squattered and quacked and flew, Gregor picked his roundabout intricate way with entire confidence, his general direction east by south. His followers trod exactly in his garron's footsteps.

Deliberately Gregor took a line that would keep them in this floundering Moss till directly north of Arnprior, a line that entailed more than the usual amount of zig-zagging and gave them fully eight miles of bog-trotting before, at last, with the sun already behind Ben Lomond, they came out on to firm ground once more, in the vicinity of Merkland.

After that it was straightforward riding through populous farmlands where humble cotter folk stared, but discreetly, silently, at the tartan-clad travellers, who spared them not so much as a glance, and into the wooded lands of Arnprior across the Glasgow-Stirling turnpike. Robert Buchanan, as befitted a substantial Lowland landowner with a hand in the America trade and a mind beyond mere cattle and rents, dabbled in this new-fangled pleasantry of enclosed parks and policies, and even planted ornamental trees – presumably for the benefit of hoped-for Hamilton grandchildren.

Arnprior House was a much more pretentious place than was Glengyle, needless to say – indeed, though only twenty-five miles apart, they might have belonged to different hemispheres, representing two utterly distinct and opposing ways of life. The one was the purely functional home of a patriarch amongst his people, on land for which he was only trustee and chief guardian; whilst the other was the private demesne of a magnate, the wherewithal for the costly support of which was earned elsewhere.

Gregor and his supporters rode up to the front door of this handsome establishment, enlarged beyond all recognition of the modest square tower-house that had contented earlier Buchanans. Here was a place where golden guineas surely would accrue to King Jamie's cause. He could see his approach being watched from more than one window – which was hardly to be wondered at since his two henchmen, aided by the promptly baying hounds, had been hallooing and bawling summons since ever they came in sight of the house, lest a chieftain of the Gregorach should be insulted by being kept waiting, even momentarily, on any man's doorstep.

Gregor was spared that, at any rate. Arnprior went in for the latest type of windows also, that opened by the entire frame being raised. One of these was raised now, on the first floor, and two female heads were thrust out – in grievous danger of being beheaded were the contraption to descend upon their fair necks.

'Welcome! Welcome, Mr MacGregor!' the feminine voices rang out. 'Gregalach! Gregalach!'

Delighted, Gregor swept off his best bonnet – with two new feathers in it, too. But that hardly seemed adequate, somehow, despite that unfortunate Mister that had crept in. So he whipped out his claymore instead, and tossed it spinning up into the air, under the young women's noses, its silver basket-hilt and gleaming blade flashing and scintillating in the golden rays of the setting sun, to catch it again dexterously as it came down – even though he cut his hand a little in the process.

'Ardchoille!' he answered them cheerfully – and for good measure the two gillies repeated the slogan loyally. 'Ardchoille!'

Another window went up, on the floor above. 'What a' God's name's to do?' That was Mr Hamilton of Bardowie, playing-cards in hand.

'It is young Mr MacGregor come visiting,' his saucy piece of a wife called up to him. 'At least, I think that is what he is doing. Though I must say, it's not very civil to throw swords at us like that!'

'Perhaps it's more cattle that he wants?' the younger girl suggested. 'Has your father one or two left, for him, do you think?'

'Dear me – I hope so. Or it will be us he'll be off with, instead! Mercy on us – what a fate! Can you conceive of it, Mary?'

'Well . . . ' Mary Hamilton was non-committal. 'The Gregorach don't really do that sort of thing any more, do they, Mr MacGregor?'

'We do not have to, whatever,' the young man said, a little stiffly, for he believed that he might be being made game of somehow. He returned his claymore to its scabbard – and tried to keep the blood on his thumb from showing. 'And you may call me Gregor, see you.'

'Oh.'

Mistress Meg's laughter spilled over. 'And you can make a kirk or a mill out of that, Mary Hamilton!' she cried.

Robert Buchanan, who knew something about the niceties and civilities required by Highland gentlemen, appeared in person in his doorway, buttoning up his long-skirted waistcoat. 'Glengyle – this is a pleasure and an honour,' he declared, holding out his hand. 'Come away in. Your fellows will take your beast to the stables, and get a bite of supper in the kitchen. Come you – and pay no heed to those lassies' havers from upbye. They're a skirling pair.'

'I like them both, sir – very well,' Gregor said, dismounting and stepping indoors, hounds at heel. 'The younger one – Mary. She is not wed, or bespoke, or otherwise embroiled, I hope?'

'Guidsakes, man – you're blunt!' Arnprior gulped, blinked, and faltered a pace, all at once. 'Lordie – you Hielantmen don't *aye* mince your words!'

Gregor eyed him enquiringly.

'Aye. I'ph'mmm. Well . . . no. Mary's a free woman, as yet. At least, so far as I know. . . . '

'That is good,' his guest commended, lifting off his shoulder-belt and claymore attached, and handing the lot to his host, as was suitable – though noting keenly enough what the man did with it.

'Did you come here . . . ? Was it to . . . ? H'rr'mm.' Arnprior hung the sword from a convenient pair of stag's antlers on the vestibule wall, and gestured a little doubtfully towards the wide square stairway. 'Oh, aye,' he said. 'This way, Glengyle.'

Gregor was fairly straightforward in most matters. 'King Jamie is for making a landing, and there is to be a rising in Scotland,' he mentioned. 'Men we will be finding in plenty, but money, it seems, will be required also.' He enunciated that word money with more than a hint of the Highlander's theoretical contempt therefor. 'You and your like have your hands on the money, Arnprior. That is why I am here. My

68

uncle has sent you this letter.' And he held out a missive drawn from his doublet.

'Eh . . . ? Good God, man! Save us a' . . . no' so loud!' Buchanan stared, and actually seemed to start backwards there on the stairs, as though to withdraw himself from all such rash and dangerous association. 'Guard your words, Glengyle, for the Lord's sake!'

Surprised, Gregor looked at him. 'Must you whisper in your own house, Arnprior?'

'Damnation – that kind of talk needs whispering anywhere!' Only as it seemed reluctantly did the laird accept the letter that the younger man still held out to him. 'What sort of folly is this you've got hold on, boy?'

Gregor frowned – as much at the boy as at the deeper implications. 'If my words do be needing guarding and whispering, sir, I'd suggest that yours could do with better choosing, whatever!' he declared strongly. 'The folly you speak of is the decision of His Majesty's Council, in St Germains, announced to us, to my uncle and myself, by Colonel Nathaniel Hooke.'

'Hooke, you say! Does that storm-cock crow? Is he here, then – in Scotland?'

'I ate with him, this midday, at Inversnaid.'

'So-o-o-o!' Buchanan was obviously impressed. 'Not six months agone I had word with him in France. . . . '

'Then you will know of how they conceive that this Act of Union will set Scotland aflame. . . . '

'Tut, man – hush you! Sssshh!' They were nearly at the first-floor landing now, and there the two young women stood awaiting them, a striking eye-filling pair, both good-looking and both attractive, but so very differently – though neither, it must be admitted, made quite such a colourful picture as the young man climbing up to them.

'Ah – so Scotland's to be set aflame, is she?' Buchanan's daughter cried down to them. She obviously had sharp ears to add to her many other evident attributes. 'Splendid – and high time, too! She's plaguey dull the way she is, I vow!'

'*I* don't think so,' her companion asserted, smiling. 'Especially when there are *MacGregors* about!'

'But aflame, my dear – the whole country! Think of it. It's Jacobite talk – I'm sure of it! A revolt – a rising? That's it – look at poor Father's face!'

'Guidsakes, Meg – hold your tongue!' Arnprior exclaimed. 'What way is that to talk! You clatter like a bell in the wind! Never heed her, Glengyle.'

'It *is* a rising, isn't it?' his daughter questioned, ignoring him.

'It is, yes,' Gregor agreed, since he saw no point in denying it.

'Oh, good! I'm glad,' Mary Hamilton declared, eyes shining.

'When?' Mistress Meg demanded. 'When will it be? I've said all along we'll have to rise. That's what's needed. The country's ripe for it, too. Even the English are . . . '

'Silence!' her father commanded hoarsely. 'Not another word. Have you forgotten, addle-pate, that I've got Killearn upstairs? And Garden. And that man Buchlyvie.'

'Stirling of Garden is a good Jacobite, is he not?'

'Maybe. But Killearn is Montrose's factor, and a Government man. And I'm no' so sure of Buchlyvie, either. . . . Come ben here, to my study, Glengyle. We'll no' can go upstairs. I'll have to read this letter. . . . '

'Leave Mr . . . *Master* Gregor with us, while you go read your letter, Father,' his irrepressible daughter urged. 'You will get the more out of it, belike. I am sure that he came all this way just as much to see *us* as to carry letters to you! Say that I am right, young man?'

'Yes,' Gregor said, readily enough – but he looked at Mary rather than the speaker.

That young woman sketched a curtsy, but said nothing with her lips.

Buchanan grunted, and scratched under the edge of his wig. Obviously he was as putty in Mistress Meg's hands. Probably, too, he felt that he could do with time to collect his thoughts and con Rob Roy's letter alone, in view of the momentous tidings. He nodded, then. 'Very well – as you will. I will see you presently, Glengyle. But, for the good Lord's sake – for everybody's sake – be careful what you say to those prattlers!' And he stumped off.

'Come, Master Gregor – and tell us all about it,' Meg cried, leading the way into a large bright west-facing room, handsomely furnished and hung with tapestries and pictures, woven carpeting on the floor-boards. One of the windows still was raised.

The young man bowed elaborately to Mary Hamilton, and she preceded him into the apartment. At his brogues' heels the two large hounds followed him – to be eyed somewhat askance by the women.

'You will have a glass of wine? You will be tired with your journey? And one or two of my cakes? I make superb cakes. . . . '

'He does not look tired, Meg!'

'You think not? Do you not note the delicate brush of shadow under the eyes, my dear? An improvement possibly, I agree – a refinement. . . . '

'I am not tired,' Gregor asserted – though he smothered a yawn as he said it. 'But I will accept your wine, Mistress, gladly. You may give the cakes to the hounds, here – they have run far.' And he took the proffered chair, and stretched the long limbs that thrust out from his red tartans luxuriously. The dogs sank down one at either side of him.

'Oh!' said Meg – and with nothing more to follow.

It was the other girl's turn to laugh, joyously. Seldom was it that her sister-in-law was thus effectively quietened.

*　　*　　*

Gregor had no intention of obeying Arnprior's unmannerly warning about being careful of his speech before these two girls. For one thing, he was not in the habit of weighing words like a huckster at other men's behest. But also he conceived it that these two were probably better Jacobites than their menfolk. Clearly this Meg had a deal of influence on her father, too, if not her husband – and he might well

71

serve the King best by enlisting the ladies to bring pressure on the others. Moreover, it had not been Gregor's experience – limited as such was, admittedly – that women were less able than their betters at keeping secrets, in things that mattered. His mother, and his aunt, for instance, were safer to confide in, he had discovered, than even Rob Roy himself.

So his fair hostesses by no means had to winkle and squeeze everything out of him – as undoubtedly they had been prepared to do. He told them all of what was to do, what was planned, and what he knew of how plans were to be translated into action. He hid nothing – save his uncle's grave fears of Breadalbane's part, which might conceivably alarm the uninitiated – only adding, as casual rider, that now he had put men's lives in their slender hands . . . including his own, of course. Which was not without its effect, either.

He got round to the money fairly promptly, explaining what was required and where it could best come from. He found his hearers quick in the uptake there, too. Perhaps they took up more even than he told them, more than he knew indeed, as is the way of women – but if so, no slackening of their interest or sympathy transpired. In fact, before Robert Buchanan reappeared, the two young women were not so much sympathisers and partisans as partners in the business – and not wholly sleeping or inactive partners either, it appeared.

So much so that when Arnprior, spectacles on nose and wig awry, but expression magisterial, suggested that Glengyle should accompany him to his study where he could inform him of what was what, Meg pricked that balloon forthwith, announced that they knew all about everything, and wanted to be informed how much her father proposed to contribute, in the first instance ? Not enough, she would vow!

Buchanan's carefully authoritative demeanour wilted noticeably under this flank attack, and for a few moments he was reduced to puffings and growls and incoherencies. He turned his reproaches on Gregor, of course, but was not permitted to get away with that, either. Nor the assertion that young females knew naught about affairs of state, were qualified to say nothing, and at least ought to respect their parents' wisdom and judgment. He eventually was reduced to confessing, indeed, that money was tight and the times difficult, security extremely doubtful, hare-brained schemes were to be deplored, and the dangers of implication grievous. In fact, that in the circumstances His Majesty would probably be well advised against the whole project – unless, of course, he came over with a large French army and coffers well filled with golden *louis*.

The outcry which greeted this level-headed and business-like assessment of the situation was such as to send the laird rushing over to close the window, to hush and shush imploringly, and to invoke Heaven's merciful deafness on Graham of Killearn upstairs.

Gregor had apt and dignified answers to give, needless to say, points to make, and morals to draw. But he got little opportunity to enunciate any of them. His companions did that for him, the one vigorously, shrewdly, mercilessly, the other pleadingly, reproachfully – but both eloquently. The young man could only sit back and listen, listen and marvel and enjoy – but also in some measure sympathise and know some small disquiet at this demonstration of masculine defeat and discomfiture, wholesale and unscrupulous.

Also, needless to say, Arnprior was forced to change his tune. First to the tune of fifty guineas. Then to a hundred. And finally to two hundred and fifty. Also to agree to use his influence, to some unspecified extent, with others of his kidney. Of course, as is frequently the way with hard-headed men of the world, he may have intended all along to come round to some such concession in the end, after being suitably cautious and sceptical. Who could tell ? After all, he was in theory a supporter of the Stewart dynasty, and his daughter presumably had got her Jacobite sympathies from him. But for all that, the process represented a noteworthy piece of ruthless female aggression, a feminine triumph, that should have been an object-lesson to Gregor Ghlun Dubh – and a warning.

The immediate objective gained, tactics gave way to strategy, in a dutifully daughter-like atmosphere. What others were to be brought in? How were they to be approached? And when?

Gregor mentioned some that his Uncle Rob had named for him to call upon – Stirling of Garden, who was apparently upstairs playing cards; Kerse of Kerse; Sir Hugh Patterson of Bannockburn; Leckie of Croy Leckie; Graham of Arnfearn; Bailie Drummond in Dunblane; and so on. He would just have to make a tour of them – and any others that Arnprior might think of.

That man was horrified at the suggestion. For young Glengyle to go traipsing the country calling on all these respectable lairds in turn would be as good as to shout aloud from the top of the Abbey Craig at Stirling what was to do. Didn't he know how kenspeckle he was – a chieftain of the MacGregors, nephew to Rob Roy himself, as notorious a Jacobite as there was in all Scotland? Did he imagine that he wouldn't set folks talking? Strange questions to put to Gregor Ghlun Dubh.

The younger man protested that that might well be so, but that he would be thought to be on the business of the Watch. But Buchanan would have none of it. Since when had Rob run his Watch like that – sending round an ambassador? And there was no harrying and rieving going on, to account for anything of the sort. And was it not directly after the Lammas mail-gathering? No – it would not do.

The ladies took over here, again. The thing could and should be done discreetly, judiciously. Only a little common sense was required, they declared. Instead of dashing around the country with his gillies and his hounds and his claymores, Gregor should lodge here quietly at Arnprior, taking sundry inoffensive trips with them in the coach to make polite calls upon the ladies of some of the gentlemen mentioned. Others of the gentlemen could be asked to visit here. Thus no Jacobite clamour would be raised, and all would be well. It was simple and obvious.

Arnprior, soul of hospitality as he was, embraced this programme with little enthusiasm. But Gregor saw distinct possibilities therein. The coach might limit his calls in some measure, of course, since not all of his quarry would be conveniently situated on turnpikes where wheels could reach them. But on the other hand, he had never experienced coach-travel; it might be a pleasant change – especially in select company. And the others could very well come to see him, indeed; on second thoughts it seemed highly suitable that they should, whatever.

Glengyle therefore signified his assent. Though it seemed doubtful whether anything of the sort was necessary, or really competent.

Time was not limitless, however, he felt bound to point out – distasteful as it was for a Highlandman to be preoccupied with mere hours and days. He had much to do, elsewhere than in this tame low country, before he made his rendezvous with Rob Roy and the rest at Kinloch Rannoch in three weeks' time. He could only spare, say, five days to this business.

Buchanan agreed that his guest's duties elsewhere ought by no means to be neglected.

The young women accepted this understandingly, too. But much could be achieved in five days, they indicated significantly.

There turned out to be a fairly unified opinion against Gregor starting his campaign there and then, on Stirling of Garden upstairs – or, for that matter, on John Hamilton of Bardowie either. They had been drinking at their play, naturally, and were likely to be in no state to deal with matters of high politics and patriotism. Another day would be more propitious. Garden was a near neighbour, anyway. In fact it would be best, probably, if Gregor did not meet the card-players at all that night, and get himself involved in all sorts of unedifying discussion and claret-inspired argument. Let these have their supper, with their host, aloft in the card-room, and the latest guest could dine down here with the ladies. For the safety of the cause.

The cause was in good hands, very evidently.

CHAPTER SIX

So commenced a week – for a week it became, of course – such as Gregor MacGregor had never before experienced, contemplated or even could have visualised. An education might be the best description of it. He made a fairly apt pupil, it had to be admitted.

There was much to be tasted, tried and savoured – beyond coach-travel. Though that had its rewarding moments, to be sure. He discovered quite a lot about women, for instance, that had not been crystal-clear to him; quite a lot about gentle dalliance that could be more dangerous than any of man's noisy challenges; pretty ways that masked unbending resolution, melting looks that represented anything but fluidity. Perhaps by inference, as it were on the rebound, he even learned a little about himself.

Achievements were not unimportant either – if not achieved altogether without his self-appointed coadjutors' help. Reluctant promises were wrung out of not a few pessimistic patriots – the fact that their cattle might always be used as a form of security for fulfilment of contract never being actually mentioned by the MacGregor. But strangely enough his successes with these fairly consistently purple-faced and heavy-paunched realists whose venturesomeness in the commercial sphere seemed to be so surprisingly more vigorous than in other realms, impressed Gregor on the whole as little more than a by-product of his week's activities. Other matters tended to bulk still larger, unexpected as this may have been.

How far these other matters managed to develop, in six days, like extra sturdy plants in fertile soil – with some little deft husbandry here and there perhaps – will be apparent from what transpired on that final day of Gregor's stay as a guest at Arnprior.

All the gentlemen named by Rob Roy – and even one or two others – had been seen and prevailed upon one way or another, with the exception of Sir Hugh Patterson of Bannockburn. This was one of the most important of all, being a man of far-flung interests and reputed zeal for the Stewart cause. But he had resisted any attempt to get him to come to Arnprior, and Bannockburn of course lay considerably farther south and distant from the Highland Line than did any of the other properties. It was on the wrong side of Stirling, country where the MacGregor writ did not run, and the Government's frequently did.

This day, then, Gregor being adamant, an expedition was made by coach to Bannockburn, a journey, by devious ways, of some twenty miles. They avoided the constrictions and possible dangers of Stirling, skirting well to the south of the town, past the Buchanan lairdship of Touch and the village of Cambusbarron, the great castle-crowned rock rearing up away to their left. They reached Bannockburn House in due course, achieved an encouraging measure of success with the wary Sir Hugh – who proved, like many of his kind, to be more susceptible to feminine charm than to Gregor's histrionics and challenges. It was on the way home that things began to go wrong. Just after they had come down off the moor and passed through the little village of St Ninians, south of Stirling, the coach, negotiating a bad stretch of the road, lurched heavily into a larger hole than usual, broke three or four spokes of its off front wheel, and came to a jarring drunken halt.

This was not Bardowie's handsome equipage, with postillions and quartette of matching greys, but an older lighter two-horse carriage of Arnprior's, less conspicuous, with an aged coachman to match. This veteran now dismounted amidst dire lamentations, to wring his hands and call upon his Maker, proclaim his innocence of all fault – and do nothing more constructive. The two young women twittered and exclaimed and were less effective than usual. Gregor Ghlun Dubh ordered the coachman to unhitch the horses, and strode off masterfully back to the village for a wheelwright or a blacksmith. So much for coaches.

Unfortunately, St Ninians, a poor inadequate bit of a place, did not boast a wheelwright, and the hulking smith whom Gregor ran to earth and dragged protesting back with him continued to protest, on the spot, that he could do nothing with spokes and wood. The Highland gentleman would have to go to Stirling.

It was a bare three miles to the town. The girls were for the coachman going, but Gregor would not hear of it, asserting that he would be as useless there as he was here. Let him be getting the wheel off. The evening was approaching, hirelings would be leaving their work and would be loth to come to their aid perhaps – he had had to convince even this miserable blacksmith in no uncertain terms. He would go himself, taking both horses so that the wheelwright could ride back on one.

The dangers of a proscribed MacGregor entering the garrisoned town and citadel of Stirling, though eloquently pointed out to him, had quite the wrong effect on Gregor of Glengyle, of course. Mary's rather faltering suggestion that she should accompany him as screen and diversion – for she was certainly not dressed for bareback horse-riding – was dismissed with scant gratitude. Let them sit peaceably in the coach and leave man's work to a man, he advised – possibly even thankful to be able to assert himself after his week of leading-strings. Where would he find a wheelwright conveniently in Stirling, he demanded of the smith?

So Glengyle trotted the two horses down the Edinburgh turnpike into the tall town that dominated from its thrusting crag the flat carselands of Forth – or such part of them as were a little too far east and south to be dominated by the still more masterful ramparts of the Highland Line that reared majestically filling all the prospect to the north. Past the huddled hovels of the Craigs he rode, and up the steep cobbled streets towards the citadel's churches and palaces and ultimate frowning castle. And tall Gregorach though he was, he knew a certain sense of smallness and loneness in the process.

He did not ride unnoticed, naturally. It was not every day that betartaned Highland notables clattered over the Stirling cobbles on what were obviously heavy coach-horses – especially with chin in the air and eagle's feathers cocking higher still. The narrow streets held their full quota of hodden-clad and beshawled strollers and idlers this fine August evening, with the day's toil over, folk leaned comfortably out of windows and gossiped in alleys. Children skirled and pointed, and even acted as escort – though that could be in the nature of a compliment, of course. There was no sort of hostility evident, even from the odd redcoats amongst the throng.

Near the foot of Broad Street a short wynd turned down, giving access to an open yard wherein a couple of carts and an old coach mouldered, wheels entire and broken lay about, and wood was stacked and littered. At the rear was a house, around the door of which fowls picked and scratched. And on a bench nearby two men sat, tankards in hand. They stared at their visitor.

One was a small wizened man, decently dressed in coat and breeches only a little patched, and a greasy cocked hat. The other was large and muscular, in uprolled shirt-sleeves and leather breeches. Both middle-aged men. Gregor addressed himself to the latter, fairly enough, bidding him a good evening and enquiring if he was Calder the wright, and announcing his need, civilly if firmly.

The man hummed and hawed, oooh-ayed and just-so-ed, and repeated the salient points to his companion whom he referred to at every other word as Bailie – and who thereupon joined in the humming. A lack of appreciation and urgency was apparent.

Patiently Gregor explained the situation, pointed out the spare horse for transport, and mentioned that payment would be prompt and adequate. But the wheelwright remained unimpressed. The day's work was done. He would see to it in the morning. And there was an inn at St Ninians. . . .

Gregor was not used to this sort of treatment – and made the fact reasonably clear.

The other mentioned, apparently more to his companion than to the enquirer, that there were other wrights in town.

The visitor expressed no interest in this information.

The wright, from ooohing and ayeing and head-shaking, became more specific. 'Since when,' he wondered, to the Bailie, 'has Hielant gentry taken to riding in coaches? I havena heard tell there's ae road fit for a cairt much less a coach north o' the Hieland Line!'

The smaller man tee-heed appreciatively. 'Ye're richt there, Deacon,' he agreed.

'An' div ye no' think yon tartans could be MacGregor, just – red an' green? Eh, Bailie?'

'Man, they could that. As you say.'

'Oooh, aye. I'ph'mmm. MacGregor.'

Gregor drew a long quivering breath. 'MacGregor it is, by God – and I am Glengyle!' he cried. He was about to say considerably more when a long tuck of drum rolled distinctly on the evening air from the castle walls above, presumably sounding for some military duty. The noise reminded the younger man rather forcibly of the possible advantage of a modicum of hateful discretion, ladies' comfort being involved. 'Come, you,' he merely said then, authoritatively.

The other did not stir. 'Is that a fact?' the wright mentioned, and sipped his ale. 'It's a bold lad this, Bailie, is it no'? An' in the deil's ain hurry!' To Gregor he said, with some dignity: 'I am Sam'l Calder, Deacon o' the Wrights' Guild. An' here's Bailie Livingstone o' this toon.'

'I am still in a hurry, whatever,' Gregor answered. But his mind was turning the situation over quickly, nevertheless. 'For myself, the coach matters nothing. But there are ladies in it. Their coach it is – not mine. I seek to aid them, just. They must be at Arnprior before darkness.'

'Arnprior . . . ? Man – did ye say Arnprior ?'

'I did. It is Buchanan of Arnprior's coach.'

'Och, mercy on us – d'ye hear that, Bailie ? Arnprior's coach.'

'Tsst-tsst,' the wizened man deplored. 'Houts, man – that's a wee thing different.'

'Oooh, aye. Just that. As you say, Bailie . . . '

It was not a little galling for Gregor to perceive the very different impression made on these smug Lowland townsmen by the Laird of Arnprior's name as against his own. Obviously Buchanan meant a deal more in Stirling town than did MacGregor – a situation that certainly seemed to call for some rectification. But at a later date, assuredly – not just now. Swallowing the words which would really have done justice to the occasion, and keeping his fists tight clenched beneath the folds of his plaid, the Highlander nodded.

'One of the ladies is Arnprior's daughter – wife to Hamilton of Bardowie. It is an ill thing to be keeping them waiting, at all.'

'Bardowie . . . ? Dearie me – Bardowie too! Man, man.' Deacon Calder was on his feet now. 'Andra!' he shouted. 'Here, Andra. Whaur the deil is the limmer . . . ?'

An answering call preceded another man who emerged from a tumbledown lean-to erection across the yard, hitching up tattered breeches behind a leather apron, a stolid bull-like workman, in no sort of hurry. To this individual, Calder gave instructions to get his tools and go with the Highland gentleman to repair the Laird of Arnprior's coach-wheel. He indicated that the man was a qualified wright and would be well able to do the work expeditiously and to Mr Buchanan's satisfaction – giving the impression at the same time that he himself, as a Trades Deacon of Stirling's Guildry, had still more important matters to attend to.

Gregor maintained a lofty silence while the man Andrew was gathering his gear – even when it transpired that the

Deacon was now assuming that he, Glengyle, had been merely a passing traveller who had come upon the coach in difficulties. That assumption, insulting though it was in its implications, might at least spare talk and gossip. He let it pass.

His leave-taking of Deacon and Bailie thereafter was as frigid as he knew how to make it.

With his silent, indeed morose companion, Gregor rode back down Stirling's hilly streets and out on to the Edinburgh road once more – keeping a suitable distance ahead of the fellow, needless to say. They collected some shouts and witticisms *en route*, and a few barking dogs, but nothing more serious.

At the coach the girls seemed to be gratifyingly pleased and relieved to see him back. Setting the wright to work forthwith, he saw no need to enlighten them on what had transpired in Stirling. There were things that even intelligent women could not be expected to appreciate.

*   *   *

The sun had set and the grey dusk was beginning to make things of mystery out of the scattered thorn trees and whins of the grassy hill above St Ninians – the same hill whereon Robert Bruce had drawn up his scratch army before Bannockburn fight of glorious memory – when, the new spokes fashioned and the hub repaired, the wheel was ready to fit on to the axle again. Gregor was assisting at this task when the drumming of hooves from down the road drew all eyes in the direction of the village. A sizeable group of horsemen were approaching – and at a spanking pace.

'Oh, Gregor! It's not . . . I hope it's not . . . ' Mary Hamilton began breathlessly, and did not finish.

'I fear it is,' Meg faltered. 'Are those not redcoats ? I fear they are. . . . '

Gregor straightened up, peering. 'Red they are,' he agreed. 'But fear you nothing, *a graidh*. Fear is not for the likes of you and me, at all.' Fine words, but the man's hand

82

dropped to the region of his hip, and he cursed beneath his breath that no claymore hung there.

With a great jingling and clatter the newcomers drew up around the stationary coach, a party of a dozen heavily armed dragoons led by a young Ensign on a handsome black charger.

Gregor got in the first word, as soon as he could make his voice heard above the din, addressing the officer. 'A good evening to you, Captain,' he said civilly. 'I take it kindly that you have come to escort these ladies to Arnprior.'

'Eh . . . ?' The other, a young man of about Gregor's own age, looked a little nonplussed. He bowed stiffly from the saddle to the young women who stood beside the coach. 'My respects,' he jerked. 'If escort is required, I can provide it. But I am here to apprehend one who calls himself MacGregor.' He turned back to the Highlandman. 'You, I take it, sirrah?'

'I do not call myself MacGregor – I *am* MacGregor!' he was told strongly. 'I am Gregor Ghlun Dubh MacGregor of Glengyle, Chief of the Clan Dougal Ciar of Clan Alpine!' A drum to roll with that would have sounded well.

'M'mmm. Indeed!' The Ensign cleared his throat. 'I . . . ah . . . well, you are our man, then. You will accompany me back to the Tolbooth of Stirling.' He spoke with the accent of the north country English. And added, as an afterthought: 'In the name of the Queen!'

'That would be inconvenient for my arrangements,' Gregor informed him, conversationally. 'And you refer to Anne Stewart in London, I take it? What has she to do with Gregor MacGregor of Glengyle, at all?'

The officer drew himself up, on his fidgeting mettlesome horse. 'Have a care how you speak, sirrah, of the Queen's Majesty! And how you flaunt the name of MacGregor!'

'Can you name a prouder, sir?'

' 'Fore God – are you crazy, man?' the other cried. 'Know you not that the name of MacGregor is proscribed?

That it is contrary to law to use it? That the whole rascally clan of you is outlawed, by royal statute? And that no man of that race may bear arms other than a blunted eating-knife?'

Gregor laughed. 'Och, och – a sad tale, that! Did not another king downbye one time order that the waves of the sea hold back?'

'Eh . . . ?' The Ensign, frowning, did not catch the allusion, unfortunately. 'There is a reward offered for the apprehension of any man who uses the name of Mac-Gregor. That reward has been claimed this day by a burgess of Stirling. You must come with me. . . . '

'Of how much, pray, is this reward?'

'Forty pounds Scots, I believe. But the . . . '

'Faugh! Forty pounds, the price of a stirk, whatever – for Glengyle! Is that not monstrous!' Gregor cried. '*Dia* – but the wheelwrighting must have fallen on ill days in Stirling for its Deacon to have to be selling his fellow-men at such paltry price! I fear that I cannot let myself go for such a figure, Captain!'

'Enough of your talk, fellow – it will serve you nothing. Sergeant Tod . . . '

'Officer!' That was Mary Hamilton, urgently. 'You cannot do this, sir! This gentleman has done no wrong. He went to Stirling on our behalf, to get us aid. For this kind action you would injure him . . . ?'

'For no kind action, ma'am – but for flouting the law!' the Ensign gave back. 'You heard him – glorying in the name of MacGregor. And look – he carries a dagger, there! He is armed. . . . '

'A dirk is part of every Highlander's dress,' Meg exclaimed. 'You must know that. . . . '

'Tut – let us not be squabbling over the small matter of a dirk,' Gregor intervened. 'You shall have it if you want it, Captain. But let the ladies be on their way to Arnprior. Here is no business of theirs.'

'The ladies have my permission to continue their journey.'

'No!' Mary Hamilton cried. 'If you take him to Stirling, sir, then we go too!'

'Exactly,' her sister-in-law agreed strongly. 'We all go.'

'But *I* am not going to Stirling, see you,' Gregor said, very softly. Louder he declared, 'The gentleman is after wanting my dirk. Here it is!' And whipping out his *sgian dubh*, he leapt like a coiled spring released.

The single great bound brought him to the side of the officer's tittuping charger. A brief jab with the point of the knife sent the already nervy brute rearing and dancing. Its rider's hand, darting down towards the heavy cavalry pistol holstered there, grabbed at the saddlery instead, to hang on. Gregor Ghlun Dubh grabbed at the saddlery too, and, bracing himself on his toes, sprang for the second time. He had been vaulting on to garrons' backs all his days – and though admittedly this charger was taller than any garron, its haunches were well down as it reared, its forelegs pawing the air. Out of the flying leap Gregor landed, tartans sailing, square on the beast's black back, behind the saddle. As he came down, all in the same movement his left arm crooked tightly round the neck of the man in front, who still was struggling to retain his seat. Bare knees gripping fiercely at the prancing horse's silky flanks, Gregor flicked the dagger viciously before the other's eyes. 'Still, you!' he hissed. 'Or . . . !'

The entire sudden outburst of violent action had occupied no more than four or five seconds. The watching ranks of dragoons were wholly taken by surprise. The Highlander was up behind their officer before they could do anything to stop him. And once there, they were not very effective – they could not be. Disciplined men, they tended to wait for orders – and no orders were given them. They tugged out sabres and pistols, but with the Ensign's black cavorting round and round, they would have been just as likely to hit their officer as his assailant had they attempted to use them. The sergeant shouted for them to close in – but a dozen mounted men closing in simultaneously on a given spot must inevitably get considerably in each other's way. More especially if the spot keeps caracoling around and lashing out.

A high degree of confusion developed around that coach. Also considerable shouting mixed with some feminine screams.

Gregor alone was not confused – for only one course was open to him. He took it forthwith. The ring of jostling redcoats was not complete, because of the coach's bulk. And since they had come up from the east, from the direction of St Ninians, the coach lay to the west of them. The angle of his left arm still all but throttling the unfortunate officer, Gregor grabbed at the reins which the other still gripped, at the same time giving a sharp flick with his dirk at the charger's arching neck. Also he kicked hard with brogue-shod heels at its heaving flanks. Under this provocation that black leapt forward instead of merely upward, had its head slewed round to brush past the coach, almost knocking over the young women, wheelwright and coachman in the by-going, jumped the trace-pole in its stride, and sent the two waiting coach-horses stampeding. Then, lengthening its pace from a scrabbling canter into a raking gallop, it went, head out, nostrils flaring, pounding along the road to the west, its double burden swaying precariously on its back.

Shouts, curses, screams and incipient hysterical laughter rose from those left behind as they stared after. But even as the sergeant's swearing pulled the mass of the dragoons out of their tangle, to spur their mounts in pursuit, high above all the uproar a ululant cry came floating back to them on the evening air.

'Ardchoille! Ardchoille!' it skirled. 'Gregalach!'

The Tutor of Glengyle had tutored well.

*　　　*　　　*

Gregor did more than skirl as he pounded along that dusty road. He laughed loud and long – which must have been disconcerting for the semi-choked victim in front, whose impression that he had been sent out against a madman may well have been reinforced. The fugitive – though that description hardly applies somehow – was not worried about the pursuit. This horse was doubly laden admittedly – but it was, quite naturally, far the finest and fleetest beast of the bunch. Moreover, he could jettison the Ensign quickly enough – and though that would be to discard his cover and lay himself open to be shot after by the dragoons, he did not anticipate much danger from pistols fired from horseback at extreme range. Indeed, he was out of range, he imagined, as it was. The redcoats would be tenacious undoubtedly, but with the dusk he could probably lose them when he cared. And only a few miles ahead lay the great wastes of Flanders Moss. . . .

No shooting developed – for pistols took a deal of repriming and charging, as well as aiming. Gregor reckoned that he was just about holding his lead. He could have thrown the officer overboard there and then – but as has been said he was a soft-hearted man, and he bore this unhappy Sassunach hireling no ill-will. Thrown to the ground at the gallop, he might well be injured – and after all, he was only a harmless dweebly sort of Englishman doing what he was paid to do, who might not be expected to understand what it meant to insult a MacGregor. If it had been a Scot, now . . . !

So Gregor waited for perhaps a mile, until they had thundered round a bend in the road – and then waited further still, for Cambusbarron village was just ahead, and it would be a pity indeed to deprive such villagers as might be out and about at this hour of the rewarding spectacle of how Government officers should be dealt with. The man's thoughtfulness had more than the one facet, it will be seen.

They clattered through the hamlet, then, Gregor giving the inhabitants a slogan or two for good measure, the dragoons pounding along strung out perhaps two hundred yards behind. A heartsome sight, undoubtedly. And round the next bend he pulled up the black a little, at the same time speaking into the ear so close to his lips – and that was nicely clear and accessible owing to the owner's cocked hat and bob-wig having landed on the road some distance back.

'I am for setting you down, Captain,' he said politely. 'And I would not like you to be hurting yourself. I will draw over to the grass, and drop to a trot, and you will jump, see you. If you are wise, that is.'

The officer may not have been suitably grateful, affable, nor even civil. But he was prepared to be wise, apparently, to this extent. As his charger was slowed down to a head-tossing sidling canter, the vice-like arm was removed from round his neck – and the dirk flickered in a last significant gesture before his eyes – he kicked heavy-booted feet free of his stirrups, swung right leg over before him and, aided by a little push from behind, slid down, to land on all fours on the grassy bank, and roll over.

'A good night to you, Captain,' Gregor shouted. 'Tell yon Deacon Calder that he'll need to work harder for his forty pounds Scots if he would . . . ' The rest was lost in the beat of hooves as the black was kicked into a gallop again.

A glance over his shoulder showed Glengyle the Ensign picking himself up a shade dazedly – and the first of the troopers just rounding the bend in the road. Seventy or eighty yards had been lost, perhaps – but the runaway could spare them. This excitable piece of horseflesh could now show its paces.

Gregor settled down to mere hard riding.

Quarter of an hour later, in the vicinity of Gargunnock, with some woodland behind him, he turned the black down a narrow lane that led through willows to the river. The sound of the pursuit was not so much a thunder or a drumming now as a mere vibration on the still air. He splashed through a ford across the Forth. Ahead, to north and west, lay all the empty spectral wastes of the great Moss. Dismounting, since this beast was no nimble-footed garron, he led his mount into it.

He heard the dragoons pounding past, across the smooth-flowing river, on the straight road to Kippen, and sighed for the folly of men.

*   *   *

It was fairly late, nearly midnight indeed, when Gregor came again to Arnprior House. He had left his fine new horse hobbled down at the water-meadows of Forth, as he came out of the Moss, and had approached the house cautiously and unobtrusively, on foot.

The household did not yet appear to have retired for the night, for lights shone from sundry windows. But there was no sign of dragoons' horses about the place. A visit to the stableyard disclosed the coach returned and in its place, and a discreet call at the back door of the mansion found it open and his own gillies waiting for him in the kitchen, with the hounds. They revealed that the coach and the ladies had come back hours before, escorted by six soldiers who had gone again with little delay. All was well – but the Laird was in a great to-do about something, apparently.

Gregor retraced his steps so as to come in at the front door, now locked and bolted for the night. His bangings thereon brought him fairly prompt entry, and thereafter he strode up to the first-floor room that he had seen to be lit up. The family was there assembled, Robert Buchanan pacing the floor.

Quite an emotional scene followed – the emotions varying considerably. Relief, joy even, praise, anxiety, displeasure and sheer outrage were all represented, and notably mixed. The young women were loud in their acclaim, Meg going so far as to rush forward and throw her arms around the prodigal guest – to the tut-tutting of the menfolk, Gregor included. Mary, though not so demonstrative, seemed only little less affected, laughing and clapping her hands and biting tremulous lips by turns. Arnprior was less appreciative, however, a man in the throes of misgivings – in fact, in a fever of anxiety. And John Hamilton of Bardowie made no bones about it – he was angry, massively angry. This, as far as he was concerned, was the end.

It seemed that there was more than the one way to view the day's lively proceedings.

A little bedevilled by this distinctly mixed reception, Gregor made a false start or two, and then, as usual, suddenly seeing the funny side of it all, burst into hearty laughter. Which commended itself to fifty per cent of the company at least. Arnprior, he assured, had nothing to worry over; nobody was going to accuse him of anything. Bardowie he considered it best to ignore entirely.

'Nothing to worry over!' Buchanan cried. 'Man – you have openly defied the Government, assaulted one of the Queen's officers, and stolen his property – all whilst a guest under my roof! And you say that I have nothing . . .'

'Sir!' Gregor interrupted. 'Do you accuse a MacGregor of *stealing*?'

'Eh . . . ? Och, well – no, no. Of course not. But *taking*, call it.'

'I could do no less, and keep my liberty, sir. And that does not implicate you, Arnprior. I let all believe that I was only a passing traveller offering aid to these ladies in their need.'

'Yes, he did!' Meg declared. 'He was splendid. . . .'

'You nevertheless involved my wife and my sister in an unsavoury and highly dangerous scrimmage, by your folly and hot-headedness,' Bardowie said heavily.

'John – how dare you!' his sister demanded. 'You are entirely at fault. It was no blame of Gregor's.'

'Of course it wasn't! We told you.' That was his wife joining in. 'The blame was anybody's but his. . . .'

'The blame was wholly his,' Bardowie insisted. 'For publicly admitting that he was a MacGregor. If he had held his tongue about that, all would have been well.'

'Shadow of God, sir!' Gregor roared. 'Were you a MacGregor – which all Heaven forbid – would you deny your own name and fame?'

'I . . . I cannot conceive of the situation arising, young man.'

'Nor can I, John – and that's a fact!' his sister agreed, hot where he was cold.

'The former Laird of Bardowie is to be congratulated on his daughter, at least,' Gregor said ponderously.

Meg all but choked. 'Oh, splendid! Splendid, Gregor!'

'Sir – this is beyond all bearing . . . !'

'Guidsakes – peace! Peace – all of you!' Arnprior exclaimed, snatching off his wig. 'Flyting at each other will get us nowhere. You, Meg – speak your goodman fairer, or hold your tongue! The damage is done, whosoever the blame. Our names will now be linked, in the Government's mind, with outlaws and rebels and Jacobite MacGregors.'

'*Dia* – some would consider that same an honour, whatever!' Gregor said, stiffly still. 'But since *you* do not do so, it is evident, I shall withdraw myself from under your roof, sir! Now! Forthwith! As Royal's my Race – this minute!'

'Gregor . . . !' Mary wailed.

'No!' Meg cried.

'Yes. Where my name is not honoured is no place for Glengyle!'

'Toots, man – don't be so touchy!' his host said, slapping on his wig again. 'There is not all that hurry. . . . '

'For yourself, Arnprior, perhaps no. But for myself, yes. Nothing else is possible, at all.' Since Gregor had had every intention of being away from the house before daylight anyway, he could be the more positive in this assertion of his due dignity.

'Well – you know best, no doubt. But I am sorry, lad. . . . '

'So am I, sir. I have to thank you for your hospitality, up till this time.' That was rigidly formal. 'And these ladies for much kindness.'

'You will explain to your uncle, Glengyle, how I am placed . . . ?'

'My uncle will know fine what is what,' the young man assured cryptically. 'Now, with your permission, Arnprior, I will relieve you of my presence. . . . '

'Where? Where are you going, Gregor!' Mary demanded.

'Och, here and there, lassie – just here and there. On

King James's affairs.' That sounded just a little too much, even in his own ears. Rather hurriedly he added a rider. 'But up beyond our Highland Line, see you, where a man can breathe clean air, and free.'

'And . . . and you will not be back?'

'Think you I have not spent overlong here, as it is?' he asked her, and held her eyes with his.

She shook her head, and bit her lip, wordless.

'The first sensible words you have spoken this night!' her brother observed flatly.

'Oh – you are hateful!' Mary cried at him. Meg moved over to put her arm round the other girl's shoulders.

'Aye,' Gregor said, with the deliberate and sibilant enunciation that he reserved for his most impressive pronouncements. 'You are the big man, Bardowie – safe behind this lassie's skirts! But, see you – you, who would not wear the name of MacGregor – come back I may, one day. And if I do, it could be to change the name of one of your family to that same MacGregor, whatever!' He bowed. 'A good night to you all!'

And while still his hearers drew gasping breaths, Gregor Ghlun Dubh swung on his brogue's heel, reached the door, slammed it, and went striding hugely down the stairs, shouting loudly for his gillies and his sword and his hounds.

If his entry had engendered emotion and babblement, his exit did no less. Above the clamour of talk the whole house shook and the candles danced and flickered as the front door crashed behind the Gregorach.

CHAPTER SEVEN

THE three men made no great journey that night – for the Flanders Moss was no place for even a MacGregor to traverse in the dark – but settled down some half-a-mile into the morass, dined off some portion of the considerable spoils of the Arnprior kitchen which the gillies had had the foresight to bring along, and slept in their plaids amongst the whispering reeds, the untroubled sleep of men more easy in their minds than they had been for a week.

Sunrise saw them picking their devious way northwards through the place's early-morning mists, Gregor, all wrath and hard feelings dead in him, rivalling the larks at their carolling. He rode his garron, and Ian Beg led King Jamie's new property, a matter which required a certain amount of care and patience, for the charger did not seem to like either bogs or deerhounds.

They fetched a course which, skirting the islanded higher ground of Choille Mhor, took them past the west end of the great lake of Menteith, wading on a spongy carpet of underwater roots amidst man-high bulrushes, and up beyond on to firmer ground. Here Gregor mounted the black charger, for the prestige of Clan Alpine, and Ian Beg climbed on to his garron. By a fortunate coincidence Duncan Og, the remaining gillie, disappearing for a little, presently made up on them, himself mounted upon a useful garron of piebald aspect. It was only Graham country hereabouts, and Gregor forbore to seek paltry details.

They climbed the long long scarps of the long Menteith hills into the heather, and rejoiced with the myriad humming bees and the whirring chattering grouse at the sweet and honest scent of it in the smile of the sun. Over the watershed, they slanted down to the birch-clad shores of

Loch Drunkie and across the hummocky moors beyond to the wide strath, where they forded the peat-stained shallows of the Black Water between Lochs Achray and Vennacher. Here, at the ale-house of the township of Brig o' Turk, they made their first halt, a dozen rough miles covered. There was quite a population at this spot, paying lip-service to MacGregor, but of mixed clans – MacLarens, MacNabs, Stewarts and the like, professional drovers in the main, whose services were much in demand for transferring the cattle of a thousand Highland glens to the Lowland markets. They were tough and broken men, handy with a dirk undoubtedly, and would have their uses in due course – but it was not such scrapings as these that Gregor sought today. He accepted the respects of all whom they clapped eyes on, and proceeded on up Glen Finglas.

At Achnaguard, the seat of the MacGregor thereof, it was a different story. Here was a gentleman of his own sept of Dougal Ciar, and a following of genuine clansmen. It was part of Glengyle's calling to know exactly how many men each laird could raise. He greeted Glenfinglas with a nice mixture of authority and respect – for he was an elderly man – and requested fifteen armed men with all reasonable expedition. When the other wondered if it was in Rob Roy's name and behalf he was told, a little coldly, that it was not. It was Glengyle speaking. The men were promised by the morrow, and Glenfinglas's own son would make the sixteenth, for good measure. Meanwhile his house was at Glengyle's disposal, and all within it.

So next morning Gregor turned off up Glen Vane, beneath the tall frowning ben of the same name, with seventeen men at his heels and one, a boy two years younger than himself, at his side. This was more in Glengyle's line than asking dour and grudging Lowlanders for guineas.

At midday they came down, over the Pass of the Faggots and through the narrows of Glen Buckie, to the lovely shut-in vale of green Balquhidder. Here was another place of divided loyalties and interests. If rights were right, it should have been MacLaren territory, but the Duke of

Atholl and his Stewarts and Murrays had gained the title to it in law, the MacGregors dominated it outside the law, and the poor MacLarens had to do the patient best they could. Here had been Rob Roy's first independent holding, where his father had set him up as farmer of Monachyle Tuarach at the age of twenty-one. From here many of his most stirring exploits had been essayed, and his name still spoke loudest of all in Balquhidder.

Gregor did not delay in the Kirkton, at the eastern extremity of the long valley amongst the mixed folk – beyond paying his kindly respects to the Minister. The upper western end was solidly MacGregor, and thither he repaired, with his trotting tail of warriors, by the pleasant cattle-dotted shores of Lochs Voil and Doine. At Invercarnaig House, across from his uncle's old farmstead, he deposited himself and his entourage with the laird thereof. One hundred and fifty men, he calculated, the Braes of Balquhidder ought to supply him. Would Glencarnaig kindly see to it? In the name, this time, of Rob Roy.

Murray, alias MacGregor, of Glencarnaig was a substantial figure, alike in person, property and influence in the clan. He was not of Gregor's Dougal Ciar sept at all, but a two-feather man in his own right, head of another branch altogether. Indeed, he might well be claiming *three* feathers one of these days – though that of course Glengyle for one would have to contest strongly.

It falls to be explained here, perhaps, that at the time the Siol Alpine – that is, the entire race of the descendants of royal Kenneth MacAlpine, founder of the Scots monarchy in the ninth century, including its senior clan of MacGregor – was to all intents chiefless. The last High Chief of Clan Alpine in the direct line, Gregor MacGregor of the house of Glenstrae, a somewhat fushionless character, had been gathered to his fathers thirteen years before, and his dying had been the best of him. His first cousin, Archibald MacGregor of Kilmanan, who succeeded, was an irresponsible and a brawling sot. That might have been borne, but having committed a pointless and undignified murder in a fit of drunken frenzy, and not having the wit to cover it with any cloak of decency, he had lit out for Ireland and had not been heard of for some years – leaving Rob Roy, who had sought to sustain him for the clan's sake, his principal debtor. Kilmanan's two sons had predeceased him, and though dead he himself might not be, he was as good as dead to Clan Alpine. And the Gregorach were the kind of people who needed a chief, and a strong chief at that.

There were no fewer than four tentative contenders for the office, chieftains of the most ancient and senior septs. MacGregor of Roro, in Glen Lyon, probably had the best claim, on parchment. This Glencarnaig would have disputed, claiming that Roro's ultimate progenitor, though elder brother to his own, had been illegitimate. Drummond, alias MacGregor, of Balhaldie, was another claimant, with moreover a fortune and Lochiel's daughter as wife to back it. And, of course, Glengyle himself was in the running. But, in point of fact, Rob Roy ruled the clan by sheer force of personality.

Therefore, it was in Rob's name that men were to be raised in Balquhidder. Gregor had his moments of vision.

Balquhidder was a hospitable convivial fertile place – if you bore the right name therein. It outdid itself in both respects towards Rob Roy's nephew, as was only seemly and proper. Indeed, the gentry thereof so outdid each other in their hospitality as in their man-raising efforts, as a matter of credit as well as esteem, that the one effort tended to interfere sorely with the other. Gregor found himself in no state to proceed, or even to efficiently count or inspect the assembled manpower, for the best part of a week. Sunday intervened, too, and the claims of divine worship by no means were to be overlooked. It was the Tuesday, then, and six days after his arrival, before Glengyle was able to disengage himself and lead his now truly spectacular tail up out of the western amphitheatre of Balquhidder and southwards over the high Pass of Weeping below the jagged peak of Stob a Choin, down to Loch Katrineside, and so on to his own Glen Gyle. As far as he could make it, in the present state of his faculties, the total amounted to between two hundred and two and two hundred and twenty men, of whom seventeen were mounted gentlemen of name and property and eleven were pipers. Or thereabouts. They made a gallant sight and sound along the shores of Katrine, at any rate, and no little impression on Glen Gyle itself.

The Lady Christian had been as good as her son's instructions. Fifty-odd of his own men had been assembled and twiddling their thumbs for the best part of a week. Forty more were waiting at Inversnaid and Glen Arklet, and at least as many again in the clachans between there and Aberfoyle. Gregor sent messengers to fetch them all in to Glen Gyle, and meanwhile set about the task of scraping together the necessary wherewithal to fittingly entertain and feed this host. He decided, without a lot of debate, that the sooner they could all be gone from Glen Gyle the better, however stimulating their presence. Moreover, of course, he had only a bare week left till his rendezvous with Rob Roy at Kinloch Rannoch.

His mother, who being of a housekeeperly disposition was good at figures, assured him that she had exactly three hundred and forty-four extra mouths to feed, before they moved off for the north the following day. A plague of locusts, she called them – which was not like Christian MacGregor. Her son could only assume that some woman's ailment had her in its fretful grip.

For some reason they did not seem to be able to travel so fast and so far as was Gregor's wont – which might mean that he would have to curtail his intended itinerary a little through the MacGregor lands to the north, now so largely Campbell-ridden. They went over to the head of Loch Lomond, up long Glen Falloch to Crianlarich, collecting adherents and refreshments on the way. Then on up populous Glen Dochart, a far cry, and into the mighty strath of Tay – Breadalbane. This was all Campbell country now, but it had been MacGregor once, before the proscriptions and the harryings and the persecutions of the clan that was to be blotted out, nameless. But there were still more sons of Gregor than of Diarmid in the humble cot-houses and crofts, even though they might call themselves Campbell before the law – and without a doubt this notable demonstration of armed might, clad in the old red tartan, did them all a power of good. Many a leaderless man dropped mattock or peat-spade or herd's crook and ran to join the pipe-led gallant throng, little bothering to ask on what business bent.

Happily the feeding and supplying of this multitude became now perforce a matter for the Campbell lairds *en route*, a source of considerable satisfaction to all ranks. The fact that the assembly was apparently proceeding to some hunting match at Rannoch on the invitation of their own chief, the Earl of Breadalbane, for some extraordinary reason, rather tied Campbell hands. And, of course, four hundred men are not to be argued with too strongly in their own right.

All this took time, and Gregor was forced, after leaving Killin, to cut short his triumphal progress along the shores of Loch Tay and turn his cavalcade up over the lofty shoulder of Ben Lawers and so down into lovely sequestered Glen Lyon. Here he had Roro to call upon, the only MacGregor of note who had managed to hold place and lands in the very heart of the territory engulfed by the Campbells, and the man with most right probably to the chiefship – not, of course, that Gregor was going to admit or imply anything of the sort. Roro, as was scarcely to be wondered at in the circumstances, was not in the habit of making displays of strength or independence, having indeed gained something of a damaging reputation, for a MacGregor, of chronic caution and discretion. But Gregor had hopes that since Breadalbane was the host in this affair, Roro's circumspection might be relaxed somewhat. And he could, if so he desired, raise at least seventy men.

Roro did not do anything on that scale, it has to be admitted, despite all his visitor's oratory. But he did send eventually twenty men and his third son – which represented quite an achievement on Glengyle's part, though it took him two whole days to work it. Another day might have achieved still more – but Gregor's time was up. Tomorrow he was due at the foot of Loch Rannoch, to meet his uncle, and pride forbade that he present himself there one minute later than noonday.

The sun was still a good hour from its zenith when, at last, Gregor at the head of his impressive company topped the final long heather ridge that marked the northernmost bounds of Breadalbane, and looked far and wide out over the long sparkling loch, the rolling hills and valleys of Struan of the Robertsons, the endless ranges of Atholl, and the vast and daunting desolation of Rannoch Moor, to the majestic peaks of Glen Coe and Lochaber. But few with him had eyes for even such a prospect. Below them, a great dark mantle of trees reached almost from their feet right down the hillsides to the water, clothing all the southern shore of the loch – the Black Wood of Rannoch, and relic of the primeval pine forest that had once clothed all Caledonia. And plain to see, from up here, in a large clearing down near the eastern end of the loch, were numerous white and coloured tents and pavilions pitched, around them a stir of men and horses and the blue plumes of wood smoke.

Gregor pointed. 'Yonder is my Lord of Breadalbane!' he cried. 'Forward the pipers. Unfurl the banners. Ian Beg – bring me my standard of Glengyle. Let us show the proud Campbell that the Gregorach has come to Rannoch! That we have a name to us, yet! Come, you!'

*   *   *

John Campbell, eleventh of Glenorchy, first Earl of Breadalbane, Viscount of Tay and Paintland, Lord Glenorchy, Benderaloch, Ormelie and Weick, and second man only to Argyll himself in the great Clan Diarmid, stood outside his gold-and-black pavilion and stared uphill. At his side lounged Rob Roy MacGregor, and at his back were ranged a dozen chieftains and leading men, few of them Campbells, Colonel Nathaniel Hooke included.

Breadalbane was frowning, whereas Rob was smiling. They made a strangely matching pair standing there, strong men both. The Earl was elderly, but gave little impression of his years. Of a pale complexion he had heavy-lidded piercing eyes, a long thin nose and a still thinner mouth that turned down notably at the corners. A small man in body, he seemed the smaller for the enormous wigs that he affected and the inordinate richness of his clothing – Lowland-style clothing. Beside Rob Roy's virile hirsute bulk he appeared the merest puppet of a man.

But there was nothing of the puppet about John Campbell. He had a peculiar reputation in Scotland, and furth of it, little of it inspired by love, but none of it scornful. The Master of Sinclair, who had cause to know, had said that he had the finest headpiece in the land, but that he knew neither honour nor religion save when they were mixed with interest. His greed was notorious, and his double-faced cunning a by-word. Yet it was declared that he could charm any bird off its bough, any man out of his allegiance, or any woman out of her virtue. He had held the highest offices in the land, was one of the richest men in Scotland, and had married an English heiress – yet he was not looked upon as a representative of Lowland interests, as was Argyll, and he was known to oppose the Union with England and had not once attended Parliament in Edinburgh while it was being discussed. At the moment he was out of favour with Queen Anne's Ministers, who no doubt found him an awkward customer, used as they were to long-spooned supping with the Devil.

He was speaking now, somewhat testily. 'Coming from that airt, Cousin, they can be only my people – or yours. I did not invite either.'

'But I did,' Rob declared easily. 'Just two-three MacGregor lads as gillies for the beating, see you. You cannot have too many beaters at a hunting match!'

'That will depend upon the quarry!' the Earl said shortly.

'And how many pipers need they to beat with, Cousin?' Breadalbane affected a semi-royal mode of address – and of course Rob was indeed his cousin, twice removed.

The MacGregor had been rather wondering that himself – though he showed no sign of concern. 'It can be wearisome work, the beating – and nothing keeps the lads in better heart for it than a tune on the pipes, Iain Glas,' he said. He was probably the only man in all Scotland who would call Breadalbane his Gaelic by-name to his face.

The Earl shot him a glance that was not all cousinly affection. 'I wonder . . . ?,' he began – and then stopped. Over a minor fold of the wooded hillside fluttering banners appeared – many banners streaming in the breeze.

The Black Wood of Rannoch was no close-grown forest, but a far-flung hummocky area of scattered pines, great-girthed noble-boughed individual trees, growing loosely out of a rich carpet of heather and blaeberries, cranberries and brackens, and even broom. There was much open space, though few lengthy vistas. In consequence, Gregor's company became apparent rather than just appeared, did not all materialise at once, or in the same place, as it came plunging long-strided down hill amongst the knowes and the hollows. Probably the effect was more striking thus than even was intended. Horsemen emerged over a wide front, picking their way amongst the tall heather clumps, and disappeared again. Pipers, singly and in groups, surmounted knolls and crests, blowing lustily, only to plunge out of sight and be succeeded elsewhere by others. Colourful banners came and went. And everywhere red-tartaned armed men emerged and broke out, so that the entire wood seemed to be full of them, ever more following over the farther ridges.

'Great God – it is an army!' Breadalbane gasped. 'What is the meaning of this?' He looked around and behind him. His own Campbell minions numbered a score or so, no more.

Sundry other proud faces in the waiting group bore just a trace of uneasiness as they watched.

Rob Roy drew a great red-furred hand over mouth and beard. 'Have no fear, my lord,' he said. 'These would seem to be my people . . . and will do as I say!'

The other's swift look at him did not give the impression of being wholly reassured by that.

Out into the wide clearing that the Earl had selected for the gathering the Gregorach streamed, and drew together and formed themselves into some sort of order, the pipers leading now, then Gregor Ghlun Dubh on his fine black charger with some two dozen mounted gentlemen at his back, and behind them most of five hundred grinning foot gillies. Almost they danced as they came down to the tents, to the lively tune of The Laird of MacGregor's Rant.

Gregor waved to his uncle, bowed towards Breadalbane and his guests, but took off his bonnet for no man. Also, he waved right and left for his host to halt, and at the pipers to cease their blowing. The latter with indifferent success. All men perforce had to wait till the solid phalanx of musicians saw fit to conform – which was not until the due end of the rant.

It was Rob Roy, however, whose powerful vibrant voice dominated all when the music ended – as indeed it was apt to do. 'Greetings, Nephew!' he cried. 'You have brought us some bonny beaters, I see! We should not lack sport. Greetings, Gregorach! You warm the cockles of my heart, whatever. Come, Greg, and pay your respects to *Mac Cailein Mhic Donnachaidh.*'

The Earl swallowed. He swallowed the Highland title of Son of Colin, Son of Duncan – which was not the one by which he preferred to be addressed. He swallowed Rob Roy's speaking first. He swallowed the possible threat of this invasion, and all it might mean. He swallowed other things, too – for the moment. 'H'mmm. You will be Christian's boy,' he said, his voice sounding notably thin after Rob's. 'You have grown aplenty since last I saw you, boy. You must have been eating a sufficiency . . . of beef, Gregor Tarbh Ban!'

Gregor blinked at that. Tarbh Ban meant White Bull. Which meant again either that his uncle had been talking – or that Breadalbane was alarmingly well informed of what went on amongst the MacGregors.

A great shout of mirthful appreciation went up as the Gregorach saw the point of the Earl's greeting. There was a Wry-mouth for you, a Campbell indeed!

Gregor laughed too. Dismounting, he stalked forward. 'My respects, *Mac Cailein Mhic Donnachaidh*,' he said. And meant it.

CHAPTER EIGHT

THE great gathering was by no means yet complete. Most of the nearer-at-hand chiefs were in, including Struan Robertson from across the loch, Cameron, Younger of Lochiel, MacDougall of Lorne, Menzies of Shian, the Stewarts of Ardshiel and Ardvorlich, Farquharson of Inverey, Gordon of Glenbucket representing Huntly, and Grant of Invermoriston. Each had come, at Breadalbane's invitation by the mouth of Rob Roy, with only one or two of their gentlemen and a handful of attendants, inconspicuousness being the watchword. Highland lairds of broad acres frequently held hunting matches, social occasions where they all could get away from their womenfolk, relax, forget their dignities, feuds and problems for a little, and concentrate on junketing, hard drinking and fine talking just as much as on hunting deer. Large numbers of retainers at such were neither necessary nor desirable. The fact that Rob Roy had thought it worthwhile to assemble a major portion of his clan on this occasion, therefore, intrigued all. Almost as much as why Breadalbane was holding it at all.

And why he should be staging it here, at Rannoch, on the very northern limit of his vast territories, where he had no castle or house. That the Earl was a slippery customer and not to be trusted went without saying. But Rob, on the other hand, was known to be honest after his lights. And he had given every chief his personal word that no hurt would come to them in attending this affair. It might be that all these Gregorach were some sort of surety for that promise. The implications of which would be interesting, indeed.

The MacGregors, of course, quite swamped the camp, and upset all Breadalbane's victualling arrangements. Nevertheless, he would not have them going off foraging for themselves, as they cheerfully offered to do, preferring apparently to meet the extra cost himself than to be at the charges of outraged tenantry.

That afternoon three more chiefs came in, weary after much garron-riding across the roughest country in these islands – Cluny Macpherson, Chisholm of Chisholm and MacDonald of Keppoch. The other MacDonalds, the Mac-Kenzies, the Macleans, and the representatives from the far north-west could not arrive till the next day at the earliest. Not all men were prepared to travel at the speed that Rob Roy and his man MacAlastair had done.

In the evening Breadalbane dined and wined his principal guests and their gentlemen in his own great pavilion with its black-and-gold Campbell hangings – a colourful occasion to which, however, only Rob and Gregor and one other MacGregor were invited. The rest of the Gregorach gentry consequently held their own celebration outside – which by the sound of it was a still more colourful and cer-tainly more lively occasion, and at which Gregor at least would much have preferred to attend. Breadalbane made an assiduous host, and though he did not unbend greatly, his witticisms and shrewd asides were well received – for the Highlander dearly loves a good talker, even when his tongue is barbed. He drank less than most of his guests, and seemed to grow the more sober as the others did the reverse.

Rob Roy, on whom liquor seemed to have no effect, kept the company amused in a different fashion, and Gregor, much aware that for once he was not only one of the youngest but the least important present, was content to sip and watch and listen. It was not often that it was a young man's – or any man's – privilege to sit down with no fewer than ten three-feather chiefs and thrice that number of chieftains of his own rank. In this tent was represented the cream of Highland Scotland, the cream of Scotland itself. Gregor was young enough to be just a little bit overawed – though as he listened to the shouts and songs of his colleagues outside he knew a certain division of allegiance. Especially when he heard a new ballad evidently in process of being composed and tried out, with many interpolations, dealing with the white bull of Gallangad.

In the great pavilion a slightly less carefree atmosphere prevailed, despite the Earl's witticisms, Rob's stories and raillery, and the effect of the wines and the whisky. The mutual suspicions and rivalries of generations were not to be wholly banished. Politics were studiously avoided – save that the loyal toast was drunk to The King, and not The Queen.

Later that night, Rob and Gregor, with MacAlastair as a pale shadow in attendance, sought privacy and cleared heads in walking the dark aisles of the wood. It was their first opportunity for confidential talk.

Rob took his nephew's arm. 'Now, young man,' he said, 'what is the meaning of it all? Why the multitude? I said three hundred – and you have brought double that. *And* a score of *duine-uasail*. And a regiment of pipers. Your grandfather did not lead as many at Killiecrankie, Greg. Why, now?'

Gregor drew himself up. 'The clan's honour demanded it, whatever,' he asserted.

'The clan's honour could have got along with less, I think,' his uncle observed. 'My object was to prevent Breadalbane from attempting any trickery, and to reassure the chiefs, who trust him but little. But this host looks like a challenge to them all, a threat, maybe. Something of an embarrassment to my own self. Did I not teach you – *est modus in rebus* – that there can be too much even of a good thing?'

Gregor thought of blustering, but recognised that it would be of no use. Not with Rob Roy, not with the man who had taught him all that he knew. He scratched his head instead. '*Dia* – it started at Balquhidder,' he revealed. 'Each of them – Glencarnaig, Marchfield, Monachyle, Craigruie and the rest – all vied with each other as to how many men they could raise. I could not deny one and accept another, without offence. They were so very . . . hospitable. The story of the bull had somehow become known. Too much was made of it, I think. I . . . och, at the end of it, Uncle, I was after finding I had more men than I needed, just. But there could be no sending them back, at all. And after that, every glen we entered added more to the tally, see you. . . .'

'Aye, Greg – there is more to being a chieftain than cocking feathers in your bonnet and strutting on your heels!' the older man said – but not harshly. Then his tone lightened, and he clapped his somewhat crestfallen nephew cheerfully enough on the back to send him stumbling forward over the pine-needles. 'But never care, lad – it may all work out for the best. We will see if we can turn the business to good purpose. And how went your errand to Arnprior?'

Gregor was on firmer ground here, and did the theme full justice. The financial account he could give made a striking enough total – though Rob seemed to be less impressed with magnates' promises than he might have been. The matter of the coach breakdown and the dragoons, of course, he turned into an epic – with all due modesty, naturally – his uncle laughing his silent laughter and only commenting that he had wondered whence came the notable black horse. Not a great deal was said about young females, despite Rob's civil enquiries. Gregor did indicate, however, that in his opinion Arnprior and Bardowie both were extraordinary poor creatures to have such exemplary womenfolk. Rob nodded sober understanding.

Then it was the younger man's turn to do the questioning. How had his uncle's mission gone? Were the chiefs rallying as they ought? None had mentioned the forthcoming campaign at the meal; were they half-hearted? What was Breadalbane's game? And how had he come to know about the white bull?

All that took a deal of answering. As to the last, Rob had not mentioned that saga of Gallangad – which ought to give them pause for thought. On the whole he was satisfied with his private talks with the chiefs and their reactions to the proposed rising. But they were not unnaturally chary of committing themselves openly to an active part in a revolt until sure of the dependability of everyone present. Moreover, few if any trusted Breadalbane himself, and only Rob's own guarantee had brought most of them here into Campbell territory. . . .

'Yes, then,' Gregor interrupted. 'And why is it here, at Rannoch, that he has chosen to have this gathering? He has a dozen castles and houses. He has better hunting than this. There is nobody here . . . '

'And there you have it, Greg,' Rob intervened. 'There is nobody here! I have thought about this, my own self, not a little. Iain Glas is a shrewd and clever man – never forget it, or underestimate him. I know none shrewder. He always will have good reasons for what he does – good for his own interest. Here are some few reasons for why he might choose Rannoch. If things go wrong and no rising takes place, the fewer folk that have seen this gathering, and his connection with it, the better! Perhaps he does not trust his own Campbells! For the same reason, he might not wish it said that he had entertained rebels in any house of his. Again, Rannoch is not all in Breadalbane, at all – at least the half of it lies in Struan Robertson's country. That might make useful explaining one day in, say, London town!'

'*Diabhol!* You believe his mind works that way? The dastard!'

'I believe that he is a man who takes every precaution – that is all. He has been so doing all his days – and seems not to have lost by it! And there is another reason that might have weighed with him. Few of the chiefs might wish to place themselves deep in Campbell country without a large fighting tail at their backs. But Rannoch, practically on Robertson land, is another matter. See you?'

Gregor nodded. 'I see, yes. I see, too, that not only do you not trust Breadalbane, but you believe him traitor. And yet you have brought all these chiefs here and put them into his hands. Why?'

Rob stopped, to lean against one of the sturdy stocky red-trunked pines that somehow had such a strange affinity with his own build and stature. 'You see things over-simply, Greg – all black and white,' he said. 'But you will perhaps grow out of that. I told you – we are dealing with a clever man in Iain Glas. It is easy to name a man traitor, and be done with him. But no clever man will turn traitor until it pays him to do so. Breadalbane is not a traitor – yet!'

'But . . . but he *may* betray us,' Gregor cried. 'I say this is madness – playing with fire, whatever!'

'All war is playing with fire – like marriage, lad! And rebellion more so. He may betray us – yes. But so may many others. What does the Good Book say – that a man can be weighed for a price? Breadalbane's will be no petty price, I warrant. He will not fail us so long as we are winning, I think – only if we are losing. Then will be our time to watch him.'

'You thought otherwise back at Inversnaid, with Colonel Hooke. You said that you misliked this forgathering with Breadalbane, doubting his attachment to the King's cause . . . ?'

'Aye – so I did. And still I would liefer have had other host than him for this gathering. I had to use some power-ful persuading to bring some of these chiefs to Rannoch. But that is not the issue, now. I have considered the matter well. Also I have had speech with the man. Hooke was right, Breadalbane sought this meeting. There was no need for him to do so. He is with us, then . . . for the nonce. Which means that he thinks that we shall win, whatever! And his name, see you, is a great accession of strength – for all men know that he does not love lost causes. He will turn many waverers. When it is widely known that he is with us – as you and I shall see that it *is* known, Greg – then King Jamie will be a deal more likely to see those golden guineas that your Lowland lairdies have so bravely promised! Breadalbane could mean Jamie's throne for him – and himself the power behind it, maybe! You are over-previous with your traitors, lad.'

Gregor stared through that half-light at his potent uncle, and wondered, his mind plunging, whether he saw feet of clay in his idol for the first time. He was shocked – shocked at many things, but worst of all at this revelation of the older man's philosophy. 'You . . . *you* do not believe it? That every man has his price?' he demanded, his voice urgent.

Rob shrugged. 'Experience has not wholly convinced me otherwise,' he said.

'But that is monstrous! It is against all that you have ever taught me. . . . '

'In precept, aye. In practice . . . !' Those great shoulders lifted again. 'It depends on the price, see you. With one, it may be two pounds Scots – or thirty pieces of silver. With another, all but the Kingdom of Heaven!'

'No!' Gregor grated. 'Not *all* men.'

His uncle smiled, then, that winning heart-warming smile of his, and his hand came out to clasp the young man's plaided shoulder. 'No – not all men,' he agreed. 'I will make an exception of *you*, Greg – 'fore Heaven I will!'

'And you, Uncle?' That was hardly, levelly, said, and the regard that went with it as level.

'I am as God made me,' Rob Roy MacGregor answered, no less evenly. He withdrew his hand, and straightened up. 'Come, you.' And he turned away, back towards the camp.

Gregor Ghlun Dubh stalked half a step behind him for most of the way, with hardly a word to either of them.

*　　*　　*

Though hunting was, of course, a minor consideration for this assembly, a gesture in that direction was made the next day. The business was arranged in two distinct phases – one for the young and vigorous, the other for the more mature and dignified. The first was practised on horseback, with deerhounds; the second from behind butts and hides, with flintlock muskets. Deer were required for both, running free for the huntsmen, and driven for the marksmen. Deer being deer, to arrange that both practices could be engaged in simultaneously required considerable organisation and very extensive territory.

For, of course, the fleet and wary red deer of the Highland hills cannot really be driven at all. At the first hint of orthodox driving they would be off, singly and in herds, streaming and drifting over the skyline and far away, free as the cloud shadows, to be seen no more of men. They had to be manoeuvred, not driven, worked upon without them being aware of the fact, impelled not constrained – and never alarmed. To achieve that, against the keenest noses and ears of God's creation, leaving eyes and instinct out of it altogether, demanded a high degree of knowledge, cunning, patience and fitness.

The scheme went thus. Sizeable quantities of deer having been located – and that was the simplest part of it – expert beaters were sent out, over a wide area, to try to work the beasts in towards a given locality, preferably a sort of bottleneck, from which they could only escape by dashing through the neck or by breaking back whence they had come. The marksmen lined the bottleneck, and the horsemen and hounds waited hidden to chase the breakers-back, In theory, at any rate. The difficulties, which were many, made the sport.

The success or failure of the day rested not really with the sportsmen at all, but with the beaters. The moving of the deer, the wildest of the wild, had to be done by merely slightly unsettling them, never alarming them, so that they drifted and fed gradually in the right direction – which had to be down-wind, of course, or the brutes would scent the waiting hunters and bolt. This meant that the beaters had at all times to be off-wind to right or left – which in the eddying air currents of the hills was in itself no easy task. They must not disclose themselves to the deer, nor let them get more than the merest hint of their wind; yet they had to cause the creatures just enough disquiet to make them move away in the required direction. This, over vast acreages of mountainside, and with different herds of deer, called for exceptional hillcraft. Compared with it, the mere shooting or riding down of the game with hounds, however exciting and difficult it might be, could be dismissed as child's play.

The MacGregors of course were there ostensibly as beaters, but it went without saying that no large proportion of them were expert enough for this task. They were sent, in the main, by devious ways that would not arouse the quarry, to block various passes and gaps and valleys, for the horsemen's benefit. Both Gregor and his uncle, though expected to be of the hunters, being old hands at the game, insisted on joining the beaters, placing themselves under the orders of local men who knew the ground and something of the wind currents. Not all their chiefly colleagues approved.

They had a fine exhilarating day of it, nevertheless, on the great heather slopes above the Black Wood, a day of physical action such as both men loved, pitting their wits and skill against a wily and worthy adversary on his own territory – or hers, rather, for the old hinds represented three-quarters of the difficulty – working in fine and instinctive harmony and co-operation with their fellow hillmen, irrespective of name or rank. And all under the spell of great skies and endless vistas and the clean scented airs of the high tops. A clean good day altogether, the object of which, in the ultimate banging of flintlocks and the hallooing of headlong hunters and the baying of racing hounds, seemed comparatively unimportant, if not actually a pity. The taste of politics and suspicion and cupidity, and worse, was for the time being washed away and forgotten. Uncle and nephew worked as a team again, with MacAlastair and Ian Beg in fullest sympathy. Coming off the hill that evening, weary, peat-stained and begrimed, their laughter and singing nevertheless rang out for all men to hear. The fact that the life's-blood of only a mere sixty-odd stags had dyed the heather, not one of them an outstanding head, and that my Lord of Breadalbane was annoyed, was of supreme unimportance.

It transpired that the proud Sons of Donald, from the west, had arrived at the camp in the interim – ClanRanald, Glengarry and Sleat. With them Matheson of Lochalsh, and MacKinnon of MacKinnon from Skye. And not with them, by any means, but a decent distance apart, the MacKenzies, under the young Earl of Seaforth and Sir Alexander of Gairloch.

The tally was now complete – for the Frasers and the Rosses, with sundry lesser clans, had made excuse, and Rob Roy had not had time to reach the Isles or the far Mackay country.

That night there was more feasting in honour of the MacDonalds and the MacKenzies – though, with the Glen Coe incident far from forgotten, the former were only frigidly polite towards their host. On the morrow, the real business of the gathering would begin.

*   *   *

The assembly was held in Breadalbane's pavilion again – however uncomfortable many of those present must have found it to be discussing politics under the black-and-gold Campbell colours. To avoid the ever-thorny problems of precedence, there were no formal placing arrangements, individuals and groups seating themselves where they pleased – though amidst a deal of shouldering, edging, stiff bowing and steely stares. No man discarded his bonnet. Apart from

'Colonel Hooke, only Breadalbane himself was hatless, in his great heavy wig – and as the heat in the tent grew oppressive he eventually laid that aside, and promptly, strangely, became infinitely more potent and dangerous-seeming, with his thin scrawny neck and bare bald vulturine head revealed.

The Earl made a brief carefully-worded introductory speech, declaring that they were all leal and good-intentioned Scots gathered for no other purpose than to further if possible the well-being and best interests of their native land. A Union with England was being negotiated, a Union that was no union but an incorporation, a swallowing up. If that was to the benefit of Scotland, well and good. But if it was not, if it spelt the end of their independence, then it behoved them to resist it. Good or bad, there was no doubt that the mass of the Scots people were against it. Which, in the circumstances, was a highly significant factor in view of the dynastic situation. Seldom indeed was the mass of the people aroused. Not for many generations had the people of all parts of their ancient kingdom been so concerned, or the Government and Parliament so out of step with the desire of the populace. Occasion and duty knocked at their doors. It behoved the Highlands to listen. He himself was an old done man – but his hearing remained to him yet, God be praised!

He then introduced to them Colonel Nathaniel Hooke, and sat down, having spoken no treason and committed himself to nothing, yet having created an extraordinary impression of crisis and opportunity. Rob Roy caught Gregor's eye – but did not hold it.

Nathaniel Hooke made a very different impact, the plain soldier, downright, unequivocal, unemotional. He read them a message from the nineteen-year-old James Stewart, subscribed at the Court of St Germains, by the grace of God, King of Scotland, England and Ireland, in which he assured his leal and trusty cousins, friends and subjects in Scotland of his love and affection for them, his gratitude for their continued loyalty to his House and throne, and his deter-

mination to come to them at the earliest opportunity. Also`
he commended to them Nathaniel Hooke, his trusted
courier and emissary, who would explain to them what he
and his Council proposed. God undoubtedly would be
with them, and would defend the right.

Rob Roy, perceiving nobody else about to do so, raised a
cheer here. 'God Save the King!' he shouted.

It was hearteningly taken up – even though men tended
to watch their neighbour's lips as they supported it.

Hooke went on to reiterate the opportunity afforded by
the widespread dissatisfaction in Scotland over the proposed Union. He told them that undoubtedly the Treaty
would be signed sooner or later, a sufficiency of the Parliament in Edinburgh having been either bribed, threatened
or compromised. There would be revolts and disorders up
and down the country. Then His Majesty would land.
Then the standard would be unfurled. Then they must
strike.

'When?' ClanRanald demanded – thus asserting the
MacDonald right to speak first and indicating their readi-
ness for the fray. He was an impatient man at any time.

'Our information is that Godolphin, and Anne's Government, expect the Acts of both Parliaments to be passed by
April next. That is in seven or eight months' time, sir. The
glens will be free of snow and floods by then, and His
Majesty intends to land about the first of May. Public
indignation should be at its pitch by then, and the campaigning season just starting.'

'The time would seem to be well chosen, whatever,'
Glengarry said swiftly, before his fellow MacDonald could
rush in with his inevitable hasty talk about delay, faint-
heartedness and the ClanRanald motto of Gainsay who
Dare.

There was a general growl of approval. Seasonal conditions meant a great deal where the clans were concerned,
not only because snow and flooding made large-scale
movement practically impossible for five months of the year
in the mountains, but because of the needs of sowing and

harvesting the winter feed for the hill cattle, on which the entire Highland economy was based, and the droving south of the surplus stock for the autumn trysts. Clan armies always had one eye over their shoulders during campaigns for these serious matters – and who would blame them? May undoubtedly was the best time for adventures of this sort, with four clear months ahead.

'Is it all Scotland that is to rise – or only the clans . . . as usual?' the young Earl of Seaforth asked.

'It is the whole country, my lord,' Hooke assured. 'I have been travelling round the country of Fife and Gowrie and Angus and Aberdeen. I have been in correspondence with many of the leading men to the south. And everywhere the cause is well received, and goes from strength to strength . . .'

'In Lowland promises!' Chisholm of Chisholm interpolated cynically.

'Promises – yes, sir. But what would you have? We do not wish to see men assembled just now. . . .'

'When you *do* wish to see men, I'll warrant it will be Highlandmen you will see, Colonel!'

'In the forefront, naturally,' Breadalbane intervened smoothly.

'His Majesty relies on the clans to give the lead, of course,' Hooke hastened to agree, casting a wary eye around the gathering. 'But there will be large numbers of men from the Lowlands. Many great lords are committed. Errol, the High Constable; the Earl Marischal; Panmure, Kinnoull; Rollo; Strathallan; Linlithgow; Winton; Carnwath; Southesk; Ogilvie; Stormont; Nairn. The shire of Fife is almost wholly ours, as is . . .'

There was such a muttering from the assembled chiefs that Hooke paused, unsure of how to proceed, unsure whether these proud Highlanders were resenting too much Lowland intervention or too little. Rob Roy came to his aid.

'That is fine, just,' he said, his vibrant voice, though seeming but little raised, sounding clearly through the hubbub. 'There will be tasks for all. Our own selves to do the fighting, and the Lowlanders to garrison the towns and hold the bridges and the like. And to keep us fed, see you . . . !'

The growling changed to a laugh, at that, and the ever-present Highland-Lowland problem lowered its ugly head for the moment.

'His Grace of Hamilton is much interested . . . ' Hooke was going on, hopefully, when again he was interrupted.

'How much is His Grace being paid for his kindly interest?' Cluny Macpherson demanded. 'King Jamie must have gold, then?'

There was another laugh, from some. Breadalbane raised his hand. 'Gentlemen,' he said, 'I take it that it is practicalities that Colonel Hooke has come to discuss with us – not personalities. I counsel that we should hold to that.'

'*Mac Cailein Mhic Donnachaidh* is right,' Rob Roy supported. 'We have not assembled from the half of Scotland to be teasing at tassels.' Though for Breadalbane to hint that gold and the price of support were less than practicalities did not fail to strike him as quaint. That others thought on similar lines was evident by the asides.

Coll of the Cows, MacDonald of Keppoch, an old and seasoned campaigner under Dundee, brought the issues back to earth. 'The clans will rise, undoubtedly,' he asserted. 'The Lowlands will assist. The populace will be sympathetic, belike. But what about King Jamie? What is he bringing with him? And what about France?'

'Aye, aye.'

'Just that.'

'Tell us that, man.'

There was no doubting the generality of the concern.

Nathaniel Hooke cleared his throat. 'His Majesty will land, somewhere on the east coast, with a sufficient force to at least protect his person,' he announced. 'Gold he will bring with him. But . . . not in unlimited quantities, I'm afraid. The King of France is sympathetic – but preoccupied with his own wars. He will help – but the extent of his help is as yet uncertain.'

'Aye,' Keppoch said heavily. 'And there you have it!'

'No, no. Do not mistake me, gentlemen. His Most Christian Majesty's support is sure. Only it is as yet unspecified. . . . '

'Then it will have to be specified, sir, in no uncertain terms!' The old chief brought down open palm on bare knee. 'Our Highland broadswords may overrun Scotland – but they cannot hold it. We need muskets, ball, powder. But above all we need artillery, to reduce the great fortresses. The castles of Edinburgh and Stirling and Dumbarton and Inverness will be held against us – and we cannot bring them down with claymores and dirks. Artillery we must have. And engineers. If the King of France does not supply them, then we are beat before we start.'

The deep rumble of agreement was eloquent.

'My lords, gentlemen – that is understood,' Hooke cried. 'King James is well aware of the need. Only details are yet undecided. There is time yet, for that. Louis will be sending many soldiers with His Majesty. He will not send them without the services that they require. Let your minds rest easy on that score.'

'And money?' Glendaruel, the only other Campbell of note present, wondered. 'A rising cannot be maintained without money. Fighting men must be paid and fed. Horses, weapons, ammunition bought. Compensation paid . . . '

'His Majesty will bring what he can. Undoubtedly King Louis will help there also. But the Court at St. Germains is far from wealthy. It would, I daresay, wring the hearts of some here to see how His Majesty must live. His clothing threadbare, footwear down-at-heel, food of the plainest.' Hooke did not actually look at Breadalbane, but his glance just flickered in that direction. 'Some French gold will come, assuredly. But His Majesty is relying, in the main, on the generosity of his loyal subjects here. . . . '

Rob Roy stood up. 'Gentlemen,' he said, 'I for one do not seek to see my country saved by foreign gold! While I have a plack in my sporran and a beast on the hill I'll not be after shouting for *louis-d'ors*!' He changed his tone, a little. 'As some of you will have heard, likely, my Lammas herds are new in. Half of all that I shall sell of them, at Crieff and Falkirk trysts, in October, shall go to the King's purse!'

That raised a cheer and flattering acclaim. But also some sidelong glancing and thoughtful beard-tugging. Not all men were so well supplied with cattle of other folk's rearing as were the Gregorach.

Rob noted the glancing, and went on quickly. 'My nephew, Glengyle, here, is just after calling on Lowland lairds in the Carse of Stirling, see you – men of the size of Arnprior and Garden and Keir, who dabble in the America trade. And Patterson of Bannockburn. Up, Greg, and tell them what these will give.' No hint there of the doubts that he had thrown on the said promises the day before.

It was a new experience for Gregor Black Knee to feel self-conscious and embarrassed before his fellow-men. But this was a distinctly special assembly. He looked round him, as he rose, clearing his throat.

'Up, the Gregorach!' somebody said.

'Up, the White Bull!' another amended. There was a laugh.

Gregor felt better immediately. Gallangad's bull was serving him well. 'I gained from these lairds promise of around 25,000 pounds Scots.' That was only some £2,000 sterling, but it sounded well. 'That was from but some eight men.'

'Promises again . . . ?' the cynical Chisholm commented.

'They are all within the area of my Watch,' Rob Roy put in mildly. 'They might possibly be held to their words!'

Gregor took a quick breath. 'You can be adding another thousand to that, gentlemen, from my own self,' he said, greatly daring. 'Scots.' And, as there was a distinct murmur from his assembled seniors and betters, he added a wholly rash, 'And if anyone wishes to buy a notable bull, the price can be added to my contribution, whatever!'

'Damnation! Were you not after giving that bull to me?' his uncle demanded. 'I tell you . . . '

The rest was lost in a great shout of mirth. Financially, at least, the day was saved. No more was heard of *louis-d'ors*.

Men were now the question. And of course men meant commitment. A chief who once had his name linked with so many men could nowise go back on it, dare not, for pride's sake, contribute one clansmen less. Rivalry, caution, ambition, suspicion and sheer vainglory played a major tug-of-war now.

Again the MacGregors were in a position, of course, to lead the way. They had 600 armed men outside there and then. What proportion of that number could be mustered for a lengthy campaign as distinct from a day or two's cantrip like this remained to be seen. But this was by no means the scraping of the Gregorach barrel. And there were always the broken men and drovers and suchlike from Balquhidder and Brig o' Turk and thereaway who could be enrolled at a price. Rob Roy said 750, at any rate – and set the standard high. Higher than he was likely to fulfil, perhaps.

ClanRanald promptly weighed in with a haughty 1,000. And thereafter young Seaforth, glaring, mentioned 2,500 MacKenzies, with a casualness that his looks belied. That brought the other MacDonalds to their feet. 700, Glengarry cried. 500, old Coll of Keppoch added. There was a brief pause as the more circumspect Sir Donald of Sleat calculated just how many would be needed still to decently beat the MacKenzies. He made it 400, and announced that figure cannily – though, successor of the Lords of the Isles himself, he could have more than doubled it. But they had outbid Seaforth and his MacKenzies by 100. That should ensure them the right of the line.

Sir John Maclean of Duart, another veteran, named 600 for himself; added that his kinsman Maclaine of Lochbuie was good for 300; and reckoned that another 100 could be got out of Ardgour. 1,000 in all.

But after this exciting interlude there was a notable pause. It was all very well for these great outland clans from the Isles and the remote north-west to commit themselves thus in their ancient rivalry. They could never be brought to heel in their distant fastnesses. If things went wrong, major punitive expeditions were never likely to reach Skye or Mull, or even Kintail and Applecross and Torridon of the MacKenzies. The MacGregors, likewise, had little to lose. They were outlawed and proscribed already, living on their wits. For more accessible and responsible folk, it was all rather different. . . .

There was much humming and hawing, much discussion and consultation and prevarication, much head-shaking and beard-tugging. Rob Roy worked hard, as did the Mac-Donalds and MacKenzies and Macleans, who were already committed. Hooke, of course, dared not intervene; and Gregor was much too junior to do more than pose as a good example. It was decided to adjourn for dinner and see what victuals and liquor could do to loosen stiff tongues and wills.

They were still eating when Lochiel's son almost came to blows with Glengarry, and thereupon threw 400 Camerons into the scales. Cluny Macpherson could not thole that, and committed himself to 450 of his folk. Alexander of Struan, the poet, had no option but to go one better, and came in with 500 Robertsons. Thereafter the contagion spread, and before the afternoon was out 17,000 men were vouched for, and half as many again hoped for, once the go-one-better-than-my-neighbour process really got going.

And, of course, with the men committed, the chiefs also were committed. The rising was assured. There only remained to draw up the usual Bond of Association, decide the assembly points, who were to command the brigades, and so on.

All that could be done on the morrow, after another hunt. Meanwhile certain clerkly ones amongst them, Rob Roy included, should draw up the terms of the Bond of Association, concoct a Loyal Address to King Jamie, and also a Memorial to His Most Christian Majesty Louis XIV of France, pointing out how ripe was the time, how fair were the prospects and how urgent the need of engineers, ammunition and artillery. Breadalbane offered to assist in this task.

Gregor wondered how many others, beside himself – and his uncle, of course, for it was not the sort of thing that Rob Roy would miss – had noticed that the said noble earl was the only man present who had not committed himself to providing some tally of men for the venture. Even Campbell of Glendaruel had offered 100.

*   *   *

The deer-hunt the next day amounted to no great shakes as these affairs went, a drizzling rain damping the ardour of the sportsmen and a fitful wind making the driving more difficult even than usual.

Gregor hunted this time with his hounds, and achieved one or two exciting kills. But he was used to better sport amongst his own hills around Loch Lomond and Loch Katrine; this Rannoch had altogether too much wood for this sort of hunting, the deer tending to bolt downwards for this forest cover instead of upwards for the open tops, as was usual and suitable. However, it all served as excuse for the gathering, which was what was required; moreover, the Laird of MacKinnon grassed a huge woodland stag of no fewer than fourteen points, past its best and creaking at the joints admittedly, but still with a spread that few had seen bettered, a trophy to take back with him for the Skyemen to make a ballad out of when compared with their poor small island deer. Not a few felt that it was a pity, however, that thi should have fallen to such a dull fellow as MacKinnon.

In the evening there was another session in Breadalbane's pavilion, to approve the form of the Memorial to King Louis, the Loyal Address to King James and to sign the Bond of Association. Louis, whose aid was so unspecified, but who nevertheless would so greatly gain in his other interests were London to be actively preoccupied with a rising in Scotland, was specifically requested, with all respect, to provide 15,000 muskets and equivalent ammunition, 4,000 barrels of powder and 12 brass field-pieces. Also

8,000 soldiers, to include an adequate number of engineers. No harm in pitching it high, as Rob explained, indicating the peculiarities of the Latin temperament. James was assured of all love and loyalty, and of the impatience with which all awaited his personal appearance amongst them – but was urged in the next paragraph that the value of his royal presence would be vastly enhanced if he brought with him the supplies and troops demanded of King Louis.

The Bond of Association was in the usual terms. It bound its signatories to reassemble at points to be decided later, together with armed forces to the numbers agreed, within twenty-one days of receipt of an authorised summons, to support with their blood, strength and treasure the legitimate title and claim of their *Ard Righ* or High King, James Stewart, against the present most calamitous and illegal usurpation.

There was some inevitable discussion and some heat engendered on the subject of who was first to sign this declaration. Not only were the MacDonalds vociferous that the honour lay with their house, rather than with, say, Seaforth, whose earldom was a mere modern nonsense not to be mentioned in the same breath as the ancient Lordship of the Isles; but there was internecine strife as to which of themselves should pen the premier superscription – Sleat claiming that he represented the senior branch of the clan, ClanRanald asserting that he was supplying the most men, and Glengarry pointing out heatedly that he was not only the eldest but the only veteran of the wars amongst them. In this pass Rob Roy it was who declared that the obvious name to be first on the Bond was that of Breadalbane, their host, who had summoned this gathering and so greatly assisted them to their decisions. No man's name would look better at the head of this historic list.

There was a moment's silence in that pavilion as the significance and worth of this suggestion sank in – for it had been pregnantly delivered. Then there was a great and general outburst of acclaim, even the Sons of Donald perceiving that here was a trap out of which the wily Campbell would find it hard to wriggle. Breadalbane's signature, first on this Bond, would do what he had so skilfully avoided doing hitherto – implicate and commit him in no uncertain terms to this venture. All men cried their approval.

All except Breadalbane, that is. With thin-lipped modesty he urgently declined the honour. He was an old man, and past days of active campaigning, good only for the conference table. He would not dream of superseding the resounding names present, scores more notable than his own. Et cetera. But Rob would have none of it – and the entire assembly supported him gleefully now. The quill was thrust into the Campbell's hand.

The Earl looked at the ranked faces around him, and then smiled bleakly. He stooped down, and signed – not Breadalbane, nor even John Campbell, but *Mac Cailein Mhic Donnachaidh*, Son of Colin, son of Duncan. And then, bowing, handed the pen to Sir Donald of Sleat.

Those near enough to see stared at that signature in silence. Rob Roy drew a long breath. Himself, he was not so clever after all, apparently. It took a long spoon to sup with the Devil, indeed.

CHAPTER NINE

THE Gregorach rode and ran southwards in different fashion from their coming. Late in the night, after that signing of the Bond, a weary courier had arrived in the camp from Glen Gyle, for Gregor Ghlun Dubh. He came from the Lady Christian, to tell her son that soldiers had descended upon Glengyle House, from Stirling, seeking him. She urged that he keep away until she could be quit of them.

The message had quite other effect upon Gregor to that

intended. He had questioned the courier and discovered that the troops were dragoons to the number of some fifty, or half a squadron, under two officers, and he had thereupon gone to wake Rob Roy and inform him that he was off home forthwith to cleanse Loch Katrine-side of such gentry. Rob had listened, nodded in the dark, grunted, and then advised against unseemly haste. Was he going to let a few red-coats spoil their sleep? Let Gregor wait, in Christian fashion, till morning, and he would accompany him. They would see to this matter in a manner befitting gentlemen.

So, taking ceremonious farewell of all the assembled chiefs, and of their host, and insisting on leaving the major part of the MacGregors, under Roro's son, to assist at the final day's hunting and to provide escort for any of the guests who might wish it – little needed as these services might be – Rob and Gregor, with their own immediate followers from Glen Gyle and Inversnaid, had set off southwards up the Dall Water, going as only the Gregorach knew how. They numbered some 120 picked men.

As the crow flies they had perhaps a bare forty miles to cover – but over no fewer than five distinct ranges of mountains. And almost as the crows flew went the MacGregors, scorning drove roads, paths and tracks, at a long-legged steady mile-eating trot, over great heather shoulders and ridges, across rolling moors, down winding glens and through quaking bogs. Over into Glen Lyon at Innerwick and out again by the savage Lairig Breisleich, the Pass of Confusion. Down into Glen Lochay, to climb once more over the massive hump-backed hills beyond into wide Glen Dochart, fording the river at Innishewan. Then up under the towering heights of Ben More and Am Binnein, down the Monachyle Glen and so into green Balquhidder. There remained only the Pass of Weeping's harsh ascent, and Loch Katrine was glittering golden below them, with the sunset flooding down Glen Gyle. Eleven hours the journey had taken them, practically non-stop, and none would name them laggard.

They slanted along the high ground, some 500 feet above the loch, leaving such horses as were with them behind a shoulder of hill, and halting at a discreet distance above the whitewashed house in the mouth of the glen, in the cover of a scooped hollow. Looking over the lip of this they could discern the rows of horses tethered with military precision in the green haugh below the house, and the blue feathers of wood-smoke drifting up from the area of the steading and outbuildings at the back. Otherwise the impression was one of undisturbed peace and normalcy, amongst the lengthening shadows of evening.

Rob Roy looked from the scene to his nephew. 'Well, Greg?' he said. 'What now?'

The younger man was grateful for that question, and for what it implied. His uncle was going to leave it to himself, as Laird of Glengyle. This was his own affair, and men were to know it.

'I am thinking that my guests downbye have probably overstayed their welcome,' he observed thoughtfully. 'All those horses will have consumed a deal of forage needed for our winter feed. It is perhaps time that the redcoats returned to Stirling?'

'It could be that you are right,' his uncle agreed.

'It seems that I will need to be having speech with the officers.' Gregor fingered his chin. 'To do so suitably and without fuss, I think it would be best if some portion of us were to be slipping down by the Yellow Burn, there, and maybe working along between the steading and the house. That would be the most of us. And another portion could be for going down the Black Burn, here, and along the front between the house and the horses, see you. And then maybe the horses could just be getting a fright, the way horses will whatever, and off with them?'

Gravely Rob nodded. 'I could see all that happening,' he admitted. 'Always supposing that the sentries that these soldiers do be setting were after looking the other way.'

'Yes, then. But supposing that small little belt of trees

and bushes to the west of the house was to be going on fire, some way, and the smoke blowing over in the wind? The sentries could be distracted, just.'

'Why not?' the other conceded.

'A gentleman might then be having a quiet bit of a talk with two officers in his own house, in these circumstances, might he not?'

'Man, Gregor – I shouldn't wonder, at all!' Rob chuckled. '*Dia* – you have been well trained, I swear!'

Gregor slid down from the lip of the hollow to inform and instruct his men, men most of them, like himself, already in sight of their homes, and wondering. Being Gregorach, they were in a brittle mood. But he soon had them grinning. He ended on a note of warning.

'It is not yet war, *a graidh*, see you. That will come later,' he explained. 'Here is only an exercise in the civilities. There is to be no killing. If use your claymores you must, let it be the flat of them. These redcoats must be taught that Gregorach territory is no place for such as them – but let us be teaching them it with all courtesy. Coll Carach – you will take the Yellow Burn, with, say seventy men. Ian Beg – you, the Black Burn, with thirty. Myself, I will come with you. A score will remain here, in reserve, to come down with much noise if it seems that they are needed. Dougal, ...' he turned with a smile to his cousin of Comar, '... you have the loud voice, as Heaven's my witness! You will bring them?' Then he glanced at his uncle. 'You ...?'

'I will be keeping Coll Carach company. And maybe lighting that fire,' Rob declared. 'An old man I am getting, just. But, see you – old or young, I have noticed here and there that dragoons, saving the officers, do be keeping their swords and their pistols attached to their saddles, and not to their persons. A strange custom – but a great convenience, on occasion.'

'Aye. You all hear that, my friends? The saddlery you will look for. Coll – you will not move in towards the steading from your burn-channel till you are hearing the curlew call three times. The same for the smoke. Is all understood?'

There was a murmur of assurance.

Gregor laughed, happily, but quietly. 'Home-coming is sweet, they say! Let us be tasting it!'

The entire lengths of the long green hillsides that flanked Glen Gyle were scored by innumerable narrow burn-channels, most of which were filled with birch and rowan scrub in their steep crevices where the winds and the cattle could not get at them. The big house lay embosomed in its trees between the outflows of two such streams, both coming down within a hundred yards of the buildings, that on the west, the Allt Buie, the Yellow Burn, actually skirting the back of the steading, into which an artificial channel was diverted to water stock and to provide for the duck-pond. Nothing was easier than for men wise in hill-craft to slip soundless and unseen down these clefts of burn-channels to within a few yards of the house, the hounds that accompanied them everywhere padding silently at their heels.

In the event, the entire business was absurdly simple, what with the excellent cover available, the deep purple shadows of the creeping dusk, and the fact that obviously the soldiers were at their evening meal. The savoury smell of roasting beef came drifting down on the westerly air to Gregor as he and his party reached the foot of their stair-way-like descent into the scattered dark pines to the east of the house – an appetising scent for ravenously hungry men who had not eaten since breakfast. That it was undoubtedly Gregor's own beef only added piquancy.

From here, peering through the trees, they had an excellent view of the area in front of the house – though of little behind it. The ground sloped down to the loch shore in two shallow grassy terraces and then a reedy water-meadow. On the second terrace the cavalry horses were tethered in two long lines. And nearby, but a little closer to the house, two corresponding rows of neatly arranged small heaps upon the ground could only represent the saddlery – though the dusk made it impossible to distinguish details. As far as could be seen, only two sentries were posted here, who strolled about casually, apparently from a base at the far end of the horse-lines. Lights were already lit in the house – which Gregor took to indicate that the officers were even now within, for his mother was less prodigal with her dips. Now and again a figure appeared in the moulded front doorway in the stair-tower – probably another sentry.

Gregor touched Ian Beg's arm, and pointed. Between the water-meadow, in which two or three milch-cows grazed, and the actual loch shore was a long dyke or raised grassy bank, built to preserve the haughland from flooding in the winter storms. 'Along behind that, with you,' he whispered. 'Line it. When you are in position, hoot like an owl. Then crawl over the bank and through the rushes of the meadow, see you, amongst the cattle. It is low-lying, and they'll not be seeing you. You will get almost up to the horses, I think. Then dirk work amongst the beasts' halters. The moment that you are seen, howl all of you like the doubly damned – get those horses bolting, whatever. Then disarm the sentries – gently, see you – and round the back to aid the others. You have it?'

'Och fine, just – yes,' Ian Beg assured. 'There is nothing to it, at all.'

'Not a thing. Go, then. And fortune go with you.'

Gregor kept back two gillies, one of them his own Duncan Og, while the others dissolved into the dusk, hounds at heel. They waited. From down at the lochside mallards quacked sleepily. Now and again a tethered horse blew through its nostrils. From far up the glen a stirk's bellow sounded faintly. Somewhere a man was singing monotonously – none of their own Celtic melodies, and therefore a dragoon.

Suddenly a pair of duck flew up from the shore, with the flap of wings beating on the water before changing into the whistle of flight. The single owl's hoot from behind the bank came almost immediately, sooner than Gregor had anticipated. Thereafter, stare as he would, he could see no sign of men, no hint of movement about the dyke or in the meadow. Was Ian delaying, holding back? Had he perhaps seen some obstacle, not visible from here? More sentries . . . ?

Then one of the cows amongst the rushes moved jerkily, out of the rhythm of her quiet grazing. He could see her moving along, now, on a line towards the house, head low but not feeding, curiosity in her gait. Some gillie would be cursing her.

That was all that Gregor required. Pursing his lips, he whistled clear and true the long liquid yittering call of the curlew, three times, trilling lonely and lovely on the evening air. Then, gesturing to his companions, he slipped forward through the trees.

Circle round as they would, there was an open space beyond the last of the pines some forty yards to the gable-end of the house. They must cross it. Their rawhide brogans making no sound, the three men paced out these yards, unhurrying – even though every instinct said to hurry, to run; in the gloom were they seen, they would be but three walking figures, no cause for alarm, but running they would have been three intruders. Still no commotion arose, front or back of the house.

Gregor reached some fruit trees under the gable-end, presumably without being observed. Against the wall of the house they waited.

Not for long, this time. They heard the crackle of fire in dry undergrowth, and in a moment or two even glimpsed the faint reflection of flame amongst the tree-tops. A man called out, enquiringly, not actually alarmed – an English voice. Another answered him, from farther away. Somebody shouted rather than called – perhaps a sergeant. The first acrid smoke clouds began to drift over, so much more pungent than the aromatic tang of the small cooking-fires.

Suddenly a horse whinnied, loud and high – and the waiting men jumped at the sound. And immediately thereafter chaos was let loose in that quiet valley under the brooding hills. Eldrich howls and yells and halloos rent the air. Hounds bayed. Shod hooves clattered and pounded. Challenges and orders and demands resounded, alarmed enough now in all conscience. A pistol banged. And then another. Steel streaked and rang.

Intrigued and concerned as he was to judge the progress of events by the noise, Gregor did not wait to listen. He slid round the gable-end and along the front of the house, behind him his two shadows. Over to the left the grassy slope was commotion materialised now, with nothing to be distinguished in the massive confusion. Gregor edged round the semicircle of the stair-tower. Only a split second after he came in sight of the door, a man appeared therein, staring out. Gregor drew back swift as thought. The man stepped out, shouting something questioning. Gregor let him get two paces beyond the line of the tower – and leapt. The general hullabaloo deadened any sound of his coming. The haft of his dirk crashed down upon the bare bullet head of the unfortunate soldier. His breath came out of him in a shuddering groan, and he sank to the ground limply.

Gregor jerked his head towards the house, and strode for the open doorway, his two gillies close at his heels, claymores in their right hands, dirks in their left.

Scared faces peered at them along the ground-floor passage, from the kitchen door. They were his own people, and Gregor waved a reassuring hand to them. He was turning to race up the twisting turnpike stair to the first floor where were the principal rooms of the house, when he halted. Hurried footsteps were coming clattering down those same stairs. He stepped back, signing to his henchmen to flank the foot of the stairway. He had not drawn his own sword, and now he put away his dirk, and folded his arms. He was in his own house, was he not?

The long spurred and gleaming thigh-boots of a cavalry officer appeared, preceding a heavy figure, down those winding stairs at an awkward run. The rest of him showed the frogged and gold-braided red coat unbelted and flying open, the long waistcoat underneath also undone, one of Lady Christian's own lace-edged napkins still tucked in at the throat to protect the cravat, and then a square-chinned cleanshaven face, brows dark but jaws still chewing. At sight of the three motionless tartan-clad figures below, two with naked claymores barring the way and glimmering in the light of the guttering dips, and the other leaning casually against the farther wall, this hurrying dragoon sought to come to an abrupt stop, did not quite manage it, slipped spurred heel on a worn step, all but fell headlong, and only recovered himself by grabbing at the rope which hung down the newel. At his back a second, younger man, coming down just as fast, collided with him, nearly pitching him farther down still. They came to a halt only a few steps above those gleaming swords. The second officer was the Ensign of the St Ninians road.

'Good evening, gentlemen,' Gregor called out to them, civilly. 'I hope that I have noways interrupted your supper ? I regret that I was not here to greet you in person. But now, perhaps, I can be making up for it ? Welcome to Glen Gyle!'

*　　*　　*

The military men were perhaps not wholly to be blamed if it took them a few moments to recover their due poise and aplomb. A series of stuttered ejaculations and appeals to the Deity came from the older man, while the Ensign first drew back as though to return upstairs, then gulped and pointed, to announce that that was the man, MacGregor himself, the miscreant Glengyle. From without the uproar maintained, if it did not actually increase. Gregor was glad to hear only three or four reports of firearms.

'Perhaps I may be honoured with your names, gentlemen ?' he suggested, politely.

The older man pulled himself together with an obvious effort. 'I am Captain Somers, 4th Light Dragoons,' he said. 'This is Ensign Davies. And you, sir, if you are James Graham, calling yourself MacGregor, of this place – then I am here to arrest you in the Queen's name. On the authority of Her Majesty's Commander-in-Chief, General the Earl of Leven.'

'Och, man – tut-tut,' Gregor deplored. 'Not so fast,

surely. Here is no sort of talk between gentlemen. If you will be returning upstairs, now, we can maybe be discussing matters like . . . '

'Damnation – a truce to your chatter, sirrah!' Captain Somers broke in. 'I am not here to bandy words.' He made as if to step farther down the stairs, perceived only too clearly how the two broadswords seemed to leap quivering to life – and thought better of it. 'What in God's name is going on out there?' he demanded, instead.

Gregor cocked an attentive ear. 'That, I take it, is some of my people trying to catch your horses for you, sir – they would seem to have broken loose, somehow. Och, but they will soon have them, safe and sound.'

'Eh . . . ? Loose?' Somers turned to look at the Ensign. An appreciation of the situation seemed to be in progress, as became good soldiers. 'Deuce take it – this is armed revolt!'

Young Davies, for a brief moment, looked almost smug. If he did not actually enunciate the words 'What did I tell you?' he managed to convey his sentiments clearly enough. 'Undoubtedly, sir,' he said.

'You!' Somers swung back to Gregor. 'Do you realise what you are doing, fellow?' he demanded. 'You could hang for this – taking up arms against the Queen's Majesty!'

'Me?' Gregor looked suitably shocked. 'I do no such thing, Captain, at all. I take up arms against no one – not even Anne Stewart, of London.' He held out his empty hands to prove it. 'These gillies of mine are apt to carry their claymores that way. A mere formality it is. Like your sentries, outbye!'

'You . . . you insolent bareshanked jackanapes!'

'Sir – under my roof, I'd suggest more moderate language, whatever,' Gregor said coldly. 'I would not wish to have my friends here teaching any guest of mine a lesson in manners.'

'Are you threatening me, sir?'

'Not so. Merely informing you, just. Indeed, I am offering you further hospitality – requesting that you go upstairs, gentlemen, and proceed with your interrupted meal. At which I shall be glad to join you, for I am hungry. And I have much travelling ahead of me this night yet – as indeed have your own selves, sirs. So I advise that we eat well.'

'You . . . devil take you, sir! What do you mean? Travel . . . ?'

'To Stirling, Captain.'

'Dammit . . . to Stirling you'll be taken, certainly. But not tonight, Graham. . . . '

'The name is MacGregor. And tonight it is. You have been away overlong as it is. I insist, whatever. In fact, I will escort you there, my own self.'

'Lord save us – are you mad, fellow?'

'I said that I feared he might be, you'll recollect, sir,' Davies mentioned a little unsteadily.

'I am concerned for your comfort, rather,' Gregor announced, head ashake. 'Our provision and means of hospitality here at Glen Gyle is limited, I fear, for such a large number of guests – however boundless our goodwill. I find that we have unhappily reached the limits of our provender. Now. It is unfortunate – but I know that you will be understanding. You must return to Stirling – tonight. When we have managed to catch your runaway horses, of course.'

'Now, by all the Powers of Heaven!' Somers swore. 'I . . . '

That was as far as he got, then. A press of men was surging in at the front door of the house, to fill the stone-flagged vestibule. All wore Highland dress, save one – a dishevelled and distinctly frightened-looking sergeant of dragoons. Rob Roy was in the forefront.

'*Dia!*' his great voice rang out. 'Pretty work! As Royal's my Race – it was a diversion, no less! How is it with yourself, Greg?'

'Passing fair. I was just after informing these gentlemen . . . Ah, forgive me. Captain Somers. And Ensign Davidson, is it? This is Rob Roy MacGregor of Inversnaid, Captain of the Glengyle Highland Watch. I was for informing them that they would be in Stirling before daylight, see you. We would see to it, our own selves, and no trouble at all. Once we have their runaway horses caught for them. Och, we can do no less.'

'Surely, surely. A good evening, gentlemen. It is a pity about the horses.'

'Sergeant Cooper . . . !' Somers got out, in a strangled voice. 'What in God's name has happened? Where are your men?'

But the sergeant only shook a woebegone head, dumbly.

'Och, your men are fine, Captain,' Rob answered for him. 'Our lads are after sharing their supper with them – a pleasing sight.'

Mystified and confounded, Somers looked behind him at his subordinate. He got no aid there, the younger man wagging his head helplessly. Whether it was the sight of their unhappy sergeant a prisoner, the potent name of Rob Roy MacGregor the redoubtable freebooter, or merely the self-evident fact that all this crew of Highlanders could not possibly have come streaming in at the front door of the house unless the troopers had been quite overwhelmed in some extraordinary fashion – whatever the cause, the fight and the spirit seemed to have drained out of the two dragoons. Gallant officers as they no doubt were, they drooped rather. This sort of situation was not provided for in any military precept or instruction.

Gregor nodded, then. 'I am suggesting that we follow the others' example, then, Uncle. Upstairs with us, and let us be eating. I think that we disturbed these gentlemen at their meat, also. We must delay them no longer. Up with us.'

He moved forward to the stair foot, Rob following. The two gillies gestured with their drawn claymores. And, heavy-booted, heavy-footed, the two officers turned and climbed sourly up whence they had come.

*   *   *

In the dining-room above there was a touching reunion with the Lady Christian – who had undoubtedly been listening at the stairhead to all that had transpired. Rob made much of her, Gregor a little less, as was but natural. She did not seem to be wholly reassured by either – but females were like that, seldom accepting even the bounty of Providence without niggling doubts. But at least she fed them, and did not argue – two essentials where women were concerned, whatever their role.

The officers seemed to have lost their appetites and refused Gregor's further hospitality, sitting like spectres at the feast while the MacGregors cleared the table. Gregor did not think much of their manners, and indicated as much, without of course being rude enough to say so.

Assured by his uncle that all was satisfactorily in hand outside, and everybody getting sufficient to eat – the soldiers having killed beef in plenty – Gregor enjoyed his meal. Then, replete, leaving Rob to entertain his guests, he hurried downstairs and outside, to cope with the further needs of the situation.

He found the troopers all penned up in the steading, and being very little trouble at all. They had been caught by surprise, cooking their meal, separated from their arms and equipment, confused by smoke and the dusk, and out of touch not only with their officers but with the sergeant and two corporals, who also liked to show their superiority by eating apart – in this instance in the kitchen, from which they had emerged too late to give any real lead. Theirs had been the pistol-shots, other than those of the sentries. Fortunately nobody was dead, or nearly so. One or two had sore heads, contusions and scratches – the worst hurt probably a young MacGregor who had stumbled over a cooking-pot of stewing beef collops and scalded his bare legs.

Already most of the stampeded horses had been caught again, or had come back on their own, none having run far, being disciplined brutes. A strong guard was sitting over the saddles and arms, having food brought by the others. The Gregorach, being used to the activities of the Watch and the droving, were good at looking after themselves in most circumstances. MacGregor of Comar had come down from the hill, with their own horseflesh, aggrieved that neither his services nor his noted voice had been required.

Gregor urged one and all to eat heartily – but to be quick about it, as he had work for them yet. He gave his instructions. All the army horses were to be saddled up. Nothing was to be taken from any of the soldiers, save actual powder and shot. Every grain and ball of that was to be taken. But no weapons. Cavalry swords were to be collected, bundled up, and carried in panniers on garrons' backs. The pistols, chargeless, could be left in their saddle-holsters. Then the troopers were to be mounted, willy-nilly, a MacGregor sitting at each man's back, dirk drawn. That would account for some fifty of them. A score more should get themselves garrons and be ready to ride. The remainder could go home. That had better be the Inversnaid people, probably. Was it all understood?

Gregor returned to his own dining-room. 'All will be ready for you gentlemen in two-three minutes,' he informed. 'But first we must all have a drink for the road, and us maybe needing it.' He filled generous glasses with amber whisky, for all present, officers and Gregorach gentlemen. 'Here is a toast for us all, my friends,' he cried. 'On your feet and let us drink to our beloved and rightful Sovereign! The Sovereign!'

There was a shout of mingled laughter and acclaim as glasses were raised and drained. Gregor had done well – enabled them all to drink to King Jamie's health, and obviously so, in the presence of these officers of Queen Anne, yet had neither shown bad manners to the guests under his roof nor left them with any excuse for not drinking the loyal toast with them. All eyes upon them, the two unhappy dragoons exchanged glances, frowning and hesitant, saw no way out of it, and lifted glasses to sip doubtfully. The joyous shouting redoubled, Gregor's own uninhibited laughter outringing all. He clapped Captain Somers on the back, next to choking the man.

'Your sentiments are sound, sir!' he cried. 'Come you, now. Gather your hat and your gear. And your sword, whatever. Yes, indeed – your sword! Stirling, it is.'

Rob Roy took leave of them at the door downstairs, claiming that a respectable man of his years was better in his bed over at Inversnaid than traipsing the countryside in the middle of the night. Moreover, they had no need of him, most evidently. He bade Captain Somers convey his respects to the Governor of Stirling Castle, and pointed out that this was the first body of troops ever to honour the MacGregor country with a visit, in his lifetime. He forbore to add that if 600 MacGregors had not been engaged elsewhere at the time, they might not have been even thus honoured.

The Captain and the Ensign, sitting their own horses and with their swords at their sides – but flanked fairly closely by Gregorach mounted on shaggy garrons, nimble if short-legged, their right hands a shade ominously hidden in the folds of their red plaids – rode away from Glengyle House, amidst the valedictory cheers of those left behind. At their backs trotted their half-squadron, more or less in parade-order, but each charger bearing a double burden – in every case the pillion-rider being noticeably the more cheerful of the two. Behind them again another swarm of garron-borne Highlanders crowded anyhow, with three pannier-ponies.

South-eastwards, round the head of the darkling loch, they rode, for Stronachlacher and the drove road for Aberfoyle.

*　　*　　*

It was approximately thirty miles to Stirling by the drove road that wound between the ramparts of the Highland Line and the northern rim of the long desolation of Flanders Moss – but a little longer by the route that Gregor led the dragoons, and by which, once their own clachan of Aberfoyle was past, they avoided all villages and haunts of men. The edge of the Moss itself received them more than once – where Gregor was urgent that all should follow exactly in the tracks of the horse in front if miry death would be avoided, himself leading. That he led on Mr Davies's former fine black charger was not actually commented upon by anybody.

Indeed there was little comment or chatter of any sort throughout, the Gregorach finding the military but surly companions.

They had left Glen Gyle after ten o'clock. Hurrying was out of the question in the circumstances, and it was almost four in the morning before Gregor drew rein near Drip Bridge under the tree-clad Hill of Drip that rose like a stranded leviathan amongst the flats of the Carse. Ahead, just over a mile away, against the already paling sky to the east, the loom of the great Castle-rock of Stirling just could be descried. He let Somers come level with him, and pointed.

'Yonder is your Castle, Captain. You will excuse us from coming farther? My people have travelled far since yesterday's dawn, and it is a far cry for dismounted men back to Glen Gyle.' He yawned, himself, as he said it.

Somers stared straight ahead of him. He did not speak, nor even glance in Gregor's direction.

The latter, who had a modicum of pride himself, knew a certain sympathy for the other man. 'Och, man – it is none so ill an ending to this ploy, at all,' he pointed out. 'You were a brave man to be entering the MacGregor country at all. More, with but fifty men to you. And you have brought them all out again, too. The first man, belike, to ever have done such a thing!'

'You can spare me your condolences, at least, Mac-Gregor,' the sorely tried soldier said tersely. 'And do not think that you have heard the last of this night's work! By God – you have not!'

'Do not be taking it so hard,' the soft-hearted Gregor urged. 'It could have been a deal worse, whatever. You have lost not a thing, at all. All your men are here. Your weapons are in the panniers, there. Also the ball and powder for your pistols. You have lost nothing.'

'Except my reputation, sir! And my self-respect. What do you think I will tell my Colonel of this night's affair?' That was a *cri de coeur* indeed, however harsh the tone in which it was uttered. 'I was ordered to bring you in to justice. . . . '

'*Dia* – what is an order, when it cannot be carried out? What will you tell your Colonel? That you braved many perils to reach your destination. That Glengyle was not at home when you got there. That he was away in the north, it was said. That you waited as long for him as you felt was safe and proper. That you left the word for him to come forthwith to Stirling Castle when he got home – and then returned your own self to report, wasting no more time. That would be the tale I would be telling, whatever.'

'May be, sir. I could well believe it. S'wounds – a likely story!'

'I think that there will be none to gainsay it! Your men will be glad to have it so.' Gregor turned. 'How think you, Ensign?'

Davies cleared his throat strongly, but did not commit himself to more positive answer.

Gregor shrugged. 'I have done the best that I can for you, gentlemen,' he said. 'I suggest that you keep this side of the Highland Line, in future – for peace's sake!' He pulled his horse round, and in his own Gaelic tongue called to his people to unload the pannier-ponies, dumping their loads on the ground. Then he ordered all the pillion-riders to dismount. They were for home.

'Good-night, gentlemen,' he said, in English again, to the officers, to all the company. 'In fair fight you might have been the end of us, whatever!' He laughed as he said it, happily, heartily, for that hour of the morning. 'Sleep you on that. Good-night!'

Not a word of response did he receive from any of them as the Gregorach turned away and slipped back into the mists and shadows of the great Moss.

CHAPTER TEN

EVEN for such as Gregor Ghlun Dubh – or Gregor Tarbh Ban, Gregor of the White Bull, as he was beginning to be known – even for such as he, life could not continue at the rate that he had been living it since that Lammas day four weeks before. Scaling the heights of experience and bestriding the pinnacles of destiny may be all very well – but there are the valleys and flats of existence to be covered also, slopes down as well as up, and even sober levels, even for a chieftain of MacGregor. Moreover, these are not only inevitable but highly necessary for the avoidance of both physical and emotional exhaustion. Gregor's need for the level plains and the quiet pastures was undoubtedly greater than he either knew or would have acknowledged.

All of which is not say that he was in any way grateful or appreciative of the quiet – or the relatively quiet – weeks that followed. Dull, he found them – thoroughly dull. Also humdrum, tedious and stale. Which was doubtless ungrateful of him, as well as foolish and illogical.

It was unusual, too, for those golden September days, the pride of the Highland year, had been always the season that he loved best in Glen Gyle – the season when the oats were harvested, the hill cattle were rounded up and brought down preparatory to the autumn trysts, when the heather was in fullest bloom, the honey was flowing, and the stags were at their best, and all the land of the mountains smiled and was glad. All that still applied, of course – but in comparison with what had gone before it seemed to have lost something of its savour for Gregor MacGregor. His thoughts tended to be elsewhere. And by no means all of them were deep in high politics, affairs of state, or battles to be fought when King Jamie landed, either. More often indeed, traitorously, they sped away southwards into the soft lush Lowland country, drawn by the magnet of a pair of dark eyes.

Not that Gregor failed to throw himself, physically at least, with a fair semblance of his usual enthusiasm, into the daily round, as was expected of him. Unlike the Lowland gentry, who would, of course, find field-work shockingly demeaning, he laboured amongst his people with a sickle at the thin oats till his long back ached with the bending and his hands were full of thistle-pricks and thorns. He rode on exhilarating round-up gallops over the boundless hills to herd the three-parts wild cattle into the glens. He stalked stags in the high corries and roebuck in the birchwoods, and lured salmon in the rivers and shallows of the lochs. He even turned his hand to compiling verse and writing it down – though this he did more privately than was his wont. The fact that in none of all this did he achieve any great degree of satisfaction was ominous.

The Lady Christian watched him at it, and sighed.

There were no repercussions from Stirling Castle. Not that he had anticipated any, strange as this might seem to anyone not versed in the situation. Though only thirty miles away, Stirling might have been in a different land. Stirling and its fortress was only an outpost of the world of government and soldiers, promulgations and parchments. Beyond the Highland Line the Governments had to depend upon the chiefs for carrying out their precepts. And if the chiefs were otherwise inclined, the precepts got no farther than Stirling, or possibly Perth. The MacGregor's south-west corner of the Highlands was particularly immune from outside interference, protected almost as much by sheer geography as by the highly practical independence of its people. The clan had been proscribed and outlawed for just over a hundred years – yet only the Campbells and other inimical Highlanders under their wing had dared to put the royal Letters of Fire and Sword into effect, even then leaving the central stronghold area of Balquhidder, the Trossachs, Glen Gyle and Loch Lomondside strictly alone. Rob Roy had been put to the horn time and again, rewards offered piously for his capture, and solemn proclamations made forfeiting his goods and chattels. Yet he was not only still at liberty and increasing in gear and substance, but officially appointed Captain of a Highland Watch – since only he could keep any sort of order along the Highland Line, and Rob's order was better than anarchy – and the Lord Justice-Clerk himself continued to pay for his protection. Captain Somers, or whoever sent him, had been bolder than he knew – and luckier. Only an army could have wiped out his humiliation – and Queen Anne had more to do with her armies in 1706.

After all the excitement of the projected rising, too, only one interlude seemed to provide any echo of it all, meantime, any relief to the feeling of anti-climax. That was a meeting of the Clan Council of the Gregorach, to elect a Captain of Clan Alpine. The meeting was held at Glen Gyle, as the most central and suitable spot – and of course Rob Roy was duly elected, there being no other real contender. A clan was normally led by its hereditary chief in war or battle, but where such chief was incapacitated by age or youth or failing in character, then it was necessary that it should have a duly appointed and accepted warrior to take over his military functions. In fact, of course, this had been Rob's unofficial position for years. But with war envisaged, and the Gregorach committed, a more explicit command was required. Had Rob not been there, who could tell what might have been the outcome, for many would have considered themselves bound, in self-respect, to seek the office. And Roro was too old and cautious, Glengyle too young, Glencarnaig unwarlike, Balhaldie untrustworthy, and so on. As it was, all were content, since Rob's fame was an asset, his prowess acknowledged and generalship proved – and moreover, as a mere second son, he had no claim to the actual chiefship, and therefore was no rival to these tentative contenders.

The Laird of Inversnaid, Captain of the Watch and former Tutor of Glengyle, then, became Captain of Clan Alpine and undisputed war-leader of the Gregorach, with all due authority to raise such numbers of the clan as the circumstances should demand. He also could now wear three eagle's feathers in his bonnet, as representing the absent chief.

The said Rob stage-managed the business beautifully, achieved all that he required, and sent everybody home happy. Gregor was particularly pleased, since his lieutenancy now could be assured. Also, he had never been really comfortable about being senior to his puissant uncle, wearing two feathers to Rob's one. It was better this way – and after all, he still remained head of Clan Dougal Ciar and in line for the ultimate chiefship.

But all that, of course, rousing as it was, represented only one day's excitement and junketing that sunny September, a very brief interlude in Gregor's deplorable humdrummery. Frustration returned.

He put up with it till the end of the month, when the harvest was cut, if not in, in all his glens, and the cattle were lowing protest in a score of valleys under the watchful eyes of the herd-boys. Then, one afternoon, he dressed more carefully than of late, informed his mother a shade curtly that he had business to attend to, stalked out, took his garron and not his black charger, and without a single gillie at heel, or even a deerhound, rode off eastwards along the loch shore.

Not a few eyes lifted from sundry tasks to watch him go, and gleamed with quiet smiles – even if the Lady Christian's were not amongst them. Even gillies will talk.

*   *   *

Already the evenings were shortening, and it was dark before Gregor won out of the Moss and rode up through the quiet farmlands. Even here, twenty-five miles away, he noted the difference in the harvest. The oats, so much heavier than his own, were all in stack and the stubbles bare.

Arnprior House was less brighly lit up than when last he had approached it. Lights shone from only two windows to the front. He indulged in no hallooing or slogan-shouting this time, quite content to wait at the front door like any unchiefly mortal, after he had banged thereon.

The manservant who opened, lamp in hand, gaped at sight of him, but admitted him hastily and hurried off with his news.

It was Mistress Meg who came flitting down the stairs amidst a rustling of petticoats, a few moments later, to greet him. 'Gregor!' she cried, 'It *is* you? How good to see you! Is all well? What have you been doing . . . !'

Gregor doffed his bonnet, and bowed. 'Och, yes – fine. Nothing at all, that is. Och, I mean – everything is good and fine. And you, Mistress Meg?'

'I'm all right. But the better for seeing *you*, my braw Hielandman! But Father is ill. That is why I am here. He has the gout again – his old trouble. And the spleen, to make it worse! So I stayed behind to look after him, when the others went.' She sighed prettily. 'And, dear me – it is a dull business.' That made two of them.

'Eh? The others went . . . ? You mean . . . ?' He swallowed, and recollected himself. 'Sorry I am, whatever, to hear about your father,' he declared hurriedly.

She gave a little laugh. 'Quite, sir. Exactly. I understand! Still – I'm pleased to see you!'

'I am glad of that,' he said, and sincerely. 'It is good to see your own self, too.'

They eyed each other then, she quizzically, he trying not to show the disappointment that he felt.

'You came a long way . . . to see Mary?' she asked.

He nodded, wordlessly.

'I am sorry, Gregor. They . . . she and my husband, returned to Bardowie just a week ago. He had affairs to attend to. Naturally I should have gone too, but for Father. I could not leave him like he is. Mary will look after John meantime. She will be sorry to have missed you.'

'Yes,' he said.

She considered him keenly. 'You are fond of Mary,' she put to him, not as a question but as a statement.

He accepted it at that. 'Fond is a poor word, I think.'

'Poor Gregor. Poor Mary. Lucky Mary! Or . . . is she? Heigh-ho!' That young woman's sighing was apt to be never very far away from laughter. 'Come upstairs, and take a little refreshment with a lonely woman, Gregor – even if it is the wrong one. We can at least *talk* of Mary!'

'Ummm,' he said, and followed her.

But they did not talk as much of Mary as he would have wished. Meg was not the one to do any such thing. Gregor did gather, however, that she was well, displeased with her brother, sorry to be gone from Arnprior, and that, if she had not actually left a message for himself, should he make an appearance, she did not lack goodwill towards him – though he had to pick out all this from the spate of his hostess's more personal chatter.

'Now – tell me all that *you* have been doing, Gregor,' she demanded, at the end of it.

'Nothing. Just nothing at all,' he assured. 'It is a long way to Bardowie Castle, is it not?'

She shook her head over him. 'Much too far for you, anyway,' she declared. 'Too far from your Highland Line. It must be thirty miles from here, forty miles south of your barbarous fastnesses, Gregor. It cannot lie more than five miles north of Glasgow. No place for the likes of you, my man.'

'Forty miles by your roads, it may be – but not as I travel,' he asserted.

'Perhaps. But all through country hostile to you and your kind. And, recollect – my husband does not feel so loving towards you as I do, Gregor MacGregor! I would not like to test him too sorely with your safety!'

'You . . . you do not sound the most respectful of wives, Mistress!'

'I had not the choosing of my husband, sir!' That was short, almost sharp.

'Ummm,' Gregor said again. 'Oh.'

There was a moment or two's silence. Then she spoke again. 'You have not told me what you have been doing since you rode away from us that night, so dramatically –

banging all the doors behind you! You need not inform *me* that you have been doing nothing. . . . '

'I have been cutting oats and herding beasts for the trysts. Dull work, see you. . . . '

'You were going to raise your clansmen, I understood – lots of them. For some mysterious meeting. Would they not obey you ? The Gregorach would not rise . . . ?'

She wormed most of it out of him, of course, before, half an hour later, thumps from above indicated that Robert Buchanan's patience had run out, and gave Gregor his excuse for leaving.

He begged off visiting the invalid, promised that he would come again, and enjoined strictest secrecy over all that he had told her.

She assured him that his information would be safer in her hands than in his own – which was probably true enough – and said that she would be writing to her sister-in-law. Had he any particular message that he would like her to transmit ?

'Tell her that I was after meaning what I said, that night – the last time that she saw me,' he declared strongly. 'Tell her . . . och, tell her to be watching out, after the Crieff Tryst is by with, Bardowie or none! Good-night to you, Mistress Meg – and my thanks.' And he clapped on his bonnet and strode off, downstairs and out. That door banged again, loud as ever.

CHAPTER ELEVEN

CRIEFF Michaelmas Tryst was the greatest cattle-fair in all Scotland. To it came the exportable products of most of the Highlands, an area covering two-thirds of the land. Other fairs, at Crieff and elsewhere, had their points, but this occasion was unique. Herds travelled from as far away as Ross and Sutherland and even the Hebridean isles, some taking as long as six weeks to the journey, and buyers came from all over the Lowlands and the North of England, from as far south as Darlington and York. Thirty thousand head of cattle, and more, would change hands at this three-day event, mainly the shaggy kyloes of the glens.

Climate and geography dictated this vast annual transference. The Highland pastures and hill grazings would feed young stock handsomely enough from April till October, but thereafter the forage died away to nothingness. The sparse poor oats and bog-hay that could be grown in the narrow glen-floors were never enough to keep alive over the winter any large proportion of the stock that could be raised in the summer shielings, and only the hardy mature beasts would survive the snows and storms and floods on the open hill. So it was necessary every autumn to dispose of these great numbers of young animals, keeping only the minimum of breeding stock to face the winter.

And there was a great demand for the stirks, as beef stock, for they were the hardiest cattle in all Europe, and moreover, brought up the hard way, they fattened most spectacularly and profitably when transferred to lush Lowland pastures.

On cattle the entire economy of the clans was based, one way or another. And Crieff Tryst represented the major harvesting thereof. By common consent and for mutual advantage a truce was called for the occasion, not only in the internecine clan feuds but in the unending bickering with the Lowland authorities.

The MacGregors' droves made an even larger contribution to the total this Michaelmas than was usual. They had had a highly successful season – which, for the Gregorach, might have a slightly different shade of meaning than when applied to other and less enterprising cattle-rearers – those connected with the Highland Watch in particular having more animals to dispose of than ever before. Rob Roy himself was anxious to make a good showing – and not solely because he had promised half of the resultant sales to King James's coffers; with war envisaged and highly unsettled conditions liable to prevail, and moreover himself and most of his clansmen away from home, it behoved a cattle-owner on the verge of the Lowland country to turn as much of his stock safely into golden guineas as was possible. Then, if his lands were to suffer the misfortune of being overrun, by whichever side, in his absence, he would have the more to show for it. Others of his kind, needless to say, thought along similar lines. The Inversnaid and Glengyle herds, linked up, made the impressive total of nearly 2,000 head.

Crieff was a stirring place those days. Droves, great and small, converged on it from all quarters. The wide haugh-lands of the Earn were a-move with cattle almost as far as the eye could see. The noise was deafening. Highlanders were everywhere, their encampments covering the green hillsides. The houses were full of Lowland buyers, factors, farmers, merchants and packmen – and every second building was an ale-house.

Tinkers and cadgers were there in their hundreds. Drovers, temporarily in the ascendant and largely drunk, swaggered at will. Lords rubbed broad-clothed shoulders with half-naked gillies. Douce townsmen looked askance at swarthy gesticulating Islesmen. Proud chieftains hobnobbed with Northumbrian dealers. Crafty gypsies outbargained urban cheapjack hucksters. Money and liquor flowed in a spate, strumpets paraded the streets – and not a redcoat was to be seen in all Strathearn.

Rob Roy and his nephew had more to see to than merely the selling of beasts. It was an ideal occasion for many ploys, including the sounding of political opinion, the converting of doubters, the threatening of backsliders, and the spread-ing of useful rumours. Before the first evening, for instance, everybody in Crieff knew that the Earl of Breadalbane was committed to King James's cause, and the Campbells with him. Also that sundry high-placed traitors were accepting bribes from England to vote for the Union. And that Scotland would assuredly rise and rend all such, whenever the Treaty was signed. And so on. Even that Rob Roy was going to give every plack he made at the Tryst to the Jacobite funds – and that others were following his example. If the resulting climate of opinion was that war was obviously near and that beef, like other things, might well soon be in short supply – and consequently cattle prices tended to rise sharply – that was only just and suitable.

In consequence, too, by the close of the first day's business there were a lot of very happy MacGregors about, and rather looking for something to do about it.

Rob was nothing if not an enthusiast, once he took up a cause. Nor was he a spoil-sport. There was always some other little thing that might be done to further King Jamie's affairs, and at the same time keep his spirited lads amused and in good heart. He approached one of the numerous smugglers who thronged the town at such a time and expended some small portion of his day's profits on a cask of finest duty-free brandy – since naturally he could not in honesty subsidise Queen Anne's Revenue – and rounded up a dozen miscellaneous pipers, of whom there was no dearth. Thus equipped, all the MacGregors that he could find marched through the streets and alleys of the old town, dark but far from deserted, to the Cross, picking up adherents on the way. At the ancient Cross the cask was set up, broached ceremoniously, and the health and success of King Jamie the Eighth drunk by all present, with musical honours. Then parties were sent out into the highways and the hedges, into every street and lane and all the roads radiating from Crieff, to hale to the Cross all found stirring, of whatever kind or degree – at the point of the dirk, if need be – to taste of Rob Roy's fine hospitality and pledge a similar toast, with a damnation to the Union included. They caught some curious fish. Some were initially diffident – but none ultimately refused. Loyalty was complete.

The business took the Gregorach most of the night, and a second cask of brandy.

Gregor slept late the next morning, and reached the saleyards without breakfast but with a sore head. His uncle was distressingly active, vocal, and seemingly on top of his form. Prices, it appeared, were even better than yesterday. God bless King James!

It was almost midday when MacAlastair, Rob's personal gillie, sought Gregor out to inform him that a lady was seeking for him, beside the Tolbooth.

'A lady!' Gregor cried hoarsely. Ladies, with any pretensions to the title, were apt to be scarce in Crieff at Tryst time.

A lady, the sombre MacAlastair agreed disapprovingly, and took himself off.

Gregor did not actually run through the town to the Tolbooth square, but neither did he daunder. He saw the coach drawn up beside the great ponderous iron stocks that were supposed to be the terror of the Highlandmen — the same coach that had spelt trouble for him two months before.

He recocked his bonnet, tossed plaid across shoulder, and pushed his way thitherwards as though Provost of the place at least.

*   *   *

Mistress Meg Hamilton was alone in the coach — which said something for her courage. She sat forward eagerly as he appeared in the doorway.

'Oh, I am so glad to see you, Gregor,' she declared, a little tremulously for that young woman. 'All these horrible drunken men . . . ! But I was sure that you would be here, somewhere. You said that you would.'

He got into the coach beside her. 'You are alone?' he demanded.

'Yes. Father is in no state to make the journey to Crieff Tryst. Besides, I doubt if he would have approved.'

'You have not beasts to sell here . . . ?'

'Of course not. It is you that I came to see, Gregor. I told

150

Father that I was going to see Jean Stirling, of Kippendavie. So I did. I stayed at Kippendavie last night.'

Gregor was puzzled, and a little uncomfortable. This young woman had gone to a lot of trouble to reach him here. Which was flattering, of course – but could be embarrassing. After all, she was somebody else's wife, even if she did not think a lot of her husband. 'Crieff, at the Tryst, is no place for the likes of yourself, Mistress Meg,' he told her doubtfully.

'Lordie – I do not need you to inform me of that!' she returned. 'But it was important. At least, *I* thought so. Whether you will do so or not, is a different matter. But I felt that you had to know. I had a letter from Mary, two days ago. Aye – I see that alters matters for you. She writes from Finnary . . . '

'Finnary! That is nowhere near to Bardowie,' the young man interrupted. 'It is in Graham country. Near to Drymen. Finnary marches with Gallangad, does it not?'

'Maybe it does. I do not know. But there she is at present. My husband has taken her to lodge with Hugo Graham of Finnary. It seems that he thinks that it is high time that she was wed – and he considers Finnary a suitable husband!'

'My God!' Gregor cried – and it was no blasphemy but a cry from the heart as he said it. 'Wed? Never!'

'That remains to be seen. But so John would have it, apparently. And besides being her elder brother, he is her only male relative, and legal guardian.'

'But . . . in the Name of Heaven – this cannot be, surely? Has she any fondness for the man?'

'She barely knows him, I think. I have met him only once, myself. He is a friend of my husband, engaged with him in some of his Americas ventures. A man of wealth and with a good estate. Moreover, a safe Whig. A match, I take it, after John's own heart!'

'But not Mary's?'

'She does not write as though it was! But does that matter so greatly? In my own case it made little difference!'

He stared at her. 'Her brother can marry her to whom he will?'

'It comes to that. One way or another. What can she do? She is only twenty – as I was. In the eyes of the law she is his property.'

'No!' Gregor denied vehemently.

'But yes,' she insisted. 'I *know*. That is the position. And you are in some measure responsible.'

'Me? My own self? What do you mean?'

'You it is that have frightened John . . . with the things that you said, that time. When you last saw him. It is because of you, I am sure, that he is hurrying Mary into this. There was no word of it previously. It is largely your doing, Gregor.'

'You believe that?'

'Yes. There is also this, I think – that he does not want any part in this rising of yours. No link with the Jacobites. Having a wife a Jacobite worries him. He would have his sister wed to a substantial Whig, for safety's sake.'

'Aye. And a Graham, sib to the Marquis of Montrose, that is the Government's own man! That will be the way of it. But, *Dia* – I think that your husband is going to be finding himself on the wrong side, at the end of it!'

'I hope so. Then, no doubt, it will have to be his wife that is the saving of him!'

Gregor looked away. 'Another Graham!' he said slowly.

'That makes it worse, does it?'

'It means that I shall be enjoying doing the business the more, whatever.'

'What . . . what are you going to do, Gregor?'

'What has to be done, just.'

'You are going to Finnary?'

'To be sure. You did not think that I would do other, did you?'

'No,' she admitted. 'That is what I expected you would do. After that – what?'

'Time enough for that,' he said briefly.

'Well . . . ' She considered him closely. 'You could

152

always tell her that her room is waiting for her at Arnprior.'

'Yes.'

'I do not know what else to say. What to suggest.' Meg shook her head. 'It is all so difficult. To know what is best. I only felt that I had to come to tell you – that you had to know.'

'Thank you.'

Obviously the man's mind was not on what she was saying. Though he was looking at her, Meg perceived that he was not seeing her. 'I am fond of Mary too, you see,' she said, then.

'Yes.' Already he had his hands on the door.

'You are going – now?'

'Now,' he agreed. 'I should have gone to her before this. I blame myself, whatever.'

Doubt grew in her. 'I hope that you will be ... I hope that I have been wise ... ?' she faltered.

He got out. 'You are for home now – Arnprior? I will find you an escort of my people, to put you down to Kippendavie at the least. There are some ill characters about at this time.'

'Thank you. You will not travel with me? Arnprior is on the way to Drymen.'

'Not by the ways I shall be taking. The roads take the long way round. I go straight. Good-bye, Mistress Meg. You are a fine woman, indeed. You should have been after marrying a MacGregor!'

'I wonder,' she said, as she watched him go.

Returned to the sale-yards, Gregor sought out his uncle. 'I find that I have business otherwhere,' he announced cryptically. 'I shall not be needing any of my people – only Ian Beg. I shall not be back, see you, before the Tryst ends. You will look after my guineas for me?'

Rob Roy eyed him shrewdly. 'Surely. Your business is urgent, Greg?'

'Yes.'

'You will be needing no assistance?'

'I think not. It is my own business, just.'

'I see. Was it Arnprior's daughter in the coach?'

His nephew frowned. 'Yes.'

'Just that.' Rob smiled. 'You will be seeking no advice from an old fellow the likes of myself, and be damned to me?' he suggested.

'M'mm. I had not, h'mm, thought of it.'

'Nor did I, lad, in like circumstances! Off with you – and do not forget that your name is MacGregor!'

'I could do no less,' his erstwhile pupil agreed.

*   *   *

Garron-mounted, Gregor and Ian Beg rode fast and far, up Strathearn, over into Glen Artney beneath the soaring peaks of Ben Vorlich and Stob a Chroin, through the Pass of Leny and along the rolling flanks of Ben Ledi to Brig o' Turk. They were on a longer journey even than that from Kinloch Rannoch to Glen Gyle. But they had no footmen to think of, and their mounts were fresh. Fifty miles, Gregor calculated the distance between Crieff and his destination, a long day's trot for even the freshest and sturdiest of garrons.

Dusk found them nearing the borders of their own Flanders Moss. Another two hours. . . .

Finnary, though adjoining Gallangad to the north, was a very different kind of property. It had its hill-farms and its moorland grazings, yes – but they were rented out to tenants. The mansionhouse itself, recently rebuilt, lay snug and sheltered in a wooded dene of the winding Cadder Water, convenient to the Glasgow turnpike, a fine place of gardens and ponds and statuary, with no single cattle-beast in sight to mar the aesthetic purity of the scene. Graham of Finnary, with revenues well invested in Glasgow, required to pay no mail to Rob Roy and his Watch. That was his tenants' affair, not his.

Gregor and his companion arrived on the scene just before nine of the evening. The big house was lit up from end to end, all downstairs windows ablaze, riding-horses stood at the front door, carriages thronged the stableyard adjoining, and the sound of music drifted out across the ornamental waters in the little valley to the Highlanders' point of vantage amongst the trees. Appreciatively they sat their tired horses, and watched. Graham had more guests than the Hamiltons, apparently.

It was an interesting situation, and a lively scene. The stir and movement indoors could be sensed, if not actually viewed. And even out of doors there seemed to be considerable activity, as coachmen and postillions shared the gaiety with the maids in the stableyard to the left.

For a time Gregor considered it all. Obviously they were going to have an extended wait. This party could go on for hours yet, no doubt. His plans were of the vaguest. He had hoped that something would give him a hint as to which was Mary's room – if necessary, a dirk at a servant's throat – and thereafter, once the house was settled for the night, he would seek to reach her there, less than simple as that might be.

But now, watching, another notion came to him – a notion that would not take so long to put to the test, and that might in the end prove simpler. It was risky, of course – but it might work, he decided. With boldness, and a modicum of good fortune that boldness merited, it might work. He mentioned the matter to Ian Beg. The funny side of it struck him forcibly as he enlarged on it – as it was ever apt to do with that man – and he began to laugh. He could hardly get it out, indeed, for mirth, and soon he had the gillie laughing too. Dignity, on this occasion, looked like being a casualty.

They settled down for a prolonged wait, content that the weary garrons should have time to rest and graze.

At length a coach-and-four drew out of the yard and up at the front porch of the mansion, the coachman climbing down and proceeding into the house. The first of the guests was about to leave. It was nearing midnight, probably.

Gregor nodded to the gillie, doffed his plaid, and laid his sword beside it. Leaving the horses to feed peaceably where they were, the two Highlanders slipped down through the trees and the bushes, waded quietly across the artificial stream below, and up amongst the clipped shrubbery and statuary beyond towards the house.

Another coach was driving round to the front door as they came up. It was to be hoped that this was the beginning of a general but gradual exodus, as was the way with most parties. The first coach was moving off, a group at the porch steps waving the guests away amidst shouted farewells. The group consisted of three men and a woman – but though one of the men was almost certainly Hamilton of Bardowie, the woman was not his sister. That would have been too much to hope for, probably.

The MacGregors, unseen in the gloom beyond the circle of yellow light, edged farther to the left, towards the stableyard entrance. Two more coaches were coming out, to line up behind the others. There seemed to be a further two still remaining in the yard, in the light of the lanterns and the flaring torches. These, like the last of the three already out, were two-horse carriages – no doubt with shorter distances to go. If they would but stay there for a little longer. . . .

Gregor moved close up to that third and last coach of the little queue. There was no need for exaggerated crawling and skulking. The shadow was deep on their side, and the statuary and shrubs were kind to men who desired not to be noticed. Anyhow, the coachman was looking consistently in the other direction, towards the porch. There was no postillion on this two-horse vehicle, of course.

With a breathed word to Ian Beg, Gregor sprang into action. He leapt lightly up on to the space between the box and the coach proper, and before the coachman had an inkling that there was anybody behind him, an arm was round the unfortunate man's neck with a choking grip – the same grip that he had used on Ensign Davies one time. The jehu was dragged over, backwards and sideways off his seat, to the ground, Ian Beg assisting at his silent downfall. In the shadows beyond the coach, the astonished man found himself hustled round behind a bush, and the point of a dirk tickling his constricted throat.

'Not one sound out of you!' Gregor panted. 'Do as I tell you, and you will suffer no hurt. I want the clothes off you, whatever.'

Already Ian Beg was tugging off the long many-caped coat, muttering Gaelic threats the while. The fellow did not struggle, either out of wisdom or sheer surprise. Gregor transferred the coat to his own broader back swiftly – and found it tight across the shoulders and chest. But the multiple capes would hide that. Its long skirts had come down to its owner's ankles – but the man was no giant, and on Gregor the coat came only to a little below the knee, leaving tartan hose exposed beneath. The coachman was wearing breeches – but the Highlandman was damned if he was going to discard his kilt and soil his limbs with any Lowlander's trousers. But there were also knee-length felt gaiters, and these might serve.

Getting the gaiters off, and buttoned up again on Gregor's more muscular calves, was not so speedy a process as the latter would have liked. The second coach drove away from the front door while he was so engaged, and the next two equipages moved up. That the third did not do so might look strange. Though its driver might have got down from his box for any of a number of reasons. Probably no suspicions would be aroused. . . .

The gaiters on, they tied up their victim. Then, before gagging him with his own neckcloth, Gregor demanded of him the name of his master.

'Edmonstone of Alderpark,' the man gasped. 'Sirs, ye wouldna . . . ?'

'Quiet, you!' he was ordered, curtly – and was silent.

Leaving him, with the gillie skulking in the background, Gregor stepped out. He picked up the coachman's cocked hat that had fallen in the struggle, and clapped it on his own head. It fitted better than the other items. Reaching the horses, he took their bridles and led the coach forward to immediately behind the previous vehicle, the driver of which, he noted, was still seated on his box. Then, leaving the horses, he strolled over to the lighted porch, as casually as he could while at the same time seeking to take sufficiently short steps so that his bare knees and tartan did not reveal themselves above the gaiters.

Another party came chattering out even as he approached, a coachman preceding them. Once again John Hamilton and the woman were with the departing guests, along with another fashionably-dressed man who was no doubt the host, Hugo Graham. None of them so much as glanced at Gregor, naturally enough.

The Highlander took a deep breath, and moving respectfully round the rear of this group, he mounted the few steps and in at the great doorway, sidelong as it were.

There was a small outer vestibule and a large inner hall, blazing with light from a great central chandelier and numerous candelabra. About a dozen people stood laughing and talking therein, besides two or three waiting servants.

Gregor saw her at once. She was standing a little way apart, talking with an elderly gallant, who waved hands, snuff-box and cambric in a positive flurry of self-satisfaction. He had never seen her looking lovelier, in a low-cut gown of ivory brocade with a filmy shawl of deep crimson. But he had seen her looking a deal happier. She had a listlessness about her that was wholly foreign to the young woman whom Gregor knew, a remoteness to all that went on around her that made her companion's complacent gesticulations seem the more out of place. Gregor willed her to look towards him, with all the willpower that was in him.

But it was a bewigged and elaborately-liveried major-domo who looked at him – and from much nearer at hand, within the vestibule. 'Weel, Cockie – an' wha're ye for?' this potentate demanded – and Gregor had just time to be struck by the markedly ordinary braid Scots voice to issue from so much exotic magnificence before realisation of the danger of his position swept over him. To announce that he was Edmonstone of Alderpark's coachman might well result in this creature here shouting out that laird's name, drawing his attention – to the immediate unmasking and downfall of his fraudulent servant. His mind racing, Gregor extemporised desperately, taking an enormous risk.

'Mr Hamilton – Bardowie – would have his sister come to the door. Miss Mary. He is out there.'

'Ooh, aye. Miss Mary. She's ower there.'

'Yes. I see her. I will tell her . . . '

'Ye'll dae nae sich thing, Hielantman,' the other asserted – and Gregor jumped at that. His voice, of course – it would never sound like any Lowland servant's accent. 'Ye'll keep your place, my mannie. *I'll* tell her.' And turning, he stalked off with all the dignity of his office.

Gregor swallowed. He had only seconds now. Would she – *could* she possibly . . . ?

The major-domo reached her, bowed and spoke, gesturing towards the doorway. Mary nodded, barely glancing in Gregor's direction, and after a moment and a word to her companion, started to walk unhurriedly towards him, her elderly cavalier still in attendance.

Gregor bit his lip, his attention almost as much on what went on behind him as before. If Hamilton and the others turned and came back inside now, before Mary reached him, there would be added complications. Fortunately, from the sounds of it, their group of guests were still lingering.

Mary Hamilton raised her eyes to look at him when five or six yards off and found his gaze directly upon her. The impact was immediate and unmistakable. Her hand went up to her throat, her lips parted, a flush flooded over face and shoulders. Gregor was frowning, shaking his head. Her step faltered.

As clearly as though he spoke to her, Gregor urged her to come on, to show no sign. He saw her gulp, dart a glance right and left, and resume her progress. Only a bare couple of seconds had elapsed. The man at her side, hand on her arm, talked away, perceiving nothing amiss. Behind them came the major-domo, strutting.

They were nearly up to him, Gregor moved a little over

to the side, the side that would ensure that the girl's escort would not come between him and her. The fellow at the back was a nuisance.

As Mary came level with him, within the arched entrance of the vestibule, Gregor turned away, to face the front door as did the others, so that for a brief moment he was moving beside her, a bare foot away. 'Your brother asks for you, ma'am,' he said, aloud. And, below his breath. 'He does not! But go to him. Say anything. Then get you away. Get you to the stableyard. Somehow. The stableyard.'

She gave no sign of having heard him. But Gregor was sure that she had heard. He let her pass on ahead of him.

He found the major-domo looking at him strangely, whether in suspicion or in mere disapproval he knew not. He walked out behind Mary and her escort, slipped away to the right, down the steps, and out into the blessed night air, stalking back to his coach. He must have seemed a very stalwart and long-striding coachman, at that. Fortunately, there was no one in front to perceive his knees.

The door of the carriage at the steps slammed shut as he reached his horses' heads, and the equipage rolled away amidst wavings. The next carriage moved forward to the porch, just as the host's group turned back inside. Mary Hamilton turned back with them.

Gregor led his horses forward the required few yards, to keep station, and leaving them there edged away into the darkness at the far side.

He found Ian Beg awaiting him anxiously in the shrubbery. 'I am for the stableyard,' he announced tersely. 'Watch you the front, here. If there is trouble about the coach, come and tell me. If you hear an owl hoot thrice – back to the garrons with you.'

Reconnoitring the stableyard swiftly from its entrance, he found the two remaining coachmen still hobnobbing with the maids around the back door. Keeping to the shadows, he moved in and round. His disguise was unlikely to avail him anything here. He halted within the doorway of a lean-to building that smelt sweetly of fresh hay.

Would she come? Had she heard him – understood? And if she did come, how was he to deal with her, here under the eyes of all these servants? Would they make an outcry? If, at the same time, the loss of Edmonstone's coachman at the front was discovered, what would he do?

There was one thing that he could try. He slipped over to the nearest carriage. The lamps were already lit. He lifted out the nearside one from its socket, to examine it behind the bulk of the vehicle. The oil-container's lid opened readily enough. Keeping his body between the light and the group across the yard, he moved back to his hay-shed doorway.

He was barely there when the skirling and chatter of the servants' voices suddenly stilled. He peered over. Another figure had appeared within the doorway at the back of the house – a female figure from which the giggling maids fell back a little in surprise and embarrassment. Gregor took a deep breath – and acted.

Turning within, he splashed out some of the oil from the lamp on to the hay with which part of the shed was filled. Then, stooping, he took a handful of dry stuff, held it to the burning wick, and as it blazed, flung it on to the oil-soaked heap.

The flames shot up, almost too well for the incendiary's safety. Brows and hair singed a little, Gregor backed hurriedly out. He raised his voice. 'Fire!' he shouted, 'Fire!' And hurried along into the shadows again as he did so.

Chaos ensued in that stableyard. Leaping flames lit up the scene, and thick smoke rolled out of the hay-shed. Women screamed. Men shouted and came running. Horses reared and whinnied and bolted. One coach went rocking right out of the yard. The other was merely dragged hither and thither.

In the commotion, Gregor slipped round the perimeter of the yard, and so to the back door. Mary now stood a few feet out on the cobbles, staring wide-eyed. Pushing past a pair of gabbling maids, Gregor reached her and grasped her elbow.

'Come!' he cried. 'Quickly. This way.' And with an arm round her middle he led her, ran her, part-carried her, across the yard, over to the entrance, and out.

She came wordless but unresisting.

Just outside they all but ran into the concerned and excited Ian Beg, who was hopping about from one foot to the other at the edge of the bushes.

'To the garrons,' Gregor jerked briefly. Had he had any available breath he would have sighed with relief as they plunged out of the area of light and down through the shrubbery towards the quiet water and the climbing woods beyond.

CHAPTER TWELVE

MARY HAMILTON was not clad for clambering up through dew-drenched benighted woodlands, but Gregor's arm was strong about her waist and she kilted up her long brocade skirts and did her best, uncomplaining, unspeaking. To cross the ornamental water the man picked her up bodily in his arms, and more than once he did the same on the hillside beyond. He was breathing deeply, then, when at last he set her down beside the placidly grazing garrons. Clutching her flimsy crimson shawl to her, she was doing likewise.

Converse was spasmodic, incoherent, difficult. 'Oh, Gregor!' she gasped. 'What . . . ? Where . . . ? Gregor!' She shook her head, helplessly.

'Everything is . . . fine now, *a graidh*,' he assured. 'Fear nothing . . . at all.'

'No. No – but . . . '

He was casting off the coachman's coat, and ripping away the leggings. 'You are all right? You are not hurt?'

'No, no. I am . . . well. But – I do not understand . . . ?'

'You were not happy . . . in that house?' he demanded.

'No,' she agreed.

'Well, then. You are . . . out of it, whatever. You are to be the happy one! Always.' He picked up his sword, and slung its belt over his shoulder. Then taking the voluminous red tartan plaid that it had lain on, he wrapped it round her person. 'That is . . . better colours . . . for you to shelter under! You will be fine now, my dear.'

'Thank you. Yes. But what am I to do . . . ?'

'Nothing at all, at all,' he assured. 'Just nothing. Wait you.' He leapt lightly on to his garron's broad back, and pulled its head round, beside her. Ian Beg came forward to assist, but his aid was not required. Leaning over, Gregor crooked an arm under the girl's shoulders, and picked her up in a single sweeping motion. to deposit her before him on the horse, seated sideways. 'That is you,' he declared, and heeled the beast into a trot.

She gulped. 'Where . . . are we going, Gregor?'

'Where would you like to be going, *a graidh*?'

'Oh, I don't know. I don't know. We must talk. . . . '

'Surely, surely. We can be talking as we go. Fine.'

'Yes – but where?'

'Arnprior is one place that we could be going to. Mistress Meg was after saying it. But maybe we will be thinking of a better. . . . '

'Meg?' Mary cried. 'She sent you?'

'Sent is maybe not the word, just. But she was after telling me where to find you.'

The girl said nothing for a little while, as they rode up out of the trees, and on to the bracken and whins of Finnary Muir. Gregor glanced behind him. The house was already out of sight, but the reflected glow of it could be distinguished amongst the tree-tops – a glow that flickered now. There was no sound of any pursuit, nor did the man expect any.

'Gregor.' Mary turned round and faced him, gripping his wrist. 'Do you realise what you are doing? What *we* are doing?'

'Fine I do, yes.'

'Riding away, like this. You are not taking me back . . . to the house?'

'No.'

She bit her lip. 'Not even if I ask you to?'

'Och, it would be hard for me to be refusing you anything that you were asking in all the world, Mary,' he assured her warmly. To add: 'So do not be asking me, whatever!'

'Oh!' she said.

'There is nothing for you in that house.'

'But . . . ' She shook her head over him. 'I am a, a prisoner, then?'

He laughed, at that, joyfully. 'A prisoner! That is it – a prisoner, just. You are my prisoner, Mary Hamilton – for always! Och, mutual it is, too.'

She had nothing to say to that, at all.

He told her then how Meg had come seeking him at Crieff, to inform him of the situation, and how her brother would marry her off to this Hugo Graham. That obviously could not be allowed to happen. So he had come hot-foot. He had said that he would come for her one day, had he not? Well, then – here he was.

The girl listened in silence, and at the end of it burst out in no paean of gratitude and acclaim. He peered down at her, wondering. So far as he could see in the gloom, she seemed to be biting her lip again.

'You did not want to marry that Graham?' he demanded, then, a little roughly.

She shook her head.

'Well, then – there is something to be thanking me for. He will not marry you now.'

'No,' she agreed, a trifle heavily perhaps. 'He will not marry me now!'

Gregor decided that she was tired, unstrung, not at her

best. Let her rest, remain quiet, be at peace. Perhaps she would sleep, there within his arms. The best thing it would be. 'Hush you,' he urged. 'Quiet, now. Everything will be fine, just fine. You will see.'

She did not deny it, in so many words – in any words at all. He had never known that one so silent. Which was strange. But women were unpredictable, ever.

*   *   *

Untroubled by thoughts of pursuit or consequences, the men trotted their garrons northwards through the night. They went by the base of Duncryne Hill again, but to the east of it this time, and down into the wide Endrick valley, through the country of shadowy hummocks and knolls, and past small sleeping homesteads. And all the time that other ride was in Gregor's mind, when he had had so different a problem and responsibility, when he was homing with a bull and not a woman. And some comparison and association rankled and rankled in his mind.

Just when he actually took the decision, it would be hard to say. Perhaps it had been at the back of his head somewhere, all the time. Perhaps there was just a hint of pique in it – a lesson for her, whatever. Perhaps there was good logical reasoning behind it – MacGregor reasoning. Perhaps, indeed, the man being a MacGregor, it was inevitable. But when, the Endrick crossed, and Drymen skirted, and they were climbing the long long braes above the little town, with all the emptiness of Flanders Moss unseen but not unsensed on their right front – then Gregor kept his garron's head due into the north, instead of turning it when he might have done, due into the east. And held to that course, as the hillside lifted and lifted, out of rough grazing, through gorse and bracken, to the ultimate heather. The great hills loomed black ahead of them.

Mary had been silent for a long time, but the man knew by the tenseness and uprightness of her carriage that she by no means slept or dozed. At length she spoke.

'We are climbing hills,' she said. 'We are in the heather. This is not the road to Arnprior?'

'No,' he agreed. 'It is not.'

'Where are you taking me, Gregor?' There was a tremor there.

'Home, just,' he told her, simply.

'Home? You mean – *your* home? Glen Gyle?'

'Glen Gyle, yes.'

'But . . . no! No!' She turned round to face him again. 'You cannot do this, Gregor. You *must* not! Don't you see – I cannot go to your house. Not this way. Oh, don't you understand . . . ?'

'The best place it is, for you,' he asserted. 'You will be safe there. My mother will look after you. I will, my own self. It is where you ought to be, Mary.'

'You said Arnprior,' she accused. 'I thought that you were taking me there.'

'I was thinking,' he justified himself. 'Arnprior would be the first place that your brother would be looking for you. He would have you away again tomorrow. You have got to be safe from him. He would be finding you anywhere in the low country, and take you away. To be safe from him you have to cross our Highland Line, where he cannot follow you. You will be safe at Glen Gyle, whatever. No Lowlander can reach you there.' His voice rose a degree or two. 'Stirling Castle itself cannot reach you there!'

'But . . . but don't you see what this means?' she cried. 'Riding away with you, like this, is bad enough. My, my reputation will not go unscathed. But to go away into the mountains with you, to your own home! It means that I am committed to you – that, that our names are linked for always. That either I become a woman of no repute, or, or . . . '

'Or my wife,' he ended for her. 'The Lady Glengyle. We shall be married, my dear, just as soon as we can hale the minister from Balquhidder!'

'We shall, shall we!' she exclaimed spiritedly. 'Who

says that we shall? It takes two to make a marriage, Gregor MacGregor!'

Astonished, he stared at her. '*Dia* – what is this? Do you not *want* to be married, now?'

'No. I do not. Not like this. Not like a, a kitchen-wench in trouble! Not taken for granted. Not without, without . . . ' She was thumping at his chest with her small fists now, for emphasis, almost unseating herself. 'Turn round, and take me back,' she cried. 'Take me to Arnprior.'

Gregor frowned. Such illogical and unsuitable behaviour was quite beyond him. 'If I took you to Arnprior, I would just be at pains to be rescuing you again, in a day or two,' he pointed out, with a noble effort at reasonableness.

'Nobody asked you to rescue me,' she returned. 'At least, *I* did not.'

'Would you rather that I had left you for Graham of Finnary, then?'

She did not answer that. 'Take me to Arnprior,' she repeated.

'I will not do that' he told her levelly. 'It would avail nothing. We will go to Glen Gyle. And we shall be married. I told you, that time when last I saw you, that one day I would come for you. To marry you. To change your name for you, to MacGregor, I said. You knew my mind. . . . '

'And what about *my* mind, sir?'

'You came away with me, tonight, knowing my mind,' he reminded her, more stiffly.

'But . . . I could do no other!' she claimed, her voice rising unsteadily. 'To do anything else would have been to betray you, to fail you utterly. . . . '

'So you were after coming away with me only to save me from your brother, woman – is that it? Me – Glengyle!' His voice could rise, too.

'Oh, do not be foolish!' Mary cried. 'You know the way it was, perfectly well. For the last time – will you turn, please, Gregor, and take me to Arnprior?'

'No, then. I will not.'

'Oh . . . !' She drew herself up, her knuckles gleaming white in the gloom as she gripped the plaid tightly to her. 'Then you will regret it, sir. You will regret dragging me off to your, your barbarous mountains like the spoils of war across your saddle-bow!'

He laughed then, but shortly, harshly. 'There has been many another bride come to Glen Gyle that way,' he told her. 'And lived to be glad of it, whatever!' He kicked up his garron into a fast and jolting trot, despite the uneven terrain, that put all unprofitable converse and argument outwith possibility. 'Enough of this,' he ended abruptly.

And ended it was.

It was a far cry yet to Glen Gyle, twenty miles as the crow flies, but half as much again by hill and heather and ford and lochside. They followed the contours of the eastern flanks of the Ben Lomond range, down eventually to ford the Duchray Water near the lonely place of Blairvaich, and so round the boggy head of Loch Ard to the drove road that threaded the Pass of Aberfoyle. In all those rough miles Gregor and the girl hardly exchanged as many words – though he asked her with stiff solicitude twice whether she was tired and would wish to lie down and take a rest? Also whether she was warm enough in his plaid? To which she made answer with merely a shake or a nod of the head. Sometimes Gregor endeavoured to sing a little, but aggressively rather than spontaneously, his heart not in it. And now and then he chatted, in the Gaelic, with Ian Beg, determinedly casual. But most of the time they rode in silence through the silent night, with only the clop of unshod hooves, the swish of the heather, the cry of a night-bird, and the age-old chuckling of a thousand streams, as accompaniment for their several thoughts.

The grey and desolate dawn began to pale the night behind them, accompanied by a chill smirr of rain, while still they trotted by the birch-clad shores of Loch Chon. Gregor drew the plaid more closely about his charge. There was no sunrise that wan morning, only the mist heavy upon crouching hills. The blue smoke of morning fires was rising above the clachan of Stronachlacher as they reached Loch Katrine. Gregor acknowledged a few greetings from the folk, his own Gregorach, but declined refreshment, with only a few miles to go now.

The great trough of Glen Gyle was shrouded in cloud and mist as they came to it that cold grey morning – and the man was a little grieved that it should be so on such an occasion. But he was too weary to care greatly. And Mary was in no state of mind for the due appreciation of scenery, anyway.

The deerhounds sensed him from afar, as ever, and came bounding and baying in joyous welcome. Thus forewarned, the Lady Christian was on the front doorstep of Glengyle House waiting, still-faced, calm, when they rode up.

'Mother,' Gregor called out, before questions could be asked, 'I have brought you home the woman that I am going to marry. Mary, she is – Mary Hamilton of Bardowie. We have travelled far, and she is tired and cold and wet. You will be kind to her, I know.'

The Lady Christian drew a deep long breath, and her hand went up to touch the still-golden hair at her brow. 'Yes,' she said. 'Of course. Of course.' Then she smiled, slowly, gently. 'Mary,' she repeated. 'Mary is a lovely name. Come, my dear.' And she stepped forward, arms out, towards the garron and its double burden.

And the girl, after a moment's lip-biting hesitation, slipped to the ground and ran, tripping over her bedraggled brocade, the two or three steps to the older woman. Into her open arms she sped, and there burst into choking sobbing tears on the other's shoulder.

The Lady of Glengyle stroked and smoothed the dark and unruly rain-wet hair, and held her close. 'There, there! *De' tha 'cur ort? Tha mo bheannachd agad,*' she crooned. '*Mhairi, Mhairi, mo chreach.* There, there.'

Considerably embarrassed, as ever by woman's tears, Gregor cleared his throat. 'H'rr'mmm. She is distraught a little, I think. Tired, like I said, see you,' he declared, rather loudly. 'Myself, I must see to the garron.' And digging in his heels, he urged his mount quickly and thankfully round the side of the house and into the steading behind.

Ian Beg looked sombrely after him.

And the Lady Christian MacGregor turned her new charge around, and led her, arm about her, over the threshold of Glengyle House.

CHAPTER THIRTEEN

GREGOR MACGREGOR's unspecified but inborn suspicion that women were strange, unpredictable, unreasonable and ungrateful beings, indeed God's most illogical creation, was more than substantiated in the days that followed – in the weeks that followed. A little piqued and tired and put out himself, he had been prepared for some small exhibition of the effects of similar influences on Mary Hamilton's part, for a brief period after her arrival at Glen Gyle – if only as an allowable and perhaps required display of feminine spirit. The last thing, after all, that he wanted as wife was any meek-and-mild milk-and-water miss. He was, too, prepared to make allowances, recognising that it had all been somewhat sudden and abrupt – though that, surely, was no fault of his. But that she should develop and maintain and continue to cherish an attitude of distant, remote indeed, reserve, of chilly aloofness, polite and calm and patient as it was utterly inflexible, almost steely, was quite ridiculous and insufferable. And that his mother, his gentle mild and reliable mother, should not only seem to acquiesce in this irritating performance but actually tacitly support it by her own demeanour, was almost as deplorable.

The whole thing was so unrealistic too, so lacking in practicality. After all, the deed was done, the milk was spilt. No display of sorrowful reproof or pained injury would alter the fact that she was here in his house of Glengyle, under his roof, and likely to remain so. She could not leave on her own, and nobody from her world could reach her here. Common sense, at the very least of it, dictated that she should make the best of what, after all, many young women would esteem a very excellent situation. Or so it seemed to Gregor MacGregor.

But not to Mary Hamilton, evidently. After the first silent day or two, when she kept her room and saw no one but the Lady Christian, she did not sulk or make scenes, admittedly. To that extent she accepted the inevitable. Nor did she actually idle or seem to pine. She found things to do, made little excursions with her hostess, and did not hide herself from the people round about. But to Gregor she was armoured in cool dignity and formal civility. All talk of marriage she either ignored or turned aside. She refused to discuss or to argue. His pleas, his reasonings, his inducements, even his threats to fetch the minister from Balquhidder and have them wed whether she willed or no – all she evaded or dismissed or rejected. There was no compromise, no weakening, no hint of response.

And all the time, strangely enough, she seemed to grow in beauty and desirability, the aura of patient sorrow and gallantly-borne tragedy actually seeming to enhance her dark-eyed chiselled-featured patrician loveliness. Everyone exclaimed at her cool graciousness and good looks – and in consequence tended to take her part. A more maddening situation for a spirited and well-doing young man would have been hard to envisage.

Gregor's well-doing was notable, too. He did not pester her, or force his attentions upon her, as some might have done in the circumstances. Indeed, presently he came to keep himself out of her sight as much as possible – and knew himself grievously the loser in so doing. He seldom actually lost his temper with her. And he wrote a letter to John Hamilton, as he need not have done, informing him of her whereabouts and that she was safe and well, and assuring him that she would be well looked after. Strangely enough, Mary did not choose to avail herself of his offered facility for sending a letter or even a message to her brother on her own, merely shaking her head and suggesting that Gregor include her sisterly regards. So he himself had to add the request that Bardowie send back certain of her effects by the hands of the present bearers. He also wrote a brief note to Mistress Meg at Arnprior; and here Mary did elect to include a letter of her own – and quite a long one. What she said therein the man would have been interested to glimpse. Ian Beg with three or four armed supporters was charged with the delivery of both missives.

The messengers brought back, eventually, an answering letter to Mary from her sister-in-law, and nothing at all from John Hamilton – no letter, no things for his sister, no message. Unless the threats and bluster and tirade to which he had subjected Ian Beg could be termed a message, and the fact that he vowed that he would move heaven and earth to lift his poor misguided and unhappy sister out of the hands of barbarous ruffians, and bring down due and terrible retribution on her abductor's head. Et cetera.

And that, of course, was not worth calling a message, much less a threat. All the heaven and earth that Bardowie could move, or considerably more highly placed folk than he was, could not winkle out his sister from Glen Gyle of the MacGregors, nor produce the retribution that he desired. The Queen's Ministers might be invoked – and no doubt were – Parliament House, the Lord Justice-General, and the Court of Session, even the Commander-in-Chief. None were in any position, or in any mood, to dispatch an army over the Highland Line, provoke the clans and stir up trouble in a Scotland already seething with discontent. And nothing less would serve – no edict or manifesto or official trumpeting would affect the MacGregors one iota –

so long as they stayed on their own side of the Line.

Gregor himself, perhaps, would almost have welcomed attempts at reprisal, or some such excitement, in the circumstances – something to make time go a little faster, some action to allow him to assert himself. Action, he felt instinctively, was his forte.

He was almost grateful, then, when after a couple of weeks of this infuriating stalemate Rob Roy came to him, apologising for interrupting his courtship – Heaven forgive him – and seeking his nephew's assistance. It was King Jamie again. Though Grant of Invermoriston had been at the Kinloch Rannoch hunting match, and had agreed to rise, his High Chief, the Laird of Grant himself, was staunch for the Government and was holding the main clan back, a serious loss to the cause, for they were strategically placed on Speyside and were having a bad effect on their smaller neighbours. But MacAlpin Grant of Rothie-murchus, one of the most potent septs of the clan, was a strange wayward man, with moreover a fondness for the theory that the Grants and the MacGregors were of one original stock. Indeed, he elected to be known as Mac-Alpin rather than Grant, much to his chief's annoyance. Colonel Hooke thought that if one of the Gregorach, highly enough placed, were to go to work on him, they might bring him in on the King's side. And if MacAlpin came in, others might follow, with Invermoriston already committed, and the Laird of Grant might find himself left high and dry as it were. And this was important, for the clan had a regiment under arms for the Government. Rob Roy himself, unfortunately, could not make the journey, for he was engaged to attend a conference of commanders at the Earl of Panmure's house in Angus. Would Greg go to Badenoch and try to win over MacAlpin for King James?

Gregor, of course, could nowise refuse. He explained to Mary, elaborately, that whatever his own inclinations, His Majesty's cause must be maintained. He would have to leave her for a little – a couple of weeks, perhaps, no more.

His mother would look after her. And she would probably never miss him anyway. As an afterthought, he mentioned that it was not really likely that he would be in any great danger. He left fairly explicit instructions with Ian Beg, who was to keep an eye on things – especially on Miss Hamilton – and with a tail of half a dozen gillies he set out next morning on his long ride northwards to the Spey.

And, though he had certain misgivings as he left Glen Gyle, he was not over into Balquhidder in the golden October sunshine before he was singing again – as he had not sung since Crieff. Which was a strange thing, too.

*   *   *

It was almost four weeks before Gregor saw Glen Gyle again, four weeks of strenuous riding, most of it spent chasing MacAlpin down the long banks of swift-flowing Spey through Badenoch's endless pine forests. The laird of Rothiemurchus derived most of his very impressive revenues from felling and floating his timber down the Spey to the sawmasters and charcoal-burners of the Moray coast. And most of the way thereto Gregor had had to pursue him, before he could catch up with him and his lumbermen and rafters, and discuss high politics. He had found the man a handful indeed, queer, fiery and more concerned with upsetting his chief than with setting King Jamie on his rightful throne. But he had got some sort of assurances out of him eventually, and did not feel that his journey was wasted.

The first snows of winter had been crowning all the world of the mountains as he rode south again, yet all the blaze of the Highland autumn lingered in the valleys. Gregor sang practically the whole long road home, and laughed at every least opportunity. His men were happy to have him himself again. He counted the last fifty miles, one by one – and did not think to name himself a fool for so doing.

He came back by the Trossachs and Loch Katrine-side rather than by the more usual route through the Pass of Weeping from Balquhidder, solely to avoid the delay that the hospitable and merry lairds of that green valley were bound to impose upon him. He reached his own place just as the last glow of light was fading out of the autumn mist-wreaths that draped most of the corries and high valleys – though the topmost peaks, snow-clad and austere, still reflected a pale sun that the rest of the world had lost.

His mother greeted him no differently from any other occasion, quiet accepting woman. But her glance slid beyond him and around. 'You have been long, long, Gregor,' she said. 'But have you not brought Mary?'

'Mary?' he wondered. 'How could I be doing that? Mary is here. Why – where is she?'

'She is up the hill. She went, as she has gone each of these last afternoons, up the hill to the Pass, to look down into Balquhidder.'

'Why? Why should she do such a thing as that?'

'Who knows, Gregor? Who knows why young people do what they do? Perhaps she was watching for somebody – somebody who would come that way, and who should have come long ere this . . . !'

'*Dia!* You mean – my own self? Watching for me?' His voice thickened. 'She would not do that . . . ?'

Christian MacGregor shrugged slightly. 'Perhaps not. You it is should know, Gregor. Perhaps it is just the view that she likes. But these last three afternoons she has ridden up there to the Pass, on a garron – alone.'

Gregor left her then, without a word, to hurry round to the back of the house and gaze uphill. There was no sign of anything but a scattering of cattle on the shadowy slopes directly above. But higher, patches of mist rolled greyly. He came back, elation and anxiety struggling within him.

'She should be down by this,' he told his mother. 'There is mist up there.'

'Yes. She has been down earlier than this, the other days. The mist may have delayed her. But she has a good garron. It will bring her home. . . .'

'I told Ian Beg to be looking after her,' Gregor declared, frowning. 'Where is he?'

'Ian Beg has done more than enough,' his mother said. 'He went after her the first two times. Then she asked him not to, the girl. She said that she did not like being spied upon. You cannot be blaming her. Besides, Ian Beg has his wife to think of. She is having another baby just now. . . . ' She shook her head. 'But Mary will be fine, I am sure. She will be down in a little.'

'I will go up and meet her, just the same,' her son declared.

'Are you not tired? And hungry, Gregor? Some food, and then she will be down. . . . '

'No. I will eat after,' he decided, and turned to leave her again.

He took a fresh garron, and set it slantwise at the steep braeside straight away, his two deerhounds at heel. The hill directly behind Glengyle House was called the Stob an Duibhe, and with two others formed the western side of the high Pass of Weeping. By climbing straight up and over the fairly easy saddle between it and its neighbour to the south-east, the summit of the Pass could be reached much more expeditiously than by the usual roundabout route. Half an hour on a garron would do it.

The higher out of a mountain valley one lifts, the more light there is of an evening. It was still not dark when Gregor reached the saddle between the hills. But feelers and wraiths of clammy mist were now eddying about him, and dense cloud cowls had come down to shroud the summits above. When he looked over into the gut of the Pass, it was as into a seething cauldron of billowing vapour.

The man paused, uncertain, the hounds questing the air. He had seen no sign of the girl. If he went down there he might very easily miss her. She might be coming up, and pass within a hundred yards of him, and neither be the wiser. But surely that was a chance that he had to take? She could hardly be lost — but she might well be frightened. She might still be down in the floor of the long Pass, uncertain at which point to start to climb out. If he did not miss her on the way up, he would be sure to find her in the Pass itself, narrow as it was.

He went down into the swirling silent gloom.

Slanting down, he stopped his garron every few yards, to listen. No sound but a strange recurrent sigh of air broke the eerie hush — but Gregor knew how effectively mist can blanket sound. Presently he called a long 'Halloo-oo!' And again, 'Halloo-oo!' Not even an echo responded, as his cry was swallowed up.

It was much darker down in the pit of the Pass. The man, at the foot, peered down at the peaty path that threaded it, seeking to discern hoof-marks. But he could see nothing in the gloom. At a particularly muddy spot, keeping his hounds to heel, he dismounted again and felt gently about the mud surface with his finger-tips. No single track of any kind could he trace thereon, horse or deer or bird. The peat-broth and gravel was smooth. And cast about as he would, right and left, he found nothing.

The conclusion that he had to come to was inescapable. She had not come down into the Pass at all — whatever she had done on the other days. Nothing had threaded that narrow way since last night's rain. What, then? Where else could she have gone?

Only the one answer presented itself. On the other side of this central hill of the Stob, a much higher ridge than the saddle that he had crossed connected it with the next summit to the north-west, Meall Mor. This link was no saddle at all, but a high stony escarpment, a narrow place of rocks and crags and pinnacles. But from it there was an excellent view down into upper Balquhidder, a better and wider vista than from the Pass here. The only other spot, in fact, on this range where there was such a view. If she had indeed come up to watch for him . . . ?

Gregor wasted no time, but set his mount to the steep hillside again, climbing whence he had just come down. That ridge, vantage point as it might be, was no place to be caught in the mist. There were drops all round it, jagged lips, out-cropping brows. The thought made the man drive his sturdy sure-footed beast hard.

A six-hundred-foot climb, the last part of it on foot, and he was up on to the saddle again. It was dark now, even though up here the mist seemed to be a little less thick than down below. He had to contour round the southern face of the Stob. It was not difficult, though steep, even in the darkness, for a man who knew every foot of the way. He called as he went – and even the sound of his own voice was lonely, lonely.

He had still to climb to reach the final ridge. He was actually in cloud, now. As the rocks grew rougher he dismounted, leading his horse. He shouted when he could spare the breath, and he sent the hounds ranging ahead.

He searched that jagged ridge, foot by foot, clambering over the rockfalls, circling the outcrops, slithering on the rubble and scree, picking a way not only for himself but for the garron that followed on so patiently. Searched, but found nothing. He had seldom felt so helpless. He did not even know that she had come here. . . .

The sudden baying of the hounds ahead of him, followed by the high whinny of a horse, sent Gregor's heart up into his mouth. He went racing forwards, shouting his presence. But no voice answered him. In a panic he came stumbling. A white garron, one of his own, stood there beside a huge rock, ghostly in the gloom, a folded plaid across its broad back. The hounds sat panting nearby. And that was all.

Really frightened now, Gregor went scrambling around in concentric circles, peering, quartering the uneven ground, calling – and cursing the darkness. There was no sign nor sound of her.

He grabbed the plaid from the horse's back, called the dogs, presented it for them to sniff, and then sent them off, ordering them to seek, seek. Noses down, twisting this way and that, they disappeared into the night. The man noted that they both were trending away northwards, towards Balquhidder, not southwards towards home.

Over there lay, first, broken rock and short precipitous

drops, worse than on this side. Then a vast gently shelving tableland of peat-hag and heather knoll and quaking bog, extending for miles at the high head of Balquhidder, the very womb of waters, where most of the streams of that green valley were born. A sanctuary for old rogue stags, the playground of the winds, and an ill place to cross at any time – in the dark and mist it could represent its own hell indeed. If she was down there . . . !

At the black edge of the abyss of it, Gregor filled his lungs to the utmost, cupped hands to mouth, and cried with all the power than was in him. 'Halloo-oo! Halloo-oo!' again and again. Five or six times he cried, desperately, half-crazedly, changing the direction of his facing a little each time. And then he stopped abruptly. Was it imagination . . . ? An echo? A ringing in his ears? One of the hounds answering him? A night bird? Or was it . . . ?

No! By God's Glory – it was none of these! It was an answering human cry, thin and tremulous and infinitely forlorn, coming from afar, somewhere half-left, out of that grim desolation. Almost beside himself, Gregor yelled again, differently now, joyfully, reassuringly, incoherently – and all in his own Gaelic. Then, urgently noting the line of that faint reply, and where on this ridge he was leaving the garrons, he started to scramble down the steeps before him, slipping and sliding, over the mist-wet rocks and ledges, the rocks at the foot of which he had so recently feared that she might be lying.

*   *   *

It took him the best part of half an hour to reach her, for it was by devious quaking desperate ways that he had to go, with scarcely a dozen consecutive yards in a straight line. He leapt and floundered and sank knee-deep. He ran light-footed, and plunged heavily. He balanced on tussocks and old heather-clumps, and tripped over bog-pine roots, jagged as fangs, and splashed through pools. And all the time Mary Hamilton drew him on, calling, calling, directing him, wisely not moving apparently. The fear that she would so move, attempt to come to him as he drew near, grew in the man. She might plunge deep in one of these black bottomless hags.

'Mary! Mary!' he cried. 'Stay still. Do not . . . be moving . . . till I come.'

'Gregor! Gregor!' From the sudden changed ring in her voice, it was evident that for the first time the girl realised the identity of the man who was making for her. Her quick high-pitched cry ended in a choking sob. She sounded as though she would be no more than perhaps a couple of hundred yards away.

That last stretch was the worst. She seemed to be stranded on what was almost an island of long heather grown up round a cluster of ancient pine-roots, and surrounded by particularly evil stretches of black treachery. How she had got there remained to be discovered – but Gregor was not able to join her without very considerable tacking, retreating and a weltering that was next to wallowing. Time and again he was almost engulfed. Then, at last, soaked, black with peat-mud and slime, gasping, he was able to reach a jutting crooked arm of root, and haul himself up. She was crouching across from him, only two or three yards away, a slight black figure only a little darker than the surrounding menacing world of blackness. The two hounds were moving shadows nearby. He leapt across to her.

'Mary! Mary, my dear, my beloved!' he cried.

She came into his wide-stretched arms, to grip and cling to him convulsively. 'Oh, Gregor!' she said – and could say no more.

*　　*　　*

For how long they remained thus, clasped to each other tightly, panting, stammering incoherences, is not to be known. In such a situation time counts for little. At length, it was Gregor's foot slipping on the precarious stance of root that caused him to move, to step aside, to loosen his hold of the girl. And immediately she sank down into the crouching position that she had been in before.

180

'What is it?' he wondered. 'You are hurt? or Unwell?'

'It is my foot. My ankle,' she said. 'I twisted it. Between some roots. There is nothing serious, I think. But it is swollen. . . . '

Promptly the man was down on his knee beside her feeling her ankle with gentle skilful hands.

'Oh, it is nothing – now that you are here,' she assured. 'Oh, Gregor – I was afraid. I was terrified. In this awful place. And the mist . . . '

'I know it, *a graidh*,' he agreed. 'It is bad. But you will be fine, now. Your leg will be sore, sore. It is swollen, yes. But nothing is broke. It will be all right. You will be fine, just fine, now.'

She almost choked. 'Oh, Gregor – I've heard you at that before!' she got out, with something between laughter and tears. 'Always I am to be just fine!'

'And so you are,' he agreed, seriously. 'Always. But . . . you are trembling! Shivering. Lassie, lassie – you are cold? Wet?'

She nodded, biting her lip. 'A little.' Great tremors were racking her, intermittently.

'Och, my dear – this will not do,' the man cried. 'See – my plaid is damp a bittie, but it will serve, maybe.' He stood up, unfastened the plaid that was belted about him for ease in climbing, and wrapped it round her. His arms lingered about her, and she leaned against him gratefully.

'See, you,' he said, as another tremor shook her, even to the rattling of her teeth. 'Warm we must get you.' And selecting a firm spot, he sat down, and took her bodily on to his lap, to tuck in the ends of the plaid around her, and hold her close to him. Then he ordered the two hounds in to him, and pressed them to lie down against them. A notable warmth came out of them, as well as a powerful smell of wet dog. The shivering girl protested at none of it.

He found her hands, and rubbed them with his own, to encourage the circulation. Then he told her to put them under his arm-pit.

Presently her shuddering and jerking died away. But

now he found that she was sniffling, regularly. Gulping too. He peered at her, so close to him.

'You are weeping?' he exclaimed. '*Och, ochan, mo chreagh. Ciod so?* You must not weep. It will all be just ...' He stopped, gulping also. 'I mean – you must not be sad, at all.'

'I am not sad,' she mumbled, and sniffed again.

'Is it sore, then? Your ankle? A shame, it is ...'

'No, no. It is not that. I am not weeping. Not really. It is just ... well, you are so good. So kind. And strong. So, so thoughtful. I ... I am sorry, Gregor.' That was a whisper.

'Eh? Eh-hey – what is this? Sorry? You?'

'Yes. I have been so foolish. ...'

'Och, wheesht, lassie. Anyone can be getting lost in a mist, whatever. Easy it is. Myself, I do not know what direction I am facing now.' Which was not strictly true, but it might well have been.

'I didn't mean that. Though there, too, you are kind. Not to reproach me. I don't know where I went wrong. I do not know where I am, indeed, in this horrible marsh – though I think that I must be at the wrong side of the hill. I had left the pony, and climbed some way up that pointed hill – yes, the Stob – for a better view down into ... well, for a better view. When the mist caught me, I thought that I knew my way down well enough, back to the pony. But – well, evidently I went wrong. I got into steep places. And the mist got thicker. I kept going down, as well as I could. I thought that I was getting down towards Glen Gyle. I knew I had missed the pony, but so long as I kept going down-hill ... But I must have been wrong. I got into this dreadful place of bogs. I knew that I was wrong, then. There is nothing like this on the Glen Gyle side. I ... I was not very clever, I fear.' She shook her dark damp head. No word of the terror that she had undergone as she floundered and struggled, lost, across that endless quagmire. Her sniff had stopped. 'How did you find me, Gregor?'

'Och, it was easy,' he lied. 'I just could not help myself, you see. I came straight for you, just. I could not help but find you, Mary. I would have found you if you had been at the other end of the world, whatever!'

She drew a deep breath, but said nothing now.

He warmed to his theme. 'You were drawing me, drawing me, see you – all the time. I could not miss you. Like the star that guides the shipmen, you were drawing me. All the way from Badenoch. My star, just. That is you, Mary my dear.'

There was the beginnings of another sniff, there.

'Och, now. There, there. Hush you, my dear one, my beloved, my fawn of the woods.' He was stroking her hair. 'Do not cry, at all, my pigeon, my dear heart. Never . . .'

And then she suddenly came to life within his arms, twisting round, her hands gripping his arm. 'Gregor! Gregor – do you realise what you are saying?' she cried. 'Listen to yourself, Gregor! You are . . . you are . . .' Her voice broke.

'I am telling you that you must not weep, just,' he said. 'You will not be looking half so beautiful if you weep, my lovely Mary. . . .'

'No, no!' she burst out. She thumped at his chest with her fists, as she had done once before – but with so very different emotions. 'No – not that! Oh, Gregor – how foolish you are! Don't you see? You are calling me beloved! Saying that you love me. . . .'

'And why not?' he demanded. 'Haven't I been loving you from the day that I set my eyes on you, whatever? In the coach, that time. Can I not say it, when it is God's own truth? A man cannot help it when he loves. . . .'

'Oh!' she cried, almost sobbed. 'Oh – you fool! You dear, beloved, adorable fool!' And abruptly her arms were up and around his neck, and her lips were pressed to his, quiver-ingly, passionately.

Gregor was surprised, naturally. But he got over it with commendable speed, and put off the questioning till a more convenient occasion. Something of an opportunist always, he took what Heaven was so liberally giving, and was thankful.

*　　*　　*

Time and place was of even less consequence thereafter. The night stretched ahead of them — for of course it would have been folly to have attempted to move the girl, handicapped as he was with her sprained ankle, over that evil morass in the darkness — and its long chill hours might have been honeyed minutes, their cramped and unpleasant stance a cushioned arbour, for all the difference that it made to them. The seventh heaven may be reached by strange routes, and curiously located.

But, in the fulness of experience, rather than of time, the man did learn, more or less incidentally and bit by bit, something of the reason for Mary's notable change of front — if reason it could be called, with a woman involved. She had, it seemed, merely wanted to be wooed. In essence, it was as simple as that. She had not been content with being just chosen, firstly, and then carried off. She had looked for gentle dalliance, apparently, tender words, the declaration of love, and her suitor's passion — and she had received none of it, only an implied admiration and a somewhat high-handed being taken for granted. Pride, it transpired in effect, had been what was wrong with her — a virtue suitable enough in Highland gentlemen but unlooked for in a woman. She herself, it seemed, had loved him all along — but it had not been for her to say so. That he had not seen fit to actually do so either was his failing. A failing for which she was prepared to forgive him, now. A little nonplussed by it all, Gregor, however, did not attempt to argue or defend himself. A practical man, he found the matter to be of only hypothetical interest now, anyway.

All of which only goes to underline something or another.

Marriage of course was a different matter — something practical, involving dates, plans and details, as well as unquestioned delights. She was not still against the idea of marriage . . . ?

Of course she was not! She would marry him just as soon as it could be decently arranged. She had all along intended to marry him — one day. It was only . . .

He would build a new wing to Glengyle House for them,

he declared, at this stage. The place was on the small side. And there were things that he had seen in his travels which he would wish his wife to have. And there were the children to think of. They were going to be very busy.

And what about the rising and the King's cause, Mary wondered, a little doubtfully?

'Damn the rising and the King's cause!' Gregor declared, quite violently. Anyway, that was not till April or May. Who could tell what might have happened by then?

Gregor MacGregor did not know what a good prophet he was.

So passed the night. They talked, they clung to each other, the plaid now rearranged to envelop them both. They embraced. They slept, in snatches, sometimes one, sometimes the other, sometimes both together. And they found no fault with any of it, even with the stiffness and cramping pains that they suffered, and the grievous emptiness of their stomachs – and the effect of strong fumes of dog thereon. They were young, they had found each other and themselves, and they were alone.

The grey dawn stealing over that black and dreary place, mist-free now, found them fast asleep, the girl curled within the man's arms, his face buried in her hair. It did not awake them. It was the shouting that did that, distant hailing, later, as a watery sun began to gleam palely above the peaks to the east. Ian Beg and the gillies were out searching for them, and had discovered the garrons on the ridge. Almost, Gregor was sorry to have to raise his voice and answer.

Even in daylight, and with hillmen to help, getting the young woman out of that tumbled sea of peat-hags was no child's play. But skill and great patience, allied to a masculine conception of gentleness and a deal of shouting, achieved it in time. A peat-stained and dishevelled crew they reached the horses, and set off downhill. And Gregor's great laughter filled all Glen Gyle ahead of them.

CHAPTER FOURTEEN

THEY were married within the month, in the ancient squat little Kirk of Balquhidder in the mouth of the valley, amidst a flurry of December snow – a chilly business, for the doors of the church had to be left open since most of the congregation inevitably had to remain outside. This had the merciful effect of reducing the length of the sermon. Most of the hierarchy of the Clan Gregor was present, as well as folks of lesser name, come at considerable difficulty through the winter glens. Apart from the bride herself, no single Lowlander was there. They both would have liked to have had Meg Hamilton up for the auspicious occasion – but Meg was now back with her husband at Bardowie, her father much recovered, and it seemed hardly feasible in the circumstances to invite her under Gregorach safe-conduct as it were, alone. And, of course, the journey in winter would have been trying for a lady, to say the least of it. Rob Roy, most suitably, gave the bride away – as a friend of the family, he said. Gregor's young sister Catherine attended her. It was a good wedding, as these things go – though undoubtedly not such as Mary's virginal dreams might have visualised a year before.

There was almost as much warlike talk thereat as there was nuptial congratulation.

But the young people were little aware of anything of the sort – or of anything at all except each other. A proper and felicitous state of affairs, which persisted thereafter likewise. The clouds of war might gather and lower over all Scotland, but for Mary and Gregor they did not obscure the sun which shone in another sky altogether. Alarms might be sounded, Government grow desperate in its bribery, riots occur in Edinburgh and Glasgow, the cry of No Union link up with the cry of King James, rumours run through the glens as they did through the streets and alleys – but at Glen Gyle other matters held sway.

They were very busy, as Gregor had said that they would be. Adjusting themselves to their new state was an absorbing task, and what energies were left over were occupied with building the new wing to the house, on Gregor's part, and in learning to become mistress of Glengyle on Mary's. In this latter business the Lady Christian was tact and sympathy itself, removing herself and her two younger children to the house of Portanellen a mile down the lochside, but making herself available every day to help and advise if desired. Mary, who had not known a mother of her own since early childhood, soon loved her more deeply than she would have thought possible.

So the winter passed. Rob Roy was seldom at home, covering the countryside, ostensibly on the affairs of his Watch, but frequently surprisingly far afield. The Watch was indeed busy, for unsettled times bring out unsettled men, and Rob was responsible for order over a wide area, many men paying him sweetly to keep the peace. Sometimes, of course, Gregor as his lieutenant had to be involved. But his uncle fondly spared him as much as possible, knowing full well that there would be demands enough later.

But as the months rolled on, a change came over Rob Roy MacGregor. A cheerful and hearty man ever, he became addicted to unaccustomed silences. Sometimes he even managed to look grim. Which was strange, for news from all over the country was almost consistently good; good for the Jacobites, that is. The clan chiefs were everywhere committing themselves; the low country lords were coming in; the populace and the burghs were seething. Petitions against the Treaty were streaming in from all quarters of the country – and being refused by the Lord Chancellor Seafield. The local militia and fencibles, and the heritors, were forbidden to meet, as required under the Act of Security, in case they turned against the authorities. Copies of the projected Treaty of Union were being burnt at market-crosses, kirk doors and other public places up and down the land.

Effigies of the Queen's Ministers hung on gallows, trees and town gates. In Edinburgh, where Parliament was signing its own death warrant, the said Ministers skulked by dark ways or rode deep in armed guards about their occasions. The country was ripe for revolt.

But it was the news that came secretly out of the castles and mansion-houses along the east coasts of Fife and Angus, in touch by sea with France, that furrowed Rob's brows – and more than Rob's. In France King Jamie's cause did not go quite so prosperously. Louis was being difficult, vacillating, playing hot and cold, promising much one day, cancelling his promises the next. James himself, a young man of only nineteen, melancholy and taciturn, brought up in an unreal atmosphere of make-believe and intrigue, was proving weak, incapable of facing up to the arrogant French king, and surrounded by ill-chosen advisers. The rivalries in his court were notorious. There were violent disputes over who was to command the expedition, the fleet, the army of liberation. The clash of personalities resounded as far as Scotland.

Spring came but reluctantly to the hill country that year, and with it April, the melting snows, and the start of the campaigning season. With it also came the fatal day, April 25th, 1707, when the Chancellor made his celebrated remark, 'Now there's an end of ane auld sang.' The completed Treaty of Union, signed, sealed and established, was presented to the Scots Parliament, which thereupon dissolved for the last time. Popular resentment reached fever pitch, mobs rose and wrecked and looted, buildings were set afire, trade came almost to a standstill.

And no King Jamie arrived, no expedition sailed, no orders were issued.

Up and down the Highlands and Islands the clans were either mustering or ready to muster. The Gregorach, being comparatively close at hand and readily available, did not need to assemble yet. Rob did not give the word. Indeed, nobody gave any word. No beacons were lit. No fiery crosses went out.

May came and went. Scotland simmered, and waited. Word came that the Duke of Berwick, James's half-brother and a Marshal of France, had been appointed to command the expedition. Then came the news that Louis had forbidden his release, as a French citizen. The Marquis de Matignon was selected in his place – and Admiral the Count de Forbin, in charge of shipping the expedition over, refused to co-operate with him. The clans waited – though some indulged in a little local raiding and innocent spoilery, just to pass the time and keep their hands in.

June passed into July, and if Scotland still waited she was off the boil now. The clansmen were returning to their summer shielings. The towns settled down sullenly. Lawlessness still was rife – but the Government began to breathe more freely.

Colonel Hooke arrived again from France, almost exactly a year after his first appearance, a disappointed man. He told of dissension, irresolution and divided counsels at St Germains, of King Louis's obduracy and haughty pride, and the rivalries of the French military leaders. They were still talking of an expedition that year, but he himself and all knowledgeable of Scottish conditions advised against it, knowing the clansmen's objection to autumn harvest-time campaigning and the closed state of the Highlands in winter. The expedition would undoubtedly sail in the spring, then – a year late, and having missed the first fever of anti-Union resentment. But who could tell how much more Scottish anger and indignation might be stirred up in the meantime by the working out of government from London, high-handed activities and contemptuous treatment? Had not Mr Speaker himself said, 'We have catcht Scotland and will keep her fast'? and the Lord Treasurer of England declared indignantly, 'Have we not bought the Scots, and a right to tax them?' Waiting another six or eight months might be no great misfortune in the end.

Rob Roy was more than doubtful. Reviving damped-down fires was ever an uncertain business, he contended. Promises and commitments made for one year might not always stand carrying over to another. There were some that he knew who would be hard to turn out a second time.

Many other Jacobite leaders undoubtedly felt as did Rob. But there was nothing that they could do to alter the case. A rising against disciplined troops and great defended fortresses, without the necessary artillery, ammunition and engineering equipment, would be useless and worse than useless. They could only wait for France.

Gregor was not amongst those who fumed and fretted and frowned. He was quite content to remain at Glen Gyle minding his own business. The exterior of the new wing to his house was completed, and very fine – but the interior, to be worthy of Mary and to come up to his own conceptions, was demanding all his ingenuity and a lot of his time. Moreover, it seemed as though Mary already might be pregnant; it would be a terrible thing if he was to go and get himself killed before he had either got the house finished or seen his own son that would be chieftain of the sept of Dougal Ciar after him.

That is what a woman, given time, can do to a hero.

* * *

But it must not be assumed that all spirit had died quite out of Gregor Ghlun Dubh, even if the range and scope of it had suffered a curtailment. As example, there was the little matter of the tax-collector, in November. Tax-collectors, like a general scale of taxation itself, were new phenomena in Scotland, and one of the earliest and most exotic fruits of the Union. But England had this attribute of modern progressive government, and Scotland must now have it too. English tax-gatherers, assessors and preventive-men were recruited by the hundred and sent north over the Border in a flood. They were less well received than either they or their masters would have wished.

Word of the presence and activities of these interlopers reached the MacGregor country from time to time, but was hardly to be taken seriously or considered in relation to such as themselves. It was with something betwixt consternation and profound offence, then, that one grey November day the news was brought to Glengyle House that one of the noxious breed had actually penetrated as far as the clachan of Aberfoyle, this side of Flanders Moss, and was going about poking his nose into other folk's affairs and generally behaving in an ungentlemanly way. That something had to be done about it went without saying. There were sundry vigorous Gregorach suggestions, that only awaited chiefly sanction.

It fell to Gregor to take the appropriate decisions – for Rob Roy was away in the Lowlands, *incognito*, on a delicate mission; no less than in mortgaging the estates, his own of Craigroyston and Inversnaid, and Gregor's Glengyle, for ready cash. That he had not felt it necessary or wise to do this previously was perhaps a significant reflection on his changed attitude towards the entire projected rising. Now, he considered, the possibility of failure and consequent forfeiture of participants' estates at least fell to be envisaged – and if one's estates might be forfeited anyway, it was no bad thing to have the cash value of them safely in one's sporran beforehand. An elementary precaution for a far-looking man like Rob Roy. So his nephew had to deal with the tax-man.

Perhaps as a result of his new status as a man of family and husbandly responsibility, Gregor went about the business in a slightly less bull-headed fashion than had been his wont. Instead of going himself, forthwith, and throwing the creature off MacGregor territory neck and crop, he sent scouts to spy out the exact position. These in due course came back to report, what had not emerged before – namely that the fellow had a couple of redcoats with him as escort, that he was working his way westwards towards the real hill country, going from house to house, enquiring after numbers of occupants, how many beasts were owned, and other property, what tribute was paid to the laird or land-owner, and so on. All of which sounded thoroughly omin-ous. If people were to be penalised for owning a few cattle, then it was past time that all right-thinking citizens rose up and put a stop to it.

Thus well-informed and well-intentioned, Gregor set out eastwards. He took only Ian Beg with him, much to his people's chagrin. Since the Union, the military forces had been much strengthened in Stirling and Dumbarton Castles, as elsewhere, entire English regiments being sent up. Colonel Hooke had sent urgent orders that no head-on clashes should be provoked on any account, meantime. These troops were all badly needed elsewhere to support Marlborough's new campaigns. If they seemed not to be needed here in Scotland, they would almost certainly be withdrawn – which was what was urgently required for the King's landing in March or April. This call, this *command*, for moderation and discretion fell in quite conveniently with Gregor's new-found mood of married responsibility. A nice moderation would be his watchword, then.

Accordingly, his plans were simple and unambitious to a degree. He ascertained that the tax-man had just begun to work along amongst the crofts at the bottom end of Loch Ard. He and Ian Beg consequently started to visit the houses at the head of the three-mile loch. They instructed the occupants in how they were to treat the tax-gatherer, how they were to be civil, not threatening, but very very distressed for him personally. How they were to assure him that he was a very brave man indeed. That there was another tax-gatherer had been working amongst them, out from Glasgow and Dumbarton, who was not nearly so brave – who, in fact, was after having a very bad time of it, to the danger of his life, who hadn't been seen for some time, indeed. The MacGregors of the hills were hard, hard on tax-gatherers. Thus and thus the story went, that they were to tell, with slight variations and embellishments, all around Loch Ard head and over the water-meadows of the isthmus to Loch Chon. Gregor returned thereafter decently to wife and fireside.

The next day he was back again, this time with an extra garron loaded with bundles of clothes and gear. He had been raiding his grandfather Colonel Donald's trophy chest. They found that the tax-man was still at Loch Ard, but near the head of the loch now. Leaving the mile or so of the isthmus between them, Gregor and Ian Beg selected one of the few empty houses at the foot of Loch Chon, a fairly isolated place. They borrowed a few armfuls of bog-hay from the nearest neighbour. Unloading the garron, they took its burden indoors.

Thereafter they spent an amusing hour or two, with hay and rope and paper and the gear that they had brought. Plus the red keel that they used for marking the cattle.

When they had finished, they shut and barricaded the door. They also told the neighbours what to say if they were questioned. And retired to Glen Gyle. Discretion and moderation could not have been better exemplified.

The next afternoon the tax-gatherer, with his two soldiers, arrived on the shores of Loch Chon, busy methodical man, now undoubtedly highly conscious of the risks that he was apparently running and the evil reputation of these mountainy MacGregors. They duly found the barricaded cottage, could gain no entrance, prowled around it, and perceived signs of recent activity. Suspecting smuggled brandy, or an illicit still, or worse, they broke down the door. And there they were confronted with three bodies dangling from the roof-timbers, two in the red coats and cocked hats of the military, that in the centre in good civilian broadcloth. And around this central figure's elongated neck hung a roughly inscribed legend which said THUS PERISH ALL TAX-GATHERERS.

As the trio staggered back from the doorway, a great outcry arose from the cover of a nearby birch-wood, shouts of 'Gregalach! Gregalach!' and 'Ardchoille!' and the like. Also a considerable baying of hounds.

The tax-man ran for his horse. But he was less active than his two guards. He had to follow them, indeed, pounding in their dust, down the drove road by Loch Ard eastwards. According to the good folk of Aberfoyle, they clattered through the clachan, much strung out, without pause and as though the Devil himself were at their heels. Which may well have been an exaggeration. But eastwards they did go, with some expedition, at any rate. And the MacGregors saw no more of fiscal authority that winter.

Rob Roy's laughter sounded just a little rueful when he returned from his journey and heard about it all. It was the sort of story which would have sounded still better coming from himself.

However, Rob also had success to report. He had managed to mortgage both estates for an excellent figure. Half of it, of all people, he had got from no less a personage than James Graham, now Duke of Montrose, himself. Montrose was land-hungry always, of course – but that a man so close to the Government, and a close-fisted man at that, should have been prepared to do the business, and to do it thus generously, was interesting. It showed that he, for his part, was no more confident than was Rob about the future, and thought it wise to maintain a link with the Jacobites.

Perhaps Hooke was right?

CHAPTER FIFTEEN

AND indeed, as the winter of 1707 passed into the spring of 1708, Nathaniel Hooke's prophecies were very adequately fulfilled. The Union grew steadily in unpopularity – not only with the mass of the people, who had always been against it, but amongst the influential circles that had supported it, the aristocratic and commercial interests that had hoped to do well out of it. Westminster's abrupt imposition of the Salt and Malt Taxes were serious blows to the Scottish economy – as they were intended to be. The trade in salted herrings to the Low Countries, Germany and the Baltic was one of the basic Scots exports. The Salt Tax hit it hard, dealt the fishing and shipping communities a sore buffet, and set the East Coast merchants growling. The Malt

Tax hit the manufacture of both whisky and ale, the drinks of the common people of both Highlands and Lowlands. The outcry ought to have been heard as far south as London. The entire farming policy of a mainly agricultural country was upset – and with it, of course, the landowners' revenues. Two more damaging taxes could not have been conceived. A duty was levied on linen, another of Scotland's staples, that ran down the looms and started riots up and down the land. And to add insult to injury, simultaneously the duty was removed from Irish linen. Then the bribes for many who had steered the Union through remained only promises, whether in cash, positions or honours. Even the Equivalent was still unpaid – that mass bait of nearly £400,000 sterling that was to compensate Scotland for having to shoulder a share of the English national debt, and which had been the carrot dangled before the noses of the growing commercial classes hard hit by the collapse of the Darien Scheme. Scottish trade with France, England's enemy, went by the board. Trade from the colonies, even when consigned to Scots ports, now had to be carried only in English ships. It was apparent that Scottish trade and interests, where they rivalled or conflicted with those of the larger partner to the Union, were to be firmly put down.

Repeal the Union became the cry from all over the land. But now there was no Scottish authority to act on the cry. Gradually the people began to look to their ancient monarchy to save them. Not Anne Stewart, lethargic and sickly in London, needless to say, but James, her nephew in France. Rob Roy's brows began to lighten again.

None of all this directly affected the MacGregors, of course. Save to push up the price of cattle, at which they made no complaint. The new wing of Glengyle House was completed and ready for occupation by Christmas – and a fine house-warming it got. And the Heir of Glengyle was born a month later, and christened Ian, amidst the rejoicings of the entire clan. Life was good for Gregor and Mary, and war could well stay away from their hospitable door indefinitely.

But that indefatigable courier and herald of fate, Colonel Nathaniel Hooke, was not to be balked. He arrived at Inversnaid and Glen Gyle again, new come from France, in late February. And this time he brought definite tidings and instructions. All – or almost all – was settled. King James would sail at the end of March or beginning of April. The fleet was already assembling at Dunkirk, some thirty frigates and transports, with five great men-o'-war as escort. Five thousand regular troops were being detached and mustered, equipped with all necessary artillery, ammunition and supplies. Even money was forthcoming. At last Louis, with the effects of Marlborough's successes at Ramillies beginning to pinch, perceived the value of a diversion in Scotland. All now would be well.

There was work for Gregor, at last. Work which could nowise be put off or shirked. The clans had to be informed and assembled. And there was no great surplus of time for the business. In four or five weeks James would be sailing.

So Gregor Ghlun Dubh, sighing, kissed his wife and baby farewell, accoutred himself with targe, claymore, pistols and dirk, and rode away northwards, not on his fine black charger, along with Rob Roy and the other MacGregor notables.

He had managed a longer honeymoon than most – but it was over now.

*   *   *

As usual, the MacGregors were acting as couriers – for none could cover the difficult upheaved country so swiftly as they. And it was the very worst time of the year for such travelling, with the snows beginning to melt on all the mountains, every stream a raging torrent, every valley flooded, and every flat a quagmire. Fords were lost beneath swirling yellow spates, fallen trees and landslides jammed the passes, soft and sodden snowfields cloaked the heights. In driving chill rainstorms, never warm or dry by day and seldom by night, the Gregorach rode, fanning out north and west. And none who saw them envied them their task.

Rob went to the west, but Gregor proceeded right up the centre of the country, through Breadalbane, Atholl, Badenoch, the Great Glen and beyond, calling on the Robertsons, the Macphersons, the Cattanachs, his old friend MacAlpin Grant of Rothiemurchus, the Macintoshes, Glengarry's MacDonnells, the Invermoriston Grants and up as far as the Chisholm in Strathglass. Turning south again, he skirted the country of the Frasers, who were refusing to come out, and the main mass of Clan Grant, but warned the Gordons, with the help of the fiery Glenbucket, and reached the Farquharsons at the head of Dee. Then south through the long empty gut of Glen Tilt, and into Atholl again. He was home four weeks to a day after leaving, weary, exhausted almost, and a deal thinner than when he had set out. He was not the first home, but not the last. One by one the Gregorach messengers returned – though Rob Roy himself, with the farthest to go and sea passages to make amongst the islands, still was absent.

All had the same tale to tell. The clans would rise, assuredly – were now rising. But few, if any, could be mustered before the beginning of May, whatever the Lowland forces might be able to do. Sheer geography and climatic conditions prohibited. Word to that effect was dispatched forthwith to Colonel Hooke at his headquarters in Fife.

The messenger returned from Fife on the same day that Rob Roy got back from the north-west. He brought a peculiar reply from Hooke, for the Captain of Clan Alpine. It was to the effect that it did not matter now that the clans would be delayed in their assembling. The expedition had indeed set sail, but it had turned about and gone back to Dunkirk. King James had contracted the measles. The attempt was postponed.

That silenced even the eloquent Gregorach.

*   *   *

Rob Roy, tired as he was, made one of his famed lightning journeys thereafter, across Stirlingshire and Kinross to Fife this time. There he delivered heated representations to

Colonel Hooke – practically an ultimatum, in fact. The Colonel assured him that all would yet be well; that this was only a very temporary set-back. The expedition would sail again later. A month's delay would do no great harm – and it did give time for the clans to gather. Rob repeated his warning, reinforcing it with some plain speaking and unpalatable reminders. The other promised to transmit the gist of it all to France forthwith.

Rob returned to his own place, and the MacGregors began to gather, in earnest.

There was a great deal to be done in the assembling and equipping and organising of some hundreds of armed men – as well as in arranging for the everyday life of the rest of the clan to continue during the absence of the bulk of its manpower. A chieftain was the father of his people, to some extent, as well as their ruler and magistrate. Gregor was kept very busy.

Mary watched all the preparations with a heavy heart. But she took Christian MacGregor as her model, and sought to be as good a warrior's wife as the other was a mother.

CHAPTER SIXTEEN

More than five hundred men were standing to arms in the valleys of the Snaid, the Gyle and in all the side glens of Balquhidder. The smell of roasting beef hung over all, with the smoke of the cooking fires, perpetually, and the sound of the pipes never ceased from morn till midnight. Races, trials of strength, feats of endurance, and the less reputable diversions of fighting-men with nothing to do, went on with unremitting vigour. It was an awesome thought to consider that similar conditions would apply in a goodly percentage of the glens of all the Highlands.

...as May 16th, and the climax of long preparations was ...and. His Majesty, recovered, had set sail. The expedition was encountering gales and contrary winds, and was being shadowed by the English Fleet under Admiral Byng. But it was definitely on its way, at long last. Thirty-six sail all told. All this information had just come by swiftest relays of dispatch-riders from London to Queen Anne's Commander-in-Chief in Scotland, the Earl of Leven – from whose entourage a judiciously placed Jacobite promptly passed it on to Colonel Hooke across the Forth.

Such was the situation that blowy May day of sun and shadow and scudding clouds when Hooke himself arrived at Inversnaid, in haste and some agitation for that sombre man. He was seeking Rob Roy, found him not, and was directed on to Glen Gyle, where Rob and Gregor were hard at work on organisation and supply. He found them, amidst the cheerful clamour of an armed camp, superintending the serious business of doling out the by no means plentiful powder and ball.

'There you are, MacGregor! I am thankful to have run you to earth,' he cried. 'You are plaguey inaccessible folk.'

'We are where God put us,' Rob answered mildly. And then in a different tone of voice, almost menacing, 'You are not come to tell us, Colonel, once more, that . . . ?'

'No, no,' the other assured hurriedly. 'All is well with the expedition. Though these thrice-damned winds from the north-west will hold it up. Always the Stewarts have bad weather! No – it is not that that brings me. I need your help again, MacGregor – the cause needs your help. Word has just reached me, through my Lord of Breadalbane, of a piece of folly which must be undone, and quickly. Two French officers on a special mission to MacDonald of Sleat and the Laird of MacLeod have been landed by some rascally sailing-master in Lorne, of all places.'

'Lorne!' Rob exclaimed. 'Amongst the Campbells? In the heart of Argyll's country?'

'Exactly. Whether by accident, wretched navigation, or evil design, I know not. But according to Breadalbane's information, they have been put ashore below the Oban somewhere, a hundred miles south of their destination in Skye. And they must be rescued, at all costs.'

'*All* costs, Colonel?' Rob repeated. 'Are they so important, these two Frenchmen?'

'They are,' the other nodded decidedly. 'Not so much the men themselves, perhaps, as what they have with them. I knew of their mission – and it is an important one, and must be completed.' Hooke lowered his voice a little. 'You will know how MacDonald of Sleat has gone back on his word, given at Kinloch Rannoch, and is not now rising? Some petty jealousy is behind it, I understand, with ClanRanald. But the effect is serious. He is the most powerful figure in Skye, and he is affecting others. The MacKinnon is hesitating. The Macleans to the south are unhappy at leaving all those MacDonalds at large behind them, with their territories unprotected. Others too. You know how it is.'

Rob knew all this only too well, being not long returned from the north-west, where he had done his best to improve this very situation. He nodded. 'What could the Frenchmen do that I could not?' he wondered.

'That is the point,' Hooke declared grimly. 'They carry, h'm, inducements, these two. Honours, from both James and Louis, for Sleat and for the Laird of MacLeod, who has always been a waverer. The price of being difficult! But much worse – money. Many hundreds of gold *louis*. Money that can ill be spared. Money that we need here. When I was in France I advised strongly against this sending of money. But others have known better. If that gold falls into Campbell hands . . . !'

He did not require to stress his point. Gregor and his uncle exchanged glances.

'Moreover,' Hooke went on, 'and perhaps as serious – these two are colonels straight from Matignon's staff. They know his plans – *our* plans. If they were to talk – were *made* to talk . . . !'

'Yes,' Rob nodded. 'This was an ill landing indeed. South of the Oban, you say?'

'Yes. At a place called Minard, on Loch Feochan, Bread-albane's message said.'

'So Breadalbane is still with us!' Gregor commented. 'I had scarcely expected as much!'

The Colonel glanced at him sharply. 'One can perhaps be over-suspicious, Glengyle,' he reproved. 'And his lordship is your kinsman.'

Gregor pulled a face, but held his tongue.

Hooke turned to Rob Roy. 'Will you go to Lorne at once, then, MacGregor, rescue these Frenchmen and put them on the right road to Skye?'

'Me?' Surprised, Rob stared. 'Man, myself I have a clan to lead, in war. I will be sending somebody to find them, never fear. But not my own self.'

'Yes,' the other insisted, in his dour sober fashion. 'You it is that should go. And I suggest that you take young Glengyle here with you. You are one of the few men who could pass through Argyll's country unmolested. Your mother was a Campbell. So was Glengyle's. You know the Campbell lairds – and I have heard you say that you have had dealings occasionally with the Duke himself. And there requires to be two of you. You may well have to separate. One may have to use guile on the Campbells while the other deals with the Frenchmen.' He smiled then, his wintry smile. 'There are not many fitted to trade guile with Campbells!'

'But the clan ... ?' Gregor protested. 'We are captain and lieutenant of our forces.'

'The clan will not suffer,' Hooke assured. 'I know your value to our cause. You will be back before any of your people are required. There will be no action for the Highland forces for two weeks yet, at the least. Here is how it is planned. The expedition will sail up the Forth to Edinburgh. Or Leith. His Majesty will land there, about a week from now. It was to have been sooner, but these contrary winds are causing delay. I have it from a reliable source close to General Lord Leven that he does not believe that he can hold Edinburgh if the King lands. He will abandon it, if there is a landing, leaving only the Castle defended, and retire on Stirling. We want him to do that. Once the Capital is ours, and His Majesty in Holyroodhouse, we have achieved the equivalent of a notable victory. So Leven must not fear to retire on Stirling. There must be no demonstration of strength in these parts, threatening Stirling, *before* he gets there. You understand? Even Perth must not seem to be threatened too soon by our forces. Once the Government troops are safely concentrated at Stirling, then the clans may show themselves. Not till then. Is that clear, now? So your MacGregors will not be into action for two weeks yet, at the soonest – ample time for you to get back from Lorne.'

After that there was no more to be said. All that Hooke had asserted about the unique suitability of Rob Roy and his nephew for any difficult mission into Campbell country was entirely true. And so long as there was no danger of them failing their clansmen, or missing any of the first heady excitement of the rising, they were both quite happy to be off on a lively-sounding jaunt of this sort, foot-loose, pitting their wits against the Campbells and leaving all this humdrum business of equipping and organising to others. They could hand it all over very nicely to Cousin John of Corryarklet, Cousin Dougal of Comar, Cousin Alastair of Corryheichen and the rest. Which would undoubtedly be very good for the said cousins.

So be it, then.

*　　　*　　　*

With only Rob's MacAlastair in attendance, Gregor and his uncle rode off early the next morning, westwards over into Glen Falloch, and still westwards, through the high pass of the Lairig Arnan to narrow Glen Fyne. Already they were in Campbell country here, and avoiding the populated lower reaches of the valley where it ran down to the head of the loch – the Duke of Argyll's own loch, with Inveraray Castle itself a bare dozen miles away – they got out of the glen as quickly as possible by climbing up to a lofty saddle over a shoulder of mighty Ben Buie, and so down by winding deer-paths through wet peat-hag country into the head of Glen Shira. Twenty rough miles covered, they rested their mounts for a little, hidden amongst the birches above the lonely farm-place of Benbuie in the valley, with the cuckoos calling from all the hillsides around. By a coincidence, that house down there was one in which Rob Roy himself was to find sanctuary, with his family, many years hence. Then on, over another range, to upper Glen Aray, and into the welter of low brown hills and bleak lochans and bogs beyond that flanked the great inland barrier of Loch Awe.

All this way the travellers had been deliberately keeping to high ground and unfrequented places, and had seen no more than an occasional upland shieling and a herd or two pasturing the hill cattle. But now they were forced to come down into low-lying and populous country. Loch Awe, stretching across their path for twenty-five miles, had either to be crossed or circumnavigated – and along its shores quite a proportion of Clan Campbell dwelt. There was no avoiding them. Rob chose to head for the little clachan of Boat of Ballimeanach, one of the many places where there was a ferry to cross the loch, but which was next to unique in having no laird's house in its vicinity. Argyll and Lorne were thicker with lairds, great and small, than anywhere else in the Highlands, the Campbells tending that way.

The travellers routed out the ferryman from his house with no sort of modesty or reserve. 'Ho! The boat!' Rob Roy shouted. 'Ho, there – the boat, I say. In the name of *MacCailean Mor* – on the Duke's business! Rascal – the boat, quickly! I pay well.' That was the way to talk to Campbells.

The ferryman came out promptly enough to that – even if he seemed somewhat surprised to note the red MacGregor tartans. He had to use his larger boat, apparently, since there were garrons to transport – which meant that he must go for a couple of men to help pull the sweeps. Rob sent Mac-Alastair with him, on this errand, just for safety's sake.

They were put across the mile of the loch in the wide old

flat-bottomed scow, with no undue delay, by a frankly inquisitive crew. Rob, far from attempting to hide his identity, boasted of it, talked largely of his closeness to Red John of the Battles, Duke of Argyll, and of the importance of his present mission – sufficiently so to embarrass Gregor, who felt that even to Campbells this was unseemly. But his uncle always knew what he was doing – and would nowise heed any frowns and tut-tutting anyway. He most handsomely paid off the ferrymen at the farther side, below the hanging woods of Inverinan. Then, heading as though for Inverinan House till the trees hid them, they turned abruptly southwards and then west to ride at all speed into the vast wilderness of little hills that lay between Loch Awe and the sea.

They slept the night in the heather, by a sad and lonely lochan, where the oyster-catchers piped and the curlews called and called inconsolably.

The next day, with the salt tang to the hill air that heralded the ocean, they spent their time working by devious ways over towards the green Minard peninsula that jutted into the Firth of Lorne between Loch Feochan and the Sound of Kerrera, seeking to avoid the valleys and all haunts of men. By late afternoon they were looking out over the wide blue waters of the Firth to the far mountains of Mull. And nearer at hand, below them, the winding rocky-shored inlet of Loch Feochan probed the valley. At its square head, amongst the flats and meadows of the River Nell, lay the Kirkton of Kilmore. Away at the mouth of the sea-loch, off the Point of Minard, according to Breadalbane's message, the French ship had set ashore its unfortunate passengers. No ship showed there now, at any rate, nor anywhere on the seascape.

There was an inn down there at Kilmore – but also, unfortunately, nearby was the castle of Campbell of Lochnell, a prominent chieftain of Clan Diarmid, and still nearer the lesser house of Campbell of Glenfeochan. They could wait till darkness, and then slip across the haughlands around the head of the loch, amongst the croft-houses, and so on to the Minard peninsula. On the other hand, if information was to be gained, that inn at Kilmore would be an apt place to gain it, sitting at the base of the peninsula as it did. Rob decided that information was necessary.

Halting in a hollow of the heather, Rob effected a transformation. Doffing his weapons, tartans, doublet and fine bonnet, he drew out from a bundle of gear that his garron carried the patched and dingy clothing of a travelling packman – hodden breeches, torn hose, grimy shirt, and stained and ragged plaid of indeterminate check. A pack too, which he stuffed with heather. All this he donned with practised ease, and told his two companions to wait for him there. Gregor thought that he might have sent MacAlastair about this business, but Rob would have none of it. So, thus garbed, the Captain of Clan Alpine went off downhill long-strided, pack over his shoulder. But it might have been observed that, long before he reached the inn in the Kirkton, he was limping heavily and with a stoop to his enormous shoulders like a dog scraping a pot. Going thus, his long arms reached almost to his ankles, and perforce he had to keep them tucked away in the dirty folds of the tattered plaid.

It was hours later, dusk indeed, and Gregor was not only impatient but getting anxious – unnatural as it might seem to be anxious about Rob Roy MacGregor – before his uncle came back uphill, actually singing, through the drizzling chill rain that had set in on the everlasting north-westerly wind. He was in excellent form. Apparently the Campbell innkeeper dispensed refreshment worthy of better folk. Which was a matter of only academic interest to one who had sat shivering in wet heather for the intervening hours.

But Rob was full of information, as well as good cheer. There was no need to go over to the peninsula and away down to Minard, he revealed. The Frenchmen had been captured, and were even now on their way, under guard, to the Duke's castle at Inveraray. *Finis coronat opus!*

The innkeeper had not required overmuch prompting, apparently – in fact, he had been agog with news. The ship had been sighted off the point six days before, evidently a

205

foreigner, and it had lain offshore in the mouth of the loch till nightfall – but had been gone by the morning. It was obvious that somebody had been landed. Campbell of Lochnell, who was a captain of one of the Independent Militia Companies, had instituted a search – and sure enough, five Frenchmen had been discovered, two days later, hiding in a deserted croft-house some miles to the north. Or at least two French officers, two servants and some sort of Irishman. Jacobite agents, for certain. They had been taken and locked up in Lochnell Castle. And only this same morning Lochnell had set out with them for Inveraray, passing that very inn *en route*.

Gregor sighed. 'We might have known it!' he said. 'What else should we have expected? And the money?'

'There was no mention of money,' Rob told him. 'And I could not be asking.'

With Rob dressed in his own clothes again, they set off southwards through the half-dark of a wet May night.

* * *

Wrapped in their plaids, they followed the road that ran south, from the head of one dark sea-loch, over high ground to the head of the next, and so on, by Kilninver and Kilmelfort and Craignish. It was a populous settled country, interspersed with ribs of low rocky hills, but they rode openly through the night, unchallenged save by the occasional dog from croft or farmstead. Rob sang cheerfully but grievously out of tune – till Gregor was forced out of sheer aesthetic integrity to put him right with his own more melodious voice, and once started quite forgot to stop.

They were making for Ardmoine, on Loch Craignish. Campbell of Ardmoine was father-in-law to Lochnell, and since the place lay almost exactly half-way to Inveraray, a moderate day's journey, and just before the track thither cut away from the drove road and through the rough hills, it could be taken as more than probable that the party would be halting there for the night. It was likely enough to take a chance on, at any rate.

The trio came to the place in the darkest part of a May night – an hour or so before the dawn. But even so, the rain having stopped, there was light enough to distinguish the tall stone house with its high chimney-stacks and pepper-box turrets, set on its own little grassy promontory jutting into the wan mystery of Loch Craignish. No lamplight showed about the house or its vicinity.

MacAlastair, on foot, was dispatched to spy out the land – and to be reasonably quick about it, for time was not un-limited, with dawn in an hour. He slipped away soundless – and his eventual returning was like a shadow materialising beside them. Briefly, factually, utterly unemotional as ever, he declared what he had discovered. Fifteen horses were tethered in the stableyard at the back of the house. Men were asleep in the stables themselves – how many he did not know. The doors of the big house seemed to be locked or barred. There was no guard or sentry set, that he had seen.

'Why should there be, whatever?' Rob demanded. 'They are safe in the heart of their own Campbell country – and MacCailean Mor rules with a sure hand. What need they of sentries? But Lochnell and his captives are here, for sure. Fifteen horses? Five for the prisoners. Lochnell himself and nine of an escort. Lochnell and the two French officers and this Irishman at least will be in the house. The others in the stables. It is our task to get them out. How think you it is to be done, Greg?'

'The stabling – is it roofed with thatch?' Gregor asked MacAlastair.

'Aha – your mind runs yet on firing stables, boy!' Rob exclaimed.

'Why not? It has proved profitable hitherto, has it not? A fire in the stable will open Ardmoine's door, I think.'

'Very well so,' his uncle agreed – who had thought along similar lines himself. 'And when it opens, we slip within. The stable roof will be of thatch, surely – even Campbells will not slate their stables, I think. But it will be damp. It may need assistance in its burning.' He sighed, and turning, rooted about amongst his gear, to produce a bottle that the others had not seen hitherto. 'A pity to be wasting good whisky – but this will help, maybe. With some hay.' Rob scratched his red-bearded chin. 'If you were Lochnell – which God forbid – what would you do with all that money, overnight, in another man's house?'

Gregor, for whom money had less importance than sundry other commodities, shrugged. 'Lock it up somewhere, I suppose?'

His uncle raised an eyebrow. 'So? I am thinking that would be . . . disrespectful! Myself, I would take it to bed with me – closer than any wife! And the man is a Campbell, mind you! Now – have we all got flint and tinder . . . ?'

Their several duties were swiftly rehearsed. The garrons would be left here. They would all take a hand at the fire-raising, but MacAlastair would be left to make the most of it, and if necessary shout the alarm when all was well alight. He would then see that the tethered horses were loosed and stampeded if possible – making sure that he kept a grip on three or four of them, to bring up here. In the dark and confusion it was to be hoped that he would pass as one of Ardmoine's men to Lochnell's people, and vice versa. Meanwhile, Rob and his nephew would move in close under the walls of the big house near the back entrance, and endeavour to slip inside once the door was opened. What happened thereafter would be dictated by circumstances.

MacAlastair leading, the trio moved quietly down across the cattle-dotted rough pasture, and through the belt of shelter trees that backed house, farmery and gardens. A few branches of dead pine picked up on the way would much assist their fire. They came without hindrance to the rear of the range of stabling and byres, which formed half a square at the landward and northern side of the tall old house. The roofing was thatch, sure enough – old reeds from the water-meadows. The walls were of stone, save for one corner, presumably an addition, where they were composed of birch planking. From the somewhat musty smell that issued from between the cracks, last season's bog-hay had been stored therein. Rob changed that smell for the better, by pouring whisky against the timbers and on to tufts of hay that projected. The reed thatching, save for the topmost layer, seemed to be as dry as their tinder.

The three men went to work with flint and steel, Gregor taking the middle of the range, using pine clusters to aid him, and MacAlastair working at the farther corner.

All that was needful was done in a few seconds. With the materials so highly inflammable there was no need for coaxing or tending – and the strong wind at last proved advantageous. As the dry reeds began to crackle noticeably, Gregor and Rob left it all, and hurried round to the front.

A small cobbled yard lay between the stabling and the rear wall of the house. The two MacGregors ran across this, aware of the stirring of tethered horses, to fetch up crouching on either side of the only back door. They were well enough there for the moment, in the dark – but whenever that thatch really blazed up, they were bound to stand revealed in the glare. Rob darted out again, over to the nearest of the horses, slashed its tether with his dirk, and led the beast back to beside his nephew, its hooves sounding painfully loud in that hollow place.

'We can crouch behind this,' he panted. 'Not attract much attention here. There will be confusion, I think. . . . '

He was right about that, at any rate. The flames were licking up from four or five points now, highest at Rob's plank building. Suddenly, with a distinct *whoosh*, this hay store turned itself into a blazing beacon, however, lighting up the entire scene in a vivid orange glare. Dense clouds of smoke were now seen to be pouring out from the thatch everywhere. Simultaneously, shouts, howls, curses and coughing rang out. Horses whinnied and began to sidle and stamp their hooves. Men came stumbling out into the yard, yelling. Sparks, blown on the wind, came flying over. Gregor had to hold in their covering horse, tightly.

Now the yard was a pandemonium of excited men and frightened horses, of wildly leaping shadows, billowing smoke, and soaring flaming fragments. And noise. For how much of it all MacAlastair was responsible was not clear.

Nothing was clear. Rob Roy, eyes streaming, ran to the closed door of the house, banging thereon with his open hands.

'Fire! Fire!' he shouted, his voice choking, affected by the smoke. 'Fire!' And went on banging.

They had not long to wait. Pounding footsteps preceding the sounds of bolts being drawn gave Rob warning, in time for him to leap back from the doorway to Gregor's side. Then the door was thrown open and two men came running out, one barefooted and struggling into a coat, the other booted but pulling up his breeches as he ran. They paused only for a moment at the sight that met their eyes. Then the booted man went plunging out into the mêlée, while the other turned back within, shouting.

The entire roof of the steading was now alight from end to end, a roaring inferno fanned by the breeze. The heat was intense, even over where the hiding men crouched. They had much ado to keep their horse held. The other beasts seemed largely to have got away from the yard by this time, either having been loosed or having dragged their tethers. In the rolling smoke and cavorting shadows it was difficult to distinguish details – especially with flooding eyes.

Three more men came running out from the house, variously garbed, and then a fourth. A woman also appeared in the doorway, wrapped in a plaid, and screeching. Rob touched Gregor's arm, and nodded.

Leaving the rearing horse to its own devices, the two of them hurried to the door. They brushed past the staring squawking woman without a word – and she did not so much as spare a glance for them. There was a long passage ahead of them, with doors opening off it, lit only by the fitful glare from behind them. Hands on dirks, they dashed along this. At the far end it opened out into a larger hallway. As they turned into this, Rob, in front, collided with another man hurrying in the opposite direction.

'Devil scald you – out of my way, fool!' this individual cried. 'What hell's work is this ?' His was the angry voice of authority. He seemed to be an elderly man, and portly. Probably the master of the house himself.

Rob took a chance. 'Lochnell?' he shouted. 'Where is Lochnell?'

'Damnation – if he's not out already, he will be up in his room!' The other gestured vaguely behind him, and up. Dimly the foot of a stairway could be perceived at his back.

'The prisoners,' Rob cried then. 'We must look to them. Where are they . . . ?'

But the laird, if such he was, was hastening on along the passage, and did not answer.

Rob hesitated for only a moment. 'Come,' he jerked, to Gregor, and led the way to the stair foot.

Side by side, three or four steps at a time, the MacGregors raced up the worn stone treads of the winding turnpike stair, slipping and stumbling a little in the darkness. But at the first-floor landing there was light, partly from a window in a passage that must face the rear of the house, whence a ruddy glow radiated, and partly from a lamp held up by an elderly woman in a nightdress who stood within an open doorway, twittering and exclaiming, one hand on her thin bosom, grey hair about her shoulders. There were two other doors on this landing, one of which also stood open.

Rob sought to moderate the manner of their approach. 'Ma'am,' he cried. 'It is the stables, just. It will be all right. Where is Lochnell?'

The lady only mouthed and gulped, the lamp swaying in her hand.

Almost certainly this would be the Lady Ardmoine. The chances were that her husband had come out of the same bedroom whose doorway she now filled. These, on this first floor, would be the principal bedrooms of the house. That other that stood open, then, might well be that of her son-in-law, Lochnell. 'Is that Lochnell's room?' he demanded, pointing.

She nodded.

Lochnell was downstairs, then – out at the fire, no doubt.

'The prisoners, Ma'am,' he questioned her, now. 'We must see to the Frenchmen. Where are they?'

'Mercy on us – what's to befall us?' the lady got out. 'Dear God – is the house afire? Am I to be left to be burned ... ?'

'No, no. You are fine, Ma'am – just fine,' the soft-hearted Gregor assured. 'There is no danger, whatever. But the Frenchmen. We must see that they are safe. Where are they, at all?'

'The Frenchies? They are in the dairy – locked in the dairy,' she gasped. 'But what's to become of us all ... ?'

'Wheesht you!' Rob cried. 'Down to the dairy, Greg! I'll be with you in a little.' And he ran into the room indicated as Lochnell's.

Leaving the lady to wail and appeal to her Maker, Gregor sprang down the stairs again.

The dairy – that would be to the rear of the house, for sure? Probably along that very passage by which they had first entered. One of those doors? Which one? As they had come along, there had seemed to be not a few. . . .

Pounding down the passage again, fairly well lit now by the lurid glare, Gregor halted at the first door. It opened to his touch. All was dark within. There was a smell of fish. And something else? Hams. A larder, only? No hint of life or movement within. He backed out.

A man was coming hurrying along the stone-flagged passage from the open back door. Gregor paused, hand ready on dirk. But the fellow brushed past, intent on his own errand, bawling something about pails and buckets.

Gregor was moving on relievedly, when swiftly his mind reacted. 'See, you,' he called after the man. 'The dairy! There will be pails in the dairy, man. That's the place – the dairy.'

The other halted, and turned back. 'Hech, hech – that is so, yes. The dairy, yes. But, *dia* – the Frenchies are in there. . . . '

'Never care!' Gregor cried. 'First things first, whatever! *I'll* look after the Frenchies for you.' He drew his claymore with a flourish. 'They'll not be getting past this! Quick, man.'

The other, an undersized runt of a man, undoubtedly a house gillie, was evidently used to receiving authoritative orders, and reacted unquestioningly to the tone of voice. Pushing past down the passage again, he stopped at the second door on the other side, and standing on tiptoe sought to reach a shelf above the lintel. Promptly Gregor was after him, and feeling along the ledge, grabbed a large key that lay there. He handed it to the little man. 'Quickly, now,' he commanded.

But the other paused doubtfully, the key in the lock. Not because of Gregor, it seemed, but on account of the noise that was coming out from behind that door. Fists were obviously beating against the panels, and shouts in French and English could be made out.

'Och, heed them not,' Gregor exclaimed impatiently. 'We'll soon quieten them. They are not armed, at all. They will not argue with my steel! Pails we must have.' And pushing the other aside, he turned the key, and kicked open the door.

There seemed to be but three men within – whose shouts died on them as they drew back before the blood-red gleam of firelight on a naked sword.

'*Bon chance, messieurs !*' Gregor cried. '*C'est bon. Vive le roi Jacques ! Vive le Grand Monarque !*' That was the best that he could do at short notice. In English, which was probably as unintelligible to the gillie, he went on. 'Do exactly what I am telling you. I am your friend. You understand. Friend. *Ami.* This man wants pails. *Seau. Buquet.* Pails to put out the fire that we have started. Let him get them quickly. Then we shall be quit of him, whatever. *Comprenez ?*'

'Indade yes. Shure, sir,' a rich Irish brogue assured him. 'Mary-Mother and all the Saints be praised! An honest Christian. . . . '

'Quiet!' Gregor rapped. And turning to the wondering gillie, he spoke in the Gaelic. 'Quick – the pails, man. I have warned these wretches. They will not challenge my sword. Get you the pails.'

In the ruddy uncertain glow that illuminated the chamber from a small high-set window barred with ironwork, it was to be seen that the place was equipped with stone shelves furnished with many bowls and pails and churns, like the dairy of any other large house. The little man scurried forward, grabbed two of the pails and edged out warily.

'Haste, you,' Gregor urged him. 'I will bring more. These Frenchies are safe enough with me. . . .'

'The door . . . ?' the gillie panted.

'I will lock it behind me,' he was assured.

The little man ran off down the passage, his pails clanking.

Swiftly Gregor swung on the captives. 'Take you pails too,' he directed. 'Coggies, bowls – anything. Anything to carry, see you. To seem to fight the fire. *Vite! Vite!* Then follow me.'

With considerable chatter and exclamation the two Frenchmen and the Irishman did as they were told, taking up receptacles, emptying the contents out of some where necessary. They seemed to Gregor to take an unconscionable time about it – and to make a deal more noise than was called for. He had sheathed his sword and got himself a large earthenware jug. Impatiently he fretted at the door.

'*Diabhol!*' he cursed, suddenly. Somebody was coming down the passage again. Had he been seen, standing in this doorway? Was it best to slam the door shut on them, himself included? The key was still in the lock. No time to take it out now. He would be a prisoner himself that way. . . .

Then, with relief, he recognised something familiar in the shape of the approaching man. It was Rob, stooping a little, carrying something fairly bulky and heavy under his plaid apparently.

'I have them here,' he called out. 'All ready. Carrying pails to put out the fire. Two French and an Irishman.'

'Good. Good.' Rob grunted. '*Dia* – this gold is heavy! Under Lochnell's bed, as I said! Man, I'm going to find dirk work difficult!'

'Damn the gold!' Gregor declared, forcefully. And in English, 'Come, you.'

Gregor leading, and Rob bringing up the rear, they hastened down the passage to the back door, clutching their various burdens. The worst of the fire was already over, with the blazing thatch fallen in at one or two points, but the clouds of smoke seemed but the denser. There was a murky hellish quality about the scene outside. But it was considerably more confused and obscure than when they had left it.

Peering, Gregor could make out only two or three vague figures amongst the eddying smoke clouds. It was difficult to be sure, but it seemed that there was more activity at the other end of the steading, the west end. A small wing jutted out there. Possibly they were trying to save that. There were no horses to be seen, now.

Strange as it might seem, it looked as though they were going to be able just to walk out of Ardmoine. Apart from the grievous fumid fog of smoke and the chaos occasioned thereby in the darkness, nobody seemed to be interested, in them or anything other than the fire. None of these people were regular soldiers, of course, just local militia, untrained and little disciplined. They had lived secure too long to compete adequately with MacGregors.

Scarcely crediting their good fortune, the five men slipped away, along the side of the house, round the corner of the steading to the east, and into the trees behind, seeking to swallow their coughing and choking, half-blinded by their streaming eyes. In the wood they deposited their pails and containers, amidst a considerable outburst of voluble French and accented English. But Rob Roy cut it short with crisp orders for silence and the saving of breath. It would be a long while yet before they could start to congratulate each other. There was much that could yet go wrong.

The validity of this warning was borne out all too soon. When they reached MacAlastair and the garrons, it was to find that he had been unable to retain a hold on more than two of the Campbell horses in the stampede – and of these one had lamed itself in the panic. In his sour cryptic way the gillie was apologetic — only to Rob, of course. The fire had gone too fast for him, and most of the beasts had broken their fetters and bolted before he had got round to them. Only these . . .

The problem before them now required no emphasising. There were five horses, one of them lame, for six men. And they would have to ride far and fast, for the entire country would be raised against them before they were many hours older. Argyll and Lorne would be buzzing like two nests of angry wasps, and it would take fast movement and sound hillcraft to avoid being stung.

Rob wasted no time in making up his mind. Quick decisions were a speciality of his, anyhow. First things had to come first. That was almost a MacGregor motto. Getting the two French colonels safely on their way to Skye was his prime task and major responsibility. The Irishman, who it seemed was only a sort of guide and interpreter — and a poor guide at that, judging by results — must take his chance. MacAlastair could take him, and the lame horse, and seek to get back to MacGregor country as best he could. The rest of them would head north with all speed on the four beasts.

Gregor was sorry enough for the Irishman to plead for him, in Gaelic. But his uncle was adamant. That was the way that causes were lost. To hold together would mean that they must go at the pace of the slowest. They would never get the Frenchmen out of Lorne that way. It was going to be no joke, as it was. Besides, MacAlastair and the Irishman would no doubt do very well on their own, anyway. They would probably be best to abandon the horse, and disguise themselves as a pair of wandering masterless men. He would leave them his packman's gear. Taking their time, keeping to the high ground, and living off the country, they would get back to Loch Lomond-side safely enough, in due course. MacAlastair had had harder tasks than that to perform in his day!

The gillie nodded terse confirmation of that.

So it was accepted, as all Rob Roy's decisions were apt to

be accepted, and the little company separated there and then, the French officers distinctly bewildered and vocal, but the Irishman less concerned than might have been expected when informed that his destination lay less than fifty miles away, as the crow flew, whereas the others had four times that amount of ground to cover.

Without ceremony or more than the briefest leave-taking, Rob Roy led his remaining three companions away at a brisk pace northwards. He had hung the two heavy leather bags of gold *louis* behind him on his own garron.

CHAPTER SEVENTEEN

THEY did not continue along the north-going road down which they had come, but quickly cut off north-eastwards up Glen Doin, following the Barbreck Burn. Ten miles or so up there lay Loch Avich, embosomed amongst its wilderness of low identical hills – and it was into that brown labyrinth that Rob would have them before the sun was fully risen.

His plan was to head north by east, travelling only by night and hiding by day, seeking to leave Campbell country, via Glen Etive, for the fastnesses of Glen Coe. It was necessary to do more than merely win out of Lorne and the Campbell territory; he had to find somebody who was actually anti-Campbell, and prepared to work actively against that powerful clan – and most of the Campbells' neighbours undoubtedly would not be prepared to do that. But the MacDonalds of Glen Coe were different from others. The iron had entered their souls. MacIan, their young chief, would do anything in his power to hurt the people who had slain his father and massacred his clansmen fifteen years previously. Moreover, with his vessels on Loch

Leven, with access to the sea, he could ship out the two Frenchmen direct to Skye. And, of course, he was a Jacobite.

Glen Coe it should be, then. But that savage valley lay a long way from Glen Doin and Craignish – a hundred miles by the roundabout routes that fugitives must take to avoid the populous Campbell glens and the great water barriers of Lochs Awe and Etive, a hundred weary miles of benighted heather and peat-hag, of rock and scree and flood. A weary wary journey, indeed.

It would be a weariness, too, to seek to set down the record of their patient circuitous seemingly endless travels, by the hills of Kilchrenan, the Sior Loch, Glen Nant and the Pass of Brander, by the high ridges of mighty Cruachan and its sisters, by the upper reaches of Glen Kinglass and the wild peaks of the Starav range and into Glen Etive. And so, at last, over the grim but happy Pass of the Lairig Gartain, out of the Campbell lands and into Glen Coe of the Mac-Donalds. Let it suffice to say that it took them five nights of most difficult heart-breaking marching and counter-march-ing, made possible only by the MacGregors' masterly hill-craft and Rob Roy's uncanny sense of direction, to reach MacIan's new-built house down beside the weed-grown shores of long Loch Leven – five nights of marching and five days of hiding, wherein they grew to know each other tolerably well, wherein the MacGregors grew to like and appreciate the laughing and debonair Colonel de Cloquet, and to utterly loathe and abominate the stiff and complain-ing Colonel Robinet – and wherein Gregor came to admire his uncle's abilities more than ever he had done. Five days and nights in which all Lorne and Argyll were looking for them, all the powers of the Duke of Argyll and his brother the Earl of Islay, Lord Justice-General, were mobilised against them, and in which never once was their presence revealed to their enemies.

So much for *MacCailean Mor*, Red John of the Battles, lately gazetted Major-General of Her Majesty's Forces.

On the 23rd of May, then, Rob Roy MacGregor handed over his two charges to MacIan MacDonald of Glencoe, who accepted them warmly and promised to have them delivered safely by sea within the week to his fellow-clansman in Skye, Sir Donald of Sleat.

The parting, and the close of the entire satisfactory mission, was marred by one brief incident. Rob would not hear of stopping overnight with MacIan, but insisted on riding away south again forthwith, by the Moor of Rannoch and Glen Orchy, claiming overlong absence from his clan as it was. In the end, in so much of a hurry to be off was he, that the Frenchmen had to come dashing out of MacIan's house after him.

'*Monsieur* – the gold!' Colonel Robinet cried. '*Mon dieu* – you forget the gold!'

Rob Roy stroked his beard, but shook his head. 'No, *mon Colonel* – I do not forget. But the gold will be safer with me than with you, I think, in this unchancy Scotland of ours. *I shall look after your louis-d'ors.*'

'*Mais, non! Ma foi* – *ce n'est pas possible. Il est* . . . the gold, it is *essentiel, de la dernière importance!* To . . . to our mission. It is the most necessary that you give the gold to me.'

'I deem it otherwise, *monsieur*. And I think that I know the situation best, see you. The gold will be safe with me.'

'*Non, non.* The gold, it is for me to give! It is not your gold. *Nom de Dieu* . . . !'

'It is not *your* gold, Colonel. It is King James's gold – Scotland's gold. And here, in this part of Scotland, *I* decide what is best for King James's cause, whatever!'

'But surely, Monsieur MacGregor,' the other colonel, de Cloquet, intervened. 'Our mission to Monsieur de Mac-Donald and Monsieur de MacLeod is *sans valeur*, valueless, without the gold . . . ?'

'Not so, my friend. If Sleat will not bring in his clan for honour's sake, he will not bring it in for gold, that is certain. And MacLeod will not fight anyhow. There is better work for the gold than that. I take it.'

'*Voleur! Brigand! Traître!*' Colonel Robinet shouted,

almost screamed. 'Miscreant – you shall suffer! *Parbleu* – you shall suffer . . . !'

'Sir!' Rob drew himself up on his travel-worn garron, thrusting forward his red-bearded chin. 'Those are no words to use to a Highland gentleman! Men have died for less! I leave you, sir – and I do not congratulate you on your manners or your wit. Good-day. And to you, de Cloquet – a pleasant journey, and good fortune.' And pulling round his mount's head, he kicked the beast into motion.

'*Dia* – I do not like this!' Gregor began unhappily. 'Might it not be best to . . . ?'

'Your opinion was not asked, boy!' Rob Roy snapped back at him. 'Come, you.' His garron broke into a canter.

Gregor looked at de Cloquet, sighed, shrugged wide shoulders, and rode after his uncle.

*   *   *

'That was not well done.' Gregor had taken a long time to come up with the older man, under the soaring smoking precipices that frowned down on dark Glen Coe – and he had been doing no little thinking in the interim. 'It ill became you,' he said.

His uncle turned to look at him. 'Still croaking, Greg?'

'I say that you should not have done it. That you have spoiled a good enterprise at the end of it.'

'Spoiled? I say crowned, rather, boy! The gold is the best of it, whatever!'

'I think otherwise.'

'Tcha! There speaks experience! Mature judgment! Glengyle – the man of the world!' Rob Roy laughed, loudly for him. 'Spare me more of your discernments, lad!'

Doggedly Gregor went on – though of all things he hated being thus laughed at. 'Nevertheless, you had no ease in the doing of it, your own self,' he averred. 'It was unseemly to leave MacIan so.' He looked sidelong at his companion. 'I believe that you intended this, from the first? To take the gold? That you were more interested in the gold than in the Frenchmen? Or the Irishman!'

'You are very free with your beliefs today, Greg,' Rob said. 'I did what Hooke laid it on me to do, did I not? And was not Hooke himself after saying that the money should never have been sent to Sleat? That it was needed here? MacDonald of Sleat would have put it in his chest, and that would have been the end of it, whatever.'

'And is it so certain, then, that MacGregor of Inversnaid will not be doing the same? Or with some of it?'

'*Diabhol!* This is too much!' his uncle cried. 'A truce to your puppy's yappings, sir! Remember to whom you speak, my God!'

'I had not forgotten,' the younger man said flatly. 'More's the pity. Nor have I forgotten that night at Rannoch, when we spoke of treason and of Breadalbane!' And he drew on his garron so that it dropped well behind Rob Roy's beast.

And thus the MacGregors rode southwards.

*　　　*　　　*

It was a silent journey that they made of it, across the boundless desolation of Rannoch Moor and down green Glen Orchy that had once been MacGregor but was now Campbell – but Breadalbane Campbell. They went discreetly still, avoiding men – for *MacCailean Mor's* arm was long – and certainly they went harder and faster than they need have done. And the barrier between them rode as fast as they did.

It was two days later, at evening of the 25th of May, when they reached home, and geography brought them to Glen Gyle first. And if it had been a silent ride, it was no less a silent reception that awaited them there. The great throng of warriors had gone from the glen – though the marks of their sojourn were everywhere evident. The women it was that greeted them, strainedly, Mary and the Lady Christian, with an unhappy Ian Beg in the background. No, the clan had not been moved to another area, they said. They had gone home – all of them. Home, just. The rising was over. King James had been – and gone. The clans were to disperse quietly to their homes. Orders from Colonel Hooke. Messengers were out, up and down the land, with the word to disperse. The King was on his way back to France. All was over.

Dumbfounded, Gregor looked from the women to his uncle. Rob's gaze was far away, but his clenched hairy fists were trembling.

'The fool!' he said softly. 'The poor weak ignoble faint-hearted fool!' It was not clear of whom he spoke – and his nephew did not question him. Then the older man's eyes narrowed, and his voice changed, notably. 'As well that we did not let go of that gold, boy,' he said. And smiled twistedly.

The Irishman had reached Inversnaid three days pre-viously, with MacAlastair, and had been sent on to Fife.

CHAPTER EIGHTEEN

IT took two or three days, and the arrival of Colonel Nath-aniel Hooke himself at Inversnaid, for the entire sorry story to emerge. Hooke came, as usual, seeking Rob's aid. An authoritative explanation of the fiasco must be got out to the clan chiefs if their loyalty was to be preserved. James Stewart still had need of the MacGregors' services, it seemed.

It was all the fault of the French Admiral the Count de Forbin, apparently. All the way north, in the face of those contrary winds, he had been nervous, with Byng's English squadron at his heels, lying off but never losing touch. He had feared a trap, outsailing, an attack whilst disembarking troops and materials. He was at odds with both King James and with Matignon the French military commander.

On the night of 23rd May the fleet reached the mouth of the Firth of Forth. The plan was for them to sail up the twenty miles or so to Leith, which they had reason to believe not be defended against them, and there disembark. de Forbin feared that once in the Forth estuary, Byng would bottle him up, that he would not get out again. He hove to off the Isle of May, in a fever of indecision, and only one frigate, which had missed the Admiral's signals in the darkness, sailed on westwards according to plan. This vessel duly arrived at Leith, found no opposition, landed a party – and could have made the port its own. Indeed, had King James been on that frigate, history would have been changed. He could have proceeded almost unchallenged up to Edinburgh and walked into his ancestors' palace of Holyroodhouse – for the Earl of Leven, afraid of the populace, afraid of the loyalty of his own troops, was packed up and ready to bolt with his Staff – or such of them as he could trust. But there was no King, no commander, no person of importance on that single ship, nobody with authority to exploit the situation. It had waited till daylight revealed that it was entirely alone in the Firth, when it had hastily re-embarked its shore party and put to sea again.

Meanwhile the French fleet had lain heaving off the May Island, while the battle of wills continued. And craven irresolution won. Admiral de Forbin decided that safety was all. He was a servant of France, not of Scotland. He refused to sail into the Forth, or to permit a landing on the nearby Fife coast at the mouth of it. He refused even to allow the King to put off in a small boat – though James, it was said, even went down on his royal knees begging, with tears in his eyes, to be allowed to land, alone if necessary, on his ancient kingdom. He was too valuable, he was assured, for any folly of that sort to be allowed – too valuable a pawn for the French, it was to be assumed. Signals to the other ships were flashed out, and the entire fleet stood out to sea, on the first stage of its expeditious return to France, with the favourable wind behind it. But before the flagship got under way, two young Scots officers of Matignon's Staff, the Captains Seton and Ogilvie, with their servants, had managed, with the connivance of sympathetic French sailors, to lower a small boat and get away. They rowed to the Fife coast, at Anstruther, only five miles away. That was how the news reached Colonel Hooke.

That was all. That was the end of all their hopes and plans and strivings. James Stewart would be back in Dunkirk by now, with the north-westerly wind behind his sails. Westminster could breathe freely again.

The MacGregors were silenced. All Scotland indeed was silenced. What was there to say?

Only this did Rob Roy eventually find to announce. Nathaniel Hooke could find somebody else to take that melancholy and shameful story round the clans. Himself, he had more profitable things to be doing. And on this occasion, when he heard about it, Gregor did not disagree with his uncle.

A disheartened man, Hooke went on his way empty-handed. Gregor did not hear, either, that he went burdened with French *louis-d'ors*.

CHAPTER NINETEEN

In the weeks that followed, Scotland waited – waited for news, guidance, reassurance, leadership, anything that she could lay hold upon. Like a rudderless ship, she yawed and veered and plunged, at the mercy of every drift and puff and current. No leadership was vouchsafed her. And all the time the Government grew bolder, more active, more resolute. And vengeful. It had had a fright. It had been made to look weak, unprepared, unsure of itself, foolish. Somebody had to pay. A display of strength was called for, now that the danger was over. Examples must be made, lest the like happen again.

There were arrests up and down the land – though not over the Highland Line. Edinburgh's numerous jails and cells were soon crammed to overflowing. Proclamations were issued demanding information anent traitorous acts, and offering rewards. Dire threats were made.

But it was largely sound and fury. Few really important people were held. Lord Drummond, admittedly, caught at the head of 200 men, was hustled away south to be immured in the Tower of London – which much offended Scotland, being contrary to the terms of the Union, and he had to be released. Dragoons called upon the Duke of Atholl, but found him confined to bed, with a resident doctor to say that he had been unable to leave his room for months. Other apprehensions hung fire. Evidence was not forthcoming. Despite the enticements and threats, the necessary evidence remained stubbornly amissing. Scotland was in surly mood, and folk would not talk. There had to be releases. Stirling of Garden, Arnprior's old friend, who had been rash enough to ride towards Edinburgh with some of his servants to meet his sovereign and had been held ever since, was freed – for the same lack of evidence. After all, it was no offence for a gentleman to ride armed about the country in unsettled times – self-preservation demanded no less. The Court of Session required more than suspicion and animus to convict of high treason, even in post-Union Scotland.

So the uneasy summer went in. Rumours abounded, even reaching to Glen Gyle. The Government found scapegoats on its own side. Various gentlemen came up from London, and sundry Scottish nominees' heads toppled.

Such was the situation as it drew near to Lammas-tide again, and the dues for Rob Roy's Watch fell once more to be collected. And in Glengyle House thoughts inevitably turned towards Drymen and Arnprior – and Mary Mac-Gregor sighed just a little, happy, busy, and secure as she might feel.

Her sighs, curiously enough, few as they might be, were answered rather remarkably. Late one golden afternoon as Gregor was scything the hay with long slow rhythmic strokes in the meadows below the house, and Mary was rolling and bouncing young Iannie in the sweet-smelling coils that she was supposed to be building, their laughter was interrupted by the arrival of a deep-breathing gillie who came out of the hills to the south and brought strange news. They had found a woman, wandering in the heather, with a lamed horse, many miles away, near the head of the Duchray Water. She had not the Gaelic, but she had made it clear that she was meaning to be heading for Glen Gyle, far from the route though she was. They had brought her, on another garron – see, there they came, over the hill. Her name? Och, yes – her name, she said, was Hamilton.

Gregor went running, then, just as he was, the hounds bounding by his side, and Mary calling messages after him. A mile or so away, over the low shoulder of hill that lay between them and Stronachlacher, a small party was approaching, three or four on foot and one figure mounted.

Stripped to the waist and covered with the seeds and dust of the hayfield, Gregor came up at his effortless lope. But he had little need to concern himself with his appearance. For Meg Hamilton was less than presentable also, her fine riding-habit stained and soaked and bedraggled, her hair unbound, her whole person mud-spattered and dishevelled. Evidently she had had at least one fall. And she looked very weary. Yet even so, her dark eyes gleamed with some hint of their old sparkle as the man came running up to her.

'Gregor! Gregor!' she cried. 'My splendid braw Hielandman! Oh, but you are a sight for sair een, Gregor! And . . . and my een are just a small bit sair, I will admit!'

'Och, never say it, Meg.' He gripped both her hands – and saw that one of them was badly scratched and mud-encrusted. 'They never looked bonnier. Fine kind brave eyes – I am glad to see them, I tell you. It has been a long time.'

'Be quiet, be quiet – or you will have them weeping tears!' she told him, a little unsteadily. 'I have contained my tears till now, on this hapless journey of mine. I must not loose them here.' She managed to change and control her voice. 'How is Mary?'

'Well, God be praised.'

'And happy?'

'I think so, yes.'

'She had better be – or I will know the reason why!' That was strongly, if unevenly, said. 'And the young man?'

'Och, a giant. A terror. A Hercules, just! And you, Meg? And . . . and your husband?'

'We have our health,' she assured briefly.

'Ummm.' They were moving on, he pacing at her garron's side. 'Yes,' he agreed, 'it is a great thing the health. You have come from Arnprior?'

'From Bardowie, really. Though I came *by* Arnprior.'

'A long road, lassie.' He shook his head. 'You should not have come alone. The wonder it is that you got this far. . . .'

'I was best alone. None of my father's servants would have been of help to me to reach Glen Gyle. I think. I dared not trust them, anyway. Not on this errand.'

'You have come on an errand, then? An especial errand?'

'Yes. I could not get a message to you – even if I could have risked sending one. I had to come myself. I have come because I think that you are in danger, Gregor. You and others. Many others. I had to come.'

'Danger? Me?' He did not manage wholly to keep incredulity out of his voice.

'Yes. You. And Rob Roy. And scores of others. Have you forgotten my Lord of Breadalbane?'

Gregor glanced at her sharply. 'No,' he denied. And that was only half true. 'What of him?'

'Do you trust him?'

Gregor ran the tip of his tongue over his lips, but did not answer her in words.

'Has he the means of betraying you, Gregor?'

'Betraying . . . ?' Swallowing, the man parried that with a question of his own. 'What do you know, woman – about Breadalbane?' he demanded, a little hoarsely.

'I know very little. Nothing certain. Nothing definite. Only scraps and pieces that I have managed to pick up from my husband's unguarded speech with two callers at Bardowie. One of them was an officer from Dumbarton Castle.

From them, eavesdropping and putting two and two together, I have gathered something. Not a lot – but enough to make me very afraid for you, Gregor. You and Mary. I gathered that Lord Breadalbane must have in his possession some paper, some document, that implicates you in . . . in what happened. Or what did not happen! Evidence to convict you of high treason – you, and your uncle, and many clan chiefs, apparently. Is there such a document, Gregor?'

Stiff-lipped, the man nodded.

'Then you *are* in danger! For the Government have been informed of it. Breadalbane is suspect – known to have been implicated in the rising that was to be. Now, he is willing to buy his immunity – and office with the Government too, it is suggested. He has been in correspondence with the Queen's Ministers. He offered them this paper, as price of his preferment!'

'My God! It cannot be! No man could be so false. So great a dastard. To betray us all – to betray the whole Highlands! I'll not believe it. Even of that fox. . . .'

'How then does my husband come to know of it?' the young woman demanded. '*He* believes it, if you do not! God forgive him, he glories in it. He hates you, Gregor – perhaps with cause. And now he sees you ruined, dead probably, and his sister free of you! He is close to many in official positions – and he is not easily misled. You will know that hitherto most of those arrested over this affair have had to be set free, for lack of evidence against them. But here is evidence, it seems – written evidence that the Courts could hang men on – hang *you* on! Oh, this horrible thing is true, I am sure. That is why I had to come. I said that I had had a message from my father, needing me. That I must go to him at Arnprior. John was going to London, anyway. He let me go – not knowing that I knew, of course, that I had overheard. . . .'

Gregor was not really listening, now. He was looking out over Glen Gyle – and seeing it as he had never quite seen it before. All the fair settled peace and seeming security of it, embosomed in its guardian mountains. But how secure was it, if this black treachery was true? It had always been inviolate, yes. His uncle was an outlaw already, yes. The Government's arm had never been long enough to reach them here. But would that still stand? After all, there was no denying that what had allowed this last remnant of the landless Clan Gregorach to remain secure was not only its inaccessible mountains and its vigorous right arms but the fact of the Glengyle sept's relations with the mighty Clan Campbell – however they miscalled them. His own mother had been a Campbell, as had Rob's, his grandmother. And the MacGregors had cleverly played off the one branch of the Campbells against the other, the Argylls against those of Breadalbane, while keeping in with both. It suited both, probably, to have the usefully disreputable MacGregors as a small buffer state between them, and many a handy turn had Rob Roy done for both houses that they would not like to have done for themselves. But now – if both were turned against them, Argyll over the matter of the Frenchmen, and Breadalbane to save his own ancient hide? Could Glen Gyle remain inviolate? If Breadalbane and Argyll let the military pass readily through their territories that flanked Gregor's own to north and west, could anything save the Gregorach if the Government was determined? If Breadalbane had done this other deed of shame, would he boggle at that? The clans might fight amongst themselves, but they kept out the invader from their glens. If Breadalbane was deliberately betraying the clans, could Glen Gyle survive, and the Gregorach become other than finally and completely landless – and leaderless – at last?

So the man was seeing his heritage, now, through suddenly different eyes. And seeing his wife and son there below them, coming hastening to meet them across the meadows, Mary flushed and excitedly happy, the toddling Iannie tumbling and squealing, naked as a trout. And Gregor felt a lump rise in his brown throat.

Meg also saw, and her voice tailed away. Then, her tone changed, she was waving to the other girl, and speaking.

'We will talk of this again . . . later. Shall we, Gregor?' she suggested.

And he nodded, gratefully.

* * *

After the two young women had fallen on each other's necks and wept a little, Meg held Mary at arm's length and looked at her through glistening eyes.

'Oh, my dear – you are looking fine, fine,' she got out. 'And bonny. Bonnier than I have ever seen you. And me such a fright!' Foolishly her hand went up to her hair, her neck. 'And the little man – he is a darling, a precious, a joy.' She snatched the chortling baby up in her arms, and hugged him to her, almost hungrily.

The fond mother laughed and blinked and gulped in turn. 'He is a scoundrel!' she asserted. 'A handful, indeed. Worse, much worse, than his father. Gregor I can manage. But this one . . . ! What shall I do with another of them . . . ?'

'Another!' That was Gregor. 'What are you saying? Another . . . ?'

'Just that, Glengyle, sir.' Mary sketched a curtsy. 'With your permission, of course. But I think that there is another of the wild Gregorach on the way! A determined pushing lot. . . .'

'*Ciod so?* And you did not tell me! *Mè!* You said no word. . . .'

'I was saving it up . . . saving it for the next time that you were hard and cruel to me, you great ogre! Then I would have tamed you. But, this . . . this is a great occasion. Dear Meg. . . .'

'*Dia* – an occasion, indeed! Here is news! Another son for Glengyle! Donald, he shall be named. After my grandfather. Meg – how think you of Donald? I tell you . . . ' Suddenly Gregor's eyes clouded, and his voice fell. 'Och yes, then,' he ended flatly.

But Mary did not notice. Moreover, Meg Hamilton spoke quickly. 'I am so glad, Mary – so very happy. You are the lucky one. But it will not be Donald, at all. It will be a girl.

230

You could even call her Margaret, if you were at a loss. . . .'

'It is a promise. Eh, Greg?' Mary laughed. 'But come — the house for us. You must be very tired, my dear — almost as tired as I was the first time I came here! Come away. I am so glad to see you, Meg, so very glad. . . .'

Chattering happily, Mary led them housewards, Gregor carrying his son. 'Is it not a lovely place — this Glen Gyle?' she demanded. 'I declare, it is worth putting up with Gregor and his brood and all his wild men, just to live here! So green, so safe, hidden away amongst its hills.'

Her husband cleared his throat, opened his mouth to speak, thought better of it, and shut it again.

'Safe, yes,' their visitor agreed levelly. 'It must always remain that, for you, Mary my heart.'

The other girl looked at her friend, her brows raised. 'Ah — you mean John? Our poor silly obstinate John? No — he cannot reach us here. I used to fear that he might. But not now. Gregor soon convinced me. And now that all the wars and troubles are past and done with, I am so glad, so happy. It was an anxious time when Gregor was going to be fighting. Always ranging the country, in danger. Perhaps it is wrong to say so, but I thanked God when the rising collapsed. It is not so easy to be a good Jacobite when you have husband and children and home at stake! But now — all is well. And your coming, Meg, crowns it all. I have only the one desire now — that you should be as happy as I am!'

'Thank you, Mary,' the other girl said. And left it at that.

Gregor set down young Ian on the threshold of Glengyle House. 'You will look after Meg, lassie?' he said to his wife. 'And you will forgive me, Meg? I have to go over to Inversnaid for a small while.'

'Now? Must you go now, Greg?'

'Yes. I have to see my uncle — about something that I had forgotten. A matter of, of trading. He would not want to be left uninformed, I think.'

'Tell your uncle, if he is looking for trade,' Meg Hamilton said, 'that he should have a word with Campbell of Invercroy.'

'Invercroy?'

'Yes. Campbell of Invercroy. I have heard that he is a warm man . . . for trade, just now.'

'M'mmm. Invercroy.' Gregor eyed her thoughtfully, and turned away. 'Thank you,' he said. 'I will not forget.'

*   *   *

Rob Roy smashed his great fist hard down three or four times on the massive table that always stood just outside the door of his house of Inversnaid.

'Fool!' he cried. 'Fool that I am! Fool thrice over. That I should not have thought of it. That Bond of Association – it ties a rope round half the chiefly necks of the Highlands! That it should have been left with Breadalbane, of all people! Who was madman enough to leave it with him? We had to be leaving early, you'll mind – to deal with your dragoons. But somebody should have had the wit to take it away – not to let Breadalbane keep it in his hands. Hooke. Struan. Cluny. ClanRanald. Any of them. The height of folly, it was! Yet I blame myself. I thought no more about it. I ought to have thought of it, whatever.'

'*I* ought to have done, assuredly,' Gregor asserted. 'For I esteemed the man a traitor, from the first. You will recollect, you said to me once, that the time to be watching Breadalbane would be when things went amiss with our cause. That it would be a failing enterprise that he would betray, not a succeeding one. Wise words. Yet I forgot them. We both forgot them.'

'Aye,' Rob sighed heavily. 'Well – now we must make up for our forgetfulness, lad. Or pay for it!'

'Yes.'

Their eyes met.

'The question is – has Breadalbane still got the Bond? Or has it left his hands?'

'I do not know. I cannot think that Mistress Hamilton can know that, either. But there is this – she hinted to me that Campbell of Invercroy may know something about it. You know him?'

'Invercroy? Yes. *Dia* – yes! He is a captain of one of the Independent Companies. Like our friend Lochnell! A good Whig. I sold cattle for his father, one time – a close-fisted old fox. The father, that was.'

'Is he of Breadalbane, then – or Argyll? Invercroy is in Benderloch, is it not?'

'Near enough. On the edge of Duror of Appin it is. He has a foot in both Campbell camps, has Invercroy. He is of Breadalbane's line, but his land is over-near to Argyll's, and he is apt to act like one of the Duke's men. As I say, he is a Whig, and a captain in the Government's pay.'

'How think you, then? Do we journey to Duror? Or to Loch Tay?'

Rob stroked his beard. 'Breadalbane is wily. And well guarded. At his castle on Loch Tay-side we could not do much with him – even with all Clan Gregor at our backs. Which would be less than wise, at this juncture, anyhow! Only cunning could serve with Iain Glas – and we have few cards to play, to that master. No, I think that we must see this Invercroy first. It is common sense, no less, to strike first at the weakest link of the chain. But we must seek to ascertain if what this young woman says is so, Greg. Whether Invercroy is indeed involved. You must question her more fully.'

'Yes. But, see you, if we could discover whether the man had visited Breadalbane recently, it would help us, would it not? Breadalbane would not travel to Duror, or anywhere else. He is claiming to be a sorely sick man, is he not? Like Atholl! And if Invercroy rode to see him at Loch Tay, he must do it by Glen Dochart – or else run the gauntlet of the MacDonalds in Glen Coe.'

'You are right,' the older man agreed. 'At the mouth of Glen Dochart it will be known if Invercroy has visited Breadalbane. That we can find out.'

'And if he has, it would be something that took him, a Whig, all that road to visit his chief who is under suspicion as a Jacobite?'

'I would not deny that, either, Greg. Hector Ban would know.'

'Yes.'

'Very well. Go you back to Glen Gyle, and find out all that you can from Robert Buchanan's daughter. We shall ride in the morning.'

'Good. I mislike the feel of hemp at my neck, whatever!'

'Wheesht, lad. They would have to be catching us, first! And they would need to be wide awake for that. It is other necks than ours that I am more concerned for. Men whom *I* invited to that gathering at Rannoch – and promised safe conduct to. My own honour is in this business.'

Gregor bit his lip at that word honour. But he did not comment. 'Myself, I am thinking of some that cannot take to the heather,' he said sombrely. 'Some nearer home, who risk more than a hanging!'

His uncle eyed him closely. 'Aye,' he said.

CHAPTER TWENTY

JUST before noon next day Rob and Gregor, MacAlastair and Ian Beg, rode down to Hector Ban MacGregor's, or Campbell's, ale-house of Farletter in the narrow western throat of Glen Dochart. No traveller that followed the lengthy transverse valley that linked the west Highlands with the east could pass old Hector's door unnoticed. And few did indeed pass it, either, without making at least a brief call within, for ale-houses were far from thick on the ground, and this one's hospitality noted.

They had no difficulty in gaining from Hector Ban the information that they needed. Yes, Campbell of Invercroy had passed that way – twice, of recent days. He had travelled eastwards about two weeks before, and had returned three days later. No, he had said nothing of his errand, or where he had been. He had had half a dozen soldiers with him. No, not redcoats – militia. On each occasion they had stopped only for a short while.

That was enough for the MacGregors. It looked as though they were on the right track. They turned westwards, up Strath Fillan, heading for Glen Orchy.

Keeping out of Argyll's territory, the four of them spent the night in the heather on the edge of Rannoch Moor, crossed it obliquely next day, and avoiding the head of Glen Coe came down into Etive, through which they had brought the Frenchmen. That second night they stayed with Mac-Donald of Dalness, and from him made sundry enquiries about Invercroy, who ranked as next door to a neighbour. Only a single range of mountains separated them from their destination now – even if it was a range that demanded no little climbing, between mighty Bidean nam Bian and many-peaked Ben Finlay.

They looked down on the House of Invercroy in its bare overshadowed glen the next afternoon – and already the tall frowning hills to south and west, Ben Finlay and Ben Vair, had blocked out the sunlight. A sad and soured place to live, that could be. They went straight down to it, openly. Here was no occasion for skulking and creeping – the approach to the establishment of a friendly laird, a Breadalbane Campbell, to whose chief they were related, and moreover with whom they were bound in terms of alliance. Right to the front door they rode, announcing Rob Roy MacGregor and Glengyle, to see Invercroy – and announcing it with considerable flourish.

The laird, who proved to be a youngish man, dark, saturnine, almost swarthy, in keeping with his home, did not altogether succeed in disguising his surprise and perturbation. But he was civil, almost over-civil, next to effusive. His hatchet-faced spouse was markedly less so. She set about preparing her visitors a meal, without enthusiasm. Neither mentioned French prisoners, my Lord Breadalbane, or the Jacobite cause.

Rob waited, talking pleasantly of this and that – though Gregor's honest tongue would not so wag – until the repast, such as it was, was set before them. Then he rose to his feet.

'Sir – before partaking of this handsome entertainment and tasting of your salt,' he said formally, 'it is only proper for us to ensure that we are in fullest accord with you. It would be an ill thing for us to be discovering afterwards that we were not in sympathy, just. That would not be seemly, you will agree? It could tie our hands, see you!'

Invercroy licked his lips, at that somewhat ominous pronouncement, his eyes flickering swiftly from uncle to nephew. 'No, no,' he declared urgently. 'There is little fear of that, gentlemen, I am sure. Sit in, sit in. We shall agree fine, I vow.'

'I am glad to be hearing that,' Rob assured, more genially. 'Nothing else is to be expected, of course – and you a good clansman of Breadalbane's.'

The other looked none the happier for this mention of his chief's name. He glanced at his wife, and then, rather longingly, at the door.

Rob did not resume his seat just yet, but began to perambulate, his patrol covering that doorway. 'For it is on Breadalbane's behalf that we are here,' he informed. 'You will have his well-being at heart, I know. And so have we, whatever – so have we.' He nodded his red head strongly, to emphasise the point. '*Mac Chailean Mhic Donnachaidh* is a sort of kinsman of ours, as you will know. His health, well-being . . . and honour, concern us deeply.'

The Campbell swallowed. 'Quite,' he got out, but without the crispness that was called for.

'Yes. And unhappily, sir, these are all in danger. It is most unfortunate. There is a paper, that has his name upon it. A paper that, in the wrong hands, might cost Breadalbane a deal, even perhaps his noble head. We are seeking that paper. For its greater safety, just. And his.'

Invercroy's knuckles gleamed whitely. 'I . . . I do not understand you, sir. What has this to do with me? I am not so deep in his lordship's confidence. . . .'

'Tut – you are too modest, Invercroy. We have it otherwise. You went to see him the other day, did you not? On the subject of this very paper. This Bond. You see, we do not underestimate your importance, sir. Where is it?' That last came out like a whip-crack.

'Eh . . . ? I . . . I have not got it.'

'So! You . . . have . . . not . . . got . . . it!' Rob stared down at him, great shoulders hunched, long arms hanging horribly loose, a potent figure. 'Where is it, then?'

'I . . . sir, I will not be questioned thus! About confidential matters. In my own house!' Campbell had risen to his feet – or almost thereto. 'You have no right, sir, no authority . . .'

'Sit down!' Rob snapped – and such was the explosive authority of that command that their host did resume his seat promptly, almost subconsciously. 'I have every right. My name – and that of Glengyle here – is also on that paper. Yours is not. We are parties to it, principals to an agreement. It is *our* Bond, as much as Breadalbane's.' His tone of voice underwent one of its lightning changes. 'Have no fear. We are concerned only for Breadalbane's safety and honour. Your chief's interests are ours. Where is the paper, sir?'

'I cannot tell you. It is nought to do with me, I say . . .'

Gregor interposed, taking a chance. 'Our information, Invercroy, was to come to you for it.'

'No,' the other denied strongly. 'No. I no longer have it.'

'Ah!' The MacGregors exchanged glances. So the man had actually had the Bond in his possession. Meg Hamilton had learned even better than she knew.

'And now?' Rob Roy demanded. 'Where is it now?'

'That I am not in a position to tell you,' Invercroy answered. Though he did not altogether look it, he was a brave man even if not a bold one.

'No?' Rob smiled his wintriest smile. 'I foresee that you may swiftly be in a position to tell nothing else – if you do not remember, sir!'

'Are you threatening me?'

'Not so. Prophesying, shall we say. You may have heard of

Rob Roy's powers . . . of prophecy? When the mood comes upon me, I am seldom wrong!'

An unlovely sound, a squawk, part choking sob, part moan, part sniff, came from the woman of the house, at the other side of the room.

Gregor eyed the plain-faced lady compassionately. His uncle did more. He bowed.

'Ma'am, I congratulate you. On your excellent woman's perception. Lady Invercroy, sir, is of a sound judgment. And she has your best interests at heart, I am sure. That is clear. You would be wise to take heed to her. What did you do with our property? The paper?'

The man shook his head. 'I did only what Lord Breadalbane told me to do with it.'

Gregor said quickly, 'You took it . . . to Inveraray? To the Duke?'

'No.'

'Where to, then? If you brought it here, from Loch Tay?' The other looked unhappy, but was dumb.

'Why else would you bring it this way? For safe keeping? It is still here, then?'

'No. No.'

'God – will you speak, man? Or shall we make you?' Rob cried.

It was the woman who spoke. 'It is not here,' she panted. 'He took it to Fort William. To Colonel Sandford.'

'*Diabhol!* So that's it!' Rob exploded. 'You gave it to the military, damn you! You rat! You wretched grovelling cur! Dealing in better men's lives! How much did they pay you for that?'

'Nothing.'

'Liar! That Bond was worth a fortune!' Suddenly the speaker had a naked dirk in his hand – though swords and pistols had been left at the front door as was customary and suitable. Now Rob lunged forward and the steel was darting under Campbell's long nose. 'How much, dog, I say?'

'Nothing – I swear it! I did only what I was told. I acted only on behalf of Breadalbane.'

'Liar!' Rob repeated savagely.

'It is true! It is true!' Lady Invercroy cried. 'Not a penny did he receive. It was his duty, his duty . . . ' She jumped up.

'The door!' Rob jerked, to Gregor – who, anticipating her move, had already leapt to deny the lady egress.

'My duty – my duty it *was*!' the unhappy Campbell asseverated. 'Duty to the Queen's Majesty. To the Government. I . . . I am no Jacobite. . . . '

'That you are not!' Rob Roy agreed. 'Your duty – to betray your fellow Highlandmen to the English! Faugh! You stink in a decent man's nostrils! You would be cleaner with the foul breath let out of you, cur!'

'No! I tell you. I did only what Breadalbane enjoined. His work it is, not mine. I was messenger only. Because I am in touch with the Fort. Because I know Sandford, the Commandant. I am Captain of a Company. . . . '

So that was it. It seemed likely enough. But it did not suit Rob Roy to accept that, yet. 'You make a traitor of your chief, then?' he challenged. 'Not you – but Breadalbane! *Dia* – let us be thanking the good Lord that we were not born Campbells!'

'What is your Commandant doing with the paper?' Gregor demanded. 'When did you take it? How long has he had it?'

'Nearly a week ago, I took it. I do not know where it is now.'

'A week!' Rob exclaimed. 'Then he could have sent it south by now?'

'I do not know. I do not know, at all.'

The MacGregors exchanged glances. What could they do? They could wreak their wrath on this wretched man – but that would avail them nothing of value. If the Bond of Association was in Fort William it was quite beyond their grasp, however bold.

'Damnation!' Rob swore. 'I ought to slit your treacherous throat, fellow!' And certainly the dirk flickered closely enough to draw a choked scream from their hostess.

'Quiet, woman!' Rob ordered, less gently than was his

239

wont with the other sex. 'Would you have your servants up, to witness your man's shame? Or his end? I tell you . . . '

Gregor interrupted. 'Invercroy could maybe be writing a letter?'

'Eh . . . ?'

'A letter, just. To this Commandant at the Fort. A letter of introduction, as you might say.'

'Ah!'

'Yes. Commending ourselves as good Campbell bravoes. Useful men for his ill work. To get us into the Fort. Once inside, we might be able to do something, whatever . . . '

'Ummmm,' Rob said.

'Yes. I do not suppose that a letter from Invercroy could get the Bond back into our hands – but if we were inside that Fort it would be a poor business if we could not be finding out where it was.'

'Surely. Surely. But, see you – I fear that *I* would be the stumbling-block,' Rob demurred. 'The pity of it, but I am over well known. And kenspeckle. Every redcoat has a description of my person, with rewards offered for my capture. Rob Roy MacGregor would not likely be mistaken for anybody else, whatever!' The man did not sound as though he wholly deplored the fact, either. 'A great foolishness – but there it is.'

'Then it must be myself, just. With Ian Beg. Or Mac-Alastair.'

'It might not be so easy, Greg, laying hands on the Bond, even once within the Fort,' his uncle pointed out. 'The Colonel-man will be holding it secure.'

'At the least we could be finding out where it was. Whether it was still at the Fort, or had already been sent south. If it is still there, then we could bring up our people, have every route out from the Fort watched, covered.' Another thought occurred to Gregor. '*Dia* – Invercroy could write that we are noted Campbell guides! To conduct the redcoats by safe and especial ways.' The young man's eyes gleamed as his imagination excelled itself. 'He could say that he had heard that the Jacobites have got wind of the Bond being at the Fort. That the party taking it south will be attacked. So he sends these trusted guides, to escort the soldiers by little-known routes through the mountains!'

'No!' Invercroy cried.

'Hush, you!' Rob Roy ordered. 'What it is necessary for you to write, that you will write!' He turned back to his nephew. 'This will require some thought, lad.'

'Invercroy could loan us some Campbell tartans.'

'But . . .'

'Silence!'

'But I tell you – it is no use!' the urgent Campbell insisted. 'The Bond is already gone. It is not there – at the Fort. It is gone south.'

'God's death! Where is it then, now?' Rob thundered. 'What are you saying? Think you that we are infants, to swallow your miserable lies? As Royal's my Race – you will find that it pays not to lie to MacGregor!'

'But it is the truth – I swear it!'

'You said that you did not know whether the paper was still in Fort William.'

'No. No – I said only that I did not know where it was, now. As I do not. But it left the Fort three days agone.'

'How do you know that?'

'Because I came back with it. With the officer that carried it south. From Fort William. As far as Duror. I took it to the Fort. I stayed there two days. Then I travelled back with the escort, by the Boat of Ballachulish, and left them at Duror, to come home. That is truth. I swear it. . . .'

'Three days back?' Gregor exclaimed. 'Then by now, where will it be? Which way went they?'

'Aye,' his uncle reinforced. 'Which route were they taking? By Duror, you say? That means that they were keeping to Campbell country – avoiding the MacDonalds. No large party, heh? Not looking for trouble? They would be going by the coast, by Loch Creran and Connel. And then, man?'

'I . . . I cannot be certain. But I think that they intended to travel by Taynuilt and Brander to Dalmally, and on by Tyndrum and Strath Fillan.'

'Aye – as I say, keeping to Campbell territory all the way. Though it is the longer road. That means that they are not sure of themselves, those redcoats. How many, man – how many?'

'A half-troop, just. Under an Ensign. All that Sandford could spare of his garrison . . .'

'So! A half-troop. Thirty men. Redcoats or militia?'

'Redcoats. Regulars. Dragoons.'

'Then they will be mounted on chargers, not garrons?' 'Yes.'

'That means that they must hold to the roads. They cannot risk the heather. Regulars on heavy chargers. They will travel the slower. Let me see, now . . .'

But Gregor already had been calculating. 'It is twenty miles from Fort William, by the ferry at Ballachulish, to Duror. Ferrying thirty men across the loch would take time, in the small boats. You would not reach Duror till perhaps mid-afternoon, Invercroy?'

'No. It was later. Evening. We did not start early.'

'The soldiers would not get much farther, then, that night?'

'No. They were stopping for the night at Duror.'

'So! They are not rushing it, then. That was three days agone. Twenty miles for the first short day. Thirty for a long one. And ferries at Creagan and Connel. Two nights back, then, they would rest at Connel. The Pass of Brander makes bad going for the surest-footed garron. I cannot think that they would risk it on chargers. They would take the longer route by Glen Nant and ferry Loch Awe at Sonachan. That would be another day's journey. So, tonight, they cannot be farther than Tyndrum. Tomorrow they will be threading Strath Fillan.'

'Ha!' Rob said, and his eyes met those of his nephew. 'Yes. Strath Fillan. I think that you have the rights of it, Greg. Thirty men . . .' He tapped his teeth, a habit that he had when thinking deeply.

'We have some hard riding ahead of us, then, this night, I think,' Gregor summed up.

'Yes. *Diabhol* – we have so! But first, lad, we shall eat. We shall need the food. Here it is, spread before us. We shall not partake of your bread as guests, cur!' he declared, to Invercroy. 'We buy it!' And reaching into his sporran Rob Roy drew out a golden *louis* which he tossed down scornfully on to the table. 'That for the food – and overpaid you are! Set to, Greg.'

Tight-lipped, smouldering-eyed, the Campbell watched while the MacGregors wolfed down the spread repast, his wife plucking at her dress and biting her lips the while. But neither stirred from their places, or spoke any word.

In a surprisingly short time the food was all gone. Rob Roy stood up. 'Campbell,' he said, wiping beard and moustaches, 'you are a fortunate man to be still alive. Perhaps I am foolish not to be making a widow of this woman, here and now. But we have more important matters to attend to, just. You will value your treacherous hide, no doubt? Well, watch it well! If a word of this visit of ours leaks out, we shall be back, see you! With time and to spare for what has to be done! You will hold that false tongue of yours between your teeth, Invercroy – or it will wag no more. You have Rob Roy MacGregor's word for that! Ma'am, I regret this upset of your house – but I regret your mismarriage more! Good-day to you.'

The MacGregors flung out of the room and downstairs, shouting for their gillies.

*   *   *

Gregor had not exaggerated when he declared that they had hard riding ahead of them that night. Tyndrum lay no more than twenty-five miles away, as the eagle might fly, but to reach it by the most direct route possible to the ablest of hillmen they must cover more than twice that mileage. And across two savage ranges of mountains, the Forest of Dalness and the Forest of the Black Mount. Fortunately they still had almost four hours of daylight, so that they won back

243

into Glen Etive, across it, up Glen Ceitlein, over the harsh pass at its head, and down to the swampy levels of Loch Dochard, before the night closed upon the hills. There-after, by following the south shore of Loch Tulla, they reached the River Orchy, difficult boggy riding in the dark-ness. At Bridge of Orchy they were on the drove road that ran southwards below the soaring cone of Ben Doran. That was well after midnight. But then they had only dogged riding ahead of them, down to the head of Strath Fillan.

There was good reason for all this effort and haste. It was almost certain that the military party which they were seeking to catch up with would be lying that night at Tyn-drum, at the head of Strath Fillan – at least it was not likely to have moved beyond there, and halting-places in that great and empty watershed of the Central Highlands were few and far between. After Strath Fillan its route would be through comparatively open and populous country. If anything was to be done about halting that column, without a large force of men to achieve it, the thing must be attemp-ted in Strath Fillan's bleak narrows. And Strath Fillan, of course, was made for ambushes. Generations of warring clans had recognised the fact. King Robert the Bruce him-self had been ambushed there, by MacDougall of Lorne, escaping with his life but not his cloak – and the spot was known as Dalrigh, the Dale of the King, to this day. What had so nearly brought low Scotland's greatest general might well prove a hazard for the Ensign from Fort William.

It was unfortunate that the MacGregors had no time to go to collect any of their clansfolk. Long before they could reach even the outskirts of their own territory the soldiers would be safely in the heart of populous Breadalbane. Anything that they might do, they must attempt on their own. Four men against thirty. Rob had known greater odds than that – but it certainly provided the travellers with ample food for thought during their long ride through the night.

They came down into the narrow strath about two miles below Tyndrum, at three o'clock in the morning, in a thin and depressing drizzle of rain that restricted even the limited visibility of the late August night. Almost automatically they had made for Dalrigh itself, scene of the most famous ambush of all. But once there, despite the mist and the gloom, it was apparent to them all that the best place for ambushing a king and an army was not necessarily the best for four men to hold up a half-troop. Dalrigh was actually the widest and flattest part of all the upper valley, a boggy haugh through which the river wound, now dotted with the shadowy humps that were sleeping or cud-chewing cattle. Four men, however bold, could do little here. But farther up, nearer Tyndrum itself, the river's channel ran through a broken rocky ravine, and at one point the drove road was pressed close to the river, now high above it on a steep bank, now low at the water's edge. Inevitably it was narrowed to a single track. That was more like the place.

Dismounting beside the murmuring river, the four weary travel-worn men held a brief council-of-war – and pooled the results of their cogitations. Certain considerations were obvious and needed not to be discussed – the necessity for cunning, surprise, exact timing, the best use of the terrain. But more specialised notions had been simmering in all four heads, and now they emerged. Cattle, said Rob Roy – whose mind tended to run on such. Fire – or at least, smoke – said Gregor, inevitably. Shouting, suggested MacAlastair the silent. Water, added Ian Beg. And in considering all four possibilities, eyes began to gleam, laughter to ripple, and weariness fell from MacGregor shoulders like discarded plaids.

They had two hours till sunrise, and probably another hour or so thereafter, before they might look for the column of dragoons. They were going to require every minute of it, they decided.

They went to work.

*　　　*　　　*

In the event, they had time on their hands and to spare.

Dawn came, with wet cloud heavy upon the hills, and if the sun rose thereafter, it made little impact up there on the high watershed of Scotland. The mist rolled and eddied endlessly around them, visibility was reduced to a few yards – and nobody came along the track from the west, from Tyndrum. Only the complaint of disturbed cattle broke the hush of early morning.

Rob and Gregor lay on a little shelf of the steep braeside, amongst the already turning bracken, with just behind them their garrons standing hidden in birch scrub. They had chosen this exact spot with infinite care, after much prospecting. On either side of them, only thirty or forty yards apart, small tributary burns cascaded down to the river, cutting quite sizeable clefts for themselves in the steep banks. A mere twenty yards below the watchers the road wound and dipped and climbed, here reduced to no more than a yard-wide track. It crossed the first burn by a carefully undermined small bridge of birch-logs. It did not cross the second at all – considerable digging with sticks and dirks and hands having gone to ensure the fact, leaving a gap that no horse would jump. Some hastily thrown brushwood camouflaged this, however, save from close inspection.

MacAlastair and Ian Beg were elsewhere, out of sight, but in no less carefully prepared positions.

Despite the tensed-up excitement of their waiting, and his occasional shivers of cold, Gregor's eyelids drooped. His uncle seemed not to miss his sleep.

Their vigil prolonged itself into hours, that seemed the longer for the countless number of Gregor's dozings-off and wakings-up. He began to fret. Had their calculations been amiss? Were the soldiers away ahead, or away behind? Were they perhaps on the wrong route, after all? Had the enemy gone directly south, by Inveraray– unusual though that would be? Or was it just that they were slow in starting of a morning?

The mist was clearing only very slowly – not that there were any complaints about that; it would assist their purposes. If there was to be any fulfilment of them, anyway. . . .

Rob Roy counselled patience. It was much more probable that they were too soon rather than too late. In which case they would just have to wait, and go on waiting. In due course their quarry would appear.

They did, too – just as Gregor was proposing a reconnaissance to Tyndrum itself to see whether they were indeed there. The thin calling of a curlew twice repeated, from a little way upstream, alerted the watchers. That was to be MacAlastair's signal, only to be given when the soldiers were in sight. And in sight, in this mist, meant very close at hand.

And now all tension and fretfulness left the two men. They reverted to calm and efficient men of action. They threw aside their plaids, loosened claymores and dirks, checked the priming of their pistols. Everything now depended upon timing – and cool heads.

The mist was hanging in white wreaths in the trough of the river, so that Rob and Gregor heard the clop of hooves and the jingle of harness and accoutrements for quite some time before the first figure loomed out of the fleecy obscurity. Both gave a nod of satisfaction. It was neither an advance-guard nor a scout, as they had feared, but a young officer – the Ensign himself. He was wrapped in a long black travelling-cloak, but the gold braid on cocked hat and on the heavy scarlet uniform cuff that extended towards the reins was unmistakable. A few paces behind him a sergeant emerged from the mist. And then a trooper. And another. They were in single file, inevitably.

The officer rode at a walking pace, hunched in the saddle, eyes sensibly on the narrow slippery track ahead of him. The MacGregors had carefully drawn heather bunches over the mud of that road to ensure that none of their own or their garrons' tracks remained. He was approaching the bridge over the first burn now. There was no reason for him to be suspicious of this; all the way down that steep-sided valley he had been negotiating identical little birch-log bridges. He crossed it, and came pacing on.

The watchers held their breaths, now, awaiting the outcome of all their plans and calculations. Everything depended upon feet, inches even, of distance, and seconds of time.

They could see eight soldiers now – ten. The officer was almost directly below them, not twenty yards from where they lay, and almost at the edge of the second burn-channel. He was drawing up his horse, perceiving now that the bridge was gone. The sergeant and three others were behind him, across the first burn, and another trooper was about to negotiate the bridge.

Rob Roy raised his pistol, took careful aim, and, as the Ensign turned in his saddle to call out something to those behind, he shot the horse through the head.

The vicious bang of that shot seemed to let loose pandemonium in that quiet valley. Though, as far as the MacGregors were concerned, it was sternly controlled and planned pandemonium. To attempt to describe the sequence of events coherently and in due order would be to essay the impossible – for a great deal happened simultaneously, and the entire action took place in the briefest space of time.

The officer's horse pitched forward, forelegs splaying under it, and its rider was thrown headlong into the burn-channel. Even as the dragoons' shouts rang out, their horses were pulled up, and hands went groping for weapons, their cries were outdone if not drowned by higher, shriller, fiercer yells of 'Ardchoille! Ardchoille!' and 'Gregalach!' – ominous slogans in any redcoat's ear. For four men, the MacGregors made an almost incredible din. Gregor's lungs were never the least of him. Much of the noise came from considerably farther up the glen – two hundred yards at least. And not only shouting. A great boulder came bounding and crashing down the braeside, back there, bringing a small landslide of scree and rubble with it – and though the troopers directly below saw it coming and were able to urge their mounts out of the way in time to avoid it, the effect of threat and disorganisation was strong. And there was a further ominous confused sound from where it had come, the sound of much movement, of snortings and clatterings.

The sergeant, abruptly in command of the lengthy strung-out column, four-fifths of which he could not see, because of the mist and the bend in the ravine, was hardly to be blamed if he hesitated, swithering between going to the aid of his fallen superior, turning back to rally the main body of his force, or attempting to deal with his immediate assailant. That he decided on the last is hardly surprising, seeing that Gregor was now bearing down on him at a breakneck pace, claymore drawn, roaring challenge, his garron sitting down on its hind-quarters, its hooves scoring deep red weals in the steep bank. He got his heavy cavalry pistol out of its holster, appeared to realise that he had no time to deal with its priming, wisely threw it from him, and dragged out his sword instead.

Then Gregor was upon him, preceded by a hail of gravel and stones. Straight at the sergeant's horse the Highlander drove his stocky garron, and though the former was much the heavier beast it could do no other than stagger back from the cannoning impact. And staggering back meant that its hooves left the slender muddy pathway. Down the abrupt slope beyond it slithered, iron-shod hooves striving for a grip and finding none. Over the brute toppled, and its rider with it, after only a single clash of sword and claymore, and down man and beast went in a sprawl of flailing limbs. Gregor's garron, carried on by its own impetus, went a little way over the edge too – but surefooted and bred to the hill as it was, it recovered itself quickly, and got all four feet back on the track again.

Laughing aloud, Gregor turned to the next dragoon.

This man had his sword out also. And he stood his ground gallantly. But he was only an ordinary trooper, good enough for the cut and thrust of a cavalry charge, but no swordsman in the way in which a MacGregor chieftain must be a swordsman. He did his best, but in half a dozen strokes his sword arm was slit from wrist to elbow, and with the seventh, a mighty back-handed swipe, his opponent knocked him right out of his saddle with the flat of his claymore.

'Gregalach! Gregalach!' the victor shouted.

There were still two troopers left this side of the burn – the man who had been crossing the bridge when the attack began had prudently drawn back. But these two, observing what had happened to their betters, and hearing the commotion behind them and the ominous noise from above, had their heads turned as much backwards as forwards. In fact, not to put too fine a point on it, they decided that they would be of more use back at the other side of the little bridge amongst the mass of their fellows. So, as Gregor yelled the slogan of his clan at them, they turned their horses' tails on him and applied their spurs.

But now a new factor complicated the situation. The noises from up above were still confused. But one of them now resolved itself into the roar of water. Down the narrow deep channel of the first burn came a wall of foaming peat-brown water, a torrent, a flood, surging and leaping, throwing out a shower of sticks and stones and debris before it. Glancing up, Gregor saw it, and shouted his mirth. Ian Beg's dam had worked, then – and the demolishing thereof! The two troopers also looked up – and desperately redoubled their efforts. The first one got across before the torrent reached the level of the track. But the second man's charger did its own calculating, and decided that it could not make it in time. It drew up sharply, haunches down, all but unseating its rider. And the pent-up frothing tide roared down, swept the undermined bridge away as though it had been made of straw, and effectively isolated the segment of track between the burns.

The remaining redcoat, glancing round at the oncoming Gregor, threw his sword away downhill in an eloquent gesture, swung his right high-booted leg over his sidling mount's neck, and leapt, landing on all fours on the slippery ground, to go sliding and glissading downwards after his sword, to the safety of the riverside below. A man as wise as his horse, undoubtedly.

Gregor and his two troopers were not the only observers of the flood. A leaderless group of dragoons had been bunched a little way back from the far side of the bridge, uncertain whether to come on or turn back. Now there was little question about it. One or two fired pistol-shots at Gregor – but they were fifty or sixty yards from him, and he took no hurt. And anyway, the soldiers' attention was further distracted. The snorting and scuffling and clattering sounds were now waxing mightily, egged on by a continuous volley of blood-curdling yells. MacAlastair, for a taciturn man, was excelling himself. Moreover, smoke was beginning to billow over and down on them, borne on the westerly air-stream, in acrid rolling clouds, growing ever denser, to thicken the mist. And out of it loomed movement, massive substantial movement, bearing menacingly downhill. New and urgent shouting from all the strung-out line of unseen soldiery rent the already tortured air.

As a substitute for a charge of mounted warriors, perhaps, a stampede of angry frightened Highland cattle may lack something. But as an alarming spectacle and a deranging influence – especially when shrouded in smoke and mist, and possibly being used as a screen for the said charging warriors – it has its own terrors. Driven on by yells and hurled fronds of burning heather from the barrier of dry stuff that had been collected up there and duly lit by MacAlastair, the brutes came thundering down the slope, heads low, tails high, great horns clashing – and it would have been brave men indeed, and braver horses, that would have stood firm in their way. The dragoons scattered left and right. But mainly left, back westwards whence they had come, for it was down to the vicinity of the swept-away bridge that the cattle were being driven. The uncertain group of men who had fired a shot or two at Gregor came to a conclusion, now, as to their immediate future, and turning their mounts round, went pushing and jostling back up the valley, no one of them being the hindmost.

All this while Rob Roy had by no means been idle –

though, indeed, little time had actually passed. When his nephew had run to throw himself upon his garron and thus to enter the fray, Rob had jumped up and plunged long-strided downwards on foot, empty-handed, even thrusting the smoking pistol back into his belt. Straight for the lip of the second burn-channel he ran, to where the fallen Ensign floundered amongst the brushwood that they had thrown in to hide the removed bridge. Down the little bank of the stream he slid, to bend over the unfortunate officer.

'Och, och,' he cried, concernedly, 'here's a misfortune, whatever! Here's no place for a gentleman! Are you hurt, at all? Your horse threw you, just. Here, man – out with you.' And reaching down a great hand, he almost bodily plucked out the young man from the branches and leafage, to set him on his feet beside him.

Unsteady feet, for the Ensign was still dazed with his fall, his brow cut, his shoulder limp, cocked hat and wig gone. 'What . . . ? Deuce take it, where . . . ? God's death, man . . . !' he muttered, and reached a shaking hand to his brow.

Rob was glancing swiftly around him, even as he supported with a hand the reeling officer. But he let no note of urgency or anxiety sound in his voice. 'A scratch – nothing more, sir,' he declared. 'You will be all right. Fine, just. A judgment, you might be calling it – eh? A judgment – for harbouring stolen property!'

'Eh . . . ?' The other peered at him uncertainly. 'What . . . what are you saying? My horse . . . was shot. You . . . ?'

'Tush, man – you'll soon get another horse!' Rob Roy reassured. Then he rapped out, 'Your dispatches? Where do you carry them?' Without waiting for an answer, he ran his hands over the other man's person, beneath his muddied cloak. And though the officer struggled against the indignity, in his dazed and shaken state he was as putty in the older man's huge hands. But there was obviously nothing like a dispatch-case attached to him. Swiftly Rob turned his attention elsewhere. The horse and its gear? Letting go of the officer, who all but fell in consequence, he strode over to the dead horse. First of all he abstracted the heavy cavalry pistol from its saddle-holster and tossed it down to the river. Then he turned to the rolled valise, strapped behind the saddle. His dirk whipped out, Rob ripped this open expertly. On top of the blankets and spare clothing was a worn black leather case, embossed with the Royal Arms. The point of the dirk had scored a line right through that official symbol.

Snatching the case out, Rob prised it open, breaking the sealing-wax which bound it, ignoring the cries of the Ensign. Inside were four or five papers. There was no mistaking, however, the one that he wanted. It was a large parchment, handsomely inscribed, and with many signatures appended. Even folded up it made more bulk than the others, mere letters, put together. Taking it out, Rob put the other missives back.

The officer had started forward, exclaiming broken-voiced. Rob Roy bowed to him, flourishing the Bond of Association.

'Hush, you,' he adjured. 'I am not hurting your dispatches. Och, no. Just this one bit paper I am taking. It belongs to . . . to friends of mine, see you. It is stolen property, and you should never have been given it, you an honourable officer. I am relieving you of a stain on your honour, just! And other men's. My apologies for upsetting your column-of-march, Ensign. And a very good journey to you, from here on.' And Rob thrust the dispatch-case back into the ravaged valise.

Then he was running up the bank a few feet, to stare around him. The cattle were in process of hurling themselves down the hill amidst clouds of brown smoke. Of troopers there appeared to be no sign. His nephew was sitting his garron about twenty yards off, laughing uproariously, twirling his claymore. Rob raised hand to mouth, and called out a long halloo, vibrant and sustained, that sounded high above the general clamour. He waved the parchment in the air, triumphantly.

And as he strode on hugely up for his garron, two other calls answered him faintly out of the din.

Spaced out along the valley, the four Gregorach set their horses to the steep braeside, leaving the chaos to sort itself out.

*　　*　　*

Three hard-riding hours later, the four men drew up their weary garrons on the rocky summit ridge of Maol an Fitheach, the Bluff of the Raven, high above Loch Lomond's head. They had not been pursued, so far as they could ascertain in the mist, but they had taken the roughest route, over the lofty shoulder of Ben Dubh-chraige and down the harsh Fionn Glen into Glen Falloch, to climb again up hither. But now the mist had gone, gathered its trailing skirts about it and lifted silently, suddenly away, and the sun shone down on a glory of glistening colour and a far-flung vista that could utterly bemuse the eye. The Mac-Gregors were not bemused, however, heavy as were their eyelids. They gazed down into the fair green sanctuary of Glen Gyle, from its farthermost head. Far down there, beside the dreaming blue waters of Loch Katrine, Gregor could just make out the white speck that was his home. He pointed to it, but his lips would frame no words.

His uncle nodded. Delving into his doublet, he brought out the crushed and crumpled Bond of Association, and opening it up, spread it before him over his garron's shaggy mane. 'There it is, then,' he said. 'There is the paper that should have set James Stewart on the throne of his fathers. There is the paper that can put a noose round scores of the finest throats in Scotland – our own included! There is the evidence Queen Anne's hangmen need to choke the life's-breath from the cream of the Highlands! See the signatures, there – Lochiel, Drummond, Struan Robertson, Cluny Mapherson, ClanRanald, Sleat, Glengarry, Keppoch, Seaforth, Duart, MacKinnon, Chisholm . . .' Rob read off the resounding list of names slowly, sonorously. 'Aye, and first of all, *Mac Cailean Mhic Donnachaidh* – not Breadalbane, or John Campbell! Who would that outlandish name apply to, I wonder? There is a paper that is worth more golden guineas than you or I could spend in a lifetime!' Almost he sighed. 'A paper worth a dukedom, and what was left of his honour, to Breadalbane. . . . '

'A paper that could have parted Glen Gyle from those that love it!' Gregor put in, unsteadily. 'That could have turned yon pleasant place into a wilderness, and driven those within it homeless into the heather. Those who trust all in me. Aye, and others similarly.'

'Aye, Greg. Even so.' His uncle nodded again. 'A potent paper, indeed.' And putting both enormous hands to it, he rent that parchment from top to bottom, And then again, and again, until the thing was no more than a heap of fluttering fragments. He tossed these into the keen air of the high tops, and they were carried away on the wind like a snow shower. 'The Bond is redeemed,' he cried. He laid a hand on his nephew's arm. 'Your Mary can sleep sound o' nights now, Greg lad.'

Gregor nodded. 'Yes,' he said thickly. 'Yes. And myself at her side. I am not a warring man, at all, see you. I am a man of peace, just . . . for all your training! An ill thing . . . for a MacGregor!'

Rob Roy looked away and away. And slowly he began to laugh, his great silent frame-shaking laughter. 'Aye,' he said. 'Just so! Gregor Ghlun Dubh MacGregor of Glengyle – Dove of Peace! So be it. Away you down to her then, man – to the Lowland Mary that has tamed you! But, see you – be at Inversnaid the day after tomorrow's noon. There is the Watch's Lammas mail to be collected – and already we are late in setting about it. Folk must not be getting wrong notions, whatever! The proper and profitful concerns of peace must go on, let kings come and go as they will! The Gregorach have work to do.'

'Very well so,' Gregor acknowledged. 'I will be there.'

And with a waved hand he was digging heels into his garron's flanks, and away downhill with him towards Glengyle House, Ian Beg at his streaming tails – and having to ride hard to keep up, weary beasts or none. And soon his great home-coming shouting was ringing round the glen-sides, back up to where Rob sat his mount, still-faced, and down forward to the populous heart of the green valley, echoing and re-echoing from a hundred hills. And presently the baying of hounds could be heard through and beyond it.

Rob Roy turned to MacAlastair, and their eyes met, and held.